Now was the time for Morgan to tell Kristen the truth. Her voice was gentle, her body warm against his. Yet he could not release the chain that held him to the past; he could not forget his revenge and hatred. He grasped at the idea that he might still be able to have Kristen for his own—to possess her. But how could he have her while the forces of fate challenged their love?

She looked up at him, questions in her eyes and the glow of trusting love on her face, and the moment slipped away from him. He would hold her now. He had time to find the answers. He would think about this problem tomorrow; for today, there was Kristen and only Kristen—in his mind, in his heart, and in his blood.

He rolled on his side, pulling her beneath him, and smiled down into her eyes. Tenderly, he caressed the side of her face, then bent to gently touch her cheeks and lips with light feather kisses. He felt her arms about him, the willing warmth of her beneath him, and he loosened the final hold on any words he might have said. His mouth possessed hers with a deep hunger that drew her into the center of it and held her.

"Oh, Morgan, I love you," she whispered.

"And I love you, beyond all," he replied, aware that he would never be able to convince her of the truth of these words if she knew that he still clung to the past. . . .

# KRISTEN'S PASSION

## SYLVIE F. SOMMERFIELD

**ZEBRA BOOKS**
**KENSINGTON PUBLISHING CORP.**

*This book is dedicated to Janet Robinson. For all her support and time, many thanks.*

ZEBRA BOOKS

are published by

KENSINGTON PUBLISHING CORP.
475 Park Avenue South
New York, N.Y. 10016

Copyright © 1983 by Sylvie F. Sommerfield

Printed in the United States of America

# One

The huge white horse galloped at full speed down the sandy beach throwing up a spray of water as he did. The laughing girl on his saddleless back looked over her shoulder at the young man whose horse was close behind her.

As they splashed through the surf, the man behind her echoed her laughter as he admired, for the millionth time, the beauty and the spirit of the girl he followed.

It was not a case, Phillip Goodhue thought, of his allowing her to win the race, for he found it difficult to keep up with her. It was the complete story of their relationship; Kristen led and Phillip tried to grasp the effervescent wisp of smoke that was Kristen. That she always managed to be elusive befuddled him. Though he found himself always swearing he would not come near her again, he always found himself hovering about her like a moth about a flame.

Ahead of them, on a pile of gray sea-washed rocks, sat another girl watching the finish of the race in order to judge the winner.

Ellen McGrath and Kristen Seaford were the exact same age; in fact had been born on the same day. Despite the differences in their social background, they were the closest of friends.

She watched the racers as they approached and smiled,

for she had known Kristen would be the winner; she always was.

When they thundered across the finish line, Ellen jumped to her feet. She ran toward them as they both slid from the backs of their horses in breathless laughter.

"I swear, I think you have stolen Pegasus; that horse flies like the wind," Phillip said.

"Come, Phillip," Kristen laughed. "Won't you give me a little credit."

"Not good for my morale, my dear." He chuckled in reply. "I'd rather think the horse beat mine than you beat me."

Kristen threw back her head and laughed; then she ran to Phillip and embraced him enthusiastically. Phillip took immediate advantage by putting his arms about her and holding her slender form close for one of the very few opportunities he would find. He did not notice the laughter die in Ellen's eyes or her approach slow.

Kristen left Phillip's arms and turned to Ellen. "Ellen,"—she turned to her friend—"would you care to race me?"

"Heavens, no!" Ellen exclaimed. "I have no desire to follow you through all that water. Look at you both, you're soaked to the skin. Kristi, your parents are going to have your hide this time."

"We'll build a fire and dry off," offered Phillip, but he was obviously enjoying Kristen's wet state for it molded the clothes she wore to her curvaceous body and thus stimulated his desire for her that had been awakened by her nonchalant hug.

"Good idea," Kristen said quickly. "I'd best not go home like this. I would hate to see the ogre when she sees me." Kristen laughed, but her eyes became serious and a shiver of distaste rolled over her.

The ogre to whom she referred was her coldly beautiful stepmother. She hated Leslie Brent Seaford with a deep and abiding passion, and she felt that her father now knew that he had been trapped into marriage and regretted it. James Seaford had been prostrate with grief when Kristen's mother had died suddenly and he had turned to what he thought was kindness and understanding from Leslie Brent. Too late, he saw the grasping cold woman for what she was. He was already married to her before he realized that Leslie had an intense jealousy and hatred for Kristen. He began to search about for a way to get his beloved daughter out of Leslie's sharp-tongued reach.

They built a fire on the beach and sat about it talking and eating the lunch Ellen had been wise enough to bring. She knew Kristen's mercurial temperament, and knew that food and personal comforts were the last things on her mind when something like a race or some other wild thing captured her imagination. Ellen watched Kristen's animated face. "She's so filled with the joy of life, she reaches for everything. I hope it doesn't get her badly hurt one day."

Kristen was tall and very slim, her boyish hips softly rounded. Her breasts rose and fell under the soft white blouse she wore—breasts that were round and firm. Her gray eyes sparkled with bright intelligence. They were wide-open windows to her mind which was quick and deep. They reminded Ellen of the gray stormy clouds that sometimes hung over the ocean. Her hair, tied carelessly back with a piece of ribbon, hung in a thick mass of golden bronze curls. Wayward, damp curls framed her oval face with its straight slim nose and wide laughing lips.

She looked from Kristen to Phillip and suffered the

7

same pangs of envy she always felt. Ellen had loved Phillip from the time they were children. She didn't know if Phillip realized how captured he was by Kristen's rare personality. But she did know Kristen felt toward him the way a younger sister would feel toward an older brother.

Phillip, at twenty-three, was four years older than Kristen and Ellen. He came from a family almost as wealthy as the Seafords which was another reason that Ellen tried her best to keep her emotions to herself. She felt it was impossible for Phillip to love a girl who was the daughter of a very poor widowed minister who lived in the village a mile or so from Seaford Manor.

When their clothes, under the hot afternoon sun, had dried sufficiently, Kristen rose. She was rumpled and wind-blown, yet she had never looked calmer or more secure. Ellen looked at her. If she had to face Leslie Seaford in Kristen's disreputable condition, she would be frightened to tears, but Kristen seemed unworried about it.

"I've got to get home," Kristen said. "We're having guests for dinner tonight. An old friend of Leslie's has come all the way from England, and I'd best be on my good behavior unless I want her breathing down my neck."

Ellen and Phillip watched her as, with effortless grace, she remounted her horse.

"Want to go shopping tomorrow, Ellen? I have to get a new gown for the party we're having for my father's birthday."

"Sure, Kristi."

"Good, I'll be around about eleven, all right?"

"All right, see you then."

"'Bye, Phillip."

"'Bye, Kristi . . . oh, Kristi?"

"Yes?"

"I think the Gracelands are having a barbecue next week."

"Yes, I know, I'm going with my . . . parents."

"Yes, I know, I was just wondering if you knew about it."

She smiled and waved at both of them, then wheeled her horse about and kicked him into motion. In a few minutes, she was flying down the beach.

"She's . . . she's so alive," Ellen said.

"Yes," Phillip agreed quietly.

"You like her, don't you, Phillip?"

"Sure I do. I have since we were kids."

"No . . . I mean . . . really like her?"

Phillip had been standing looking down the length of beach while Ellen watched him intently. He was almost six feet tall. His hair was so blond it hovered on the edge of being white and it was in extreme contrast to his deep bronze skin that told of many days in the sun. His eyes were a soft crystal blue. They were contented eyes, for Phillip had a rewarding life. He was the youngest child of a family of four. The oldest was a brother, then two sisters, then Phillip, who was pampered and cared for by all. Despite this, he had an easy-going sense of humor, and his character included a fine sense of honor and responsibility that most people would have found surprising. Now he turned and looked down on Ellen's upturned face. A small frown put creases between his eyes as he took the few steps to her side and dropped down beside her on the sand.

Ellen was tiny; she stood just five feet tall and everything about her was in miniature perfection from her heart-shaped face to her slender legs. Her hair was black and her eyes were large and honey colored with small gold flecks. She looked directly at him now with a questioning gaze.

"Ellen . . . you've always sat back and let Kristen be first in everything, haven't you?"

"She is . . . Kristen is so great. I know you care for her."

"I'm not denying that." He grinned. "I care for her, and I admire her, like a beautiful summer day, or a thunderstorm, or like the magnificent way the ocean can overpower me, but . . ."

"But what?"

"But she's not the woman for me."

"She's not!"

"No, she's not. I know the kind of girl I'd like to have for my own, permanently, and she has so many good qualities of her own that if she'd say she'd be my woman, I'd never think of Kristen or any other woman again."

"Qualities . . ." she stammered, feeling a flutter deep within when Phillip reached out and brushed strands of her hair from across her face. He did not withdraw his hand, but instead, he gripped her hair and drew her closer.

"Qualities . . . like . . . she has beautiful brown eyes with little gold flecks, and her hair feels like satin. She's so little I could put her in my pocket, but," he whispered, "I'd rather hold her in my arms."

Ellen was spellbound by a dream that seemed to suddenly be coming true. Phillip was reaching for her as she always dreamed he would. His strong arms closed about her and, with a soft murmured sigh, she closed her eyes and felt his mouth capture hers in a kiss that spun her world out of control and left her clinging to him as if he were the only solid thing in existence.

"Phillip," she sobbed as she suddenly pulled away.

"Ellen?"

She looked up at him, tears fringing her dark lashes. "Don't play with me, Phillip, please. I can't hide how I feel about you. But I know I'm a nobody in your world, and I won't be played with."

"You damned little fool," he said with a gentle smile. "You should never stand in anyone's shadow, Ellen, and I won't have anyone calling the woman I love a nobody—not even her." He reached out, took hold of her shoulders, and drew her to him. They knelt, facing each other, and he smiled as he put both arms about her, holding her firmly.

"Now, suppose you say that again."

"What?"

"How you feel about me."

"You know how I feel. I'll bet you've known for a long time."

"I suspected . . . no, I hoped, but I want to hear you say it."

"All right . . . I love you; I guess I've loved you since we were children. I can't believe this is happening to me. I always thought you and Kristen . . ."

"Ellen, can't you really see? It was never me and Kristen. Oh, we come from the same social world, but we want different things. She wants . . . I really don't know; I guess adventure. She's always looking about the world for excitement. Sometimes I feel sorry for the man who falls in love with her. He'll have to be made of iron and he'll have to be someone strong enough for Kristen to respect. I only know one thing: it's not me. I don't want a woman I have to tame. I want a woman who loves me enough to want to share a life with me—just me. Do you Ellen? Will you share the rest of your life with me?"

Ellen could not speak the words, but the tears on her face and the smile on her lips combined with the nod of her head, spoke for her.

"I love you, Ellen. I'll be good to you, I promise," he whispered as he bent his head to kiss her again. This time, she put her arms about his neck and her soft parted lips told him more than words could ever say. Her small slender body melted against his lean frame and his hands slipped from her waist to the curve of her hips to hold her more firmly against him.

As the two lovers knelt together on the beach, the sun was just kissing the horizon and everything was bathed in the red glow that lit the world. Phillip pulled her down beside him on the blanket near the fire. He lay beside her looking down into her love-filled eyes. It made his heart expand within him, and he realized he had made the right choice. Here was a woman of gentle giving, a woman who could bring him peace and contentment. He gave one fleeting thought to the wild little gypsy called Kristen, but then, in the touch of soft arms and lips, he forgot everything but the sweet creature in his arms.

Their eyes held as his hands began a slow discovery of the soft sweetness that lay beside him. He touched his lips to her cheeks, her eyes, and then again took her soft pliant mouth with his. There was more to consider than the difference in their ages. Phillip, as a son of a wealthy family, had gotten most things in life he wanted—including women.

He slid his hand down the soft curve of her body to her slender legs; her soft warm thigh felt silken beneath his exploring fingers and he felt her tremble.

His lips traced a fiery path down her throat to the soft flesh above the neckline of the blouse she wore. Gently, he pushed it from her, revealing the perfection of her curved breasts with their small pink nipples. As he tasted them, he heard her gasp partly from fear, but more from the pleasurable sensation his wandering lips had given her.

"Oh, Phillip," she whispered softly, "I love you."

The sun had dipped beyond the horizon and the new moonlight bathed her slim body in pale white. He held his breath as he slipped her skirt away to reveal her perfection to his hungry gaze. "You're so very beautiful, Ellen, almost too beautiful to touch."

"But I want you to touch me, I want you to love me, Phillip; but most of all I want you to know how much I love you."

Wordlessly, Phillip removed the clothes that seemed to bind him. His heated body thrilled at the cool touch of hers as he again pulled her down beside him.

This time, his hungry mouth took hers with a firm fiery passion and she moaned softly as her arms came about him, caressing the hard muscles of his back and shoulders.

Phillip controlled her senses as his hands and mouth elicited responses from her body she never had known existed. She wanted to pull him within her, to hold his lean hard body forever captured.

She felt the strength of possessive arms and the heat of passionate lips that searched her body for the profoundest depth of her need. She writhed in an agony of wanting . . . wanting . . . wanting such as she had never known.

Then they were one, his body lifting her senses to fly among the clouds, to soar to the heights of passion. Their bodies were molded to each other, their arms clung, and their lips shared a oneness that joined them irretrievably and forever.

He held her in silence for a long time as they both spiraled down to reality. He held her and caressed her, unwilling to ever let her go again.

Before the sun set Kristen arrived at the stables of the Seaford home. She dismounted and turned her horse over to a groom with explicit orders for his special care. Then she walked across the lawn and entered the back door of the huge mansion. The Seaford wealth was one of the greatest in the colonies of America and James Seaford had never been afraid to use it. He built the finest house, set the finest table, enjoyed the finest wine, and spoiled his one and only child by giving her everything money could buy—spoiled her in a way, for Kristen, despite the fact she could have everything she ever dreamed of, was a compassionate and honest person. An outgoing girl, she made friends easily, and at nineteen, she had already had the best education money could buy and had refused several proposals of marriage.

She crossed the foyer and started up the stairs when a cold voice stopped her. "So, you have finally come home, and in your usual condition."

She turned and looked down at the beautiful blonde woman who stood in the library doorway.

"Hello, Leslie," she answered coolly.

"Kristen, really, can't you ever dress or act like a lady?"

"When the need arises. For now, I see no one for whom I'd act so."

"We have a guest for dinner," Leslie answered through a frigid smile. "Do you think you could try not to embarrass your father by acting like a child for one night?"

"You needn't worry about me, Leslie. I can act the part

14

of a lady as well as you do. And of course, as authentically as you do."

Leslie's smile faded to a look of fury. She turned, walked back into the library, and slammed the door behind her. Kristen continued up the stairs to her room where she closed the door and locked it behind her; then she threw herself across the bed and tried to control the deep fury that held her.

Leslie Seaford stood inside the library door and looked across the room at Jeffrey MacIntire, who smiled in return.

"From what I hear, Leslie, you and your husband's daughter do not like each other."

"Don't worry about me, Jeff; I can handle myself. I'll take care of my part of the bargain and you take care of yours. In time, we'll unite both these fortunes and we'll be sitting on top of the world. See that you take care of your end."

"I'll be here for three weeks. In that time, I will charm the father and sweep that wild little girl off her feet."

She chuckled as she went to him. She put both her hands on his face and pulled it down to hers, kissing him expertly and thoroughly. "Just don't forget, Jeffrey, love, to whom you belong."

"Are you worried, Les? Are you afraid I might take this planned marriage seriously? After all, once I am married to her, I need only get rid of her father and the fortune is in my hands."

"No, Jeff,"—she smiled slowly—"I'm not worried. You forget, my dear, I know a great deal about all of your dealings, a great deal you would rather the law didn't know . . . and I have enough proof to hang you. No, I'm not worried, Jeff."

Jeff smiled, for both he and Leslie knew that what she

15

said was the truth.

Leslie Seaford was an absolute beauty. Everything about her was golden and flawless. Her gleaming blond hair, her tawny eyes, her pale golden skin were an almost perfect combination. In addition, hers was a lush slender body that could drive any man to distraction. She used all her expertise to get whatever she wanted and she very seldom failed.

She had started a campaign to convince James Seaford that Kristen should be married. He had finally agreed with her when he had realized that Kristen was no longer happy at home. Now, Leslie planned her next move—one that would give her the Seaford fortune and Jeffrey MacIntire.

Before they could speak again, the door opened and James Seaford came into the room. Leslie went to him smiling and kissed him. After a year of marriage to her, James may have been wise to her character, but he was completely enslaved by the sheer beauty and physical desirability of his young wife. The introductions over, James sent for Kristen who reappeared. She had bathed and dressed very carefully. She had spent time on her hair and dress so that when she entered the room, even Jeffrey was taken by surprise by her sweet innocent beauty.

The dinner went beautifully. Kristen was entertained by Jeffrey's charming stories of all his travels. She was charmed by him for he was an outlet to a world she desperately wanted to know.

If he fooled Kristen, he fooled her father as well. To James, he seemed a gift from heaven. He saw his daughter smile, saw her relax and enjoy a man's company, and slowly his mind began to open and he began to listen to Leslie's subtle hints that Jeffrey was the right man for

Kristen to marry.

Although she would not say anything to anyone but Phillip, it was Ellen who sensed something in Jeffrey that she could not trust. "I . . . I just don't like him," she told Phillip, one night after they had spent the evening at the Seaford home.

"Well, what is it you don't like about him?"

"I don't know."

Phillip laughed and drew her into his arms. They were returning to her home in his carriage and he had stopped for a few minutes to enjoy a stolen kiss or two and some intimate caresses.

"We've accepted their invitation to go to the barbecue with them. Maybe then you'll get to know him better and get over this. After all, Kristen is our friend and if she likes him, we'd best accept him, too."

"I guess you're right." She sighed, but still, somewhere deep inside a gnawing worry began to grow.

Daily, Jeffrey spent more and more time with Kristen. He took her riding and to parties. She enjoyed his company. Not once did he make an overt gesture toward her. He treated her with all the charm he possessed and he seemed to accept her just as she was.

Leslie watched their day-to-day contact with a shrewd eye and she knew beyond doubt their plan was succeeding.

It was close to the end of the three weeks and Jeffrey knew he had to press his suit now. He would have liked nothing better than to take Kristen home as his bride. He had already promised himself, no matter what, that before he had to eliminate her, he would enjoy Kristen's rare beauty. The prospect of taking her to his bed was more than inviting to him. Kristen never knew of the times in those three weeks that he had released his desire for her on the lovely body of Leslie Seaford.

No matter how she tried, Ellen could not stop the feeling from persisting that if she did not do something, Kristen was going to make a mistake; she wanted desperately to do something to delay them.

When Jeffrey finally spoke to James, he convinced him that he loved Kristen, that he wanted to take her home as his bride.

James, under Leslie's subtle prodding, agreed. Seeing only the man he wanted her to see and not knowing the cold heartless man who wanted only to ruthlessly possess first her, then her fortune, Kristen accepted Jeffrey's proposal.

The time came for his departure and Ellen was desperate; then she went to Kristen. "Kristi, can I ask you to make a great sacrifice for me?"

"Ellen, you are my dearest friend; of course, you can."

"You know Phillip and I are going to marry."

"Yes, he told me. I'm happy for you. You and he were made for each other; I've always known that."

"I . . . I would be completely happy if . . ."

"If what?"

"The wedding is in two months."

"And?"

"Kristen, could you stay, just long enough to be my maid of honor? It would not be the same if you were gone."

"Jeffrey wanted us to go to England with him."

"I know, but . . . oh, Kristi, it's only two months. After the wedding you could go. Besides, it would give you more time to . . ."

"To what?"

"To . . . to get your trousseau together."

18

Kristen thought for a while. If she didn't go back with Jeffrey now she would be able to enjoy the wedding and then have the fun of the ocean voyage all to herself. It was an exciting thought. It never occurred to her that if she had truly loved Jeffrey, it would have upset her to see him leave alone. All she could think of was the excitement of the trip and days of sun and sea that she would have to herself. To his dismay, and Leslie's, she decided to stay for the wedding.

"But, my dear," Jeffrey said, "I wanted to take you with me, to share this trip with you."

"Oh, Jeffrey, it will be for only two months, and Ellen and Phillip are my dearest friends. I will come immediately after."

"I'll send one of my ships for you. When is the date of the wedding?"

"May the sixth."

"Then I will have a ship here on the seventh of May and you will come to me."

"Yes, Jeffrey, I will."

Jeffrey had kissed her several times, but they were chaste kisses for he was afraid he would frighten her. None of the kisses, including the one he gave her on the dock as he bade her farewell, did anything to waken the dormant passion that lived within her.

She did not really question why it did not upset her when he left.

As the days went by, Kristen began to notice that her father was becoming thinner and paler. He seemed suddenly to begin to age.

The wedding of Phillip and Ellen was a joyful affair. Kristen laughed and danced and thoroughly enjoyed herself. When Phillip and Ellen had left and she and her father and stepmother were on their way home in the carriage, the conversation was light and Kristen was humming to herself when suddenly her father gave a low murmured groan and fell forward into her lap.

She gave a shriek and grasped him in her arms. She held him so until the carriage came to a rocking halt.

They carried James Seaford to his bed and called the doctor, but within a few hours, Kristen, stunned by the news of her father's death, was plunged into an agony of blackness for she had loved him dearly.

When the day came for the will to be read, they gathered together, Leslie confident that she would be a wealthy woman at the end of the day, and Kristen still listless and in shock from the suddenness of her loss.

Reginald Murkton was a gruff-voiced lawyer who had been a friend of her father's most of his life. He unfolded the will and began to read. Reginald's voice droned on and on over the small bequests James had left, mostly to loyal servants, to friends, and to his church.

"And," Reginald's voice went on, barely heard by Kristen, "to my wife, I leave the sum of fifty thousand pounds. The balance of my estate is to go to my daughter, Kristen Seaford."

Leslie sat stunned. All her plans crumbled. She had worked so hard making James's death look as though it were from natural causes. She had intended to eliminate the need for Jeffrey and to have the fortune for herself. Fury went through her and she turned her malignant hatred on Kristen.

The only alternative for Leslie now was to get Jeffrey and Kristen married as soon as possible. When the ship arrived that Jeffrey had sent, Leslie told them to wait; then she began to convince Kristen that she should take a short trip to help her get over her grief.

"Maybe a few months would help heal the pain. Then

you and Jeffrey could return."

"And what of you?" Kristen asked, for her disdain of Leslie had not lessened. Still, Leslie had been her father's wife, and she felt she owed her something.

"With your permission, I will stay and take care of the house until you return. Then you can decide what you want to do. You may be happy and decide to stay in England."

After two weeks of frustration on Leslie's part, Kristen agreed to go. It took her several more days to pack her things and to decide what she would take with her. Leslie was seething with resentful hatred when she, Phillip, and Ellen went to the ship with Kristen.

Kristen was surprised when, just before she boarded the ship, she heard her name called and she turned to find Reginald Murkton, her father's lawyer, beckoning her to him. When she went to his side, he smiled at her.

"I've come to wish you bon voyage, my dear, and to tell you I hope for the best for you."

"Thank you, sir; it was very nice of you to come and see me off."

"Kristen," he began, his brow furrowed with deep lines of worry.

"Something is bothering you; is it something that concerns me?"

"Well, yes . . . I . . . I would like your permission to . . . well to . . ."

"To what?"

"To continue the medical investigation into your father's death."

Kristen was startled. "Do . . . do you think there might be something wrong?"

"I can say no more, child; it is only a feeling I have. Did you notice anything different about your father in the past few months?"

Kristen remembered just how thin and pale her father had become, and now she was frightened. "Maybe I should stay here. If there is anything wrong, I should be here to help."

"No . . . no, child. It will look . . . I mean it will be easier for me to look about . . . sort of quietly."

"You do suspect something . . . someone," she said in alarm.

"Kristen, will you take my advice? It is safer for you to go and it will make it easier for me to look around."

"You're afraid for me?"

"Yes, I am. Will you humor me and go? I will write to you and tell you exactly what I think and what I am doing. It would be better for my nerves if you were somewhere safe. Being married, you will have someone to protect you."

"All right, but you will write . . . soon?"

"Yes, I promise."

She hated to leave; reluctantly, she went aboard the ship and she stood at the rail and watched the coastline recede from view slowly. She was both afraid and excited—afraid that there was some substance to the shadow in Reginald's mind, and excited about the new adventure she was facing. She tried to think back over the months and as she did, a feeling of guilt touched her. She had been so wrapped up in her enthusiasm for life that she had not noticed the ebbing of the existence of another whose life was as dear to her as her own.

She remembered her father and all the things he had done for her during her childhood years. He had always been kind and gentle with her, tried to give her everything to make her happy. How had she rewarded him? By not even noticing he was slipping away from her, she thought.

Guilt stabbed her again and again as she unfolded all her memories and examined them carefully. In her self-pity, she felt the tears sting her eyes, and she promised to try to be a good wife to Jeffrey, to try to share her life with him and to do nothing selfish to hurt him as she must have hurt her father.

She made herself all kinds of promises about how she would be in the future. She wanted to throw away the old frivolous Kristen and to be the kind of woman Jeffrey would want. It never occurred to her that it would be completely against her honest outgoing nature to be the kind of woman Jeffrey MacIntire would want. And she did not yet know of the rendezvous that awaited her on the open sea. It would lead her into a wild new adventure, an adventure she could never imagine in her wildest dreams and an adventure that would change her world as nothing else had ever done.

# Two

The two huge ships circled each other, one a hawk and the other its helpless prey. The captain of the merchant ship, *North Star*, cursed violently and shouted orders in a vain effort to elude the sleek ship that pursued him. That he could not have carried enough guns to defend himself, he knew; but he doubted if he had enough guns even to escape capture. He knew who he was up against just as well as his crew did. He also knew his crew expected the orders to shorten sail—orders that would put them in the hands of the notorious Captain Black and the crew of the *Falcon*.

The *North Star*, heavy with cargo, lumbered along, listing in the deep troughs of the waves from the damage already done to her. Debris lay scattered about the deck and small fires were being extinguished in several locations. Captain Willoughby looked about him, his face suffused with anger and a feeling of helplessness. His second in command stood at his shoulder, his own face white from worry, mostly worry that Captain Willoughby would sacrifice everything before he surrendered. He was wrong; Captain Willoughby cared for the welfare of his men too much to endanger them any further. He hoped to save his ship from any greater damage.

"Strike all sails, Mr. Donlevy," he said grimly. "Bring her about and run up the white flag. We have no choice but to surrender to that devil before he blows us from the sea. God curse him!''

"Aye, sir," Donlevy answered. Then he shouted his orders and within minutes grappling hooks were flung from the pirate ship and they were being boarded.

Captain Willoughby waited proudly on the quarter-deck, his hands folded behind his back and his face grim. He refused to leave the quarter-deck and go to meet a man he considered a scoundrel.

The notorious Captain Black swung his legs over the rail and dropped lightly onto the deck. He looked about him; then he spotted the captain and his face creased in a broad white grin. While his men followed his orders and made the ship secure, he made his way to the captain's side.

"Ay, Captain Willoughby, I presume," came the deep laughing voice.

"I am, sir," the captain answered angrily, "and you need not introduce yourself to me, I know who you are . . . Captain Black."

"Captain Willoughby?"—Black laughed—"I'm sure the terrible things you've heard of me are not all true. Some of the stories have been somewhat exaggerated."

"Exaggerated!" the captain sputtered angrily. "You captured the *Dolphin*, damned near sank the *Prescot*. You're responsible for the damage done to the *Empress*, that almost made her a complete loss and now, after what you've done to me, you expect me to believe the stories are exaggerated! B'God man, you have unmitigated gall."

"I admire your seamanship, Captain," Black said coolly. "If you want to be safe sailing the sea, do so on a ship from another line, for if you sail for the MacIntire line again, I shall blow you from the sea."

The words were said calmly and coolly, but in a voice

25

deadly serious. Captain Willoughby squinted his eyes and gazed at the younger man closely for a few minutes. The thoughts that tumbled about in his mind began to fit together. All the ships that had been attacked, including his, had belonged to the MacIntire line of ships.

"So," he said softly, "you have some sort of a vendetta against the MacIntire line."

"I shall see it destroyed . . . personally. I just hope you're wise enough to command a ship from another line."

"Why do you attack the MacIntire line?" the captain said calmly.

"My reasons are not for you or any other to know, with the exception of Lord Jeffrey MacIntire. When you return, tell him for me that I will see him ruined, that I will sink any other ships he puts on the sea. I am repaying an old debt and returning to him something that has been long overdue, and I shall not rest until I consider the debt paid in full."

"What can a man have done to deserve such violent hatred?"

"A deed," Black said softly, "that you would not believe, as all others did not, but a deed that was done by him, and a deed that will one day cause the fall of his empire and ultimately . . . his death."

"You blasted scoundrel, Lord Jeffrey MacIntire is a most honorable and beloved man. Why, no man in his right mind would believe the accusations you made against him."

"I know," Black said quietly. "If I could have taken the proof of what he is responsible for to men of justice, and had him shown to the world for what he was, we would not be standing here today. You would be captaining another ship. I would be home, and Jeffrey

MacIntire would be hanging in front of Newgate Prison where he belongs."

"Really, sir! I think you are quite insane."

Captain Black chuckled happily. "Perhaps you are right, sir; perhaps you are right."

A seaman approached them. "Cap'n Black, your orders are carried out, sir. The cargo's been ruined."

"Good," he replied, then laughed at the captain's rumble of anger. "Get the men locked below and have all our men reboard the *Falcon*."

"Aye, sir."

"By the time you free your men, sir," he said to Captain Willoughby, "we will be gone. Take my advice and find another man's colors to sail under. The next time you might not be so fortunate."

Captain Willoughby watched him turn and walk away. It would have amazed him could he have followed the young pirate captain to his ship, for he would have seen a transformation he would not have believed.

The tall bearded Captain Black went below deck after he had given the orders that would take the *Falcon* to a small secret cove on the coast of England. He closed the cabin door behind him and, with a soft smothered laugh, he walked to a chest of drawers that had a large square mirror atop it.

The mirror reflected a strong masculine face, with deep blue eyes fringed with thick black lashes. His unruly black hair was no longer hidden under a red scarf. His skin was a deep bronze, and his nose, rather hawklike, matched the predatory white smile that touched his broad sensuous mouth. Slowly and deliberately, he reached up and began to pull the mustache and beard from his face. Once they were gone, his face seemed younger and even more handsome.

27

"Morgan, old chum," he chuckled, "we've pulled it off again. I should imagine old Jeffrey will be absolutely apoplectic this time; maybe if we hurry we can be there to see the effect."

He threw back his head and laughed; then he began to remove the clothes he wore: the tight black pants that hugged his long muscular legs, the white shirt and black vest and the high black boots. In their place, he donned the black satin breeches, waistcoat, white ruffled shirt, and green jacket of the English dandy. In a few minutes, he had changed from a domineering pirate to an English gentleman. He made a mock bow to himself in the mirror. "Farewell, Captain Black," he said softly, "and hello, Lord Morgan Grayfield, Duke of Mayerlyn."

During the early evening hours of the following day, a coach with Lord Morgan Grayfield came to a rocking halt in front of Mayerlyn Manor.

Morgan disembarked, then gave orders for the coach to wait. As he stepped inside the door, he looked toward a huge open stairway down which an older version of himself was walking.

"Father, good evening."

"Morgan, where in heaven's name have you been, Son? I hate to be late for the ball."

"Is Mother ready? I've the coach outside."

"Yes, she'll be down in a moment. Morgan?"

"Yes?"

"I'm glad you were able to talk your mother into going tonight. Maybe between the two of us, we can help her forget."

"Forget, Father?" Morgan said softly, his blue eyes darkening. "None of us will ever forget. Not what

28

happened or who is responsible for it. I know I never shall."

"Morgan, you and I are the only two who know what was in that letter. I don't want your mother ever to find out. She has enough grief to bear. There is no way we can prove what happened or why. He's too respected, too rich, and too powerful. There's no way to reach him. Can't we just try to help your mother through this?"

"I'll help Mother in any way I can; you know that. But if the opportunity ever arises that I can make Lord Jeffrey MacIntire pay, I will take advantage of it."

"There's no way. Do you think I would not do it if I could? The letter held no direct proof and the law would never consider touching him. He holds the courts in the palm of his hand, and the bastard has the king's ear. There's no way to touch him."

His father's anger upset him and he clapped his hand on his shoulder.

"Father, don't worry. I've put the whole thing away for tonight. We'll make it as pleasant for Mother as possible. She's been looking forward to this ball. I'm sure Lord Jeffrey will be there, and I," he said softly, his eyes glowing with a warm blue glow, "I shall behave like the gentleman I am, and not try to kill the man. Maybe . . . just maybe something will happen on its own to make things a little more just."

"Morgan, I know you and Charlotte were close. Are you sure she didn't say anything to you before . . . before the night she left?"

Morgan did not want to lie to his father, and this occasion was probably the only time in his twenty-eight years he ever did so. But if he told him the truth he knew it would not help the situation and could only cause his

29

parents more grief.

"Don't you think if she had said anything to me, left me some kind of message, I would have done something about it?"

His father sighed deeply. "Yes, I suppose you would have."

Before either of them could speak again, a soft feminine voice spoke from the top of the stairs. "Morgan, where have you been?"

Morgan looked up and smiled at the slender woman who was coming down to meet him, both hands extended. He took them in his and kissed her.

"I've been over to Jamie's checking out the new horses he's just bought. I must say you do look pretty tonight."

"Thank you, dear," she said softly, but her hands still clung to his and it hurt him to know why.

He and his sister Charlotte, although several years apart in age, had been as close as a brother and sister could be. But Charlotte was gone, and his mother could still not control the need to hold him close to her, lest some terrible thing should reach out and snatch him away.

Charlotte's death had been sudden and only he and his father knew exactly how, why . . . and who was responsible.

He could still remember the day her slender body had been found on the beach, a beach upon which they had played as children. There were all kinds of places along the beach that they had used as secret hideaways as children.

Jeffrey MacIntire, despite the fact that Morgan had taken an instant dislike to him, had found a more susceptible person in Charlotte. She had fallen deeply in love with him and for a time the whole family had thought they would be married. Jeffrey was an extremely handsome and very wealthy man and was considered a good catch for any girl. But the marriage never came to be. Although the Grayfields welcomed him into their home, and Morgan suspected Charlotte met him somewhere at night, still he did not propose. Then, the news was publicly announced that Lord Jeffrey MacIntire was to marry Kristen Seaford, a girl from a very wealthy and politically influential family.

The day after the announcement, Charlotte disappeared. No matter how hard they tried, they could find no trace of her; then, three days later, her body washed ashore and with it, in a packet tied about her waist, was a suicide note.

Morgan knew Charlotte, and he knew she would never have killed herself. He was the only one in the family to view the body and he was quick to notice the bruises on her face and her throat. But there was no way he could prove his suspicion that Jeffrey was responsible. The suicide note said she simply had nothing to live for and preferred to die. Somehow, Morgan knew Jeffrey was responsible, but there was no way to point an accusing finger at a man in his position.

Then one day, a few weeks later, Morgan had gone out for an early-morning walk. He walked among the rocks and sand that Charlotte had loved. There, in a small niche in the rocks, a favored place of Charlotte's, he found the pictures and the diary.

The sketches, all of them of her family and the places she loved . . . all except one. It was a quick sketch of Jeffrey . . . and it had been crisscrossed with black lines as if she were extremely angry.

The diary never mentioned Jeffrey by name, but it said something even worse . . . "I am expecting his child. I

31

shall go to him today and tell him and we will be married. Dear Diary, why am I so very frightened? I hope . . ."

It was left unfinished. No one but Morgan would know, but it was all clear to him. Jeffrey had had the opportunity to marry more wealth and power by marrying Kristen Seaford, so he had simply dropped Charlotte. Then Charlotte had discovered she was pregnant. Jeffrey panicked when Charlotte threatened to expose him to his future bride, and he killed her. Morgan vowed that someday he would get revenge, on both Jeffrey MacIntire . . . and Kristen Seaford.

It was some time before he figured out just what he would do, time that he spent helping his mother hold together the pieces into which she had shattered at the news of her daughter's death.

Now he had all the means gathered together, and for the past six months he had struck with deadly accuracy at Jeffrey's source of wealth, his ships that brought him wealth from all over the world.

As Captain Black, he had damaged the MacIntire line severely and as Lord Morgan Grayfield, he had been there to watch the effect of his plans. He was playing a dangerous game and he knew it, but he knew he could reach Jeffrey no other way. He told no one in his family or among his friends what he was doing. He had had the ship built in a foreign port and had acquired his crew man by man. They were men of his own choice, and men he knew were completely dependable. He rewarded them well after each mission and secured their complete loyalty.

Now he was anxious to get to the ball; he had taken patient hours to convince his mother to go. He wanted to see Jeffrey's face when he found that another expensive cargo had been lost. Morgan knew that with this fourth strike, he had caused severe loss to the MacIntire line and the idea excited him.

"If you're ready to leave now, Mother, I've the coach outside."

"Yes, yes," she said with a smile. "I'm ready."

Morgan smiled at her with deep affection. Amelia Grayfield was a slender woman with fine bones and a skin like porcelain. She had gifted him with her blue eyes and thick mass of black hair. There was an air about her of the delicate aristocrat and her family had always respected her gentility.

His father, Merideth Grayfield, tall and still slim at forty-eight, was just as dark-haired as she, but he had the golden eyes of a magnificent lion. His father always had been a figure of authority, yet Morgan and Charlotte had both known that he loved them completely.

They walked to the coach together and rode, mostly in silence to the MacIntire residence. Morgan had to admit it was probably the showcase of the homes in the county, but he could not appreciate its beauty when his heart was filled with black hatred for the man who possessed it.

Jeffrey MacIntire had been the head of the MacIntire empire since the untimely death of his parents the year before. He had one sister, a shy, pretty girl, who lived in the shadow of the strength and power he wielded. Lady Jane MacIntire was a sweet-natured girl and she and Charlotte, being almost the same age, had become friends. Sometimes, Morgan would catch Jane looking at him with such a look of intense sadness in her eyes that he began to feel Jane knew much more than she would ever say. He felt sure of it, just as he felt sure she lived in absolute terror of her brother's anger.

No matter how hard he tried in the months following his sister's death, he could not get Jane alone long

33

enough to question her. Jeffrey had maneuvered her, as he always did, so that she was never given the opportunity at social functions to speak to him, and Morgan had sensed that she had been forbidden to visit the Grayfield family.

Tonight, besides wanting to see Jeffrey's face when he heard of the loss of his cargo, he wanted to try again to speak to Jane alone. He had to find out what, if anything, she knew of the situation between Jeffrey and Charlotte.

The ballroom was crowded with prestigious people, people whose wealth and influence could somehow be useful to Jeffrey. Morgan, for the first time, began to wonder why he and his family had been invited. Surely they were of no use to Jeffrey; he must realize that they had no love for him, in fact were suspicious of his part in the death of their loved one.

Jeffrey stood, with Jane beside him, to welcome the guests as they entered and even though the emotion was wiped quickly from his face, Morgan did not miss the sudden look of surprise and the quick unguarded look of disapproval he cast at Jane who refused to meet his eyes.

"Lord and Lady Grayfield," he said with an easy smile that went no further than his lips. "How good it is to see you again. We have missed your company very much in the past few months. Jane and I are sharing your grief at your loss and we welcome you to our home."

"Yes," Jane echoed softly, "welcome to our home."

"Thank you," Merideth replied. He shook hands with Jeffrey while his mother kissed Jane lightly on the cheek. Over his mother's shoulder Jane's eyes caught Morgan's for a minute. The look was so filled with desperate pleading that Morgan could not mistake it for anything other than a plea to speak to him when the time was right. He nodded and was rewarded by her quick hesitant smile.

Morgan could not, would not, shake the hand of the man he felt responsible for his sister's untimely death. Instead, he bowed formally and offered his arm to his mother.

"Good evening, Morgan," Jeffrey said with a frozen smile on his face. "If it's convenient, I would like to talk to you later . . . in private."

The last thing Morgan wanted was to be alone with him. The opportunity might prove too much and his emotions might show just a little too plainly. He wanted no seed of doubt to lead to the exposure of Captain Black . . . at least not yet. But there was no way out of it now.

"At your service, sir," he said.

Jeffrey nodded, but Morgan did not like the look in his eyes. Morgan had never underestimated Jeffrey's quick mind, and he knew that one slip on his part could cause him to be hanging in front of Newgate.

Jeffrey MacIntire was probably the most handsome man at the ball. Morgan tried to look at him objectively. He was an inch or so shorter than Morgan's six feet two, broad of shoulder and narrow-waisted. His perfect features were accented by a bronzed skin. But they were just a little too perfect—everything unflawed, everything in perfect symmetry. The flaws were on the inside, and the cold, calculated glow of his brown eyes reminded Morgan of this.

He could see why girls fell at Jeffrey's feet, but he knew that Jeffrey was not the kind of man to give warmth in return. He was one of the takers of the world.

As the evening progressed, Morgan watched to see if he could get an opportunity to dance with Jane, and maybe get her alone for a moment.

It had been obvious to him that Jeffrey had been

35

surprised at their arrival and he felt it had been Jane who had issued the invitation.

Although in conversation with some friends, he heard only half of what they said, and kept an eye on Jeffrey. He was rewarded for his attention when a man entered the ballroom who was definitely, by the way he dressed, not an invited guest. He made his way to Jeffrey's side and spoke quickly to him. Jeffrey's face became red, and Morgan could see his body stiffen and his hand clench in anger. Obviously news of his recent loss had just been brought to him. He followed the man to the door on the opposite side of the ballroom. Morgan smiled to himself as they entered the room and closed the door behind them. He was so engrossed in his thoughts he did not realize that Jane had come to his side until she spoke.

"Morgan," she said softly.

He turned and looked down at her. Her wide hazel eyes were frightened and she cast a quick look toward the door behind which her brother had just disappeared.

"Jane." He smiled. "I've been planning to ask you if you would spare me a dance this evening."

She tried to smile, but failed. "Morgan, I have to talk to you; it's important."

"Come." He took her elbow and guided her toward the terrace doors. "We'll take a walk in the garden."

They walked out through the wide doors to the terrace and down the curved stone steps to the garden. He could feel the tension in her body seem to relax. Finding a bench in a secluded spot, he led her to it.

"Jane, what is it? You seem . . . frightened."

"I am, Morgan."

"Can I help?"

"You are the only one who can."

"What is it?"

"Sit down . . . please; you tower over me." He sat down obediently beside her and took her hand in his.

"I'm sorry if I frightened you, Jane. Tell me, what is the matter?"

She licked her lips. "Sometime tonight, my brother is going to ask you for a favor."

"A favor . . . me?" he said doubtfully.

"Yes. There's been a lot of trouble with his ships and he's got to have something . . . special delivered. He's going to ask you to have your father use one of your ships for safe passage."

"I'm afraid I'd refuse him; in fact, I can't believe he would have the nerve to ask me."

"It . . . it was my idea, Morgan."

"Yours? I don't understand." He saw now that she was close to tears and was twisting her hands nervously in her lap. "The invitation tonight, you sent it, didn't you, without his knowledge?"

"Yes."

"Why, Jane?"

"Oh, Morgan," she gasped and grabbed his arm with both hands. "I've got to get away from here; I've got to get away from him before . . ."

"Before what?"

"I've never meddled in his affairs. I've kept my mouth closed about everything that happens in our home. I would have continued so, but . . . oh Morgan. He wants me to marry . . . to marry Clyde Rupert."

"Clyde Rupert! Why he's . . . at least seventy, and I've heard some stories about him that aren't too pleasant. Why would he want to marry you off to that old lecher?"

"He," she said softly, "will make a great profit if I

37

do it."

"And you don't matter?"

"I imagine not. There are not too many things that stand between Jeffrey and his wealth and power."

"Yes," Morgan replied, "I know. What do you want of me, Jane?"

"Accept my brother's offer; at the last minute I will come to the docks and leave with you."

"Where will you go?"

"I have an old widowed aunt in Ireland. If I could just get to her . . . Please Morgan, help me."

"What is it he wants me to deliver?"

"You are to go to America and bring back his bride, Kristen Seaford."

"I . . . I'm to bring him his bride?" Morgan looked at her for a moment; then he threw back his head and laughed heartily. Jane watched him in wonder. "His little virgin bride," Morgan said almost to himself, "and he wants me to deliver her safe into his warm waiting arms!" Again he laughed.

"Morgan, please, will you do this for me?"

"It depends."

"On what?"

"On what you can tell me about Jeffrey's involvement in my sister's death."

Her face went white and he thought for a minute she might faint; then suddenly she stood erect and she seemed to gather herself together.

"I shall make you a bargain, Morgan. When I am safe in Ireland, I shall tell you whatever you want to know . . . all that I know."

"And if I refuse?"

"I shall tell you nothing."

"Well," he said gently, "the lady has more iron than

I thought."

"I'm fighting for my life, Morgan. Do we have a bargain? Will you help me?"

"Yes, yes, Jane. I will, and when you are safe I expect you to keep your side of the bargain."

"I will."

"We'd best go back in before either of us is missed. And besides,"—he chuckled—"I wouldn't want to miss Jeffrey's offer for anything in the world."

They were not back in the ballroom more than a few minutes when the library door opened and Jeffrey came out. He was looking about the ballroom and Morgan saw the relief cross his face when he saw that Jane and Morgan were on opposite sides of the room. Slowly, reluctantly, he approached Morgan. "Morgan, can we have that private talk now?"

"Of course, anytime."

Jeffrey led the way to the study. There, he offered Morgan a drink. When he took it, Morgan could see that his hand was trembling a little. He realized just how important this must be to Jeffrey and how upset he was at the loss of another cargo, at knowing his ships were unsafe to use to bring his bride to him.

"Morgan," he began, "I know our families have been . . . estranged over this tragic incident. I . . . I want you to know how very sorry I am that it happened."

"Yes," Morgan replied softly, "I know how sorry you must be."

Jeffrey flushed and started to speak again when Morgan interrupted.

"Jeffrey, you want something from me. Drop the amenities and tell me what it is."

Jeffrey smothered his anger, but Morgan could see it took tremendous effort. "One of my ships has been

39

attacked by that . . . that pirate, Captain Black. It is the fourth time in the past few months. I must curtail the activities of my ships until we have blown this bloody bastard from the sea."

"It doesn't seem so easy to me. Maybe"—Morgan smiled pleasantly—"you should consider going into some other trade."

Morgan was amused at Jeffrey's determined effort to control his temper. He inhaled deeply. "Morgan, I need a favor from you."

"Oh?"

"Yes, I . . . I'll offer you anything you want for the use of one of your ships for one voyage."

"One of my ships?"

"Yes."

"For what kind of voyage?"

Again it was obvious Jeffrey did not want to tell him. "I only want the use of your ship; it's . . . it's a private matter."

"No one uses my ships. We haul and deliver any kind of a cargo, but nobody uses my ships."

"Blast it, man, it's for one voyage. Just to America and back."

"No one," Morgan said firmly, "uses my ships. Tell me what you want and maybe I'll deliver it for you."

Jeffrey glared at him for a minute, and Morgan sipped his drink with an expectant smile . . . and waited.

"All right, all right!"

Jeffrey picked up his drink and took a deep swallow. "Do you have a ship that can leave for America by next week?"

"The *Sea Mist*."

"Who's the captain?"

"Owen MacGregor."

"Do you know I expect to marry soon?"

"Yes . . . I know."

"I need someone to go to America and bring Kristen to me. I cannot take the chance of Captain Black waylaying one of my ships and finding her."

"Tell me, Jeffrey . . . is her family tremendously wealthy?"

Jeffrey looked at him coldly and said through gritted teeth, "Yes, tremendously, why?"

"They would probably pay a tidy ransom for her if she was captured."

"I want to marry the girl, not pay a ransom. Will you have Captain MacGregor go for her?"

Morgan stood up, letting Jeffrey wait as long as possible; then he smiled. "Yes, yes, I'll have MacGregor go for her. He'll sail on the morning tide next Tuesday."

Jeffrey smiled and sighed in relief. "Thank you, Morgan."

"Don't thank me." Morgan grinned. "The price will be quite high."

"I'm willing to pay anything you ask."

Morgan smiled and walked to the door; then he turned to look at Jeffrey again. "I'll remember that," he said quietly and closed the door behind him.

After the ball was over, Morgan took his parents home; then he sat for a while and made some plans. The next morning, he sent a note to Jane to tell her where and when to be aboard the *Sea Mist*. After that, he went to Owen MacGregor and told him what he had to do, and that he should expect Jane.

After that, he went home and told his parents he was going to visit his friend Jamie Price for a few days, and he did go to Jamie's, but only to tell him to cover for him as he had done four times before.

Then he left for the secret cove where the *Falcon* was moored.

When her sails were filled and he was on his way, he stood at the rail and thought . . . thought of what he planned to do when he captured Kristen Seaford, the unfortunate future bride of Jeffrey MacIntire.

# Three

Owen MacGregor had captained one of the Grayfield ships for seven years. At thirty-two, he was young to have worked his way up from cabin boy to captain so rapidly. He was a brusque no-nonsense Scot who considered his loyalty to the Grayfield line the most important thing in his life.

Owen was tall, taller than the average Scot; he stood well over six feet and was built like a wedge of solid oak. Owen had boasted many times that he had never experienced a sick day in his life. He had the strong heavy muscles of a man who had spent his life in the outdoors at strenuous labor.

His tanned face was square-jawed and firm, and only softened by the deep blue of humorous eyes. His reddish gold hair was unruly and just a little longer than fashionable; yet it complemented his rugged features.

He was a firm man who lived by rules and expected others to do likewise. Consequently, he ruled his ship with an iron grip tempered by a fine sense of humor and understanding. He found it easy to reach women with his wide smile and laughing eyes. With joy, he gave and took love, never leaving a woman unhappy or sorry that he had crossed her path. He had an immense capacity to give even more than he received, but he also had the capacity to slip away from any threat of permanent involvement.

Owen had come from an extremely poor home. He had done without most of the things essential to a good life; but always he had been surrounded by love. He was the oldest brother of three and had three sisters besides. They were a boisterous, affectionate family and Owen drew his personality from this environment. He had yearned to go to sea from the time he was a boy and had worked diligently toward making a life there.

He had been second mate on a rather ancient ship when he had crossed the path of Morgan Grayfield. They had founded a friendship on mutual strengths and ideals, and Morgan had offered him the captaincy of one of his ships. That offer had cemented Owen's friendship for Morgan and his own deep admiration for Morgan's ability. Their friendship was rewarding for both men.

Now Owen stood at the rail of his ship, the *Sea Mist*, and exercised a rigid control over his impatience. He had his orders from Morgan. He knew he was to go to America to bring Kristen Seaford, future bride of Jeffrey MacIntire, here for the wedding. He also knew of the double life of Morgan Grayfield, his constant harassment of MacIntire ships, and his reason for it. He knew all the plans for his ship to be taken by the *Falcon,* and he had his route mapped and his rendezvous point well-marked.

He was waiting now for Jane MacIntire to board. He could not understand Morgan's reason for sending Jane when he realized that Jeffrey could have been responsible for Charlotte's death.

Owen had never met Jane, but he was already prepared to dislike her as much as he did her brother. He cursed softly to himself as he realized that if Jane didn't come soon, they would miss the tide and lie landlocked for hours.

"Damned females, they dinna seem to have any mind

for proper timin'," he muttered to himself. "Where the hell is that cursed woman?" Owen had complete command of the English language, but he also had an unconscious habit of slipping into a Scottish brogue when he was angry or excited about something.

He thrust his hands deep into the pocket of his jacket and slowly began to pace, mentally preparing a few words to say to this woman who was a lady, but at whom he was now furious. Owen was certainly less comfortable with the gentry than his own people and he allowed himself the privilege of thinking words he knew would never be spoken.

He remembered Jeffrey MacIntire, an arrogant cold man, handsome beyond belief; but he had sensed the heartless man beneath the exterior. He had also heard stories of Jeffrey that had chilled him. He had met many evil men in his lifetime, but he had not run across a man as cold and ungiving as Jeffrey.

Owen began to fantasize the sister. She would be a lady of extreme beauty, he thought; yet there would be a cold heart inside that lovely exterior. His thoughts were constructing her when a closed carriage drew up to the lowered gangplank and stopped. He walked over and waited for the cloaked and hooded figure who was disembarking. She was much smaller than he had imagined she would be and when she walked up to stand beside him, the top of her head came only to his shoulders.

He could not see her face because of the hood that covered her head and cast her in deep shadows. "Captain," came the soft quiet voice, "I'm so very sorry to be late; please forgive me. It was very difficult for me to get away."

"We've still time to catch the tide. Do you have

much baggage?"

"A little."

"I'll take you to your cabin, and I'll have the baggage brought aboard. If you will come with me?"

She nodded and followed him as he turned away. As they proceeded, he snapped crisp orders and men began to move about rapidly, many of them casting quick surreptitious looks at the figure in the black cloak.

Owen stopped in front of his own cabin. It was the only quarters on the ship that he thought would have enough comfort for a lady who was used to the best. He did not tell her it was his. "This will be your cabin, ma'am. I'll have your baggage brought down. Now, if you'll excuse me, I must be on deck to get us safely out of the harbor."

"Yes," came the soft reply. "I'm very grateful to you, Captain. I don't want you to have to go out of your way for me. I'll be fine."

He still could not see her face in the shadowed hallway, but her gentle voice and the soft scent of her perfume was beginning to arouse his curiosity.

"If there is anything you might need . . ."

"No, Captain, I'll be fine, thank you."

He nodded and watched her open the door, step inside, and close it between them. He went on deck, and for the next hour he concentrated on getting his ship free of the harbor and into the open sea.

He decided to double-check and make sure everything was all right with her before he retired for the night. He went below to her door and raised his hand to knock. But the knock was never sounded. His raised hand hesitated at the soft sound he heard emanating from within. Muffled sobbing came to him; she was crying as if her heart were breaking. It caused Owen to stand in silence, for if there was one thing with which Owen MacGregor

46

could not cope, it was a woman in tears.

He wondered what was the reason for them, for if Jane MacIntire was like her brother, he would hardly expect to find her in tears. It made him wonder if there was more to Jane MacIntire than anyone knew. Morgan had told him nothing about her except that she was to be taken to her aunt in Ireland.

Slowly, he turned from the door and went to the cabin he shared with his first mate. He lay on his bunk for a long time before he slept, hearing in his mind the mournful tears. He wondered if she would stay in her cabin for the entire trip, and if he would have a chance to talk to her, for more than curiosity had been roused by her helpless tears. There was a deep inherent chivalry that was imbedded in him and once it began to rear its head, it would not be ignored. If there was some way he could help her, ease the pain of whatever it was that made her cry so, he would try to find it. He kept placing one of his beloved sisters in her place. Once his imagination caught hold, he pictured all kinds of reasons that she might be desperate for help . . . and he also wondered about the real reason behind her nocturnal escape from England—and Morgan's part in it.

He was up before dawn, which was usual for him. He went about his duties with half of his conscious thought, for the other half was with the girl in his cabin. His orders given and his time free, he drifted toward her cabin. He rapped lightly on the door.

"Yes?" came the soft reply.

"It's Captain MacGregor, ma'am. May I speak to you for a moment?"

"Yes . . . please, just a moment."

He heard her moving about for a few minutes, then the sound of her steps approaching the door. She hesitated,

47

then she opened the door and stood before him.

What Owen expected was so different from what he found that he stood in momentary shock. He had expected a cold hard duplicate of Jeffrey MacIntire; what he saw was a young woman of exceptional beauty. She was like a fragile rose, her features delicate and unflawed. But hers was not the perfection of Jeffrey; she was a sweet and warm reflection of him, yet the complete opposite of her brother. Her hazel eyes were wide and slanted up at the corners to give her an innocent, expectant look. Although she wore her hair in severe braids wrapped about her head, it was a glossy auburn and, undone, would have fallen to her hips. Her mouth, although wide and full, was held tightly compressed as if she were still afraid of something. She was delicately boned, the fine lines of her face muted and soft; and she was slender, almost bordering on thinness. Her small hands were clasped before her and he noticed that they trembled a little.

He became aware that she was regarding him as if he were an ogre. He smiled his most charming smile. "I've come to check and make sure everything is well with you. Morgan would have my hide if you wanted for anything."

He was rewarded by a tremulous smile, after which Owen held his breath in the expectant hope she would do so again for it had illuminated her hazel eyes and given her face an inner glow.

"I am fine, Captain. You are very kind, but I do not want to be any trouble to you."

"How"—he chuckled—"could a wee thing like you be any trouble? From the size of you, I would say you ate next to nothing, and it is certainly no trouble to a man on a long voyage to look at such a pretty face."

"Thank you, Captain."

"My name is Owen MacGregor, and I consider myself a good friend of Morgan's. That should at least put us on a first-name basis, especially since we shall be sailing together for a week."

Again she smiled, and Owen MacGregor was captured, held by a woman in a way he had never been held before. To his surprise, he found himself wanting to hear her say his name in her soft velvet voice.

"Owen . . . do . . . do you know why I'm here?"

"No. Morgan told me only that you were to be delivered to your aunt in Ireland before I go on to America to bring back your brother's bride."

"Then you know who I am?"

"Jane MacIntire."

"You know my brother?"

"Yes," he answered shortly, and the answer told Jane immediately that Owen and Jeffrey were certainly not on friendly terms. It gave her a feeling of intense relief, and it showed plainly in her eyes.

"I am so grateful to Morgan for this opportunity to get away. If I can get to my aunt's, Jeffrey cannot force me to come back."

"Force?" Owen said. "Why would he want to force you to do anything?"

Owen was thinking again of his sisters. In his mind he could never fathom forcing one of them to do anything.

"He . . . he wants me to marry. It is a thing of money. I . . . I would have been a reward for a joint business venture."

"But surely, if ye dinna want the man, ye brother wouldna . . . force ye?"

She looked at him and for the first time, he noticed the golden flecks in her eyes, and he also noticed her unshed tears.

"Yes," she said in a soft choked voice as she turned from him. "If it meant enough profit he would force me to mate with the devil."

A low growl of anger from Owen made her turn again to look at him. His granite face looked as if he were about to explode with fury and his blue eyes flashed angrily. "It is unnatural for a brother to treat a sister so. My God, is the man a monster?"

"I cannot tell you—it is too painful—the things of which I'm sure. I can only say that many have suffered at his hands, and that I am so very frightened of him that I had to escape or perish."

"Perish?"

"If . . . if Morgan had not found a way for me to escape . . . I would have done away with myself. It would have been much better than to live with all I would have been forced to accept."

At that moment, watching her pale face and hearing what she said, Owen would have gladly murdered Jeffrey MacIntire if he had had him there. He could see that Jane was very upset and saw no reason to upset her any further.

"You're safe. I'll see you get to your aunt's. There's no way he can touch you now. Why don't you rest awhile, then come on deck; the day is bright and the air is clear. Later we can have lunch. In a few days, you will be in Ireland. Enjoy these few days with an easy mind that neither Morgan nor I will let him near you again."

"Thank you again for all your kindness . . . Owen. I'm sure you have gone far from your path to aid me. I am grateful, but I really do not want to be a bother."

"You're not a bother, and"—he smiled—"I should very much enjoy your company for the short time it takes to get to Ireland. Won't you please me by coming on deck

50

and by sharing what would otherwise by a very dull lunch?"

She looked at him intently as though reading his mind, then again she smiled a bright and relaxed smile. It was a smile that reached out and took hold of Owen and was not to leave him peace for many days and nights.

"Yes, I would like that."

"Good, I'll see you on deck."

"In a few minutes, as soon as I make myself presentable."

Owen could have told her that he didn't see how she could be any prettier, but he held his tongue and left, closing the door behind him and whistling lightly through his teeth as he went on deck.

It was a little over five days before they sighted the coast of Ireland, five days that were a joy to Owen for he took pleasure in showing off his ship to Jane and in sharing Jane's company. He was a humorous, light-hearted man by nature and Jane would have been light-hearted also had she not led the kind of life she had. It wasn't long before he changed her tense face to one of bright smiles. For Jane, it was a new experience being able to laugh freely with a man instead of remaining mute and in fear.

The night before they docked, Owen and Jane walked slowly about the deck of the *Sea Mist*. If all went as planned, tomorrow, Jane would be safe with her aunt and Owen would be on his way to America. For the first time in his life, Owen found it difficult to say to a woman what he really wanted to say. It would have done him a world of good to know that Jane felt the same as he. They walked in silence, each of them groping for the words.

"Tomorrow it will be a short trip from the dock to your

aunt's home," he said.

"Yes."

"If you don't mind, I should like to accompany you ashore." He hesitated. "After all, I had orders to deliver you safely. That means right to the door."

She stopped walking and turned to look at him. "Owen, you have been exceptionally kind to me. I cannot tell you when I have felt so relaxed or laughed so much. You have gone out of your way to make things easy for me. I do not want to press you any further. It is surely an imposition to take more of your time for me."

His blue eyes remained steady, held by the soft touch of moonlight on her face and the soft gold flecks that glimmered like fireflies in her eyes. He reached out a huge callused hand and touched a tendril of her hair that had escaped. His heart flooded with an urgent need to keep her near him; he felt as if some unseen hand were reaching out to grasp her and take her from his world. His heart so full, he retreated to his Scottish accent. "Aye, lass," he said softly, "dinna ye ken why I would do so? Dinna ye ken that I canna find it in my heart to let ye go?"

It was so. Jane, held away from developing any relationships outside of Jeffrey's control, did not understand either the warm intent gaze or the soft fluttering deep within her when his gentle voice reached out to caress her.

"Owen," she whispered, "why am I suddenly frightened?"

"Fear of somethin' ye dinna know; but dinna be afraid of me, lass. I mean ye no harm. I find ye more beautiful than any lass I've ever known. I know ye need time to ken of what I speak. I'll not hurry ye. When this trip is over . . . if I can come back . . . will ye welcome me, lass . . . ? Will ye share your time with me? Will ye let me show you just how much I care for ye?"

Her eyes, wide and searching, held his for several seconds; then she said in an almost inaudible whisper, "Yes, Owen, come back to me. I feel I have searched for someone like you all my life. Come back to me and help me find my way."

He smiled. "Ye'll niver regret it, lass; I swear, ye'll niver regret it." He drew her slowly and very gently into the safety of his strong arms. His mouth, firm and hard, brushed hers in the most gentle of kisses.

Jane had been kissed before, fumbling kisses by the suitors Jeffrey had brought around. None of them had prepared her for the warmth that flowed through her and the sudden need that turned her weak. Owen did not for a minute question his emotion; he knew it for what it was. He as overjoyed when her slim white arms crept up to his broad shoulders and then about his neck. The sweet curves of her slender body pressed against his huge frame searching for something all her feminine instincts told her was there.

Owen knew he had to stop what was happening before he was past the point of stopping. In his mind, he was taking advantage of a girl who was helpless and had no one else to protect her. His own sense of morals forbade his doing so; besides, he wanted more from her than a fling in the cramped quarters of his cabin. He held her a little away from him and smiled. "I'll take ye back to your cabin. The day will come early. The sooner I get ye to your aunt's, the sooner I'll get this mission over. Then I'll be back to claim ye and I'll no be lettin' ye go again."

He slid his arm about her waist and they went back to the cabin where he kissed her good night, pushed her gently inside, and pulled the door closed. For one moment, he couldn't believe himself. He chuckled as he walked back on deck. Any other time, he would have shared the bed with a woman without hesitation. "This time, is different," he thought; this time he had found the one woman with whom he wanted to share the rest of his life.

For a few minutes, his mind went to Jeffrey MacIntire. Knowing him for what he was, he realized it would not be long before he searched for Jane. She needed his protection. He vowed to get this mission over as fast as possible, because if anything happened to Jane, he knew he would somehow search out Jeffrey MacIntire and kill him.

The dawn did come, too soon for both of them. He helped her get her baggage into the small cart and lifted her up onto it; then he climbed up beside her. Taking up the reins, he put the horse into motion.

"Do you know exactly where it is?"

"Oh, yes, Owen. I've been to Aunt Kathleen's many times. It's a small farm not far from here."

They rode along in silence, she gazing about in fond remembrance of childhood days spent on this emerald island, and he thinking of the long days and nights to come without her.

When they pulled up in front of the small farmhouse, Owen lifted her down and she turned toward the house smiling.

"Aunt Kathleen!" she called. But the bright smile faded from her face when a tall man stepped out on the porch, puzzlement on his broad honest face.

"Good day, miss, are ye lookin' for someone?"

"Why," Jane replied in surprise, "I'm looking for Kathleen Grady. This is her farm. I'm her niece, Jane

MacIntire from England."

"Oh, miss, I'm sorry," the man said, and his face registered his troubled mind. "Mrs. Grady passed away, miss."

"P-passed away?" Jane said, her face going pale.

"Yes, miss, over a year ago. A letter was sent to Mr. MacIntire and he gave orders to sell the farm since it was left to you. I bought it and we sent the money to him. He said he was going to put it aside for you."

Jane felt as if her world were crashing about her. With no place else to go, she would be forced to return to her brother. Owen reached out and put his arm about her shoulder when he saw her face pale and her tears begin.

"It's all right, Janie, love, it's all right."

"Bring her inside; let her sit for a while," the young farmer said.

Owen led Jane inside and sat her on a small stool in front of a crisply burning fire.

"I'll get ye a cup o' hot tea, miss," the farmer said as he moved toward the kitchen. "Nora!" he called.

"Yes, Sean," came a feminine voice from the kitchen. "Would you fetch a cup of tea?"

Owen knelt by Jane's stool, a worried frown between his eyes. "Are ye all right, love?"

"Yes, yes, I'm all right. . . . Oh, Owen, what am I to do?" Her voice was a hoarse whisper.

"Do? Why, lass, ye'll come wi' me," he answered softly and was just as surprised as she for the thought had only occurred to him the moment he spoke it.

"With you?"

"I've still time before I'm due in America. If you agree, I'll take ye to Scotland, to my family. Ye'll be safe there until I can come for you. Hush, love, don't cry," he added helplessly as tears brimmed her eyes.

She reached out her hand, laughing through her tears at the distressed look in his eyes. "Oh, Owen, God must have given me my whole lifetime of blessings when he gave me you."

He chuckled, relieved that the tears were gone. It was the first time a woman had ever referred to him as a gift from God.

The man and his wife brought her a cup of tea which she obediently sipped.

"Ye say," Owen questioned the man, "ye've bought the place and the money was sent to England?"

"Aye, sir. When the will was read, the farm was left to the young miss. When they wrote to England, word was sent back in the young miss's name to sell the farm. It was a rare opportunity for Nora and me to have our own place. We bought it and sent the money on to the young miss in England. Please, sir, don't tell me we been doin' wrong? Has the money not gotten there?"

"Oh, it got there all right, I surmise," Owen said angrily. "It just got to the wrong hands . . . and I suspect that . . ." He hesitated in front of Jane and Nora to give voice to his opinion of Jeffrey MacIntire. "Are ye feeling well enough to return to the ship, Jane?"

"Yes, Owen, I'm fine." She rose and handed the cup to Nora. "Don't worry, either of you," she said gently. "The farm is yours. Is there money due to be paid yet?"

"Yes, miss," the young man said worriedly. "We still owe a tidy balance on it."

"Well, you no longer do. If you will give me a paper, I shall make out a deed to you. I don't want you to send another shilling to England."

Owen smiled, his heart filled with pride for her. He was also pleased that Jeffrey MacIntire was going to get what was coming to him, and he was delighted at the thought of

56

the look on Jeffrey's face when he found out that Jane had deeded the farm and he would be getting no more money. Jane rapidly wrote out the paper and handed it to the young couple who gazed at it in complete disbelief.

"But . . . is it legal?"

Jane looked at Owen questioningly. "I'll sign it as a witness," he supplied, and did exactly that.

The young couple, so delighted with their good fortune, asked Owen and Jane to share a meal with them. They agreed and it turned into a bright and laughing affair.

The ride back to the ship was pleasant for they kept laughing together over the happiness they had given others.

Owen was both happy and miserable to have Jane with him again on board ship for the short trip to his family in Scotland—happy because just being near her made him so, and miserable through the long sleepless nights he wanted to share with her and couldn't.

Their arrival at Owen's home overwhelmed her because of its atmosphere of boisterous joy. His brothers accepted her as Owen's woman without listening to any of their words and his sisters fussed and pampered her until her head swam with pleasure. She had never been in such a household before. She stood and watched Owen as he laughed freely and wondered how it would have been to be raised in such a family. His eyes caught hers across the room and read them perfectly. He made his way to her side. Filled with sympathetic gentleness, he took her hand in his. Owen knew what he felt and he wanted to share it with the woman he loved. "Do ye know, lass, you've the bonniest eyes in all God's creation and that I love ye dearly?" He whispered the words as he pressed her small hands in his.

"Owen . . . I've never been happy . . . really happy in my life until now. Do you know how very lucky you are?"

"Since I've met you . . . aye."

"No, I mean . . . this . . ." She gestured about her with her free hand.

"This what?"

She sighed and smiled again. "I'm glad you've never known the difference. It's made you what you are and I,"—her voice softened—"I love you just the way you are."

"I'm glad." He chuckled. "I have to leave on the morning tide, but I want ye to be ready when I get back. We'll be married the day I return if ye're willin'?"

"Yes, Owen, I'm very willing."

He bent forward and brushed her lips with his, wanting to pull her close and crush her in his arms and hold her forever.

He kissed her good-by the following morning. "I love ye, lass . . . remember. I'll be back soon."

"Please hurry, Owen. I feel safe when your arms hold me."

The trip to America was uneventful, but he knew what was lying ahead when he had put Kristen Seaford aboard. He had been so wrong about Jane that he hesitated to make an opinion about Kristen Seaford before he knew her. He wondered what kind of woman would marry Jeffrey MacIntire or if she even knew what kind of man he was. He made his arrival known and had to wait over a week for her to board. When she did, he was surprised at the quiet subdued person she seemed to be. *Seemed* to be, for he sensed some inner current in her that she was

58

trying her best to hold completely in check.

This was the woman Morgan had planned to kidnap and now Owen was having some misgivings. Now that love had turned the tables on him, he was thinking of Jane being in her position. He knew Morgan was not the kind of man to do the girl any harm. He just wanted to stop the wedding and warn the girl of what she was getting into.

He prepared to leave the shores of America behind knowing that in a few days his ship would cross the path of the *Falcon*. He would put up some token resistance, but eventually, he would submit, let himself be boarded, and let Kristen be taken from his ship so he could go and give the word to Jeffrey and tell him that he would have to wait for Captain Black's blackmail orders.

Owen was torn. He felt loyalty to Morgan, love of Jane, and concern for Kristen. When Captain Black struck, Owen MacGregor would have some words for him.

# *Four*

Escorted by one of Owen's men, Kristen went to her cabin. She had not met the captain yet, but she looked forward to doing so. For despite all that had happened and her sincere efforts to be subdued and ladylike, an intense excitement held her. She had always admired the white-sailed ships, often fantasizing a trip on one. Sitting on the cliffs at home overlooking the beach, she had watched them, their graceful white sails lifting and falling with the ocean's currents, as they moved sedately by on the horizon. Now that she was aboard one, it took all the control she had not to dash on deck and enjoy the full breeze as it lifted the deck under her feet and carried her out to sea.

Striving to remain as calm as she could, she unpacked several of her older dresses. She took off the good traveling dress she was wearing and donned a plain blue cotton gown under which she wore several less petticoats than usual. She knew a lady should never appear in public with her hair down, but she was too impatient to fuss with it. Quickly, she took her mass of red-gold hair, twisted it atop her head, and held it with a few pins. She slipped her feet into the oldest pair of shoes she had and laced them about her slender ankles. Taking an old worn cape, she threw it about her shoulders and left the cabin.

Owen, standing on the quarter-deck easing his ship

from the harbor and into the sea was surprised when her bright head appeared from the companionway door. Surprised, but a little worried. Most ladies, by the time a ship left the smooth waters of the harbor and hit the strong currents of the open sea, were a little green about the gills and if she were going to be ill, he preferred it to be in her own cabin and not on deck. He made his way toward her and watched her bright-eyed smile as he approached.

"Good morning, miss. I'm Captain MacGregor."

"Good morning, Captain. It is a glorious day, and your ship is very beautiful."

"Thank you. . . . Are you all right? Your cabin, I mean," he added lamely when he saw her quick amused glance.

"I'm not ill, Captain; nor do I intend to be. I intend to enjoy every minute of this fabulous journey before . . ." She stopped and her cheeks turned pink for she had a feeling this hard-faced man with the amazing blue eyes, read her thoughts, and she had been about to say before she was married and forced to stay at home.

"What is the name of this beauty?" she asked.

"The *Sea Mist*."

"Very pretty."

"Yes, I named her after a small cove at home. It's a beautiful cove where a green sea flows in—like an emerald. But she's hidden by a soft mist every morning and every night."

"Where is home?"

"Scotland."

"I should have known by the sight of you." She laughed. "And I did think I detected a Scottish burr there for a minute."

He chuckled in helpless response to the laughter in her

eyes and her bright easy manner. Again he wondered how a beauty like this with such a sweetness about her could bring herself to marry a man like Jeffrey MacIntire. Surely she did not know him well. Over the next few days, he planned on watching her. Maybe her looks were deceiving. Maybe she knew what Jeffrey was and was happy with him. But, he wondered, if that was not so, what in the world could he say to stop her?

He offered her a guided tour of the ship and laughed outright when she could hardly control her excitement. They walked about and she stopped often to be introduced to one of the men and to talk with him for a minute. She was so unaffected and genuinely enthused that he could see the men warming to her. They all, including himself, tried to answer the bubbling questions that she asked about everything in sight. He had the quick thought that he would like Jane to meet this woman, for she was exactly the kind of influence his little Jane needed to pull her free of the oppressive past that had made her so still and quiet, so reserved and full of fear.

When he thought of Jane, he thought of Jeffrey, and when he thought of Jeffrey, he thought of Morgan, and again he wondered what his plans were for Kristen.

Somehow, he thought, he had to get Morgan alone for a few minutes to tell him that he was clearly wrong about Kristen. Maybe the two of them could convince her of what she was walking into. Maybe Morgan could take Kristen to Jane in Scotland; there, at least, she would be kept safe from the hands of Jeffrey MacIntire.

He was brought back to reality when he realized Kristen was speaking to him. "I beg your pardon, miss—" he began.

"My name is Kristen," she said with a smile and a

gentle hand on his arm.

"Kristen," he repeated obediently.

"And yours?"

"Oh . . . Owen . . . Owen MacGregor."

"Owen, I do hope we'll be friends. I'm sure I should be on friendly terms with a captain who sails one of my future husband's ships."

"I'm sorry, Kristen, but the *Sea Mist* is not off the MacIntire line."

"Oh?"

"No, I'm employed by Lord Grayfield."

"I don't understand."

"It seems," he began, hating the deviousness of it all, "that your future husband's ships have been plagued by a notorious pirate. To make sure of your safety, he hired this ship from Lord Grayfield and asked us to bring you to him."

"A pirate," she said softly and lowered her lashes to hide the excitement in her gray eyes. "Who is this pirate, Owen?"

"He goes by the name of Captain Black, and he captains a sleek, swift vessel named the *Falcon*."

"Why is this ship any safer than one of his?"

"Well . . . it seems the pirate has a personal vendetta against Mr. MacIntire. He's vowed not to let a ship of his cross without takin' her. Mr. MacIntire felt you would be a lot safer on a ship of another line. The pirate would not know and that way, you would be safe."

"I see. Do you know anything about this personal vendetta against Jeffrey?"

"No," Owen lied valiantly, but Kristen was too adept at reading men's eyes not to know. Curiosity bubbled in her, although she sensed that Owen was not going to budge from the story he told.

They continued their tour of the ship, but Kristen's mind was only half on it; the other half was wondering about a mysterious pirate named Captain Black who had a grudge against her future husband. Also, she was wondering just what Jeffrey could have done to arouse such hatred.

She had supper with Owen and found she enjoyed his company. Kristen had always enjoyed a deep sense of humor in anyone and Owen was blessed with one. She found herself laughing over episodes that he told of his young life, sparing himself nothing.

"Tell me, Owen, are you married?"

"Not yet," he replied, "but if I have my way, I soon will be."

"How wonderful. What is the lucky girl's name?"

Owen almost choked when he realized fully what a trap he had fallen into. "Jane," he gasped . . . the only name that would come to his floundering mind.

"Jane what?"

If he told her the last name, it would bring more questions, questions he did not dare answer. He grasped the only name he could think of, her deceased aunt's. "Jane Grady."

"Very pretty name. Is she as pretty? Tell me about her, Owen."

Owen could have happily talked of Jane all evening and as he always did when he was nervous or excited, his English lapsed. "Ah, she's the bonniest lass this side o' the ocean or t'other. She's got eyes like honey wi' little gold stars tha' dance in 'em like fireflies. She's a tiny mite o' a thing no higher than my shoulder. Skin so soft like the petals of a pink rose and . . ." He stopped, embarrassed at his musing.

"Don't be embarrassed. It would be wonderful to be

loved like that by someone. I envy her."

Now Owen's curiosity was aroused and again he began to wonder about the relationship between Jeffrey and Kristen. "Why should you feel so? Dinna ye love . . . Jeffrey MacIntire the same way?"

Kristen seemed suddenly to be startled by what she had said.

"Yes . . . yes of course, I do, and he loves me as you love your Jane." Her eyes darkened to a stormy gray because of an emotion Owen could not read or understand. If he had not known otherwise, he would have wondered if Kristen was being pushed into this marriage by someone.

"Well, Owen, thank you for the lovely tour of your ship and a pleasant dinner. I think I shall retire now."

Owen rose. "Shall I walk you back to your cabin?"

"No, I know my way and I shall enjoy the walk. Good night."

"Good night," Owen said, and he watched her walk away with a puzzled frown on his face. Why should a pretty young girl, about to be married, suddenly seem so unhappy? For no matter what she said, Owen had seen her clouded gray eyes. Again, he began to think of a way to talk to Morgan before he took Kristen. He wanted Morgan to be kind to her, not frighten her, and he knew Morgan's mind was running to hot revenge, not a pleasant interlude. He worried about what Morgan had in store for her.

Kristen walked slowly along the deck. She enjoyed the soft breeze, and the stars in the black night sky seemed so close she could reach out and pluck one. The rise and fall of the ship and the whisper of the water against its side were relaxing and she stopped for a moment to lean both arms on the rail.

Her thoughts fled back to Owen's professed love for his Jane. Did Jeffrey love her like that? If he did, then why did she feel this terrible urge to run away? To go somewhere where Jeffrey couldn't find her. She remembered Owen's story about the pirate and, as she looked out over the moon-dappled ocean, she wondered just where this mysterious man was and why he hated Jeffrey so much that he vowed to sink any ship of his he found. As she walked back to her cabin, she promised herself she would ask Jeffrey about him at the first opportunity. She went into her cabin and undressed, then slowly she began to drift off to sleep and into a world of dreams.

She was wearing a blue dress and walking along a beach. Jeffrey walked beside her and they were laughing together. Suddenly, a huge black-cloaked figure loomed in front of them. He grasped her arm and pulled her to him, enclosing her in the folds of the dark cloak he wore. Jeffrey seemed confused, as if he didn't know what to do about it. She called to him to come to her, but he stood watching them drift away. Kristen began to struggle in the man's arms, but she could hear his soft laughter as he drew her tighter to him. She could feel herself pressed against an iron-hard body as gentle hands began to pull away the clothes she wore. She struggled until she heard a deep masculine voice whisper to her. "Don't fight me, love. This was meant to be . . . this was meant to be . . . this was meant to be." His voice faded away and Kristen leaped to startled wakefulness, trembling and with warm tears in her eyes. It was several minutes before she had regained enough control of herself to lie back on the bed and renew her search for dreamless sleep.

At the same moment, many miles away, another ship moved slowly toward a rendezvous point. Morgan paced her deck and breathed in the soft night breeze. He also enjoyed the calm starlit night.

In two days, he would cross the path of the *Sea Mist* and he was surprised at his own impatience to see the bride of Jeffrey MacIntire. Instead of wearing the false uncomfortable beard he had usually donned for disguise, he had allowed his own to grow from the day he had first planned the abduction. Thinking of the abduction, he went over in his mind the plans he had made. He had found a secluded small island; he would take Kristen Seaford there and hold her until he could send a ransom note to Jeffrey. The ransom was to be a staggering amount and he felt it would come near ruining Jeffrey financially. It never occurred to him that what he was doing might fit in well with Jeffrey's plans to acquire the Seaford fortune, for with Kristen declared dead, Jeffrey and Leslie could claim that Leslie was the sole heir and marry.

He intended only to frighten Kristen, not to hurt her. Frighten her enough that she would run back to Seaford Manor and stay. Morgan should have known that the fickle heart of fate sometimes turns man's best laid plans against him.

He paced now, aware he was unable to sleep. It was a new thing for him, this uncomfortable feeling that something unusual was about to happen. He enjoyed the excitement of chasing and capturing a ship, so it was not that which held him in this unusual suspense. He thought of what Kristen Seaford, wealthy heiress, would be like. Arrogant, he imagined, a proud disdainful person, who felt that wealth should be held by a few. To combine the wealth of the MacIntires and the Seafords would create a formidable power in the world. Maybe, he thought, if he frightened her enough, he could change her way of thinking; maybe he could make a different person out of a spoiled little girl.

Again, as often happened when Morgan was on such a mission, his thoughts went back to Charlotte. He thought of his sister with pain and that did a lot to strengthen his idea of revenge against Jeffrey MacIntire. As far as he was concerned, Charlotte's death could be laid at only one doorstep. He reflected on the possibility that Kristen did not really know Jeffrey, but doubted that for he remembered how infatuated Charlotte had been with Jeffrey.

He spent the night in a seesaw of confusion about Kristen's involvement in getting Jeffrey to discard Charlotte for her. In defense of his own plan, he finally decided that she was as cold and money-hungry a person as her future husband, and, as such, she shared his guilt. She would also, he decided, share his fate.

Morgan was proud of the *Falcon*. He knew she could not be surpassed for maneuverability on the open sea, and as for speed, she was the fastest he had ever seen. He had had her built specifically so, for he had known the purpose for which he intended her. He had not been disappointed, for she had, with ease, run down and taken every prize that he had sought. He laughed when he remembered the anger and the frustration in the eyes of the captains whose ships he had taken. Anger and surprise when he did not take either their cargos or their ships as prizes. Maybe some did not know, but he was sure Jeffrey had the idea that his personal destruction was the aim of Captain Black. There was such a hatred in Morgan for Jeffrey that he was surprised Jeffrey did not feel it, and he was sure that eventually, Jeffrey would put together two and two and come up with the inevitable four. He was curious as to what Jeffrey would do about it when he did suspect the truth. There was no way he could prove it, for Morgan and Captain Black could not be connected by appearances.

His thoughts were interrupted by the approach of his first mate and he was surprised to find that dawn was nearing and it was time for the change of the watch.

"Mornin', sir."

"Morning, Jeremy."

"Looks like it's goin' to be another pretty day."

"Yes, is everything shipshape, Jeremy?"

"The *Falcon* couldn't be better, sir, and the men are impatient to get going."

"Another day or so and we'll find our prize. It should be easy."

"It always is, sir." Jeremy grinned.

"You remember, and remember to tell the men, I absolutely forbid any unnecessary bloodshed. I want no deaths on my conscience."

"Aye, sir, we know. It's been your orders every time; we didn't figure they'd change this time."

Morgan's smile flashed and he chuckled. "I want to drive him from the sea. I can do that without having blood on my hands."

"You've got him mad enough to kill you should he ever find you out. Knowing Jeffrey MacIntire, I'm sure he wouldn't be as considerate of you as you are of him."

"I'd probably be hanging from the tallest gibbet he could find."

"That you would, sir, that you would."

"Well, I'm going to get a little sleep. Keep her on course, Jeremy."

"Aye, sir," Jeremy answered and he watched Morgan walk away.

Morgan went to his cabin and discarded his clothes.

Then he threw himself on his bunk. The soft sound of his laugh could be heard as he envisioned what the unsuspecting Kristen might be doing at the same moment.

Kristen was already up, dressed, and on deck to enjoy her favorite part of the day—dawn. Often, at home, she had risen early and ridden her horse along the beach at the break of day. She had braided her hair carelessly letting the long braid hang free. The dress she wore was the oldest of those she had brought and she wore it so she would not have to worry about the salty sea spray. Her gray eyes were clear and filled with sunny laughter as she traded quips with the men on deck. They smiled as she walked by, each of them imagining her as his own wife, child, or sweetheart. She had worked her way into their hearts with her effervescent disposition and her ability to talk to each of them about what interested him most. More often than not in the past two days, she had played the part of listener. Owen decided, by the time Morgan came, she would have captured enough hearts to make it hard for him to surrender her very easily. In fact, he began to worry that some of them might want to fight for her to the death.

Owen watched her walking toward him. He enjoyed her free-and-easy stride and the way she dressed for the situation instead of lacing herself into the stiff clothes of the ladies of the day. To his practiced eye, he would have guessed there was not too much under the green dress she wore, other than a couple of petticoats. She came to his side, the breeze whipping fine tendrils of her hair across her smiling face.

"Good morning, Owen. Isn't it the loveliest of days? I feel so well I could shout for joy."

"Aye, lass, I can see that; you're fair toward overflowin' wi' sunshine."

"Oh, how lucky you men are to be able to be so free all the time. If I were a man, I would sail my own ship to every part of the world, and see all there was to see."

"No, lass, it's not all you would think it to be. I've sailed the sea since I was a boy. I'm nigh on thirty-two now and I can tell you that the day comes when you become lonely and long for the gentle comforts of home and one who loves you. I came close to missing all that and I'm glad I've found a safe harbor in which to drop anchor and live peaceful. Everyone needs someone to reach for and hold when the nights are long and lonely."

"You're thinking of Jane?"

"Aye."

"Will this be your last voyage, Owen? What will you do?"

"No, it won't be my last voyage, for all I really know is the sea. But the voyages will be faster and shorter, for my heart has the need to cling to the woman I love and maybe, if God is willing, to have sons of my own to share my old age with."

"I think," she said softly, "that I envy your Jane just a little. Maybe we will meet someday."

"Aye," Owen said gently. "Maybe sooner than you think."

Kristen looked up at him, puzzled slightly by his last words. She was about to question him when he pointed toward the calm sea.

"Look, lass, 'tis good luck. We're being followed by porpoises."

She turned her attention to the water and stood in profound admiration of the graceful leaps of the sleek gray porpoises that bounded from the ocean on either

71

side of the ship. Owen was happy when her attention left him, for again he felt he had stumbled over his own tongue. He cursed Morgan for a moment and was even tempted to try to give enough of a fight to discourage him from boarding the *Sea Mist*. He might have done so, had he not known that Morgan did not discourage too easily and that all he would accomplish would be to rouse his anger—and that anger, combined with what he already felt, might turn toward the unsuspecting Kristen.

Kristen, true to her word, threw herself into enjoying her brief span of freedom. She laughed, talked, and began to learn not only the ship's jargon but the way the magnificent white-sailed structure worked.

She ate her lunch sitting on the hatchway cross-legged, listening to one of the old men on the ship spin a tall sailor's yarn for her benefit. When the story was finished, Kristen threw back her head and laughed gaily. As the day wore on, Owen was becoming more and more tense. He knew that anytime after the next day's dawning, he could expect to sight the sails of the *Falcon*.

Owen, his first mate Robert Morse, and his second mate James Prescot, sat with Kristen over dinner. They were entertaining men and Kristen leaned back in her chair listening to them talk. She could not remember many times in her life she had enjoyed more than this. She felt a peaceful lethargy creep over her and she was about to excuse herself and go to bed when she began to notice Owen more closely.

She had soon picked up the knowledge that Owen was generally a relaxed and easy man. She also noticed that his accent only crept into his conversations when he was excited . . . or very nervous.

Now she noticed that not only was his accent thick, but

that the hand he held around his glass of wine was so tense its knuckles were white. His other hand plucked nervously at the napkin beside his plate.

She also noticed that he was watching her surreptitiously, his mouth grim. This was not like Owen at all, and it was this extreme deviation from his normal attitude that drew her attention. She rose from her chair and smiled at him.

"Owen, would you walk to my cabin with me?" All three men rose to their feet, two to bid her good night, and Owen to offer his arm to her.

They left the small cabin and walked slowly down the deck. The ship was quiet, for at this time of night, on a clear sea, there was need only for a skeleton crew.

They walked in silence for a few minutes, enjoying the breeze-filled night and the large golden moon that had just risen over the horizon. It bathed the ship in its pale white light.

"Owen?"

"Yes?"

"What is wrong?"

"Wrong? Why do you ask that? There is nothing wrong with me. What man could complain when he is strolling about his ship wi' a beautiful lass like yourself?"

She stopped and looked up into his face, a face he tried to keep under control—too much control, because it was firm and hard, and for the humorous Owen, this was out of the ordinary.

"Owen, is it anything to do with me?"

Owen sighed deeply. There was no way he could tell her without betraying a friend and endangering further his beloved Jane.

"Kristen . . . I want you to know that I admire both

73

your beauty and your fine spirit and that I would never let anything harm you."

"I know that Owen. If I did not trust you completely, I would not seek out your company so frequently. I would remain locked in my cabin."

It was a devastating blow to Owen to hear these words, for it only made a bad situation worse. He was bound completely and there was no way out of it, but "be damned" he thought, no matter what Morgan had decided to do, he was not going to let him hurt a girl who would have no idea what was happening. He wanted to tell her everything, and to turn the ship from its designated course; yet he knew he couldn't do that to Morgan who trusted him, too. Instead, he made his decision. He would tell Morgan tomorrow, change his plans, and then take Kristen to Jane and let her tell Kristen about Jeffrey MacIntire. Then both Jane and Kristen would be free. He was sure that Morgan would listen to him. He took Kristen by the shoulders.

"You trust me?"

She nodded.

"Then leave everything as it is. Trust me to make everything all right. Then I shall take you to meet Jane and all the problems will be solved."

She looked at him in silence for a moment, while he waited for her decision; then she smiled. "Of course, Owen. I shall do whatever you wish."

"Thank ye, lass, ye'll no regret it."

She reached up and kissed him on the cheek. "Good night, Owen."

"Guid nigh', lass," he whispered; then he watched her walk away. Satisfied, he went to his bed knowing that what he had chosen to do was the right thing.

He lay for a while planning on what he would say to

Morgan to explain the situation. He felt Morgan might understand because he intended to offer his services to attack Jeffrey's ships in return for Kristen's freedom.

He planned well, and it might have happened that way, except fate had another situation in mind and fate would not be cheated.

## Five

The day dawned more beautiful than ever. Owen kept one eye on the horizon and one eye on Kristen. He knew that at any moment the lookout would sight sails, in fact he was surprised Morgan had not crossed their path before now.

As the day wore on, Owen became more and more tense; he couldn't for the life of him think of what was keeping Morgan.

Toward early afternoon, low gray clouds could be seen. "A storm," Owen thought angrily. That was all he needed. He couldn't change course or Morgan would not find him and the storm lay directly in his path.

He was leaning on the rail, his eyes intent on the gathering storm, and his mind on what he would say to Morgan. He was so lost in thought he did not hear Kristen come up beside him until she spoke.

"Good morning, Owen."

He turned to look at her. The bright open smile on her lips and in her eyes upset him now. Against the morning sky, her bright hair gleamed. She had tied it back carelessly with a ribbon. Her clear gray eyes seemed to him to penetrate his guilt. It made him uncomfortable.

"You're worried, Owen. What's wrong?"

"There's a storm coming. It looks like a fierce one."

She turned to look at the approaching storm, then back

76

to him. It suddenly struck him that her eyes were like the weather. When she was happy, they were clear crystal gray. When she was worried, as she was now, they darkened like the deep gray clouds that moved rapidly toward them.

"Ye're not afraid, lass?"

"No, of course not. I'm sure you know what you're doing. I'll not be afraid until I see you are." She laughed.

Her statement added more fuel to the fire of his guilt and made him mutter a silent curse under his breath.

"It would be best, lass, if ye'd stay in your cabin until we pass through this. It would only put more worry on me and the men to be concerned for your welfare in such weather."

"As you wish, Owen. I don't want to cause any problem. Can I stay on deck until the storm hits?"

"Aye, but ye'll promise me to go below as soon as I say . . . no arguments?"

"No arguments," she responded quickly.

Owen left her then to go about the business of preparing his ship to face the coming storm. He shouted firm authoritative orders, and men leaped to the rigging. Sails were tied securely to the spars—just in time.

Kristen felt the lifting breeze touch her and saw the mounting waves. She would have enjoyed staying on deck to face the storm. She felt exhilarated, caught up in the challenge to the ship of the sea and storm.

She stayed at the rail savoring the salty taste of the sea spray until a young sailor came to her side.

"Cap'n says would you go below now, ma'am. It's goin' to blow fierce and he wants you to be safe."

"All right," she said reluctantly. With one last look she made her way down to her cabin. She opened the door to step inside and suddenly she was thrown from her feet as the storm struck with full force.

She gave a yelp of surprise when she tried to stand only to be knocked down again. Instead of trying to rise, she crawled to her bunk and sat upon it, clinging to the wood frame that was bolted to the floor, grateful for its feeling of motionless security.

Now the storm struck with a violence she could hardly believe. She wondered how Owen and his crew could survive on the sea-washed deck.

To Kristen, it was a fury of a storm, but to Owen and his men it was a thing they had handled many times before.

Owen's first mate knew all the details of the agreement between Owen and Morgan. It might have been better if he had not, for it would have changed completely the situation that followed, the situation that delivered Kristen to Morgan.

Several things happened simultaneously. They reached the edge of the storm; a piece of splintered mast fell, struck Owen, and knocked him completely unconscious; and the *Falcon* lay waiting for them as they appeared out of the gray clouds.

Trying to make a decision as quickly as possible, the first mate ordered Owen to be carried to his own quarters to be cared for. He hoped Owen would waken soon; but until he did, he would be forced to put up some kind of fight against the *Falcon*. He ordered the sails unfurled and set a course that would turn him away from the attacking *Falcon*.

Kristen, hearing the storm lessen, made her way toward the deck. She arrived amid pandemonium and no one really noticed her.

She gasped in shock as she watched their elusive

tactics as they ran from the threat of the approaching ship.

She watched the tall sleek ship as it continued again and again to outmaneuver the *Sea Mist*. As the others did, she knew it would only be a short time until they were stopped. Her heart thudded painfully as she realized she could be the prize the pirate was after. She reached out to one man who was rushing past her.

"Where is Captain MacGregor?" she shouted above the noise.

"He's been hurt, ma'am; they carried him below."

"Hurt! How badly?"

"I don't know," he said as he pulled away from her. "You'd best go back to your cabin. I'm afraid we're going to be boarded by that damned pirate."

Thinking of Owen's kindness and the beauty of her time on his ship, Kristen turned to glare over her shoulder at the nearing ship. It was near enough now that grappling hooks could be thrown. They were, and slowly the ships were drawn together. She watched in fascination as men swarmed from one ship to the other. Pressing herself flat against the companionway door, she shook, not only with fear but with anger.

She saw Morgan as he swung easily from the *Falcon* to the deck of the *Sea Mist*. As his feet touched the deck, she saw him take complete and absolute command of the turmoil about him with a few crisp orders.

Anger boiled within her; yet she could not take her fascinated eyes from him. To her, he looked immense, his tall lean body strong and overpowering. She saw the flash of his white teeth as he spoke commands. Even across the crowded deck, his intense masculinity was a force she could feel. It caused a strange stirring deep within her.

It was her he wanted, she thought, and she pushed aside her feelings of attraction for the tall handsome pirate and allowed her hatred to boil to the surface. He had wounded, maybe killed Owen, her friend. Probably he was wounding or killing others for her, and for his revenge on Jeffrey. Why? Why? What dreadful thing did he think Jeffrey had done and why did he choose to punish him through her, an innocent person? Determination grasped her. She would not let him get away with it.

She slid slowly toward the door handle, but as her hand reached for it Morgan saw her. He pointed and said a few words to the man beside him who started toward her. Quickly, she grasped the handle and pulled the door open. She climbed down the steps as rapidly as she could, ran to Owen's cabin, and closed and bolted the door behind her. As she threw the bolt home, she heard the man who had followed her slam against the door. The bolt held. What surprised her was that from the lack of sound, the man seemed to have left. She searched about for a weapon, and found a sword that hung against the wall. She drew it from its scabbard and held it with both hands. Facing the door, she waited for whatever he planned to do next.

Jeremy came to Morgan's side, panting and with a smile on his lips.

"Jeremy?"

"She's locked herself in Owen's cabin. I don't think the lady is the gentle type who takes well to kidnapping."

Morgan chuckled.

"One small woman, Jeremy?" he questioned teasingly. Jeremy laughed in return.

"You go get her. I've no taste for draggin' screaming women from one place to the other."

Morgan laughed again and walked purposefully toward Owen's cabin.

Kristen waited, unable to tell what was happening. She held the sword and watched the closed door. It was not too long before she heard heavy steps approaching and stopping outside the door. After several minutes of silence Kristen's nerves were stretched taut, and she would have given a great deal to know what was happening.

Morgan studied the door closely and realized that although it was heavy enough to resist force and the bolt was in all probability the same, the hinges were old and rusty. With one well-placed slam of his foot, the hinges gave. Another thrust and the door swung inward. Kristen and Morgan stood facing each other with only the sword between them.

He stood and looked at her, a half-smile on his face and his eyes glittering with amusement at her fragile defiance.

She stood, backed against the wall, both hands holding the heavy sword in front of her. Her gray eyes were filled with storm clouds and her slim body trembled with rage at him. His eyes appraised her beauty with a touch of surprise. He had expected someone very different. He absorbed her rare beauty and immediately began to form a defense against it. In his mind, Jeffrey's woman could only be of one type—a cold calculating person as he was.

"You had best put down the sword or I shall be forced to take it from you. I would not like to hurt you."

"Liar!" she spat. "Why would you attack a ship, injure Owen, and do so much damage? Leave me alone. If you take one more step, I shall kill you."

He chuckled. "I must compliment Jeffrey; for the first time, he's shown some taste in his women. So you think

81

you are to be Jeffrey's little bride, well I am afraid you are wrong. Put down that sword, you are going with me."

"Never! If I can't kill you I shall kill myself before I let you touch me."

"I think not, my lady. I think you need a little taming, and I don't think old Jeff should have the pleasure of doing it."

She gasped at his open threat and he saw fear leap in her eyes, yet he had to admire the way she stiffened and brought the sword up toward him.

He did not believe for a minute she had the courage to use the sword. This was a drastic mistake on his part. Kristen was so afraid and yet so angry that she did not even consider any kind of surrender.

He took several firm steps toward her, then cursed and leaped back as she swung the sword upward. He looked down at the long ragged slash across his shirt and saw the bright red spots begin to stain it. He had come close enough to the point for it to slash a ragged cut about six inches long diagonally up his chest. He looked at the blood for a minute in complete shock; then anger filled his eyes. With one quick movement he drew his sword from its scabbard and struck hers with a blow so forceful that her sword flew from her hand and her whole arm tingled with pain at the force of it. In a moment, he was beside her and reached to grasp her. Again, what he expected, was not what happened. Most women would have retreated before his attack, screamed, or maybe even fainted. She did none of the three. Instead, she doubled her fists and struck out at him, several of the blows landing. He yelped at their force and grabbed her in his arms, confining her arms at her sides. He should have found a way to trap her legs for she kicked and writhed in his arms.

He found he was enjoying the feel of the soft curvaceous body he held bound so tightly against him. He was about to say a word to try to calm her when he again gave a surprised yelp of pain. She had sunk her teeth into his shoulder. He dropped her momentarily, then grasped her again. His hand touched the fabric of her dress and held. The tearing sound and her startled cry of fear held him momentarily spellbound. He had, in one swift move, torn away nearly the entire bodice of her dress. Her hands flew to shield herself from his gaze.

This was getting out of control, and he had not intended to hurt her or frighten her so badly. He would have moved away and tried to talk to her, but her fury and her fear were beyond reason now. He stepped back and she attacked.

Her strength was no match for his, but in her unreasoning anger and fear she did not try to rationalize.

To keep himself from more harm, he bound her to him again and held her so tightly she could not move. In fact, she could barely breathe. Then he was in for another shock. He looked down into her fear-filled gray eyes. Her slim rounded body pressed against his stirred him to a sudden blaze of desire. It was unexpected and he held her for some time before he recognized in her trembling lips and tear-filled eyes the fear she felt.

Why would she feel so? he rationalized defensively. A woman who had known Jeffrey should recognize desire when she saw it. He tightened his arms and heard her soft gasp and quiet sob of desperation. He did not believe, could not believe, she was the sweet innocent she appeared to be. It did not fit into the mold his mind had made for Kristen Seaford.

She was alarmed at the feel of his hard body against hers and the iron strength of the arms that held her.

"Let me go, please," she said softly. "If it is ransom you want, I have money. I'll give you anything you want, only let me go."

Mentioning her wealth was the worst thing she could have said. She saw his blue eyes cloud with anger and another emotion even he did not realize.

"You and Jeffrey," he snarled, "so much alike. Money is your life isn't it? You care nothing for the lives of others. Well, this time, my little rich girl, your money will do nothing for you."

Her lips were soft and moist below his, her body warm and firm in his arms. Her gray eyes, clouded and filled with fear, were the victims of his anger. With one arm he held her, and with the other he grasped the back of her hair and pulled her head back. His lips descended to hers in what he intended to be a kiss of punishment and anger. At their first touch she opened her mouth to protest.

His lips were hard and demanding against hers. He tasted completely the parted lips that were soft and pliant beneath his. Then something seemed to go wrong. He felt a stirring deep within him, and the sudden flame of it coursed through him. His lips became gentle and the arms that held her released their crushing pressure as he began to lose himself in her gentle sweetness.

She moaned softly as, for the first time in her life, she felt the burning touch of desire. Something in the center of her being seemed to burst into a million brilliant fragments and she tumbled into it, lost in the intense heat that threatened to consume her. She struggled weakly, and suddenly the realization of what was happening came to him. He had never raped a woman in his life and was overwhelmed with shock at his desire to do so now.

That he wanted her more at this moment than he had ever wanted a woman in his life left him shaken and angry—angry with himself for being so vulnerable, and angry with her for her ability to turn the tables on him.

He thrust her away from him with a curse and she stumbled back, her eyes wide with shock. Unaware of her rare and fragile beauty, she stood before him, the torn dress and disheveled hair creating a picture he would carry in dreams a long time. He had to shake her out of her shock more for his protection than hers, for he found himself wanting to take her in his arms with gentleness and ease her fear. He wanted to hold her . . . kiss her . . . love her. . . .

"I'm sure you bedded Jeffrey with ease, but I am more particular," he said in seeming coolness. "You're too skinny a whore for my taste even if you are rich."

Rage leaped to her eyes and her cheeks grew pink with shame and anger. She grasped the remnants of her dress and held it against her. Her eyes burned with the tears she refused to shed. He saw the determined proud lift to her chin and wanted to reach out and touch her. "I would die," she gasped in a hoarse strangled voice, "before I would ever let you touch me again. What kind of animal are you that you feel the need to take a woman by force and against her will? What is it you want, to prove your manhood? If so, you have failed. You are not a man, you are a beast."

He smiled to himself. He could handle her anger better than her gentleness. He grabbed her and despite her struggles, he bound her with a piece of rope he had brought along. He knew he could not take her on deck in her half-dressed state so he took one of Owen's cloaks and put it over her shoulders. Then he pushed her roughly ahead of him.

When he came on deck pushing her ahead of him, Jeremy's smile faded. He saw her disheveled state and her tear-stained face. Her gray eyes, wide with shock, took him by surprise. He looked at Morgan with a deep frown. This was not like Morgan to manhandle a woman. Morgan had always had a way of melting the coldest heart. He came to their sides, speaking to Morgan but watching Kristen's frightened face.

"Shall I take her aboard, sir? Everyone's ready."

"Go aboard, Jeremy," Morgan replied. He felt ashamed at Jeremy's obvious thoughts. "I'll bring her."

"Yes, sir," Jeremy said quietly, but Morgan could see his look of disapproval as he turned away.

Morgan turned and lifted Kristen effortlessly in his arms. He held her against him as he swung onto the deck of the *Falcon*. He took her down to his cabin and dumped her on his bed. Her arms bound behind her, the cape fell open and she lay before him, defenseless and extremely beautiful.

He gave a low muttered curse as he turned away. He left the cabin and slammed the door behind him.

Kristen could feel her trembling body relax and she surrendered to her fear. She turned her head against the pillow and cried. She was not prepared to admit that her fear was not of him . . . it was of herself. For the first time someone had reached to the depths of her being and touched her. She was afraid if he did so again, she would not be able to withstand the force of his attack.

The *Falcon* was underway and the sky had darkened before Morgan returned. He found Kristen asleep; her nervous tension and exhaustion had overcome her. He stood looking down on her slim body. Her disheveled clothes were tangled about her and her bright hair covered his pillow. She looked so small and defenseless that she again brought a softly muttered curse to his lips.

Gently, so that he would not waken her, he unbound

her hands. He saw her stir with relief and she mumbled softly in her sleep.

"Father," she whispered.

He sat on the edge of the bed and took one of her small hands in his. He saw the angry red marks on her wrists and massaged them gently. He heard her again sigh and relax into a deeper sleep. His hand brushed the length of her silky soft hair. As he watched her he wondered just what kind of a woman Kristen really was. If she gave him a chance he intended to find out.

He covered her with a blanket, and admitted with a chuckle that he had done this for his own peace of mind, for her half-naked body distracted him.

He went to a closet and took out another blanket; then he took off his boots, wrapped himself in the blanket, and lay down beside her. In a few minutes, he, too, slept.

Owen stirred, groaned, and forced himself into a sitting position, holding his head in his hands.

"Oh, my head is filled with demons fightin' with sharp swords. What happened?"

"You got a pretty good rap on the head with a bit of debris. Knocked you cold. You been out for over an hour."

"The storm?"

"It's over. We've a bit of damage, but nothing we can't fix."

"Good. There's been no sign of the *Falcon* yet has there? We should be crossin' her course soon."

"Sir . . . the *Falcon*'s been here and gone."

"What!" Owen almost shouted, then he winced as the pain cut through his head. "What do you mean 'been here and gone'?"

The first mate was startled by Owen's look.

"Oh, God." Owen groaned and buried his face in his hands.

"Is somethin' wrong, sir? I thought this was goin' along with your plans?"

"Did he say where he was takin' her?"

"Said it was a secret he wasn't tellin' anyone. He just said he'd contact you in about three weeks. He left you this note to give Jeffrey MacIntire."

"Three weeks," Owen groaned. "Three weeks of takin' his revenge out on a girl that's innocent of all this. My, God, I'll never forgive myself for this." His face became hard. "And if he harms that girl, I'll never forgive him either."

The first mate was told to go and see to the repairs. Owen lay back on the bed and said softly, almost as an afterthought, "And I'm sure little Jane would never forgive me if she ever knew of my part in all this. God, I hope she never has to know. I've got to find out somehow where he's taken her. Maybe I could keep him from doin' that child any harm . . . maybe."

Owen gave immediate orders for them to make all speed toward home. He would take the word to Jeffrey, then try to find some way to search out anyone who might have any idea where the notorious pirate, Captain Black, would anchor the *Falcon*.

It took a little more than a week before Owen and the *Sea Mist* reached harbor, an agonizing week for Owen. He did not feel any better when his ship entered the harbor and he could see the carriage that sat on the deck awaiting him. Jeffrey MacIntire had come for his bride.

The morning after Jane had boarded the *Sea Mist*, Jeffrey had risen and descended the steps to breakfast. He was thinking about the bargain he had made with Morgan Grayfield, a man he thoroughly hated. In the morning light, he was no longer sure it had been wise to take Jane's advice and ask for Morgan's help. After all, it was Morgan's sister he had once been engaged to marry— engaged before he found that the Seaford money was greater and that his old mistress, Leslie, had opened the door to it for him.

He remembered Charlotte—naïve, trusting Charlotte, who had given herself to him so easily. How he had laughed with Leslie at her conquest. How foolish she had been to believe her tearful confession of pregnancy would change his plans. She had pleaded, begged, and when that did not sway him, she had threatened. He knew he could not allow her to tell anyone. He had even been magnanimous enough to offer her a way to rid herself of the unwanted child. She had no business attacking him when he had found her an easy way out. Her death was an accident. He struck her several times to stop her screams and she had fallen and struck her head. He couldn't let her death mar the plans he had to wed the Seaford money, so he had taken her body aboard his small sailboat, tied the suicide note about her naked body, and dumped her over. Now, no matter what anyone might have thought, he was rid of her.

But Morgan's cold blue eyes irritated him. They seemed to reach within him and read what he didn't want read. He would never have suggested Morgan send one of his ships for Kristen if it hadn't been for that accursed pirate, Captain Black.

Of course he knew the man had a personal vendetta against him, and he also knew just how effective it had been. Jeffrey was near to ruin.

He smiled to himself. The tide would turn when two of his plans were completed. One, the marriage with the Seaford money, and the other, the arranged marriage of his sister to Clyde Rupert. What the old lecher wanted with his shy little sister, he didn't know; nor did he care. He only knew Clyde had offered to pay and pay well. He had watched Clyde's lascivious eyes on his sister, mentally undressing her, and knew he could name an exorbitant price—and he did. Clyde had accepted and Jeffrey had promised he would have her within a month.

"How do you know she will agree?" the old man had asked.

"I have not asked her to agree," he had replied arrogantly. "She will do as I say or I shall have to teach her obedience. I have done so before. Do not worry; she will do as I say as I expect she will obey you."

"Yes," the old man had replied softly, "she will learn to obey my every command."

At these thoughts of Jane, he called to a servant girl who came to him, her eyes wide with fear.

"Yes, sir."

"Go up and tell my sister I expect her to be at the table for breakfast within ten minutes."

"Yes, sir."

She literally ran from the room. It was several minutes before she reappeared. This time there were tears in her eyes and she trembled like a frightened rabbit.

"Well?"

"Sir . . . Jane is gone."

"Gone, what do you mean gone?"

"One suitcase, some of her clothes . . . they're gone. . . . She's gone, sir."

Jeffrey was so angry now he could hardly contain it. He ran from the room and up the stairs as the young maid whispered softly, "I hope you never find her, you monster. I hope Miss Jane has escaped forever."

He had set up a search for her for the next several days,

90

but it was as if the ground had opened and swallowed her.

He paid no attention to the absence of the *Sea Mist* for three or four days because he knew it had gone for Kristen. It was only when he had exhausted every other avenue that his mind turned to the *Sea Mist* as the only means of escape she had had. With deep burning anger he waited for the *Sea Mist*'s return for he expected not only the delivery of his bride but the return of his sister or the answer to her location.

After he had begun to think of the *Sea Mist* he began to wonder if its captain, Owen MacGregor, had any connection to Captain Black . . . or even if he might be Captain Black himself.

He dwelt on this thought until he remembered the description of Captain Black, and it in no way described Captain MacGregor. But if he wasn't the pirate, some instinct told him, he might know much more than he was saying. He would, he promised himself, have a long talk with Captain Owen MacGregor . . . as soon as he returned.

Now he sat in his study waiting for the carriage he had sent to bring Captain MacGregor to him.

Owen made his ship secure; then with reluctant steps, he entered the carriage that would take him to Jeffrey MacIntire.

He knew he would have to lie well to deceive this man. He also knew he would have to exert all of his control to contain his desire to beat Jeffrey thoroughly and to shout his possession of Jane to him and to the world.

He was escorted to the study, and within a few minutes he stood face to face with Jeffrey.

"Gossip and news has preceded you," Jeffrey said coldly. "I have heard you were attacked by our pirate friend. Is that"—he motioned to the still-angry scar on Owen's head—"a little memento of the occasion?"

"Yes," Owen said thoughtfully, "you might say it was."

"And Kristen?" Jeffrey asked softly.

"He has taken her," Owen replied bluntly.

"The bastard! I shall see him hung if it is the last thing I ever do. What does he want? Why doesn't he come here and fight me? The bastard! The filthy coward. She wasn't harmed, was she?" he asked anxiously. "He did not seem to want to do her any real harm, did he?"

"I'm sorry, Mr. MacIntire, but I never saw either him or his ship. I was unconscious at the time. When I finally regained my senses, he, the *Falcon,* and Miss Seaford were already gone."

"Then you did not know his plans?"

Owen reached into his pocket and withdrew the folded note.

"I imagine this was meant to explain his motives. He left it with my first mate."

Jeffrey unfolded the note and began to read. As he read, his face became redder and redder until he seemed about to explode. Suddenly, he crumpled the letter in his fist.

"He wants to ruin me! He wants every last cent I own. Oh, it will be such a pleasure to destroy that bastard when I catch him."

"*If* you catch him," Owen reminded.

"You have doubts?"

"You do not seem to be doing very well so far. How many times is it he's attacked you successfully, now? Six . . . seven? No one seems to be able to find any trace of him."

Jeffrey's eyes narrowed as he watched Owen. "Yes,"

he said softly. "He always seems to know of the comings and goings of all my ships. How would you account for that, Captain MacGregor?"

Owen shrugged. "Obviously, he has some kind of a spy system. Maybe someone close to you."

Jeffrey did not speak for several moments; then when he did, his voice was soft and conversational. "Close to me," he murmured. "Captain MacGregor, the night you left, did you carry any passengers?"

"Passengers?"

"Yes, did anyone book passage on your ship?"

"No, sir," Owen replied honestly. "No one paid for passage on the *Sea Mist* that I know of. There really is no room for passengers on her."

"Ummm . . ."

"Why do you ask?"

"A . . . ah . . . friend of mine is having some . . . ah . . . difficulty with his wife. I thought, as she has not been seen since that night, she may have booked passage on your ship and gone to America."

"I can honestly say, sir, that I delivered no passenger, male or female to America. My only mission there was to bring your bride here. No, there was no one on my ship when I arrived there and no one but Miss Seaford when I left."

"I see. Thank you for all your effort, Captain. I am sure you will thank Morgan for me when you see him; at least until I can thank him more appropriately."

"Aye, sir. I'll tell him."

"Good."

Owen was grateful to leave Jeffrey's presence before he could untangle the words Owen had used and ask him more pointed questions.

Owen began a surreptitious search for anyone who

might be connected with Morgan. He knew all the friends Morgan trusted and he felt if he could find just one, it would give him some lead to where he might begin the search for Morgan and the *Falcon*.

It was only two days before he began to realize he was being closely watched. Of course, he knew the only one who would be watching his every move would be Jeffrey.

It was clear he did not believe all Owen had said, and that he suspected a connection among Owen, Jane, and the elusive Captain Black.

He cursed the trap he was in. Even if he did find news of Morgan, he would not dare go to him for he was sure Jeffrey would have him followed. It even occurred to him that he could not go to their expected rendezvous in three weeks unless he found a way to rid himself of the shadow of Jeffrey MacIntire.

Another more terrible thought occurred to him. Unless he could get away, he would not even dare to return to Jane for that would be telling Jeffrey exactly where she was. He would die before he let him find her.

He lay on his bunk, wrapped in thoughts of how he could find a solution to the uncompromising situation in which he found himself.

# *Six*

Kristen stirred, then drew herself closer to the warmth near her. She was lost in a deep pleasant dream. She was a little girl again, secure in the warmth of her father's arms. He held her close and she could feel the comforting sound of his deep breathing.

Night filled the small cabin. Morgan had heard her thrashing about moaning softly as if she were a lost child. He had turned and gently drawn her into his arms. He wanted only to comfort her, but he enjoyed the soft feel of her. She slept, clinging to him. He caressed the silken strands of her hair that fell across his chest. He inhaled the perfume of her; it touched a hidden sense within him. He could feel the warmth of her slim body penetrate the shirt he wore and he could feel her soft breasts pressed against him.

Again he wondered about the mystery that was Kristen. How could she love a man as unfeeling and degenerate as Jeffrey MacIntire? He knew she would never believe the reason behind her kidnapping. He had thought it would be a simple thing, to hold her, maybe frighten her a little, and return her to her home. He wanted her to hate Jeffrey, to hate the man who had caused her such grief. It was not working as he had planned. She was not a fragile little girl to be frightened and to run. She had attacked him in anger and shame; in fear and distress she had fought him.

He drew her closer to him, angry at his own thoughts. He fought to blank out the sympathy he felt. He fought to blind himself to the sight of her beauty. He fought to close his senses to the scent and feel of her. He fought by remembering Charlotte and her death. He fought, and very slowly, he won.

When the first rays of sun explored the small cabin, Morgan was already up and dressed. He sat at his desk, pretending to be working; yet he watched her as slowly she stirred to wakefulness. Suddenly, the realization of where she was and what had happened returned to her. She sat up abruptly. He lifted his head to look at her. The sun entered the small window behind her and turned her hair into a blazing golden flame. The torn dress, forgotten for the moment, revealed her soft creamy skin. His breath caught at the picture she made.

Determinedly he made his voice cold and harsh.

"So your majesty, you have finally decided to arise. I see you are used to servants bowing and scraping. Well, it won't happen here. If you'll kindly get out of my bed, I will have my breakfast brought. If you're a good little girl you can share it. If not,"—he shrugged—"you'll go without until dinner."

He saw her clear gray eyes darken and her lips tremble before she pressed them firmly together to contain her fear. She gathered the torn dress about her and lifted her head proudly to gaze at him. "I want nothing from you except to be returned to my home. I do not care what you think of me. I hate you, you cold-hearted monster. All I want is to see the last of you. I hope they hang you for this and I will be glad to dance at your hanging."

He threw back his head and laughed, knowing that her

anger at him was the only thing that stood between them, and he needed it as much as she did.

He rose from his chair and walked toward her. Now he would make sure that she would carry that hate long enough to keep them both safe.

She watched him approach, fascinated by the overpowering sense of size and masculinity that exuded from him. Her eyes told him she was aware of him whether she knew it or not. It was an awareness he needed to kill.

Casually, he dropped down beside her, watching her draw away from him. "Now why be so shy, your ladyship?" He grinned. "We are alone. I'm sure old Jeff wouldn't mind sharing a little." He reached up and, with a quick motion, flipped the torn dress from her fingers and casually caressed one breast.

She gasped in shock and drew away from him as far as she could on the narrow bed. This time her eyes held a genuine fear and he wondered in surprise if no man, even Jeffrey, had ever touched her before.

"Suit yourself," he said with a shrug. "I've plenty of time. We'll be sharing this cabin for the next few days. There's a lot of time."

That, he thought with finality, should keep her as far away from him as she could get.

She watched him stand and walk to the door.

"I'll send you some water if you care to bathe, and I'll see if I can gather you some clothes. I wouldn't want you walking around among my men like that. I might find I have a mutiny on my hands."

He left, closing the door firmly behind him. Kristen huddled in a ball; the intense fear that had struck her at his words and at his casual touch left her weak and shaken. She closed her eyes and allowed the hot tears to overtake her.

This was the way Jeremy found her when he entered with the tub and hot water Morgan had told him to bring. At the sight of her, Jeremy jumped to the obvious conclusion. Morgan had taken her, without care, without love; and for the first time in their years together, Jeremy became thoroughly angry with Morgan.

He prepared the tub for her and laid out the clothes Morgan had gotten from their cabin boy. He worked in silence, watching her. She sat motionless on the bunk, the blanket about her; and her eyes, wide and still filled with tears, gazed thoughtfully out the window. He could tell her mind had slipped away from the miserableness of her enforced situation.

He could not believe Morgan was responsible for the look of abject misery on Kristen's face. To him, she seemed like an injured bird, unable to fly.

Morgan, as far back as Jeremy could remember, had found women easily. He had enjoyed the company of more pretty girls than Jeremy could count. Never had he treated one without gentleness and consideration.

There was nothing he could say to comfort her for she seemed not to know he was there. Instead, he held in his anger and left the cabin.

Kristen knew that he was there, but she said nothing for she expected no more mercy from him than she had found at the hand of his captain.

Slowly, she shook off her lethargy and rose from the bed. She went to the tub of water. It was warm and inviting. Beside it lay several large squares of cloth to dry with and a bar of soap. Next to this lay a pile of clothes and it took her a few minutes to realize these were the clothes, sent by her captor, in which she would have to dress for the balance of this journey. A journey that would lead her where? From the arms of the man who would have been her husband into the arms of the man who not only hated Jeffrey, but her as well.

She picked up the clothes and was surprised to find knee-length pants and a white shirt. Boys' clothes!

Angrily, she threw them down, but she knew he would be vicious enough to drag her among the crew in her tattered dress. He wanted to humiliate her. Well, she thought grimly, I will not let him succeed.'

She took off the dress, threw it aside, and stepped into the tub. She relaxed and allowed the water to ease her tension.

After she had lathered herself clean, she washed her hair and wrapped it in a towel. Rubbing herself briskly dry, she drew on the pants which were nearly a size too small and hugged her rounded hips like a second skin. The shirt, also too small, was stretched taut across her breasts. It was a good thing there was no mirror for what she would have seen would have shocked her.

Unbinding her hair, she rubbed it dry. Then she took a brush she found on the dresser and brushed the tangled golden mass until it sparkled.

She let it hang loose and free and turned toward the door. Her spirits rejuvenated by the bath and clean clothes, she went forth now to face her captor and was prepared to fight him in every way possible.

On the quarter-deck, Morgan stood with both hands on the wheel. Jeremy stood beside him and it took only a few minutes for him to sense Jeremy's scowling disapproval.

Morgan chuckled. "What's on your mind, Jeremy? You knew what we were going to do before we left."

"Aye, sir," Jeremy said through stiff lips.

"But you don't approve of something?" queried Morgan.

"Aye, sir."

"Do I have to pull it from you piece by piece? You knew I intended to kidnap her."

"Aye, sir."

Morgan sighed in exasperation. "You knew I intended to frighten her away from Jeffrey."

"Aye, sir."

"All right, Jeremy, what has your hackles up?"

"She's a pretty little thing and she's scared stiff. You never should have taken advantage of her like that. I've known you a lot of years and I've never seen you resort to rapin' scared little girls. That ain't frightenin', that's hurtin'. I don't like to be a party to such a thing."

"Rape . . . she said I . . ." Morgan sputtered in shock.

"She didn't have to say. I ain't blind. Her dress all torn and cryin' like that. The poor thing is scared so bad, she can't talk. What the hell came over you to use her like that? You hate Jeffrey that much that you can take it out on a little thing who can't even defend herself? I'm sure as hell disappointed in you. In fact,"—he glared at Morgan—"I don't think I'll stand this watch. The company ain't so nice."

He turned and walked away leaving Morgan staring after him in shock.

And if that shock was not enough, Kristen appeared at that moment and walked toward him. He could not believe the vision he was seeing, or the fact that the cabin boy's clothes could be turned into something so breathtaking.

As she walked down the deck toward him, all work ceased when she passed, and men stood to stare in open-mouthed wonder at the goddess who walked among them.

Morgan realized he had to do something before he lost control of his entire ship. He called one stunned man to him.

"Take the wheel," he commanded.

The man took hold of the wheel, but his eyes still followed Kristen as she walked toward them.

As rapidly as he could move without running, Morgan went to Kristen's side, grasped her by the wrist, and literally dragged her behind him to the security of his cabin. He pushed her in and slammed the door behind him. He leaned against it and watched the rage in her break to the surface.

She whirled about to face him, arms akimbo and her breath heaving in short gasps. Her face was pink from the rapidity with which he had dragged her along, and her gray eyes, darkened to almost blue-gray, were flashing anger like streaks of lightning.

"How dare you treat me like this? You monster!"

"Don't you know any other names?" he said casually. "You're becoming repetitious."

"Animal! Beast! Thief! You filthy—"

"Now, now, my lady. Don't get carried away."

"What is it you want from me? You force me into these terrible clothes, then drag me about this ship like a . . . a . . ."

"Trollop," he supplied with a grin.

"Ohhh!" she screamed, and before he could move, she leaped at him with nails prepared to rip at his face.

He caught both wrists and with little effort pinned her arms behind her. He smiled down into her angry, tear-filled eyes. He rapidly became very aware of many things. Her soft moist lips inches away . . . the round breasts held against him . . . the slender body he held so easily in his arms.

He bent his head and touched her lips with his, more to frighten her into silence than anything else. He was completely unprepared for the effect it would have on

101

him. Her lips were salty with her tears and they trembled beneath his. It was meant to be a touch, a gentle touch, and he did not even know when it got out of hand. Vaguely, he heard her soft whimpered moan as he crushed her to him. His mouth sought hers in a kiss that deepened with each second. He forced her lips apart and ravaged her mouth, searching for the flame that matched his own.

She writhed helplessly in his arms, and it did more to rouse him than to stop him.

Reluctantly, he lifted his head. When he did, she sagged against him; and, resting her head against his chest, she cried. The tears were from frustrated anger and the touch of a challenging emotion she had never felt before.

"I hate you," she sobbed. "I will kill you if I ever get the chance. Why? Why are you doing this to me? I have done nothing to you. Can your hatred of another be so strong that you must destroy all those near him? Will hurting me make you feel better or stronger?"

She lifted her head and glared at him with an angry look so intense that he could feel it go through him.

"What kind of a man are you to prey on someone innocent and to call it revenge? Why do you not fight the one you hate instead of punishing someone who does not even understand the reasons why?"

Guilt and anger warred in his mind. The urge to hold her gently, to tell her he was sorry for frightening her, battled with the doubts he carried. He was not really sure she did not know the man she was going to marry. He had known the wiles of many women and knew they had the most innocent way of achieving their goals. If it is an act, it is a very good one, he thought. She very nearly had him convinced she was completely innocent, not only of the kind of man Jeffrey was but of any kind of man in general. He had to keep up the charade until he knew for sure exactly how it was between her and Jeffrey.

He pushed her from him and walked a few steps away from her while he regained his own control. When he turned to face her again, his eyes held the same mocking amusement she had seen before.

He looked at her and had to admit she made the most fetching picture in the clothes she wore, but he knew he could never let her go on deck as she was now or the ship would stand small chance of reaching their hideaway.

"Much as I enjoy your appearance, my dear, I must insist you wear something a little more modest."

"Damn you!" she fairly shouted. "It was you who made me wear these clothes."

He chuckled. "I had no idea you would fill them so . . . delightfully. My cabin boy did not look quite so . . . round and pleasing in them. A slight mistake on my part, but I will rectify it quickly."

"What do you suggest I wear now, you miserable beast! Nothing?"

"Interesting thought," he said suggestively in a deep voice as he took a step toward her.

She retreated rapidly, her defiance quickly changing to fear that he might touch her again. It surprised him that it annoyed him, mostly because the desire to hold her again lingered just below his conscious thoughts. A desire to hold her and not see fear leap into her gray eyes, but . . . No! he would allow no such thoughts to dominate him. He would do what he had come to do—stop Jeffrey from making an advantageous marriage. He turned to a chest and flung it open. He drew from it a shirt and pants of his own.

From another drawer, he took a pair of scissors. In a

few quick snips, he shorted the legs of the pants and the sleeves of the shirt. Then he threw them at her and saw her look of hatred as she deftly caught them.

"Change," he commanded gruffly. Then he was caught by complete surprise as she bundled them into a ball and threw them back, catching him nearly in the face before he could react.

"You can go to hell before I take orders from you."

"You will change," he said threateningly, "or I will change you myself."

She defiantly lifted her chin, turned from him, and went to the bed, where she wrapped a blanket about her and sat down firmly—her back to him—and gazed in silence out the window.

Amazement followed by blinding anger overtook him. In two quick strides, he crossed the room and lifted her bodily from the bed. Despite her kicking and thrashing, he ripped the blanket from her.

Determinedly, he held her as he ripped the front of the shirt open. In several quick jerks, he tore it from her. His hand went to the waist of the pants that were already straining at the seams. In a quick motion of his arms, they gave.

She did not scream for she knew no help would come, but she fought him wildly with every ounce of strength she owned. When the clothes had been torn away, he held her naked thrashing body against his for a moment. Then he threw her roughly against the bed and straddled her. His weight held her firmly against the bed.

Leisurely, as if he were dressing an obedient child, he drew the shirt over her head. He grasped her flailing arms and thrust them into the sleeves.

Once he had the shirt on, he set about drawing on the pants. When he was done, he stood erect and looked down on her. She lay suddenly quiet. Heavy tears rolled down her cheeks; yet she refused now to even look at him.

He turned toward the door, his anger rapidly cooling before his guilt. He heard a soft muffled sob. He put his hand on the door, but could not resist turning to look at her again. She lay as he had left her, her eyes closed and the silent tears on her cheeks. She seemed so small and vulnerable he nearly went to her to gather her into his arms.

He gripped the door firmly, refusing to see what was so apparent.

"I expect you to be on deck soon. I would not want to have to come and get you. Then I might be angry enough to throw you overboard."

He left, slamming the door behind him.

With a low moan she turned on her side. In agonizing shame, she lay, her pride threatening her senses. Slowly, she began to think. In the fury of the preceding moments, she had lost all grasp on reality. Now she began to gather herself together again. He had shamed her, deliberately tried to damage her pride. He wanted her broken and crawling at his feet. Never! she thought. She would not allow his revenge against Jeffrey to succeed by letting him do this to her.

Slowly, she rose to her feet. The clothes he had forced on her were so large that she had to grasp them to keep them on.

She stood contemplating them; then she smiled. She would go on deck; she would wear what he had so brutally thrust on her. She would not let him see for a minute the depth of his success.

Walking to the chest from which he had taken the clothes, she knelt and lifted the lid. She searched until

105

she found what she wanted.

A needle and thread, a long scarlet sash and several long dark slim ties. Quickly, she cut the collar from the shirt, then she folded the edge and sewed it down. She drew one of the long ties through this and when she slipped the shirt back on she drew the string taut. It drew the shirt in gathers about her neck.

Tucking the shirt into the overly large pants, she folded them across her waist and wrapped the red sash about her several times from beneath her breasts to her hips.

When she had done this, she took the scissors and cut the pants so that they ended just below her knees, leaving her slim legs exposed. It was a surprisingly attractive outfit when she finished.

She drew her hair over her shoulder and braided it, circling the end of the long thick braid with another of the black ties.

She slipped on her own black slippers. Then she stood erect and looked at the closed door. Gathering her courage, she walked to the door and opened it.

Morgan stood on the quarter-deck. He had been watching for her to appear. It worried him now that he had pushed her beyond what she could endure.

He was ignoring as best he could the quiet Jeremy who refused even to look at him.

I'll give her a few more minutes, he thought; then go and get her. Damn, he thought, what in the hell has come over me to treat her so? It was the thought of her and Jeffrey that enraged him, but that was the last idea he would allow to enter his mind.

The minutes marched along and he began to worry about her. One quick glance at Jeremy's closed silent face did not do his thoughts any good. He turned the wheel over to his mate and started toward his cabin, hoping he would find her angry instead of in silent tears the way he had left her.

He had only taken a few steps when the companionway door opened and she stepped out. If either of them could have read the other accurately their battle would have been over, but he saw only the smile of bitter anger and defiance and she saw only the threat of more brutal anger.

He went to her. She watched him come. Never would she let him know that she trembled violently, wanted to cry out to him, to beg him to let her go. She held herself under rigid control, but it was no more severe control than he held over himself.

"I see you have finally acquired some wisdom. You can make yourself at home anywhere on the ship as long as you get in no man's way."

"I will get in no one's way," she replied coldly. "Especially yours. The farther I stay from you, the better."

She moved past him and went to the rail. She stood with her back to him and did not see the appreciative glance he gave her slim figure. She did not see the warmth in his gaze, but Jeremy did. With a small humorous chuckle, he turned away. My captain, he thought, has run across a reef that threatens to sink his ship.

Kristen's normal bright disposition did not take long to reappear. Jeremy went to her and spoke gently with consideration. Within two days, she and all the crew knew she was not only under their captain's protection, but Jeremy's as well.

She stayed as far away from Morgan as the size of the ship would allow. When they did meet, she did her best to speak little and to ignore him as much as she possibly could. It grated on Morgan's nerves that she could be laughing with someone or in friendly conversation with Jeremy only to freeze at his approach.

Jeremy was enjoying Morgan's discomfort immensely. He felt in this case, Morgan deserved what he was getting.

It surprised Kristen that she was enjoying herself immensely. The crew treated her with happy affection, each pointing out things of interest and telling her stories of themselves, their pasts, their presents, and their futures.

Jeremy enjoyed her company and did not for a minute believe Kristen was aware of Jeffrey's past or the reasons for her abduction.

He knew long before Kristen and Morgan ever suspected that the two were aware of each other and drawn to each other by a force they could not ever hope to fight. He knew Morgan wanted Kristen by the way his gaze would dwell on her when he thought she was not aware.

He also knew that Morgan would be the last to admit it. He knew of Charlotte, and he knew Morgan's hatred of Jeffrey would make him cling to thoughts of revenge. What worried him was thinking that he must have taken her the first time, and wondering just how long Morgan's desire for her could be held back by thoughts of revenge, or for that matter, how long it was going to be before Morgan saw it for what it was and admitted . . . that he did not want to return Kristen Seaford to Jeffrey MacIntire . . . ever.

The days passed and soon Jeremy told Kristen they would be sighting land. "Where, Jeremy?" she whispered softly.

"I can't tell you, the captain wouldn't like it. All I can

say is it's an island, and there'll be nobody on it except us."

"The captain . . . Jeremy . . . what will he do with me when we reach land?"

"Hold you till he gets the ransom or . . . what he wants."

"Jeremy . . . why does he hate Jeffrey so?"

"It's best you ask him, Kristen."

"I . . . I'm afraid of him."

Again Jeremy was struck with anger at the man he cared so much for and his careless treatment of this child.

"Kristen . . . you don't know the captain. Right now he's got some dark thing eatin' at him. He ain't this way. Maybe someday you'll be able to see that this is a dark side of him. There's a side of him that's good and kind. Don't let what you think you see frighten you. He won't hurt you anymore."

"Good . . . kind. I find that hard to believe. He has been hard and brutal. I do not think I want to see any other side of him. All I want is to go home."

"Home, you mean to marry Jeffrey?"

"No," she said quietly, "I want to go home. I will not marry Jeffrey. I have just found out how little I know him. No, I do not want to marry anyone. . . . I just want to go home."

Jeremy smiled. She had finally turned from Jeffrey; now he hoped she would turn toward Morgan, see him for the man he really was. He thought maybe Kristen was the one thing Morgan would need to help him from the path of destructive rage he was on. If they could only find each other, maybe all of this would not have been for nothing.

They stood together at the rail talking; neither of them noticed Morgan who stood watching them.

He saw her smile at Jeremy, saw the breeze blow

strands of hair across her face; her slim body was dressed in the outlandishly beautiful costume he had forced on her.

In his mind, he felt her slim naked body writhe against his, tasted the sweet moistness of her lips again and again until it drove him to a thick hungry desire for her.

Angrily, his desire blended with his hatred for Jeffrey and his claim on her.

He was caught in an emotion he did not want, and he wondered, if Jeffrey paid the ransom, would he be able to return her to him?

# Seven

The island was a place Morgan had chosen at the beginning, when he was first faced with the problem of hiding the beautiful but easily identifiable *Falcon*.

It was about six miles long and about two miles wide. At its very center was a tree-covered range of hills that tapered down to a long white sandy beach. Halfway up one of the hills he had built a small three-room house. Just below this was a long narrow building that held supplies for the *Falcon*. He did not want his ship traced through the buying of supplies.

The *Falcon* was anchored not far from shore in a quiet secluded lagoon. Jeremy helped Kristen into a longboat. Morgan had gone ashore in another boat ahead of them. When their boat was dragged up on the beach and they alighted, Jeremy led her up the sandy beach toward the small house.

When they reached it, Morgan was already there.

"Jeremy, go and have the *Falcon* checked from bow to stern. I want her in good shape for our next trip."

"Aye, sir," Jeremy said, but Morgan was amused by the fact that Jeremy really was hesitant about leaving Kristen alone with him.

Jeremy was, to Morgan, his mentor and conscience. He was old enough to be Morgan's father, and had, in fact, guided him through many things. It almost made him

111

laugh outright to see Jeremy's worried look and to realize the source.

"Jeremy," he said softly, "there will be no problems."

Jeremy's gaze held his.

"I trust you, lad."

"I know," Morgan said softly. "See about the *Falcon*."

"Aye, sir." Jeremy turned and left. After his retreating footsteps died away, Morgan and Kristen stood and looked at each other across a very silent room.

She watched him as a mouse would watch a very hungry cat. He took a step toward her and she immediately took one away.

"This is ridiculous!" he snapped. "I have no intention of harming you. For God's sake, woman, don't act as though I intend to ravage you. I've never used force on a woman in my life and I've no intention of starting now with you."

Angrily she pulled back the loose sleeve of her shirt to show him several angry black-and-blue marks on her arm. "I have several more of these as proof of your very gentle nature."

His eyes narrowed as he looked at the bruises and a quick sense of guilt touched him.

"I did not mean to do that. You should have done what I told you to do and that would never have happened. The fault is yours."

"The fault is mine?" she almost shrieked. "You injure my friend, abduct me from my friends, tear my clothes from me, haul me here without a word as to why or what I can expect, and you stand there and tell me the fault is mine. If it could be my choice, I would see you in hell before I would do as you tell me."

Morgan sighed; he could see in her frightened state that no words he might say would wipe away her fear.

Time would prove to her he meant her no physical harm.

"There is a bedroom in there." He pointed at a closed door. "And a kitchen in here. I am going to care for my ship. I will come back later to see if you are all right."

He left, and she contemplated his last words that meant to her only one thing: he meant to come back later and finish what he had started on the ship.

She ran to the door and pulled it open. Standing on the porch of the cabin, she watched him walk to the beach. Morgan expected her to gather herself together and be quieted by the time he returned. Then he planned to talk to her, to try to end her fear of him, and to let her know he only intended to hold her here for a time, then send her safely back home.

He did not count on Kristen's independence, or obstinacy. She had no intention of letting him manhandle her again. Of course, Kristen did not think for a moment beyond defending herself from his violence.

She began a swift search of the small house. Opening the door he had first indicated, she saw a small room with one window. It contained a large four-drawer dresser against one wall and a chest at the foot of a large and very comfortable-looking bed. It was obvious there would be no weapons of defense here, and a bedroom was the last place she wanted to be with him. Quickly closing the door, she went to the other. There she found a fireplace with cooking utensils hung above it, and a table with two chairs. The cupboards, she noticed, were well-stocked with food. Anyone could remain here for a long time. She did not choose to do so.

Quickly she searched the kitchen and found several wicked-looking knives. Choosing a large one, she carried it with her.

113

She returned to the main room and drew a chair near the small fireplace. Then she sat down to contemplate exactly what she would do, and what she would say to help gain her release when he returned. First she must force him to keep his distance from her; then she would promise him any amount he wanted to return her to her home. She would tell him she had no intention of marrying Jeffrey; since her wedding plans seemed to be the cause of this, maybe they would be the end of it.

Time moved slowly by and the sun began to near the horizon. She was hungry and got up to return to the kitchen, meanwhile listening for the sound of his footsteps. She found bread and cheese and cut herself a huge chunk of each. In another cupboard was a bottle of what she thought was wine. It seemed to be the only thing to drink so she carried it along, too.

She sat in front of the empty fireplace again and opened the bottle. She bit off a large bit of the cheese and bread; then she took the bottle. Since there were no glasses she could find, she decided to drink anyhow. Tipping the bottle she took a large swallow and nearly choked as the fiery liquid coursed through her.

She gasped for breath, then felt the warmth of it seep through her body. It made her feel good when the first touch of flame was gone.

She continued to eat until the pieces of bread and cheese were gone; but by that time, over half the bottle was gone, too. In a half-drunken state, she began to feel waves of self-pity. Hot tears filled her eyes and rolled heedlessly down her cheeks as she mourned her tragic luck and her meeting with Captain Black. After each thought of him, she took another sip, and after each sip, she thought of him.

When another hour or so had passed, the last rays of

the setting sun found her curled in the chair, the knife in her lap and the bottle in her arms. She did not hear Morgan's approach, or the opening of the door.

In the half-light he could barely make out her form in the chair, and he did not understand her silence.

Quietly, he lit the candle on the table. Holding it up he walked to her and stood looking down. A thread of quiet laughter emanated from him as he realized, from looking at the bottle, that she was completely drunk.

He bent down and, taking the bottle from her hand, he held it before the candle, and whistled softly.

"My God, you've drunk over half of this bottle. I wonder if you thought it was wine." He smiled down at her. "My love, you are going to be sorry for this in the morning."

He set the candle and bottle aside and bent over her. It was then he saw the knife clutched in her other hand. He knelt before her and gently took the knife from her, surprised at the unwelcome feeling of tenderness that swept over him. He saw the tears on her cheeks and the vulnerability in her slender form. He reached out and brushed the tears away gently.

"Tomorrow, little one," he whispered. "Tomorrow I'll do my best to take away some of your fear. Until then . . ."

He rose and bent over her, gently lifting her from the chair. She sighed deeply and her head rested against his shoulder. Her arms clung to him as if in her dreams she were reaching for comfort and safety.

He carried her to the bedroom and laid her gently on the bed. He would have removed her constraining clothes, but he knew if she found herself naked in the morning, it would only confirm her fear and make her believe he had taken advantage of her helplessness the

115

night before.

He sat on the edge of the bed for a moment and looked down on her relaxed sleeping form.

She was more beautiful than he had ever thought she would be. Her features, softened in sleep, made her look even younger than she was; yet he estimated she couldn't be more than eighteen. Again he was puzzled by her. She seemed so unaware of the kind of man Jeffrey was. He wondered if it was some kind of game she was playing with him to gain her release or if she truly did not know the reasons behind all that had happened.

She stirred restlessly and her brows drew together in a deep frown. Again tears escaped from under her closed lids.

"No," she murmured. "No, don't . . . please."

If he had felt guilty before, his attack of conscience only worsened as he realized she was still fighting him in her dreams.

At the age of twenty-six, he thought he had tasted just about every kind of woman that existed, but this uncertainty was new to him. He had prepared himself to hate her and found he could not. He had prepared himself to be cold and unfeeling, but found he was feeling more than he had bargained for.

He took her hand in his and felt her cling to him. When she touched a source of warmth and security, it seemed to comfort her. She drifted again into a deep and dream-filled sleep.

Gently, he disentangled her fingers from his and rose from the bed, ignoring his deep and very real desire to lie beside her and hold her in his arms.

He left the room and closed the door behind him. Going to the table, he took the rest of the bottle and sat in the chair from which he had just taken her. Slowly, he sipped from the bottle and thought of all the things that had happened to draw him and this woman child together.

Several hours later, he took some blankets from a closet and made himself an uncomfortable bed on the floor. He chuckled at himself, for it was not like him to sleep in such an uncomfortable place when the promise of a much softer one hovered near.

"I must be getting old." He laughed, but the warmth of the desire that flowed through him at the thoughts he still carried of her told him definitely that age was not his problem.

He could have slept comfortably in his bed on board ship, but he would not leave her alone, even though he knew she would come to no harm. His makeshift bed's discomfort made him sleep light. That was why he heard her stir and begin to waken as the first rays of the sun touched the small house.

He opened his eyes and listened for the sound that had wakened him. It came again, a soft despairing moan. He got to his feet and went to the bedroom door and opened it. She lay facing him in a curled heap of disheveled hair and tear-filled eyes, her complexion hovering near the color of the green sea beyond them.

"You've poisoned me," she gasped. "I'm dying."

"No, my love, you're not dying. You are only paying the price of drinking nearly three-fourths of my best bottle of whiskey. It serves you right."

His eyes glittering with amusement and the taunting half-smile on his lips were all she needed to put the crowning touch on her misery.

"Oh," she moaned. "How can you be so miserable and unfeeling? I hate you. Please go away and leave me alone. I would rather suffer this pain forever than to share a

117

room with you another minute."

He chuckled and moved toward her. She made every effort to escape from the other side of the bed before he got to her, but the pounding in her head and her extreme nausea made it impossible.

He grasped her and effortlessly lifted her body in his arms. With quick firm steps, he left the bedroom and walked to the front door.

She moaned softly again as terrified thoughts filled her mind about what he planned to do to her. Death seemed at the moment to be the most pleasant way out of her misery.

Behind the cabin was a swiftly moving stream that started somewhere near the top of the mountain and rushed to the sea. It was cold and crystal clear and banked on both sides by grass-covered ground.

In several places it widened and deepened so that one could swim in it; in fact, Morgan had many times.

He laid her on the bank at the edge of the stream, then proceeded to dunk her head in the water. She came up thrashing and sputtering only to be doused again and again.

To her surprise the throbbing in her head began to recede, but the ache was replaced by pounding fury. She fought him as he prepared to dunk her again. Taken by surprise by her violent, unsuspected attack, Morgan slipped and fell into the water. This time, it was his turn to register shock and surprise, and despite the way she felt, Kristen lay on the bank and began to laugh. Her laughter built until she could hardly breathe.

Closing her eyes, she laughed until the tears came; then suddenly her laughter ended in a shriek as he lifted her and with cold deliberation, threw her into the water.

She surfaced to see him standing on the bank, hands

on hips, grinning amiably at her.

Suddenly the whole situation seemed ridiculously funny to her and she returned his smile.

"We are even, I hope?" he said.

"Hardly, Captain. I still owe you much."

"We could at least call a truce until we're into some dry clothes and have a meal. *If* it is all right with you. I promise I will not get within five feet of you at any time. After we eat and dry off and I get a chance to talk reasonably, we might be able to bring an end to all the hostilities."

He watched her as she contemplated his offer, and could not believe his feeling of relief when she nodded her acceptance of his terms.

He stretched out his hand to help her from the water, then let it drop as she deliberately ignored it and climbed to the bank by herself. It was then he received another shock.

The shirt he had forced upon her was nearly sheer with its wetness. It hugged the naked body beneath it as if it were her skin. It left nothing to his imagination at all.

Following his gaze she looked down at herself. It was as if she stood naked before him.

Embarrassment and shame made her cry out. She spun on her heel and ran to the cabin, giving him a very interesting bit of scenery to follow as she did.

Inside, she grasped one of his blankets, threw it about her, and turned to face him as he entered behind her. She looked like a hunted doe held at bay by a vicious dog.

"I thought we had a truce?" he said mildly.

He stood by the door watching as she began to gather herself.

"I have more clothes in the other room. You are

119

welcome to them until we can get you something more suitable." He chuckled. "But I must insist, my dear, that you take a little better care of them. The supply is not inexhaustible, you know."

She smiled at his attempt to relieve her anxiety, and began to relax.

"You do have some scissors here? I'll make something of my own."

"Yes, but anything you need, Jeremy can supply. He keeps a store of the most amazing things. I'm sure he'll come up with something. Are you ready to eat?"

"I'm famished. Where is the food?"

"Jeremy prepares it here usually, but since he's not here, he must be cooking on board. We'll go there."

"I can't."

"Why?"

"I can't go there like this." She looked down at the blanket about her.

"No . . . I suppose you can't. Well, Jeremy will have to bring the food here."

"How will he know?"

Morgan held up a finger and winked at her; then he stepped onto the porch. From his pocket, he took a small mirror. Holding it up so that it caught the rays of the sun, he sent a flashing signal to the *Falcon*. In a few minutes, the blinking light was returned.

It took Jeremy and the cabin boy less than half an hour to arrive with the food. As the cabin boy set the food and utensils out on the table, Jeremy smiled and eyed both Morgan and Kristen. Morgan smiled to himself as he realized Jeremy's imaginings. He already thought Morgan had raped her on the ship. Now her wet hair and blanket-wrapped body inflamed his indignant anger at

Morgan for what he thought was deliberate and brutal mistreatment.

Jeremy turned accusing eyes on Morgan who kept his face impassive with what he considered noble effort.

"Will there be anythin' else ye'll be needin' . . . *sir?*" He stressed the word firmly so Morgan would know of his displeasure.

"Yes, Jeremy," Morgan replied nonchalantly. "Do you have some needles and thread and maybe some cloth that Kristen can work with? She's in need of some more clothes. It . . . ah . . . seems she had a little . . . ah . . . accident this morning."

"Accident?" Jeremy questioned suspiciously.

"Yes . . . accident. She fell into the stream."

"Fell?"

"Yes."

"In the stream?"

"Yes."

Kristen's cheeks pinkened as she saw clearly how Morgan was playing with Jeremy, and the thoughts that were in Jeremy's mind. Her anger at Morgan returned. To think he could so easily imply such things and allow Jeremy to think them infuriated her. Morgan saw her gray eyes begin to cloud with anger. He recognized the storm that was coming. Quickly he motioned to the table and smiled at Kristen with his best-controlled gentleman's smile.

"I know you are hungry, Miss Seaford. Please, do sit and eat." He turned to face Jeremy as Kristen went to the table.

"That's all we need, Jeremy. You can send the boy back for the dishes later."

"Aye, sir," Jeremy replied through stiff lips. He

121

turned and left, letting the door close rather noisily on Morgan's soft chuckle.

He returned to the table and sat opposite her.

"Jeremy is an excellent cook. I suggest you try each thing for he will look forward to a compliment or two on his return."

He studiously ignored her gaze as he began to fill her plate. She watched him closely. He was a puzzle to her. A pirate, yet with obvious breeding he could not hide. Against her will, she had to admit he was extraordinarily handsome. His thick black hair, still damp from the water, curled in a wayward mass. There was a humorous glow in his deep blue eyes that she could discern even though he didn't smile. Yet when he did smile, she held her breath at the way it seemed to reach out and enclose her in a bright field of warmth.

He set her plate in front of her and she began to eat, more to avoid meeting his eyes than from hunger.

"Eat," he said. "I'll be back in a moment."

He rose and went into the bedroom. In a few minutes, he returned. He had changed his clothes, and now he draped the wet ones over a chair. Then he returned to the table and began to eat.

They ate in silence for a few minutes; then she spoke hesitantly.

"Who are you?"

He raised one questioning brow.

"I know what you are, or what you say you are, but . . . who are you, really?"

"I am as I say I am—a pirate who seeks revenge on a blackguard who deserves to die for what he has done."

"What could Jeffrey have done to a pirate to bring on such vengeance?"

It seemed for a minute he was going to answer her;

122

then he smiled wickedly. "Need I tell you anything of the man? After all, did you not promise to marry him? You should know more of his character than any other."

It was meant to be a jibe at her, but he was surprised to find her eyes darken with an emotion he could not read. Within her, she struggled with the thought that in her time of weakness and distress she had promised to wed a man she didn't know. If Morgan had not taken her, she would, in a few days, have tied herself forever to a stranger.

She looked at Morgan, and her eyes widened with the knowledge that she was glad. The sudden relief surprised her. To cover her emotions, she questioned him again.

"You have asked Jeffrey for ransom for me?"

"Yes."

"And . . . if he pays it, you will return me to him?"

"Yes."

"Even if . . . if he is what you say he is, you would give me to him? Are you any better than he? You shouted to me about the love of money, yet with enough money to make Jeffrey suffer, you would push me into the arms of a man you choose to call a villain."

Stung by her accusation, and the truth of it that struck him wordless, he remained silent. His silence to her meant acquiescence.

She rose from the table, forcefully holding back the tears in her eyes.

"No, Captain Black, you are no better than Jeffrey. If it is money you choose over honor, then take mine. It is worth it to receive such a lesson about men. Take mine, for I do not choose to be returned to or to marry Jeffrey MacIntire or any other man. Take my money and let me go home."

She said the last words softly; then she turned, drew

the blanket tighter about her, and with a cold scornful look left the cabin.

He rose and went to the door. He stood in the open doorway and watched her walk to the beach.

Slowly a half-smile touched his lips and a satisfied look glowed in his eyes.

He had felt deeply the words she had uttered, reacting to some with guilt and some with anger. But the ones that still whispered seductively in his head and returned the humor to his eyes were . . . "I do not choose to marry Jeffrey MacIntire."

# *Eight*

Kristen walked down the path to the ship, her thoughts a jumbled turmoil within her. What kind of man would deliberately steal her from someone for whom he felt such hatred and disgust, then at the drop of a few coins return her to face such a man? At that moment she hated both Jeffrey for getting her into this, and Morgan, for opening her eyes to such cold-blooded using.

She reached the beach where Jeremy and the cabin boy sat before the beached longboat.

Jeremy had seen her coming, for one of his eyes was always on the cabin. He watched the dejected droop of her head, and when she approached, he saw the tears in her clouded gray eyes. He stood up when she approached and saw her reach within to summon up a hesitant smile for him. He smiled in return.

"Is there something I can do for you, miss?"

"Could . . . could you take me back to the ship? I need to do something about my clothes and . . . Jeremy, is it possible I could have enough hot water for a bath?"

Again he smiled and it warmed her to see the gentleness in his eyes.

"Aye, miss. You just come with me. I'll see to it you get an undisturbed bath, and if you like, I'll help you with the clothes."

"Thank you, Jeremy." She rewarded him with her

warmest smile in appreciation of his kindness.

"Come along, Toby," he said to the cabin boy, no older than ten, who stood watching Kristen with undisguised admiration for her rare golden beauty.

"Toby," Jeremy said sternly and the boy leaped; his face reddening in embarrassment. He nearly ran to help Kristen into the longboat.

"But," Toby began, "what about the captain?"

"Toby," Jeremy said, "at this moment I'd be happy to let him swim to the ship—aye and maybe have a shark take a small nip while he's on the way."

Toby's eyes widened in disbelief. This was Jeremy, the captain's closest and most trusted friend. He could not believe Jeremy could say such a thing. Jeremy chuckled, knowing Toby's near-worship of Morgan could never accept such a thought.

"Come, lad, I didn't mean that; but that boy surely does need something to shake him awake."

"Yes, sir," Toby said, relief flooding his face. He should have known Jeremy would never turn on Morgan even for a lady as beautiful as the one who sat in the boat.

Slowly and in complete silence, they rowed to the ship. Kristen was deep in her own thoughts and did not feel Jeremy's intent sympathetic gaze on her. Again he was filled with disbelief that Morgan would treat a pretty young thing like Kristen so coldly and unfeelingly.

He remembered the young Morgan who had played on the beaches with his sister. He remembered the love Morgan had felt for Charlotte. She had been several years younger than Morgan and he had protected her from any form of hurt like a young gladiator. Jeremy remembered also a pain-filled Morgan who felt he had failed to protect the sister he loved from her final hurt, the hurt that had taken her life and left Morgan filled with suffering and

126

thoughts of revenge.

Jeremy sighed. If only Morgan could put aside the hatred that ate at him and see Kristen for the rare sweet thing she was. Silently, he prayed something would open Morgan's eyes before he hurt Kristen.

The longboat bumped along side the *Falcon*, bringing both Kristen and Jeremy out of their thoughts. Gently, Jeremy helped Kristen aboard and walked with her to the cabin.

The torn dress lay on the floor, mute evidence of all that had happened to her there. Kristen bent and picked it up.

"I'll fetch ye a needle and some thread, miss. In no time we will have it fixed."

Kristen held the torn dress in her hand, but in her mind, she saw Morgan's angry blue eyes glaring at her. She shivered at the thought and again Jeremy misread the evidence. He was sure that rape had been committed there by a man he never could imagine performing such an act.

"I'll send ye a bath, miss, and if ye don't mind, I can sew a fair stitch. I'll repair it while ye're havin' your bath."

"Thank you." She smiled and handed the dress to him. "I'm grateful for your kindness, Jeremy. There's only one more thing."

"Yes, miss?"

"My name is Kristen; my friends call me Kristi. I hope we'll be friends, Jeremy."

"Thank ye, miss. I'll be proud to be called your friend."

He nodded, took the dress, and left the cabin. Slowly, Kristen sat down on the bunk. She was surprised that her thoughts returned to the blue-eyed pirate she had just

127

left, that she was wondering what he was doing and thinking now.

After a short time, Toby returned with two sailors. They carried a large tub. It took a determined Toby several trips to fill it with warm water. But when she smiled and thanked him warmly, that was reward enough for him. He followed Jeremy's orders to the letter.

"I'll be right outside, my lady," he said solemnly. "Jeremy says I'm to stand guard to see no one disturbs you while you're bathin'."

He left, closing the door behind him, and stood with his young shoulders braced against the jamb, a very determined glint in his young eye.

Kristen sank into the water with a grateful sigh. She lay back in the tub to enjoy the warmth of her bath. But when she allowed her mind to drift, she suddenly found it lost in thoughts of dark blue eyes and strong arms. By the time she had bathed and washed her hair she felt much better. It was the absence of his disturbing presence that contributed to her sense of well-being. In fact, she felt she could have enjoyed the new sense of freedom she felt if it hadn't been for the dark specter of Morgan.

As she wrapped herself in a towel, a soft rap sounded on the door.

"Yes?"

"I've your dress, miss," came Jeremy's voice.

She opened the door and he handed the dress to her. When she looked at it, she was amazed at the neat precise stitching that made the gown nearly as good as new. She donned the dress and sat on the edge of the bed, towel-drying her hair.

After it was nearly dry, she searched among Morgan's things until she found a comb and brush. She brushed loose the tangles, then drew her long hair over her shoulder and braided it. The braid hung thick and heavy to her hips. Tying the end with a bit of material she tore from the shirt she had been wearing, she completed her preparations.

Then she returned to the bed and sat down wondering what she would have to face next. She sat for some time until a feeling of confinement drew her to her feet and toward the door. She wondered if he had returned to his ship, and if he would have some objection to her walking the deck in the beautiful sunshine. No matter what, she thought, I cannot bear this confinement another minute. If he wanted her locked away, he would have to drag her back by force. The thought barely entered her mind before the realization followed that if he wanted to, he could do just that and there would be no one to come to her aid. A soft tingle of fear touched her.

Just as she stepped on deck, Jeremy approached her.

"The captain has signaled, Kristi; he wants the longboat on the beach. I . . . I imagine he wants you back, too."

She knew, if Morgan had given the order, it would do her no good to argue. Yet she hesitated because she did not want to be left alone with Morgan in the cabin.

Wordlessly, she walked to the rail and prepared to descend to the longboat. Jeremy helped her, and Toby scrambled rapidly down behind her. Only a few minutes later they drew the boat up on the sand. Reluctantly, Kristen climbed out and stood looking up at the silent cabin. She felt unsure of herself and strangely frightened at what might await her there.

"Jeremy," she said softly, "could I just walk for a while. There's no way I can escape. Please, just let me be alone for a while."

He felt a sympathy for her seeming helplessness. "Aye,

129

Kristi, I see no harm in ye takin' a walk. I'll send Toby for ye after a while. I would talk to Morgan anyway."

She smiled her thanks and turned to walk slowly down the beach. Jeremy watched, and again the anger touched him at the thought of what Morgan could have done to make her so desolate.

He turned, and with Toby at his side, started up the hill to the cabin.

Morgan stood in the doorway. He had watched the slow progress of the longboat as it left the ship. He saw Kristen as she stepped ashore and spoke a few words to Jeremy. Then he watched as she turned and started slowly down the sandy beach.

The early afternoon sun glistened on her golden hair, and she seemed so small and defenseless.

"Defenseless." He chuckled, remembering her wild attacks and the force behind the few blows that had connected. "Anything but defenseless. Don't be taken in by her sweet shy look, Morgan, old chum. I've a feeling there's more fire there than can be imagined from the looks of her."

He was still watching her rapidly diminishing figure when Jeremy stopped beside him. His eyes followed Morgan's.

"She's a nice gentle lass," Jeremy said softly. "Not one accustomed to mistreatment."

Morgan's gaze swung to him, amusement sparkling in his eyes. "Contrary to what you believe, Jeremy, I've not laid a hand on her; nor do I intend to. I have one thought in mind—revenge on Jeffrey. When that is done, she's free to go . . . untouched."

Jeremy's gaze held his, seeking to see within. "Ye've never lied to me, boy."

"And I won't begin with Kristen Seaford," Morgan said softly. "Rest easy, Jeremy; she's safe with me. I've no intention of harming her."

After a few minutes, Jeremy nodded. "Was there somethin' you was wantin' from the ship, lad?"

"Just her. You can go back now. Take the boy with you. There's weather in the air. If anything comes up, I want someone aboard who can keep the *Falcon* out of danger."

"You think it's goin' to blow?"

"No, but I don't want to take any chances with the *Falcon*. If it stirs, I'll come as fast as I can."

"Aye, lad. I'll see to her care."

Jeremy and Toby walked back to the longboat and started for the ship. Jeremy was relieved. Morgan had never lied to him about anything and he was pleased to know Morgan intended to return her to her home safely, without letting his need for revenge against Jeffrey do her any harm.

From where Kristen was sitting on a huge outcropping of rocks, she could see the longboat heading for the ship and she knew she was again a prisoner, alone on an island with this dark angry man.

She did not want to return to the cabin; a strange new emotion claimed her body and her thoughts. She named it fear; yet it was a thing she had never felt before.

She left the rocks and walked to a crop of trees that looked out over the calm blue sea. She sat in the shade of the trees and absorbed the calm serenity about her.

She thought of Jeffrey and tried to evaluate honestly her feelings for him. It surprised her to find that not only were there no feelings, but a dark blue angry gaze came between her and her memory of Jeffrey.

She closed her eyes and allowed him to walk into her

131

mind. She could feel the pressure of his mouth on hers, and the iron band of his arms about her. She remembered the emotion that had burst within her and let her anger grow at her weak near-submission to him. She knew he had tried deliberately to frighten her and her thoughts blazed with resentful anger. Never, she thought, would he complete his revenge on Jeffrey by her submission. Never would she let him know of the trembling weakness of her wayward memory. She thought of how casually he could treat her kidnapping, and of the obvious fact that money was his desire. He would like nothing better than to laugh at Jeffrey and to let him know of her fear and capitulation. The blow to her pride was so severe that she felt it burn through her like molten flame. If she could have faced him at that moment she would have been overcome with the desire to see him dead.

She inhaled deeply, trying to control the thoughts that brought her too close to tears. Never again, she vowed silently, would she weep where he could see. Never again would she allow him the satisfaction of knowing he could reach within her guard and touch that vibrant emotion. She disavowed her response, refusing to acknowledge it or the quiet voice from within that denied her thoughts.

Morgan did not go after her, deliberately choosing to give her time alone. Maybe she would get over some of her deep fear of him. He realized, reluctantly, just how much it irritated him to see fear leap into her eyes when she sensed his presence. He wanted her at ease with him, talking to him comfortably. It was the only way he knew to readjust her thinking about him and about Jeffrey. He still remembered her words about Jeffrey and going home. When she returned he was going to find out if what she had said expressed her true feelings or just temporary anger at the position she was in.

Kristen had felt the warm lethargy creep over her. Soothed by the soft sound of the sea against the white sand and the whispering breeze in the trees behind her, she allowed herself to slip into a half-dream state. It was so beautiful here, and she felt as if she belonged to this vast blue-and-green world more than she would belong in Jeffrey's world as his wife. She could not see herself restrained, having to always act the mature lady, never being allowed to let her freedom-loving soul expand and grow.

The sun began to dip toward the horizon, but now Kristen didn't notice for her head rested against the tree and her hands lay still in her lap. Her thick lashes rested on her cheeks as she sank into a peaceful deep sleep.

Morgan began to worry, thinking she had gone too far, maybe slipped from the rocks and fallen, or—his heart began to beat heavily—maybe, like Charlotte, had eased her fear and pain in the sea. When that thought struck him, he could not force it from his mind.

He left the cabin and started down the beach. No matter what the outcome, no matter what fear she felt toward him, he had to know if she was safe.

He trailed her footprints to the outcropping of rocks where he had first seen her sitting, but it was several minutes before he spotted her sitting among the trees. He walked to her on silent feet, and was very close before he realized she was asleep.

Slowly and quietly, he walked to her and looked down. Was this fragile-looking creature the one who had attacked him with bared sword and claws? She looked young and very vulnerable, and again he was struck by the thought that she was definitely not the type of woman with whom Jeffrey would choose to spend the rest of his life.

He stooped down, resting on his haunches before her. With a gentle hand, he brushed some wayward hair from her face. She stirred at his touch, and suddenly her eyes opened wide. For several moments, they were caught in a timeless silence. Her wide crystal gray eyes held his; they were filled with an awareness of him, and he did not want to shatter that look.

She gazed up at him, more conscious of his presence than any other thing around her. His blue eyes were gentle, and drew her within them and held her.

All her senses were aware of him, the sight of his lean body bending near her, the masculine clean smell of him. A tingling awareness of his strength overwhelmed her at the memory of his hard arms about her and his lips taking hers and awakening a fire she had not known existed. She wanted to cry out, to move, to break this spell with which he held her, but she could not.

Again, he reached out and brushed his fingers along her jawbone and down the slender column of her throat until he could feel the pulse that beat frantically there. He knew that she quivered not only with fear, but with the touch of an emotion she had never felt before.

He took her hands in his and stood up, drawing her up with him. With one pull she was in his arms. He held her close to him and heard a soft murmured sound as he bent his head and took her mouth with his.

The need for her burst through him like liquid fire, and his gentle kiss turned seeking and possessive. He forced her lips apart expertly and heard her soft moan as she returned his kiss.

Joyously, his heart surged; she was his! But the joy rapidly diminished as he heard Jeremy's last words. "Ye've never lied to me, boy."

"I've no intention of touching her," he had said. Yet at this moment he wanted her more than he had ever wanted a woman before.

He had to gain some control of himself before he did damage that could never be undone. Roughly, he shoved her away from him. She stepped back a few steps and gazed at him in shock, as if this were the first moment she was really aware of his presence. She misread the look of need in his eyes for one of anger, and felt he had only kissed her to prove to her she was the kind of woman he had accused her of being.

Shame and embarrassment washed over her, for she was all too aware of how easily she had nearly surrendered. She had felt the depth of his passion and had lost control because of the blazing urgent need that had overwhelmed her and carried her along in a current she could not control.

She sobbed as she realized he must be laughing at her for the easy way she had nearly given herself to him.

He saw her pain, felt it himself, as she lifted her eyes to his. There was no way he could tell her how he felt, for if he did, he would take her here on this beach in the red glow of the setting sun and be damned with Jeffrey and the rest of the world.

She spun on her heel and started back to the cabin, but not before he had seen the tears on her cheeks and the deep pain in her eyes.

There was nothing he could do but follow her, allowing her to feel the pain of his thrusting her away. He knew if he tried to explain he would only make matters worse. It was best they had this barrier of anger between them, he thought. It would protect her from him and . . . maybe protect him when she was sent back.

He opened the cabin door to find the main room

135

empty; then he heard her move about in the bedroom. With a sigh, he sat down in the chair trying to form a plan to ease the situation and to get her to talk to him. Damn, he thought violently, like a boy with his first woman. Why the hell did I do that? But he knew the answer, just as he knew that he must control his desire for her.

He forced his mind to Charlotte and Jeffrey, and after a while he again held the reins of his hatred.

When Kristen finally had her emotions in some semblance of control, she decided she could not face Morgan again tonight. She could not stand to see the arrogant laughter in his eyes or to hear him taunt her about her foolish near-surrender.

She decided to let sleep lead her over this painful bridge. She undressed and went to bed. But it was not to be so, for as soon as sleep claimed her, so did dreams, and in her dreams, Morgan came to her in gentleness and love . . . and she could no longer resist.

When she awoke the next morning it was to the sound of laughter. Slowly, she got out of bed and dressed. Walking to the door, she opened it a crack and looked out.

Morgan was seated in the chair with his feet propped on a stool. Jeremy and young Toby were loading the table with food and she felt the nudge of hunger as the aroma of the breakfast dishes reached her.

No one noticed the half-open door. They were laughing at something that must have been said by Morgan before she woke. Miserably, she wondered if the laughter was at her expense. Could he have been amusing them by making fun of her obvious foolishness. She was surprised at the pain this idea brought.

It was Morgan who noticed her presence first. He rose from the chair and walked to the door.

"Good morning. Come out and have some breakfast." He smiled warmly at her, but she was still suspicious about the source of the laughter.

She walked past him without a word, not daring to look up into those mocking blue eyes—eyes that followed her across the room wondering how she could manage to look so beautiful fresh out of bed. He restrained his thoughts of her in bed for they did his peace of mind no good at all.

His mind on her, he did not notice Jeremy's amused look. No one knew him as well as Jeremy did, and Jeremy had been convinced a long time ago that Morgan needed to find the one woman who could tame him and settle him down. He wondered if this gentle little woman-child could be the one. There was no doubt that Morgan's mind was filled with her, but he worried that she might be another passing fancy as all Morgan's other women had been. It was Toby who eased the silence; he jumped to his feet with a bright welcoming smile for her. He was a solidly built young boy who gave promise of growing into a handsome man. His hair was reddish gold and a mass of tousled curls. He had sea green eyes that sparkled with youth and happiness. He had a round face split by a broad mouth that smiled easily, and a bridge of freckles marched across his nose.

"You can sit here, miss."

"Thank you, Toby." She smiled.

She was surprised that the captain's first mate and cabin boy ate at the same table as he as if they were family. It was not long until she began to realize they considered each other so.

As the conversation began to flow about her, she began to see their camaraderie and affection for each other. They included her in their conversation and laughter as if she belonged to them. She was aware of Toby's near-worship of Morgan and saw Morgan look at the boy with amused affection. It confused her. How could a child love a man who was at least a pirate and at most . . . she didn't know what?

"Would you like to go swimming later?" Toby asked.

"Why yes, Toby, I'd like that." She smiled. "But I've nothing to swim in."

"Ah, well," Morgan laughed, "I see I must sacrifice more of my clothes. You will turn me into a pauper just trying to keep up with your heavy use of my apparel."

They laughed together and despite her decision to ignore him, she felt herself drawn again into the warmth of his smile.

She spent most of the afternoon swimming with Toby in the deep blue lagoon, and Morgan, after telling them he could not go with them, spent the afternoon watching from a distance. He had claimed other work to do, but Jeremy was pleased at the way his eyes drifted toward the slim figure that played in the surf of the island.

They came home laughing and tired and ravenously hungry. After a huge supper, Jeremy and Toby returned to the ship, and Morgan was deeply annoyed to watch her smile fade and to see the wary fear reappear in the shadows of her gray eyes.

She and Morgan stood on the shore and watched the longboat return to the ship. She had had the urge to plead with Morgan to let her go back aboard with them. She was too aware of his presence next to her, and she felt the renewal of her fear as he took her elbow and they turned back toward the cabin.

They walked in silence, she wondering what she would face next, and he in deep thought. She had no way of knowing that he was even more aware of her closeness than she of his.

"Kristen, I think it is time we talked," he said firmly. He meant the words to be gentle, but even to him, they sounded stiff and formal.

"What do we have to discuss? I am your prisoner."

"Yes, you are my prisoner . . . temporarily, but I see no need for you to jump like a frightened deer every time I look in your direction."

"You see no need of fear?" She stopped and looked up at him. "Can you say, Captain, that you have given me no cause to fear you? I still carry the marks of your . . . gentle touch. I still do not know what you intend to do to me. I cannot help but fear what you will do next."

"We will be here two weeks before Jeffrey's answer is brought to me. I promise you, you have no need to fear me again. I will make you as comfortable as I can, and I will not give you cause to worry. We meant you no physical harm." He grinned. "Most of our problems have been caused by misunderstanding. I thought you meant to kill me and was only defending myself."

"I did," she answered honestly. His disarming smile touched her, enclosing her in the warmth of it.

"Then, madam,"—he laughed as he extended his arm to her—"shall we return home?"

She smiled, feeling relaxed for the first time since she had been taken from Owen's ship. She took his arm and they walked together to the cabin.

Later that night when she closed the door to the bedroom between them, she went to the bed and slept, relaxed and at ease.

He sat for a long time contemplating the new Kristen. Sweet and smiling she left him with the need to draw nearer and know her better. It was a long time before he slept.

# Nine

For the next three days, Kristen surrendered to the pleasure and beauty of the island. Her hair brightened under the sun and her skin began to turn golden brown. She spent most of the time swimming or fishing with Toby, and Morgan, using all his will power, kept as much distance between them as he reasonably could.

It was a difficult thing, for when her easy relaxed nature was allowed to blossom, she became irresistibly beautiful to him. At the end of every day, he would find important business on board ship and stay there until he knew from the absence of light in the cabin that she slept. Then he would go ashore and sleep on his uncomfortable bed cursing himself for not sharing her bed yet, knowing he could not stand to see her happiness change again to anger, or the open way she smiled at him close and her eyes darken with fear.

Jeremy watched his frustrated abstinence with deep amusement. He knew Morgan all too well not to know he felt some deep and special emotion for Kristen. He knew that Morgan would have bedded any other woman long before this.

A dark and violent storm was brewing within Morgan, but not nearly as dark and violent as the one that would throw them together.

The fourth morning of her captivity, Kristen left her

bedroom to find Morgan waiting for her.

"Jeremy's signaled. There's a little repair problem on board. Toby's coming with the boat. We'll go on board and eat there."

She agreed.

"Kristen?"

"Yes?"

"If you would like, after breakfast, I'll show you the other side of our island. There's a string of interesting caves and a lovely view from the high rocks."

She could not read the look in his eyes, yet she felt he had reached out to touch her. She did not even understand why she agreed so quickly, or why she felt such a tingle of warmth at his quick smile and outstretched hand.

They had breakfast with Toby and Jeremy and several others of the crew sitting on the deck. Kristen shared their laughter and good-natured fun.

It was a pleasure for Morgan to watch her; yet he barely controlled his desire to take her away from the crowd and share time with her alone.

Jeremy held her as long as he could with amusing stories. He enjoyed Morgan's glare and his obvious annoyance.

As soon as he could, Morgan took Kristen and the longboat and rowed ashore.

"Keep the *Falcon* out of trouble, Jeremy." He laughed as he left. He had no idea how those words would be carried out in the next few days.

When they dragged the boat ashore, Morgan turned to her.

"Kristen, if we walk up past the cabin it is less than an hour's walk to the top. From there you can see for miles. We can do that or take the boat around the coast and walk

141

back from there. The choice is yours."

"Let's walk to the top," she replied.

He nodded and they started up the path. Passing the cabin, they came to the small stream. He found the narrowest part of it and measured it by eye. He could, as he had done before, take it in one leap, but he was sure Kristen could not.

She, too, stood for a minute and looked at it.

"I could wade across."

"It won't be as deep for me as for you," he replied. He turned to her and suddenly she was being lifted in his arms, and before she could protest, he waded across the knee-deep stream and deposited her on the other side. They continued their walk. He pointed out beautiful flowers along the way and told her their names. At one point, he plucked a vibrant red flower and handed it to her. She placed it in her hair tucking it over her left ear. He chuckled softly not wanting to tell her that a bright red bloom tucked behind a girl's left ear meant she was a maiden looking for a mate. He was sure she would not appreciate this explanation.

When they stood at the top of the hill, Kristen gazed in silent wonder at the beauty that spread before her. She could see the ocean, its colors blending from deep blue to green, for miles.

"Oh, how very beautiful."

"Yes, I've stood here often and never tired of the beauty and peace of it."

She turned to look at him. "I asked you once before who you were. You do not seem to be a . . . a pirate."

"What do I seem to be?"

"I don't know. A man of quality, a man who has been educated . . . a . . . a man who has an appreciation of the rare and beautiful things in life."

142

"Why thank you, my lady. I haven't been complimented lately." He grinned, his eyes crinkling at the corners.

"Tell me about you."

"No," he replied, "you tell me about yourself first."

"There is not much for me to tell. I was raised in America. I lost my mother and was raised by my father who spoiled me atrociously." She laughed.

"Yes," Morgan agreed, "he should never have allowed you to go on this journey alone."

Her smile faded.

"My father died . . . just before I agreed to marry Jeffrey and come to England."

"Is that why you agreed to marry him?" he asked softly.

She looked at him for a few minutes in silence, then accepted the truth herself. "Yes," she replied almost in a whisper.

He moved close to her, feeling the hurt that touched her. "Kristen, you have to love someone to be able to share your life—love and know that person."

"And I don't know Jeffrey?"

"No, you don't."

"And you do?"

"Yes."

"Why, Morgan . . . ? Tell me why. Why do you hate him so?"

"Would you believe me if I told you?"

"I don't know; but I'll never know if you don't."

He sighed. "There was once a very pretty girl, like you, who made the mistake of falling in love with him. He chose to marry a girl with more money and position." He went on to tell her of Charlotte's death and the evidence that pointed to Jeffrey. Not once did he let her know the

143

connection between himself and Charlotte.

"Was she someone you cared for?"

"Yes . . . I loved her very much," he said firmly, "and I will see that he pays for it."

She watched the coldness in his eyes and shivered at the intense hatred that glowed there. She could not understand her feeling of tenderness and sorrow when she saw it. She wanted to reach out to him and wipe away that pain-filled look.

"I'm sorry, Morgan," she said simply.

He looked at her as if he had been drawn back from some dark place and had just realized her presence. He smiled. "I brought you here to see the caves, not to cry. Come on. The walk down is easier."

He reached out a hand to her and she put hers in it, letting him lead her down the path to the beach and the promised caves.

They walked along the sand enjoying the touch of the salty breeze and the warmth of the sun. Slowly, the beach narrowed as huge rocky cliffs appeared beside them. When Morgan stopped, he pointed out the huge mouths of caves that ran all along the cliffs.

"In that large one there are ancient paintings on the walls. No one knows who made them or, for that matter, when or how, or what has become of them. Want to go see?"

"Yes."

He took her hand, helping her climb up the side of the rocky cliff to the entrance of a cave. As they stopped at the opening, Morgan's eyes were caught by the horizon. Kristen's eyes followed his.

"What is it?"

"I think we're in for some bad weather later. There're storm clouds on the horizon."

"Will it come soon?" The quiet way she said it drew his attention to her.

"Afraid of storms?"

"I wasn't until we had one aboard Owen's ship. I can still remember the violence of it. It was frightening."

"You needn't be afraid. We'll be back to the cabin before it hits here."

They walked into the cave and Kristen gasped in surprise. A pale inner glow lit the interior eerily.

"Where does the light come from?" she asked.

"I don't know; something in the walls, I expect. Beautiful, isn't it?"

She looked about. Ancient paintings, preserved forever, lined the walls with animals and human forms.

"They must tell a story of some sort," Morgan said. "But I have been here many times and I can't make out what it might be. Maybe someone will come along someday and be able to read it."

"Have many people come here?"

"None as far as I know. It's kind of my own private hideaway. I'd like to keep it for as long as I can."

"I can understand that. I should love to have a place all my own that I could go to when I felt the need of solitude."

They stood so close they were almost touching and his eyes were intent on her.

"Feel free to share my hideaway anytime you choose. It will be a secret between the two of us."

He said the words softly; yet she could feel the gentle warmth of his words enfold her. She felt such a sense of peace and belonging that she stood spellbound looking up into his smiling eyes. Gently, he reached out and touched her cheek with his fingers. Her lips parted in a breathless mood of closeness. His hand slid to the back of her head

145

and very gently he drew her toward him. Softly, like the wings of a butterfly, his lips touched hers.

All her past thoughts fled before the golden warmth that enfolded her. His arms came about her and he bound her close to him, so close he could feel the pounding of her heart. Slowly his mouth began to claim hers in a deeper and deeper kiss. Her lips parted and her arms crept up about his neck. Again the heat of this strange new emotion gripped her and her wayward body assumed control over her thoughts. She felt as if every bone in her body had melted to a burning flowing river.

He lifted his lips from hers and looked down into her half-closed, passion-filled eyes. Taking her face between his hands, he began to kiss her eyes, cheeks, and lips with gentle kisses that made her murmur softly out of her need to feel his demanding mouth claim hers again.

Despite all his determination not to reach out for her, and his claim to Jeremy that he would not touch her, he could not resist the need to hold her even if it was just for a moment. He held himself in complete control for he knew he would never take her on the dirt floor of a cave. No, he thought, for her it had to be perfect. One does not take the woman one loves as one would take a whore . . . anytime . . . anyplace.

Love! The thought struck him violently. Of course he loved her, there was no longer a doubt in his mind, just as there was no doubt he would not ever return her to Jeffrey's arms. Not as long as there was a breath in his body.

"Kristen," he murmured against her soft parted lips. "You are so very beautiful . . . so beautiful."

He took her mouth again with his, searing her with the flame of his passion, branding her forever his.

Kristen became suddenly aware that again she was

surrendering to him without thought. How easy it must seem to him. All he had to do was to reach out and touch her and she became weak and pliable in his hands. Maybe her vulnerability had often amused these men. How often she had seen the glow of laughter in both his and Jeremy's eyes. Gathering all her will she stepped away from him. Her change from willing acceptance to sudden rejection took him momentarily by surprise.

"Kristen," he said softly as he reached to draw her to him again. She backed out of his reach.

"Don't. This may all seem to be an amusing game to you, to take Jeffrey's woman so easily, to make me want you, then to laugh . . . laugh at the easy way you've made another conquest. I'm sure you've had many, but I will not be numbered among them. I refuse to be used as a means for revenge. I refuse to allow you to make me love you, then use it to show Jeffrey just how easy it has been."

"Kristen, you don't believe that?"

"What else am I to believe? I know your hatred of him. I know you would use any means to get revenge, but . . . not my love, Morgan . . . please . . . not that way. I couldn't bear it."

He smiled. "Then you do feel something for me? You do want me as much as I want you? Your kiss did not lie to me?"

She again felt the warm touch of tears in her eyes, tears she refused to shed before him. "Heaven help me," she said softly. "I do."

She spun about and ran from the cave. Descending swiftly, she almost fell down the rocks to the beach. She was standing on the sand before she noticed that the breeze had changed to a sharp biting wind that whipped about her, and dark clouds were nearing the island.

She heard Morgan coming down the rocks and began to walk back over the path to the cabin. She did not know what she would do when she arrived; she only knew she could not let him touch her again. She was not strong enough to withstand the desire to surrender to him.

She was only walking a short time when he caught up with her. To her surprise, his face seemed dark with worry and he grasped her hand and began to pull her along rapidly.

"Morgan!"

"Kristen, we've got to get back to the cabin before this thing really hits. It's a hurricane."

"A hurricane?" she shouted above the rising wind.

"I don't have time to explain. If we can't get to the ship, Jeremy will take her out beyond danger. We've got to get back to the cabin."

He began to run, dragging her after him. She could feel the wind rising in intensity. In fact, it would have forced her from her feet if Morgan had not been holding her.

They reached the stream, and without a word, he swung her up against him and leaped across. Dropping her to her feet, he again took her hand and began to run.

By the time they reached the cabn, the wind had risen to howling ferocity. She could hardly breathe and the rising gale was throwing about bits of dirt and debris that stung the skin. She was exhausted and frightened by the time he dragged her through the door and slammed and bolted it behind them. He ran to the windows and drew the shutters closed. After making sure everything was secure, he turned to her.

That she was frightened he knew, but he was not sure of what she was frightened of most: the storm . . . or him.

He went to her, watching her eyes, knowing that she

148

was aware of him, yet realizing that her fear was of the storm.

He stood close enough to touch her, but he didn't. Instead, he spoke softly to her.

"Kristen, I want you to believe me. I love you. Those are words I've said to no other woman. I want you. I won't let you believe that what I feel for you has anything to do with Jeffrey. No matter what else comes of this, I will never return you to him. I want you to trust me, just for a while. I love you, Kristen."

His voice died to a gentle whisper and he stood holding her eyes with his, trying to tell her what he felt, praying she could feel, as he did, the rightness of their being together.

She could feel the intense power of his magnetism for her; she sensed the urgency in his words and in his eyes. Again she could feel a breathless warmth enclose her and she swayed toward him. It was the only incentive he needed. In a moment she was in his arms and his mouth was claiming hers in a demanding kiss that whirled her world beyond her grasp and left her only his hard, lean body to cling to.

Twin storms raged, within and without, but Kristen was no longer aware of the violence that raged against the small cabin. She knew only the tumultuous upending of her world. Sensations flooded her, sensations she had never felt before. Morgan felt her total surrender to him, and with a happy laugh, he swung her up into his arms and carried her through the half-dark cabin to the bedroom. Again he could feel the trembling in her. Slowly, he cautioned himself. He did not want to spoil this special time by frightening her with the intense need that burned within him and threatened to overcome him.

149

Gently, he held her against him, inhaling the sweet fragrance of her and letting his hands caress her slender hips, drawing them closer. Again and again he touched her soft parted lips with his, stirring the flame he sensed within her. Her eyes were closed and she clung to him, the only stable thing in her recklessly whirling world.

Nimble fingers loosened the hooks on the back of her gown and he slid it down to her waist. He touched her lightly, caressing her soft rounded breasts. His lips whispered against her skin, her slender throat, and soft rounded shoulders, then lowered until he captured a taut nipple. His tongue flicked against it drawing a deep sigh from her.

Tenderly, he nibbled gently at the soft curve of her waist as he drew the rest of the dress away.

His mouth returned to hers, hot and demanding, and her mouth responded now, returning his passion with wild abandonment. Tongues warred with each other to draw the deepest fire of their need.

Her mind whirled and crashed against the arousal that blazed within her. The beating of his heart matched the pounding of hers.

She clung to him as she felt herself lifted again and gently laid against the soft pillows of the bed. Through half-open eyes, she saw him quickly strip and cast aside the clothes he wore. Then his heated body was against hers, and he savored the cool soft flesh that lay against him.

She closed her eyes, panting and breathlessly aware that the overpowering magic of his hands and lips had again begun their mystical control of her body and her mind. Her body reacted with instinct to this new and wondrous emotion that shattered her reserves and brought to vibrant life one and only one thought:

Morgan . . . Morgan who reached within her and touched the center of her being and burst it to a million hot flames that licked at her senses until she felt she could bear the magical beauty of their love no longer.

The ecstasy of their coming together drew a moaning cry from her as her body arched in response to his movements. Her flame matched his. She was woman, all woman from the beginning of time and he was the mate ordained for her. Time and place had no consequence as they blended into one and caught the rapture and beauty of the fusing of their love.

She wanted to draw him within her, to hold forever; he crushed her to him as if he could make her part of him by the force of his need. She was his! His mind shouted and his body was released from all thought of anything but her possession.

Their worlds careened out of control and they filled each other with the timeless possession and flow of love that made them one.

She gasped and nearly ceased breathing as her world seemed to burst into a million fragments and she tumbled among them, lost forever to any other reality but him.

For a while, they lay silently together, each unable or unwilling to break the fragile dream that held them.

He held her close to him her cheek resting on his broad chest. Her hand lay against the dark skin of his chest and began to caress it gently, enjoying the taut feel of the muscles beneath it. Never had she felt so much a woman, never had she felt such peace and contentment.

He raised himself on one elbow and looked down at her. Gently, his hand caressed her, and he bent his head and kissed her, quick light kisses. He was pleased with the way she reached to hold him to her and the response in her lips that clung gently to his.

151

"Kristen," he murmured. "No matter what else happens believe that I love you beyond all else."

She reached up to hold his face between her hands, and the warmth and desire he saw in her eyes told him all he needed to know. She had accepted the truth of his love completely, and with no restraints or doubts.

"Morgan?"

"Yes?"

"What will become of us?"

"What do you mean? We love each other. You belong to me and I to you. You do not believe for a minute I will return you to Jeffrey?"

"No . . . but . . ."

"But what?"

"Our worlds are so very far apart, Morgan. No matter what I feel for you, can I live my life as the wife of a pirate, never knowing if one day you will be caught and . . . hung? I don't think I could bear it if anything were to happen to you. Can you not think of giving up this wild dangerous life?"

His mouth twitched in contained amusement. She thought he was a pirate for profit and had no other means.

"Morgan, don't be angry with me, but . . ."

He laughed and bent to lingeringly caress her lips again.

"Angry with you? Impossible. I love you and need you too much to be angry. Say what you are going to say."

"I . . . I have money . . . don't look at me like that. It would only be a means to help you find a way to make an honest living."

"You would give up all your wealth for me?"

"Of what use is money to me if I were to lose you? Morgan, please, think about it. Come back with me," she said hopelessly. "No one will know you are what you are. I will say you rescued me."

He laughed and drew her body tight against him. It made him wild with happiness and desire to know she would give up everything she had for him.

"I will think about it, love," he whispered against her hair. "I will think about it, but not now. Now there is only room in my mind for you."

Looking up into his eyes, she could see nothing but warmth and desire for her. The look of amusement was gone and the heat of his gaze sent a warm tingle through her. She could feel her body respond to the need in his. Her hands drew his face down to hers and their lips blended again in a warm kiss. She was surprised and confused that her mind and body responded to him again with such a deep desire to yield she could not contain it.

His mouth played gently, teasingly with hers, drawing forth a soft murmur of protest as her body sought his. She moved against him, her skin seeking the touch of his and her breath warm against his skin. The shattering storm gave her no fear now; for she had never felt safer in her life than in the embrace of the strong arms that held her. Again the magic of his gentle caresses and the fire in his kisses blinded her mind and body to everything but the need of him. He lifted her passion to soar with his and then to dip into the wild sea of surrender.

In the safety of his arms she slept and they clung to each other even in slumber. She wakened several hours later to a deep silence. He lay beside her relaxed in sleep. Rising on one elbow, she looked down into his sleeping face. He seemed so much younger, his face almost boyish and vulnerable. She looked down the length of his hard lean body and grew warm at the remembrance of their fiery joining.

His body was dark against the soft creamy gold of hers. Possessively she laid one hand on his hip and slid her fingers gently up the smooth skin to his waist. Taut hard muscles rippled under the smooth skin. She let her mind touch the memory of the feel of him when he had possessed her.

Now her hand gently caressed his lean ribs and moved up over the heavy muscles of his chest. It was only then that she lifted her eyes to meet his and found they were holding hers with such a look of intensity she could not speak. He slid his arms about her and drew her across his body. She looked down into his eyes and a slow half-smile of possession touched her lips.

"The storm is over," she said softly. "All is silent."

"No," he replied as his hand gently caressed her hair. "We are in the center of it. Inside the storm all is quiet and still, yet there is more to come."

"But I am safe here," she replied softly.

"Yes, love," he whispered. "You are safe here and I shall keep you so always."

"Should we not be prepared? Surely Jeremy or Toby will come to see of our welfare?"

"No, love, at the first sign of the storm, Jeremy took the *Falcon* to safety. Since he did not see me coming, he knew I would care for my safety and yours. I doubt if he will return the *Falcon* in less than a day or so."

"Then we are marooned here?"

"Yes."

"For another day or so?" She smiled seductively.

"At least." He grinned.

"There is not another soul on our island but us and no one to come to interrupt our solitude." Her voice died to a soft whisper as she saw a burning flame ignite behind the blue eyes that held hers. He reached up to draw her closer to him.

"Heaven help the one who dares to cross that threshold now," he said, and he caught her lips with his as her laughter reached him and her arms came about him. It was an interlude that would brand her for always with the depth of his love.

They remained inside until the storm again swept around them and passed. They rose, and amid much laughter, gentle touching, and occasional kisses, prepared a meal which they ate without realizing the quality of the food.

They went to the beach where he abandoned his clothes then teased and cajoled her into removing hers. He laughed at her shy blushes and proceeded to turn them into laughter as they cavorted in the soft rolling waves like children.

Later they lay together on a soft grassy hill that overlooked the beach. They talked secretly together of nonsensical things and laughed as lovers do. Then they walked along the shore in the glow of the setting sun, then returned to their cabin.

These were two days of pleasure; all of their waking hours spent exploring their island and the brilliant fiery passion they felt for each other.

He tried to keep her mind from the future, yet he knew her thoughts were there for he could read her clear gray eyes like the open pages of a book.

He also knew that she worried about him and that thoughts of her own future had not occurred to her, except for her awareness that their lives would be permanently entwined.

There was no way he could let her go, either home to America or to England, for with her would go the knowledge of who he was. It would not take long for her

155

to know of his double identity, and once she knew, Jeffrey could soon figure it out. Yet his need for Kristen, and hers for him, would be too much to be kept secret. He could not let her go; yet he could not tell her who he really was yet.

Once Jeffrey held the knowledge of who he was, he would soon be exposed. With Jeffrey's power, Morgan would be hung, for he could not yet prove that the death of his sister should be laid at Jeffrey's door.

He had to keep his identity a secret until he found a way to get the proof he needed. He had to destroy Jeffrey before he could ease his mind and find happiness with Kristen.

He had another week before Jeffrey's message would be brought. Deliberately, he closed his mind against telling Kristen the truth. He had clung to the idea of revenge against Jeffrey too long to be able to let it go now. Somehow he would find the proof. Kristen would understand, he rationalized; he could not let Charlotte's death go unavenged.

They stood, two days later, on the cliff and watched the *Falcon* sail back into the lagoon untouched by the storm they had outrun.

Jeremy and Toby rowed ashore to assure themselves that Kristen and Morgan had weathered the storm well. Jeremy was not in the cabin an hour before his astute eyes saw the difference in Kristen. He looked at Morgan whose hungry gaze was watching Kristen, in laughing conversation with Toby, and he knew that they were lovers.

Later, when Toby and Kristen had gone to the *Falcon* to try to find some more clothes that Kristen could alter to fit her, Jeremy stood and looked at Morgan, his knowledge written on his open face for Morgan to read.

156

"Think what you will, Jeremy," Morgan said softly. "I love her and I intend to hold her for as long as I can."

"Aye, boy, just long enough for her to find out who you are. What will you do then? Ye can't send her back to Jeffrey, and ye can't hold her once Jeffrey's message comes."

"I'll find proof. . . . I'll get to Jeffrey before she finds out. She thinks I'm a pirate." Morgan chuckled softly. "She has even offered to give up all her wealth for me if I will cease being a pirate and become a gentleman."

"Isn't the love of a sweet thing like that enough to take you from this path of revenge you are on?"

"No!" Morgan said, anguish deep in his voice. "I cannot let her death be for nothing. I cannot let that bastard get away with murder."

"Morgan, lad," Jeremy said miserably, "a time comes to drop hatred and revenge and allow somethin' good to take its place. If she finds out ye've lied to her about this, she may think ye've lied about all things. It might be a pain that would kill the love she has for ye. Are ye willin' to take that kind of a chance?"

"I won't let either of them go," Morgan said determinedly. "I'll hold her here until I find the proof I need. When I take her back to England; it will be after Jeffrey has been punished for his deeds . . . and . . . it will be as my wife."

"Whose wife? Lord Morgan Grayfield's, or Captain Black's—the pirate?"

"As the wife of the man who loves her."

"But not enough to trust her with the truth?"

"Jeremy," Morgan said softly, "I can't let her go now. I can't tell her the truth yet. I need more time with her to teach her that my love will care for her. If I tell her the truth she might believe these last two days were part of

157

my revenge. It was what she thought at first." He turned to look at Jeremy. "Give me time, Jeremy. Let me have her love until I'm sure of it. Then I'll tell her the truth. Just give me some time."

Jeremy sighed in defeat and watched Morgan walk to the beach to meet the incoming boat. From the distance he heard happy laughter as Morgan swung Kristen from the boat into his arms.

His eyes darkened with worry. "Aye, lad," he said softly, "but I hope it ain't enough time for ye to do yerself more harm. I hope ye don't lose what ye're too blind to see before ye open yer eyes and realize revenge ain't worth the loss of love."

# *Ten*

Golden days followed, rare and beautiful sun-kissed days in which Kristen gloried. The *Falcon* lazed in the lagoon, their only contact with the outside world, yet neither of them felt the need of any contact other than each other.

Each moved within the presence of the other as if no one else existed. They would walk the beaches, arms entwined, enjoying their closeness. They would light a fire on the sand at night and cook fresh fish for supper, then lie on a blanket and share the beauty of the moon-dappled water and the joy of being together.

Morgan answered her many questions about his past as best he could without telling her the truth of his identity. He spoke of his parents with warmth and a deep affection she could feel, and again she began to wonder how a man, raised with such love and affection, could have turned to the nefarious trade he was in. She remembered his story about Charlotte and was amazed at the pang of intense jealousy she felt for a dead woman who had inspired him to such vengeance. She loved him deeply and completely and she vowed to try again and again to turn him from this life to one they could share in happiness without constantly watching for a hand that could one day reach for him and separate them completely and for eternity.

They sat now on the grassy cliff beneath the shade of

some trees. He had his back braced against the bole of one, a knee bent, and his arm resting upon it. She lay with her head in his lap, and his other arm rested possessively on her waist. His firm brown hand was still; yet his touch bespoke a protective and possessive attitude.

Her eyes were closed and she was enjoying the feel of his presence. His deep serious eyes were contemplating the beauty of the view without really seeing it. His mind was worrying again over the problem of Kristen, the truth, and their future. He would not allow the thought of sending her back to Jeffrey to enter his mind, yet how could he let go of the need to avenge Charlotte's death? If he returned with Kristen, in moments Jeffrey would figure out the identity of Captain Black and have him hung for piracy. There was no place he could take her that Jeffrey wouldn't know.

He wanted to explain to her who he was, but he feared she would think it all a part of his revenge. Picturing her turning from him in anger or pain, he cast that possibility from his mind.

He envisioned her eyes darkening with pain, saw her draw away from him, thinking his love for her was a lie. What he had imagined seemed so real to him that his hand spasmodically gripped her in a strong possessive hold. His grip was fierce enough to arouse her from her pleasant dreamy state. She opened her eyes and looked up at him. Seeing his face drawn and hard from some violent inner thought, she was startled and wondered if it had anything to do with her. A panicky thought struck her: was she still part of his vengeance or was her love for him enough to carry him away from those dark thoughts, away from the violent life he led?

She had pictured in her mind the story she could piece together from all he had told her. Jeffrey, rich and handsome; Morgan, poor and in love with Charlotte. Maybe she had chosen Jeffrey because of his wealth . . . as Morgan had accused him of choosing her, and Morgan had become enraged. At her death, he had chosen to believe Jeffrey guilty of it. He had chosen then to seek some kind of revenge on Jeffrey. After this followed the dark thought that his love for her might be shadowed by the need for revenge. As swift as it came, she pushed it aside. No! He loved her! It had nothing to do with anyone or anything else. He loved her and she loved him, and with this new and beautiful thing she would draw him away from all his dark thoughts. They would one day share the Seaford fortune and he would have no more cause to carry hatred in his heart. She would fill it so full of love there would be no room for anything else.

Slowly, she reached up and laid her hand against his face. His attention turned to her, and his eyes lightened at her clear gray gaze of love.

The hard muscle of his arm loosened and she could feel his gentle touch as he caressed her lightly. She put her arms about his neck as he lifted her to lie against him so he might enjoy the feel of her slim soft body in his arms. She bent her head to touch her lips to his, gently running her tongue across his firm mouth. It gave him great pleasure to know she sought him with the same fierce passion that he felt; yet their closeness renewed his black fear that her love could be snatched from him so easily.

His arms bound her to him and he kissed her with such a sudden blazing need that it startled her.

"Morgan?" she questioned as she lay against him. "What is it?"

Her voice gentle, her body close against his, now would be the time to tell her the truth. Yet he could not release the chain that held him to the past; he could not forget

161

his revenge and hatred toward Jeffrey. He grasped at the idea that he might still be able to have both: the fall of Jeffrey and the possession of Kristen.

She looked up at him, questions in her eyes and the glow of trusting love on her face, and the moment slipped away from him. He would hold her now. He had over a week to find the answers. He would think about this problem tomorrow; for today, there was Kristen and only Kristen—in his mind, in his heart, and in his blood.

He rolled on his side, pulling her beneath him, and smiled down into her eyes. Tenderly, he caressed the side of her face, then bent to gently touch her cheeks and lips with light feather kisses. He felt her arms about him, the willing warmth of her beneath him, and he loosened the final hold on any words he might have said. His mouth possessed hers with a deep hunger that drew her into the center of it and held her.

"Oh, Morgan, I love you," she whispered.

"And I love you, beyond all," he replied, aware that he would never be able to convince her of the truth of these words if she knew that he still clung to the past.

He tasted her lips again with sweet lingering kisses. His mouth strayed from hers to nibble gently at a delicate ear, then roamed down the slim column of her throat to the soft round flesh that rose above the ties of her blouse. He pulled loose the tie and brushed the shirt down from her shoulder. His mouth created little flicks of flame against her taut rounded breasts. He nibbled gently until he heard her soft murmur of pleasure; then he captured an erect hardened nipple in his mouth and lightly sucked until he felt her stir in his arms, impatient that his hold on her restricted her movements. He held her immobile, slowly driving her frantic with desire for him.

With one hand he loosened her sash and reached

162

inside the overlarge band of her pants to gently caress her and trace small heated patterns across her flesh. He heard her soft moan of pleasure as he pushed the restricting cloth away and his lips followed his hands. Still he held her writhing body tightly, his hands about her slender hips. He could feel her urgent need of him and his passion was flaring to a heat nearly out of control, yet he held himself back. He would carry her higher' and higher, drawing from her a need to match his own, trying to tell her that she belonged to him and only him.

He heard her whispered words of love and felt her searching for him with blind hot passion. He released his restrictive hold on her and they came together with a brilliant force that tore everything from their conscious thoughts but each other and the love they shared.

They clung to each other as they tumbled down into the oblivion and peace of completion. He could hear her ragged breathing as she trembled in his arms. No spoken words could touch the miracle of pleasure they had shared with each other. He rolled on his back and drew her against him while the wild beating of his heart regained some control.

"Morgan?"

"Yes, love?"

"Let's not ever leave here. Let's stay and forget the rest of the world. It doesn't matter what you've been or done. We could make a beautiful life here."

"You'd give up all you have for me?" he said softly. "All the things your wealth could get for you?"

She rose on one elbow and looked down into his unfathomable eyes. Gently, she bent, and brushed her lips across his.

"What does wealth matter if I do not have you? Maybe . . ." she began hesitantly, her eyes pleading for

163

him to understand. "Maybe it has been a hard life for you, being a pirate. Maybe wealth might seem to be important to you, and . . . losing someone you loved as much as you must have loved your Charlotte has blinded you to anything but revenge. But Morgan, we could be happy, I would do anything to turn you away from anger and revenge. Forget Jeffrey, Morgan. Let our love be enough. We could begin a new life. One day the world would forget a pirate."

Morgan floundered between his need to tell her the truth and his still-deep remembrance of Charlotte—and Jeffrey's involvement in her death. He could not forget. He could not put the past out of his mind, and worse, he could not speak the words that might turn Kristen forever away from him. Once she knew who he really was, she would surely believe that he had only made love to her out of revenge against Jeffrey for she would know that money had not been a part of it. What else would be left for her to believe except that he had taken her to prove to Jeffrey he could not hurt him?

He sat up and, without speaking, began to dress; then he walked to the edge of the cliff and stood trying to draw his thoughts into some order, trying to find a way to finish the job he had started but to keep Kristen, too.

Silently she watched him; then she drew on her clothes and went to him. She laid her hand gently against his broad back. Tears hovered in her voice and terror filled her heart as she said softly, "Is it that you do not love me enough to put aside this life and share mine with me?"

He turned and looked down into the dark shadows of her tear-filled gray eyes. "Love you!" He put his hands about her waist and drew her against him. She closed her eyes and rested her head against his chest, feeling the solid beat of his heart and savoring the hard muscular arms that held her. "Let me tell you how much I love you. I love you so much I feel you are a part of my body. I love you so much that if you laugh I want to feel the pleasure of your joy, and if you weep, I want to taste the salt of your tears. I love you so much that sometimes I cannot believe what I feel. It overpowers me, urges me to hold you and keep you always."

"Morgan, what will we do? After you, I could never think of another. You won't let the fact of my wealth stand between us? I know that Jeffrey is wealthy, and that you have nothing but your ship and your ability. It is enough for me. . . . Is it enough for you? You . . . you won't let your pride send me away?"

He cupped her face in his hands and kissed her gently over and over until she clung weakly to him.

"Let us share these few days together. Trust me, Kristen, I will find a way for us to be together. Somehow I will find a way to solve whatever problems we have. I will not let you go—to Jeffrey or to any other man. Will you have enough faith in our love . . . in me . . . to trust me for a while?"

"I do trust you, Morgan," she replied. "I will wait if I can be sure that we will be able to share the rest of our lives together. There is nothing else more important to me, than to know you love me as I love you."

"I'll think of something," he said determinedly as he took her hand and they began to walk back to the cabin.

He would never forget the days and nights that followed. He knew Kristen in every mood: the gay careless Kristen whose eyes were bright with laughter as they shared the sun-filled days, the passionate Kristen who claimed him completely as they shared the star-filled nights, and the sweet gentle Kristen who spoke to him of love in every way.

Often they would walk the beach at night with only the stars for company and the gentle sound of the ocean to whisper to them of the night to be shared.

Toby, whose world had expanded to include Kristen in the sphere of people he loved, shared some of their days with them, as did Jeremy.

There were times when Kristen would catch Jeremy watching Morgan with a strange look on his face, a sad look that nudged her curiosity. If anyone knew about Morgan's past, it would be Jeremy, who had been with him from the start. She promised herself to try to question Jeremy at her first opportunity. Knowing his loyalty to Morgan, perhaps he would tell her nothing about him. "But," she mused, "perhaps . . ."

The occasion came the next day. Morgan left her and Toby on the beach and went to the *Falcon*. He told her he was needed for some trivial thing, but he spent some time alone in the cabin trying to organize a tentative plan that had seeped into his mind.

Jeremy packed some extra food and went to the cabin. He meant to leave the food there and take Toby back to the ship, but he did not find them at the cabin or on the beach below.

Curious, he set out to find them. Kristen and Toby were exploring some of the caves on the far side of the island and it took Jeremy almost two hours to find them.

He walked along the stretch of sand searching for them; then he heard his name being called. Looking up, he saw Toby and Kristen standing in the mouth of one of the caves. He waved and watched them make their way toward him. Watching Kristen walk toward him with her free, easy stride and open, trusting smile again made him upset with Morgan and the lies he was telling her.

He could not believe now that Morgan would deliberately deceive the girl just to get revenge on Jeffrey. Morgan had never lied to him and he could still hear Morgan's voice when he had told him that he loved Kristen and intended to keep her. He had urged Morgan again and again to forget his revenge, to tell Kristen who he really was, and to marry her.

"She'll never believe me now, Jeremy. She will see all this as part of my revenge. No, I've got to find another way."

"What other way is there but the truth?"

"I don't know yet, Jeremy," he had replied grimly. "I only know I will find it, for neither heaven nor hell will take her from me now."

He remembered Morgan's hard blue gaze and knew that for the first time in Morgan's life, he was caught in a situation he was not sure how to handle. Yet he knew, as sure as there was a God in heaven, Morgan would never let Kristen go.

"Jeremy, hello!" she called.

"Good afternoon, miss. You sure are lookin' pretty today." Jeremy still could not bring himself to call her Kristen.

"Thank you; has Morgan come back with you?"

"No, but I brought some food. Are you and the mite here hungry?"

"I am." Toby laughed.

"Well, run on ahead and get somethin' started." Jeremy chuckled.

He and Kristen followed, walking slowly. Soon Toby was out of sight. They walked in silence for a while.

"Oh," Kristen said softly, "how I love this place. It's so . . . so peaceful."

167

"Aye, it is that," he agreed.

"You and Morgan have come here often?"

"Aye, it seems to be the captain's favorite place, besides,"—he smiled—"it is not on most of the maps so it ain't likely many knows where it is. The captain, he kinda likes havin' a place of his own to run to when things get hard for him."

"Jeremy . . . have things been that way in Morgan's life? Hard I mean."

"Everybody has hard things to take in a lifetime. I don't suppose it's been any harder on Morgan than on others."

"I . . . I know he must have been very poor, for money seems to mean a great deal to him, and . . . Charlotte . . . he must have loved her very much. Jeremy, can you tell me about her?"

Jeremy was silent for a while.

"Charlotte," he said softly. "She was a sweet and pretty thing. Always laughin' and happy, always trusting."

"What did she look like?"

"She was a tiny thing, all smilin' blue eyes and hair black as night."

"Did he . . . did he love her?"

"Aye, miss, he loved her, but not the way you're thinkin'. Morgan loves you in a way he's loved no other woman. The love he had for Charlotte was different. Some day he'll tell you about it. It ain't my place to be talkin' of her without him knowin'."

"What about his family, Jeremy, are they living?"

"Aye, both of them."

"It must be difficult for them to know their son has turned to piracy."

Jeremy laughed aloud.

"They'd not be knowin' a thing about it, miss, and the captain would die before he'd have them know. They're proud of the boy and he'd like to keep it that way."

"What are they like, Jeremy?"

"Fine people, fine. They're a warm close family. Morgan loves them and they love him more now that . . ."

"That what?"

"That he comes and goes so much," Jeremy added lamely; yet Kristen felt sure it was not what he meant to say.

"Jeremy . . . can you tell me what happened between Morgan and Jeffrey? What started this terrible vendetta?"

"No, miss, I can't . . . I won't. The captain, he has his reasons for what he's doin', good reasons." He stopped and looked into Kristen's clear gray eyes. "I know it's hard for you, havin' all the questions and none of the answers. Give this thing some time. The captain, he loves you, of that I'm sure. Give him time to work it all out. Trust him, miss, and you'll find out everything will come right. He'll find a way. I know now he's found you he'll never let you go."

She sighed, then smiled up at him. "I trust him, Jeremy," she said softly. "I love him and I want him to be happy. I don't think he can be happy as a pirate. I feel he is so much more than that. I would gladly give him all my wealth if he would just put aside this life and let go of this dreadful hate that seems to drive him."

"You offered him that?"

"Yes, I did."

"And he refused, so you can see it isn't just the money. You're a sweet, loving woman; just keep loving him. Believe me, I'm sure it is the one thing that will set his world right. He needs you maybe more than you need him. Miss?"

"Yes?"

"No matter what anyone ever tells you, don't believe anything bad about the captain. He's a good man, and one day soon, he'll find his way out of this and the two of you will be together."

"You love him, too?"

"Aye, like my own son."

"You think what he's doing is right?"

"No, miss, but I'll stand with him for the reason behind it. Will you remember what I'm sayin'? Stand by him, miss; you won't regret it."

"I will Jeremy, I will."

"Good." Jeremy took her arm in his. "Now let's go back to the cabin before Toby burns it down tryin' to cook somethin' for us."

She laughed and they headed back.

Morgan came to eat with them and they shared a relaxed supper. Kristen waited in the cabin while Morgan walked to the beach with Jeremy and Toby.

Once on the beach, Jeremy sent Toby out of the range of their voices; then he turned to Morgan. "What are you going to do?"

"Do? About what?"

"About the way that girl loves you. Are you goin' to tell her the truth or keep lyin' to her."

"Damn it, Jeremy, I don't know what I'm going to do yet."

"Then if you can't tell her the truth, let her go. She has already said she has no intention of marryin' Jeffrey. Send her back to her home in America. She's too nice to be used like this."

"I can't."

"Why?"

"Because," he said quietly, "I love her and I want her here."

"Then tell her the truth."

"Again, I can't."

"And again, I ask why?"

He turned to look at Jeremy. "Jeremy, old friend, try to understand. I'll find some way to work out what is between Kristen and I; there's an answer and I'll find it. But I won't let Jeffrey go free after what he has done. Don't you see, Jeremy, I can't. I can't let Charlotte have died for nothing."

"Morgan, sometimes it's best to give up the past and let it die. Charlotte would not have wanted it this way."

"I let her die, that's enough."

"Let— You blame yourself for her death?"

"I do. Who knew Charlotte better than I? I saw what was happening. I suspected it was Jeffrey, but I let it go. I thought, maybe one day she would see him as he was. I didn't realize that day would be her last day to live. I owe her this debt, Jeremy, to see he doesn't go unpunished. She can't rest and neither can I until it is done."

"Revenge is a two-edged sword, Morgan. Most times it kills the wielder as well as the victim. Is it worth the loss of Kristen's love?"

Morgan's anguished eyes looked out to sea, not seeing the beauty of it, but the memory of the girl who had died and the one he loved. Would her love remain if she knew the truth?

"It's a chance I have to take, to hope she understands why, to hope she loves me enough by the time she learns my identity that it won't matter. I will tell you this, Jeremy: I will never let her go, but I cannot let him go either. Somehow I will find the way. Until I do, Kristen is here, and here she will stay."

"You mean you're keepin' her here! What if he pays the ransom? He'll expect her to be returned."

Morgan grinned. "Someone should explain to him that one shouldn't trust a pirate. I will be around to watch his face when he finds he's lost all his money and Kristen as well."

"Then what? Where will you be able to take Kristen? Where will you be able to find any happiness? Lord Morgan Grayfield is known everywhere, and the Mac-Intire power reaches too far for you to escape it. When she shows up somewhere with you it won't take him long to have you hung. You know he'd enjoy nothing more than to know who Captain Black is. Finding out who you really are would give him the greatest pleasure."

Morgan's face hardened. "I'll pick the time and place for him to find out. On that day, I'll tell him who I am, for it is a confrontation he'll never walk away from. At that time, I will have ruined him financially; then I intend to kill him."

"Morgan, boy, what if you're faced one day with a choice?"

"A choice?"

"What if you have to choose between your revenge on Jeffrey and Kristen. Will you be able to live with the choice?"

"It won't come to that."

"But if it did," Jeremy said softly, "how would you choose? Think about it."

Jeremy climbed into the boat and soon he and Toby were pulling away from the shore. Morgan watched them, and for the first time he was unsure of the path he was on.

He turned and walked up the path toward the cabin.

Inside he was met by soft warm arms that clung to him and willing lips that met his with passion. The soft feel of her in his arms pushed every other thought from his mind.

She gasped in surprise as his hard arms crushed her to him, and his mouth claimed hers in a kiss that seared her soul. She was aware of some deep strong emotion that was different in him.

He held her face between his hands and kissed her again and again.

"Love me, Kristen," he murmured. "Love me." The poignant plea touched her deeply; it was as if he were reaching in desperation. She clung to him, surrendering completely to his need.

"I need you, Kristen, to believe in me, to love me."

"I'm here, Morgan," she whispered. "I'm here."

He looked down into her eyes, his gaze deep and penetrating. To her it seemed as if he searched for something. She was held breathless and motionless by the flame of hot passion in his eyes. Then suddenly, she was lifted in his arms.

In the soft warmth of the bed, he claimed her, his lips drawing from her an all-consuming desire, his hands possessing her completely. She was lost to all reality, knowing only that her fiery need for him had branded her forever, and that no matter what else happened, she would be his always.

He no longer thought of right and wrong, of good or evil; he knew only the magic softness that was Kristen, the harbor of safety that was his love. He closed his eyes, absorbing the sweet scent and feel of her, then he pressed himself deeply within her. With a low groan of intense satisfaction, he lifted her body to meet his. Tongues of

173

flame licked through her, turning her world crimson, and she called out his name over and over. She gloried in the way he seemed to need her, and she desired nothing more to answer that need with the unquestionable assurance of her love.

For a long time, they lay together without speaking. He held her against him, one hand gently caressing the long silken strands of her hair. After a while he could feel her body relax against his and he knew she slept. But sleep eluded him. His mind whirled from thought to thought trying to find the answer.

White moonlight entered the room as he lay in silence listening to the soft brush of the ocean on the sand and the gentle breathing of the woman who lay quiet and secure in his arms.

Suddenly his arm tightened about her, and she stirred restlessly in his arms. He smiled as he tightened them more and began to kiss her gently—her cheeks, eyes, and the curve of her slender throat until he felt her waken.

"Kristen," he whispered against her throat. "Kristen, my love, my sweet, will you marry me?"

Her sleepy eyes half-open, she clung to him for a moment; then suddenly she sat up, her eyes wide open. She looked down at him. "Morgan?"

"What?"

"I . . . I thought you said . . ."

"Said what?"

"I thought you asked me to marry you," she whispered. "I must have been dreaming."

"And," he replied gently, as he drew her close to him, "do you dream of such a thing?"

"Yes, always, I dream. I dream that you and I go away somewhere alone; I dream that we marry. I dream that we have children and live happily ever after . . . like the fairy tales I was told as a child. Yes, I dream of you . . . always of you."

"It was no dream, love. Will you marry me? We will go away. I know of a small house in the mountains several miles from Devon, England. It's small and isolated, but we could share it, live there together. Will you marry me and come to my castle away from the world? At least until I can straighten out my life. Then . . . then you will be mine for all the world to see."

"Oh, Morgan," she whispered softly as she slid down against him and put her arms about his neck. "Don't you know I would go anywhere with you, anywhere, as long as you hold me and tell me you love me?"

"It would mean that you would be alone for a while, that I would have to leave you for a little while. I will find a way to change my life and make our future. Would you wait for me?"

"Yes, if it means you will turn your back on being a pirate. If you would be reasonable about my money. If we could make a good future together. Morgan, I love you. I will do whatever you think necessary if it means we'll be together for always one day."

"Yes. Have faith in me, Kristen. Some way, somehow, I will make a life for us."

"Then that is all I need to know," she said softly. "Love me, Morgan, and let me tell you how much I love you."

"Kristen . . ."

He held her close to him and their gentle kiss slowly filled her with the warmth of his love.

"I love you, Kristen . . . believe me, have faith in me. . . . I love you."

It was meant with all his heart, but these were to be words that would one day burn within his mind and heart, words that one day would take him from the height of pleasure to the depths of despair. These words of love would one day turn to hate, and almost take from him the one person he loved beyond all else.

# *Eleven*

Jeremy listened in open-mouthed shock. He could not believe what Morgan was telling him.

"Get the *Falcon* ready to leave on tonight's tide, Jeremy. I expect to touch the coast of England before we hear from MacIntire. By the time his answer gets to us, Kristen and I will already be married."

"Married! You come home married to her and you'll be dead and hangin' by nightfall."

"I've no intention of anyone finding out who I am yet, and I've definitely no intention of hanging. Kristen and I have a long life to share together and I intend to be alive and well to share it."

"There's no way of keepin' them from knowin' you're the pirate that's been runnin' them ragged if you and Kristen marry. Jeffrey's not a stupid man. What are you goin' to tell him? That you rescued her? Not likely."

"You're right; I've no intention of telling him that. I've no intention of telling him anything. He'll never see Kristen again."

"Where can Lord Morgan Grayfield hide in England? Is there anyone who doesn't know you and your family?"

"Why should I hide? Kristen will be quietly safe at the hunting lodge; at least until I find some way to straighten this out. In time, when everything's over, we'll go home. Then I'll tell her who and what I really am."

"You just can't let loose of this hatred, can you, boy? Why not let her be found, then you and she can meet and marry in England. She still is some part of your revenge, isn't she? But of course, if you do that, it means you have to let this go, and you just can't do that, can you?"

"Jeremy, it will all work out. I can't just let him walk away." His voice softened. "Charlotte deserves more than that. I can still see her as she was the last time we were together. She was so young . . . so sweet. To have met a death like that—I don't want suicide attached to her name."

"No, Charlotte didn't deserve what happened. She was young and innocent of what was going on, but . . . so is Kristen."

"I don't intend for her to be hurt by all of this. The less she knows the better. She'll forgive me when I tell her and"—he held up a hand to ward off Jeremy's next words—"I will be the one who tells her."

Jeremy sighed, his eyes saddened by knowing that Morgan was blind to what could happen. Blinded by his own hate. He only prayed Morgan's eyes would be opened by Kristen's love before he lost her. He knew if Morgan did he would suffer regret and pain for which he was completely unprepared.

"All right, Morgan, the *Falcon* will be ready. We'll leave on the tide."

"Thanks, Jeremy."

Jeremy watched Morgan walk away, his step light and a soft tuneless whistle on his lips.

He went back to the small cabin. Inside he closed the door behind him and leaned against it smiling at Kristen who crossed the room and walked into the circle of his waiting arms.

"We'll be ready to leave in about an hour. Kristen . . .

178

I want you to write a letter."

"A letter . . . to whom?"

"Jeffrey."

"But Morgan . . ."

"Write and tell him you have changed your mind about marrying him, and that after we set you free you intend to go home."

"Do I?" she whispered. "Intend to go home?"

"You'll never be out of my reach again, my love. I'm taking you to a place where I can be near you while I try to get our lives rearranged. Will you wait, will you go with me?"

"Yes, Morgan, you know I will."

"It won't be easy for you, and I hate to leave you for any time at all, but I promise you one day it will all be worth the waiting. I love you, Kristen."

"I know," she said softly. "I know that you are changing your whole life for me. You won't regret it, Morgan. I'll try to make you as happy as you've made me."

Guilt kept him silent as she drew his head down to hers; then he lost himself and the thoughts he did not want to face in the magic of her kiss.

The sun was a red ball on the horizon when the sails of the *Falcon* filled with a strong breeze and the ship left the haven of the small uncharted island.

Four days later, it entered the small cove where it had hidden so many times before.

Morgan and Kristen, accompanied by Jeremy and the cabin boy, Toby, who had turned himself into Kristen's gallant protector, took a small boat and left the cove, going down the coast.

Morgan's family had a hunting lodge, well isolated

179

from the everyday world as a place of retreat. It was to this secluded place that Morgan took Kristen.

It was large for a hunting cabin; large, comfortable, and prepared to accommodate any number of guests for any length of time.

"Morgan," Kristen said softly as they stepped inside. "Will . . . will I be alone for long?"

"You won't be alone. Toby is staying with you. I'll only be gone for a couple of weeks."

"I . . . I hate to act like a baby, but . . . I . . . I've been so alone since my father died. I've found you and . . ."

"Shhh, love," he whispered as he drew her into his arms and held her. "I'll come back soon; but before I go, we are sending Jeremy for the minister from the village that is only a few miles from here. Before I go, you will be my wife. You will, won't you?" he asked gently.

"Yes . . . yes, Morgan."

Jeremy left for the village, but they were all to be disappointed, for the man who was minister to the village was away from his home, comforting a dying friend, and could not come.

"I'm sorry, Kristen," Morgan said miserably.

"It's all right, Morgan. When you get back, I'll be here and you won't be able to get away from me ever again. Come back soon."

"I will love, I will."

He was gone too suddenly for Kristen. And it took all her effort to control the sudden sense of dark loneliness that threatened to overcome her.

"Come, Toby, I know all boys your age are continuously hungry. Shall I fix you something to eat?"

His face beamed in a wide grin and he nodded, pleased that his goddess was smiling again.

Morgan and Jeremy made their way back to the *Falcon*.

Making sure that all was secure there, they took the small boat and in a few hours, Morgan stepped ashore on Jamie Price's property.

Jamie was not surprised to find Morgan at his door for on occasion he had found him there at the strangest times. All of their lives he and Morgan had been friends, and he was the only person in English society who knew the dual role of pirate Captain Black and Lord Morgan Grayfield.

"Morgan, come in. I'll pour you a good strong drink. You look tired."

"I am, but I want to get home tonight. What have you heard, Jamie?"

"Need I say that Jeffrey is about to explode with fury? If he ever gets his hands on you, Morgan, he will personally see to your hanging."

Morgan laughed. "Yes, I imagine so."

"What have you done with his future bride? Have you collected the ransom for her? If you have, he'll probably not be able to afford a wedding."

Morgan took the proffered drink, then motioned toward a chair. "You had best sit down, Jamie. I have a long story to tell you and the shock might be too great for you."

Jamie sat, but the expectant smile he wore faded to a worried scowl as Morgan began to talk. By the time Morgan had finished, worried lines creased Jamie's brow.

"God, Morgan, you're in one hell of a position. If Jeffrey gets wind of any of this— Morgan, why don't you let all this go? Take the girl and make a happy life together. He just isn't worth it. Let the past go."

"You too, Jamie?"

"Me too?"

"Jeremy keeps saying the same thing. I won't be

181

satisfied until I see him dead."

"You know as well as I do, Charlotte would not have wanted it this way."

Jamie sighed when he saw the closed angry look in Morgan's eyes. He stood up.

"Well, I guess it's another trip to London for me. I expect you want it to be well known you've spent the last few weeks with me."

"That's right. I want to be there when Jeffrey gets Kristen's letter. I want to see the last of his plans disintegrate."

"What then, Morgan?"

"I'm not sure yet. But if my plans go well, within a month or so, Jeffrey will be invited to the wedding of Kristen Seaford and Morgan Grayfield. That should just about be the finishing touch; that should just about make him angry enough to challenge me or to leave himself open for me to challenge him. One way or the other, I mean to destroy him . . . completely."

Jamie's eyes became filled with pity. "And you think that will ease the hurt of the memories or the pain of your guilt?"

"Guilt?"

"Do you think I don't know you blame yourself for Charlotte's death? It won't work, Morgan. In the first place you are not guilty of anything, and in the second place, revenge never works out. You kill him but Charlotte is still dead . . . and you will still carry that misplaced guilt within you."

"What would you suggest I do?"

"Let love take the place of guilt. You have damaged Jeffrey, nearly destroyed him financially. Let it go at that. Take your woman and turn your back to the past. Be happy."

"I can't, Jamie . . . I can't."

Again Jamie sighed deeply. "I'll help you all I can, Morgan, as I always do, but I can't help feeling I'm doing you more harm than good. Come on, I'll get a carriage ready. We'll go to London and make your presence known."

They left for London within the hour and after arriving amid chatter and laughter that drew attention, they again left for Morgan's home.

It was after they had arrived, been made comfortable, and eaten a meal that they prepared for their visit to Jeffrey. In silence they rode, first to the docks to see Owen and then to Jeffrey's home. Morgan was surprised at his reception from Owen. What he had expected was far from what he received.

Owen was seated in his cabin contemplating a maneuver he was planning that would enable him to get away from the surveillance Jeffrey had put on him, to get the *Sea Mist* free of the harbor, and to get back to Jane and his wedding as soon as possible. He was deep in thought when the door opened and Morgan and Jamie walked in.

"Morgan! Damn you, man, I've been waitin' a long time for word from you. What the hell have you done with that lass? I thought ye'd get word to me before this. Ye have na hurt the lass have ye, boy?"

"Whoa, Owen." Morgan laughed. "Let me explain."

"Ye should ha' wakened me and let me talk to ye before ye took her. Morgan, if ye've harmed that child, ye'll answer for it. She's not what ye thought she was."

"I haven't harmed her, Owen. Now will you sit down and let me explain all that's happened?"

Owen sat, but the look in his eye was still tinged with wary anger.

"First, Owen, what happened with Jane? Did she get to

183

her aunt in Ireland all right? What has Jeffrey had to say about it?"

Now Owen chuckled and his eyes lit with amusement. "He's fair to bein' about to burst, he's so angry. But the lass ain't in Ireland, and it will be a long time before he sees her again; never, if I have my way."

"Tell me what happened. Where is she?"

"Wi' my family, in Scotland."

"How did this come about?"

Owen shrugged, but his smile was broad. "As soon as I can wiggle my way out from under her brother's spies, I intend to return. I also intend to make the lass my wife as soon as humanly possible."

"Well," Morgan said softly with a devilish smile that matched Owen's. "It seems we are guilty of taking both Jeffrey's women away from him; for you see, I intend to marry Kristen Seaford."

Owen whistled gently. "Suppose you tell me how all *this* came about. Surely you ain't marryin' that lass to get back at Jeffrey MacIntire?"

"Hardly. I would do a lot to get back at him, but marrying is a little too much. I love her and I intend to marry her just as soon as we get one little problem straightened out."

"What little problem is that?"

Morgan explained all that had happened between him and Kristen and Owen sat in silence for a while.

"He'll hang ye . . . or she will."

"I think with Kristen's letter, and my other plans, Jeffrey's time is up. I'm going to pay the man a visit tomorrow, after he's had time to get Kristen's letter. I want to be there to watch."

"How are you going to get around him addin' two and two when you and Kristen marry? It won't take him long to figure out who you are."

"I'll figure out a way."

"Well, good luck to ye; for me, I intend to leave for home soon. I'll invite ye to the weddin' if you can get away to come. In fact 'twould be nice to have a double weddin' if ye could get out from under all these problems."

"Sounds like a good idea."

"Morgan . . . Jane is uncommonly afraid of her brother. I suspect she knows many things that might be able to put a stop to him. If I can get her to tell me, maybe it is something ye can use as protection if the need ever arises."

"I'd appreciate your finding out anything you can; it might work as leverage in getting him to let Kristen go if the need comes up."

"I'll do what I can. She hates to talk of the man and I can see the fear in her eyes when she speaks of him."

"Thanks, Owen, for all your help, and for bringing me Kristen. It's one of the best things that have happened in my life."

"Take care of her, Morgan. In the time I've known her, I've found her to be a sweet gentle thing. That kind of a woman is rare in a man's life."

"I'll care for her, Owen, and one day soon we'll come to Scotland to visit you."

"'Twould be good. I should like to be able to apologize to her for deceivin' her like I did."

"I'm sure she'll forgive you."

He held out his hand to Owen who took it in a firm grasp.

"I hope things work out well for you, Morgan, but if it were me . . ."

"Don't say 'forget him,' Owen. I can't and I'll just

185

have to go along with the plans I've made. What about your shadow outside?"

"It might be fun to play wi' him for a while, but I want to be gettin' back to Jane soon, so I'll just make a late-night visit to him when he's unsuspecting."

"If you're gone before I see you again, give Jane my best and send me an invitation to the wedding. It's one I wouldn't want to miss."

"Thanks, and good luck to you and Kristen. I hope you work everything out and find a way to spend the rest of your lives together."

"See you at the wedding, Owen," Morgan said.

He and Jamie left the ship, boarded the carriage, and left to have their first confrontation with Jeffrey since Morgan had taken Kristen.

When they were announced at Jeffrey's home, they were taken to the library where they waited only a few minutes for Jeffrey to join them.

Morgan's astute eyes could see immediately that Jeffrey was under a terrible strain and he enjoyed the fact that he was responsible. The only thing that annoyed him was the fact that Jeffrey didn't know it . . . yet.

"Morgan?"

"I've been spending some time at Jamie's and I hadn't heard that our pirate found my ship as well as yours. Have you heard from him?"

"The damned blackguard has sent me a ransom demand that is nearly impossible."

"But you've raised it?"

"Yes, I've raised it. I have also raised enough to put a sizable reward on this pirate's head. No matter what it costs, I will have his head if it is the last thing I do. I have spoken to the king, but unless Captain Black attacks a ship that belongs to him, he will do nothing."

"I've been told by Owen that Jane has gone away."

Morgan was startled now by the satisfied look on Jeffrey's face.

"She's gone for a short trip, but now that I know where she is I have already sent a ship to bring her home."

Morgan kept his face impassive, but his heart leaped at the thought that Jeffrey knew where Jane was, was making a move to bring her home, and Owen didn't know about it. He would have liked nothing more than to find out how Jeffrey knew, but he was afraid to ask for fear of raising more suspicion in Jeffrey. It was Jamie who spoke.

"How did she leave? You haven't been sending any ships out lately."

"I have my suspicions about that. All I know for sure is she arrived in Ireland at our aunt's home. She was foolish enough to sign a paper for the sale of our deceased aunt's home. There were . . . other signatures on the paper. Signatures that told me exactly where Jane has gone. Our ship left two days ago to bring her home to where she belongs. She has obligations to our family and has already been promised in marriage. This little affair will be over soon and she'll be here to fulfill her obligations."

"If I were she, I would run away from the groom you've chosen, too." Morgan smiled.

"Clyde Rupert is a very influential man. He will give my sister a firm place in society."

"And a lot of money," Morgan said quietly.

"Only the Grayfields would sneer at so much money," Jeffrey said defiantly. "My sister needs to make an advantageous marriage."

"How about her feelings? Don't you think it would be an unbearable thing for a girl as young and pretty as Jane to be married to a lecherous old man like Clyde? And what about the nasty rumors about the man?"

"One can hardly believe rumors. This is my family affair, Morgan," he said softly. "I'll take care of Jane."

Before Morgan could reply there was a knock on the door.

"Come in."

"Mr. MacIntire," the butler began. "There is a message for you, sir."

"A message, from whom?"

"I don't know, sir. A man just dropped it off at the door."

"Did you know him?"

"No, sir. He looked like a sailor, sir, from his clothes, but I've never seen him before."

The servant handed the letter to Jeffrey, a familiar letter to Morgan who found himself tense as he awaited Jeffrey's reaction.

Jeffrey tore open the letter and began to read while Morgan silently watched. Jeffrey's face first went white from the shock, then red with anger, anger he tried to control and hide from the eyes that were watching.

"Not bad news, I hope," Morgan said.

"No," Jeffrey said. "Nothing I cannot handle." He rang for the butler and handed him the message. "Take this message up to Mrs. Seaford."

Morgan and Jamie were both startled at the name.

"Mrs. Seaford?" Morgan said. "I thought . . ." He caught himself before he said the words that would have revealed that he knew more of Kristen's life than he should have.

Jeffrey's preoccupation with the letter and his intense anger at the news it brought, overlooked the slip. "Mrs. Seaford is Kristen's stepmother. She arrived just yesterday. She is very alarmed by Kristen's kidnapping.

188

As executor of Kristen's estate, should anything have happened to her, she has put the entire estate in my hands to help me buy back my future wife."

"I see," Morgan replied. "I should like very much to meet her."

"Yes . . . yes, of course," Jeffrey said. He looked at Morgan for a moment as if some thought had suddenly struck him; then he sent for Leslie.

There was not much conversation while they waited for Leslie to come. Jeffrey seemed to be deep in thought and Jamie, a worried frown on his face, watched him for he felt the thoughts were directed at Morgan. Some sense told him these thoughts were not good. He tried to discuss other things, but it still made him nervous when Jeffrey answered him in an absent way while his gaze remained on Morgan.

Even though Morgan had been told a little about Leslie by Kristen, he was unprepared for her youth and beauty. He thought, being Kristen's stepmother, she would be a much older woman, and he wondered what her connection with Jeffrey could be.

"Mrs. Seaford," Jeffrey said, "this is Lord Morgan Grayfield and a friend of his, Lord Jamison Price. This is the gentleman to whom the *Sea Mist* belongs, the ship that came for Kristen. It was one of Morgan's captains, Owen MacGregor, who captained her when the pirate attacked. Morgan, Jamie, this is Kristen's stepmother, Leslie Seaford."

"My pleasure, Mrs. Seaford," Morgan said politely and Jamie murmured a greeting.

"Good day, gentlemen. This is a very tragic circumstance under which to meet."

"Tragic?" Morgan questioned. "Jeffrey has told us he has sent the ransom for your stepdaughter. She should

189

be home soon after that."

"Oh, Lord Grayfield," she said in a deeply sorrowed voice. "I wish I had your optimism. Kristen was such a fragile, delicate child. I can't believe she has withstood the attack by pirates, and God only knows what has happened to her since. I shudder to think of it."

Fragile, Morgan thought humorously. Delicate! Hardly the words to describe the way Kristen had fought him, or the warm passionate woman who waited for him.

"Have faith, Mrs. Seaford, why I have a strong feeling your stepdaughter is closer to home than you think she is. This pirate captain has never killed a man before; I hardly believe he would kill the girl."

"There are things," she murmured softly, her eyes downcast, "that are worse than death."

If Morgan and Jamie initially were taken in by the gentleness of her act, Jeffrey was amused by it. Morgan glanced his way for a moment and was stunned to silence by the glitter of laughter in Jeffrey's eyes. It was then he put two and two together and came up with . . . Jeffrey and Leslie.

"Well, I must go," Morgan said. "If I can be of any help . . . delivering the ransom or maybe bringing Miss Seaford home, you will call on me? It would be my pleasure to help put an end to this and give the villain justice."

Jamie could have choked with laughter at Morgan's double-pointed words.

"Thank you, Lord Grayfield," Leslie said.

"Yes," Jeffrey replied quietly, his gaze again centered on Morgan. "I'm sure I can call on you for any kind of help."

After the door closed behind them, Jamie laughed aloud. "Deliver the ransom . . . rescue Miss Seaford . . .

Morgan, old chap, you have always had a great deal of nerve, but this surpasses all."

Morgan chuckled. "Jamie, I'd like to do both. Deliver the ransom and bring Kristen home. I just neglected to tell him whose home I would bring her to."

They laughed; then Morgan's face became serious. "Owen."

"What about him?"

"He's got to get out of here now. Jeffrey knows where Jane is and has sent a ship to bring her home. Owen's got to stop them."

They went to the docks as rapidly as possible. Owen was surprised to see them again, but his face grew pale as they hastily told him what was happening.

"Owen, you've got to leave now."

"What about my shadow?"

"Let him go and tell Jeffrey. It doesn't matter now. All that matters is that you get home in time to keep them from dragging her back here."

Owen nodded and they left his cabin. "Thank ye, Morgan. I appreciate your warnin'."

"Get there in time, Owen, that's all the thanks I need. I wouldn't want him to drag her back to face what he plans for her."

"Dinna ye worry, lad. He'll no get his bloody hands on her."

"Good luck, Owen."

They left the ship and stood watching her white sails unfurl as the *Sea Mist* sailed from the harbor.

"Do you think he'll make it, Morgan?"

"If anyone can, Owen will. I pity the man who puts his hands on Jane. I've seen Owen angry. He could break a man in two with his bare hands."

"What's your next step, Morgan?"

"I'm going home now and for a few days I'll remain in sight until I can find out what the connection is between those two."

"Those two? Jeffrey and Mrs. Seaford?"

"There's more connection there than we know yet. Think of it, Jamie, if something happened to Kristen, who would inherit the Seaford fortune?"

"Her stepmother, of course," Jamie said softly.

"And if there's a connection between the two," he mused, "Jamie, they're hoping Kristen either dies at the pirate's hands, or . . . or maybe they plan on doing the job when she comes home. One thing is sure, kidnapping her was the best favor I could have done her, for I think her loving future husband and her stepmother had other plans for her."

"Morgan, there's another thing."

"What?"

"I think Jeffrey is beginning to get a bit suspicious of you."

"Me!" Morgan laughed. "Jamie, you're seeing things. He has no idea the pirate is me."

"Morgan, do you not think the pirate has been described to him often enough? Even without the beard, it's possible you might have struck a familiar note between the pirate and you."

"You sound like a scared old woman. He has no idea who I am. Come along, let's go have dinner and a few drinks at my house. Then I've got to make some plans. We'll watch over our two friends closely for a while. It would be nice to find out what their connection is and what plans they might be making."

"How do you plan to do that?"

"Well . . . Leslie . . . she's young and pretty. Maybe she might be interesting to spend some time with."

"If she's what you think she is and if Jeffrey's guilty of all we think he is, you're playing a very dangerous game, my friend. If they ever find out about you, your death is sealed, and if you won't think about your own safety, think of Kristen's. She needs you, for if all you suspect is true, you're the only one who stands between her . . . and death."

"I believe Jeffrey is guilty. I'll find out where Leslie Seaford fits in. No power on earth will get to Kristen. No matter what else happens, I'll never let Kristen fall into Jeffrey's hands."

They rode to the Grayfield mansion where Morgan's enthusiastic parents happily greeted them both.

A large dinner was provided and the four of them sat laughing and talking together.

"Morgan, you spend so much time away from home lately," his father said. "I've begun to suspect there's a woman somewhere who's caught your interest."

"Good heavens." His mother laughed. "That would be wonderful. It's time you settled down. I would like grandchildren one day before I grow old."

"You, Mother?" Morgan chided. "You're as young and beautiful as you were when I was a little boy. You've a long time before you grow old."

"I thank you for the compliment, my son." She smiled. "But I refuse to let you turn my head and change the subject. There is someone, isn't there? You have changed in the past few weeks."

"Yes . . . yes, there is someone. I love her and I intend to ask her to be my wife one day soon."

"Who is she?"

"Mother . . . I can't tell you right now. There is a small difficulty we must overcome. Have patience and one day, I'll bring her here."

"Difficulty? She . . . she's not married?"

"No, Mother." Morgan laughed. "She's not married."

"Then what . . . ?"

"Trust me, Mother. It will all work out. One day soon, I'll bring her here. You will love her as I do. Until we are free, will you trust me?"

His father stood up and raised his wineglass.

"Of course we will trust you, and we will wait, though I admit not with much patience. Until then, my son, here is a toast to you and your future bride."

Morgan smiled his gratitude and lifted his glass to join the toast.

Several miles away, two others were sharing a drink. With a glass in his hand, Jeffrey stood contemplating a low-burning fire with a half-smile on his face. Leslie came to him and he put his arm about her waist.

"What are you thinking of, Jeffrey? You seem pleased with your thoughts."

He took a sip from his drink, then bent his head and kissed her deeply and passionately. When he released her, he was pleased at the hot passion in her eyes, a passion he intended to share . . . soon.

He explained the letter he had received and watched her frown.

"Don't worry, my dear, when Kristen gets released, we will be there to greet her. I don't intend to let her or her money slip through my fingers."

"Where is the exchange to take place?"

"At sea . . . so he can be sure we're not playing any tricks."

"Then you really intend to pay it?"

"Temporarily. But we'll find him, and when we do, we'll get my money back."

"Our money," she said coolly.

"Yes . . . our money."

"How do you think you'll find him? You've been unsuccessful before."

"Yes," he said softly, "but there's some connection between Kristen and this Owen MacGregor . . . and I've got a suspicion there's one between Owen and Morgan. I have a strange feeling Morgan knows much more than he says."

"You don't think he's the . . . ?"

"Pirate? No, but I'll bet my last sovereign he knows who he is. This would fit in well with his need for a little revenge against me."

"What are you going to do?"

"Do?" He smiled as he pulled her again into his arms. "First I'm going to make love to you . . . then I'm going to spread a little honey to catch our pirate."

"I like your suggestions," she said, as she raised her mouth for his kiss. "First things first."

He laughed as he closed his arms about her and parted her lips with his.

## Twelve

Jane woke slowly, luxuriously aware of the first sense of security and belonging she had ever had. The room in which she slept was far from the luxury she had always known; yet she had rested better than ever before.

It was a small room with one window that looked out over the most breath-taking beauty she had ever seen. It was bare of all but the essential things: the large bed in which she slept, a chest for her clothes, and a small stand that sat by her bed and held a pitcher and bowl for washing. It was not adorned with any decoration, yet it was scrupulously clean. The curtains that hung from the window glistened white in the first morning sun, and the thick quilts she lay under still smelled as if they had just been brought in from an airing outdoors in a fragrant breeze.

She thought of Owen, Owen who had opened the door to contentment and happiness for her by bringing her here and offering her his and his family's warm open love. She remembered his family's boisterous and happy acceptance of her. In the few weeks she had been with them, they had tried to erase her past thoughts and the pain that accompanied her memories.

James, Owen's father, was the model from which Owen had been created. Tall and broad of shoulder, his age of fifty-two sat well on him. Jane could tell almost at once that he was soldier-trained, and she wondered why he was now farming. His red-gold hair had faded just a bit, but when his blue eyes smiled at her, they were so much like Owen's that she could almost feel Owen's presence.

His mother, Margaret, was a small woman with wide brown eyes and skin white as cream. She seemed delicate, but Jane suspected she was the iron core around which the family moved. It was obvious in no time that her opinion and thoughts were deferred to most of the time.

Owen's brother, Ian, was younger than Owen by two years. At thirty, he was a combination of both his parents. He was two inches shorter than Owen, but at six feet, he was still a formidable man. He had his mother's deep-midnight black hair and her wide brown eyes. He was a slow-moving man who studied everything with patience, made his decisions . . . and then stood by them immovably. He had chosen as his bride a young tawny-haired girl from a neighboring village, a girl whose wealth would have put her beyond a young farmer's dreams. But at first sight, he had wanted her, and with determination, he had fought for and won her . . . without too much hesitation on her part for the dark-eyed Ian had won her heart the first time she had seen him. In the five years they had been married, she had never regretted it. They had one child, a girl who had her mother's tawny hair and her father's dark eyes and quiet patient disposition.

Douglas, at twenty-seven was a handsome laughing boy with a happy-go-lucky nature. He was tall and slender, yet completely masculine. Girls found his quick witty charm nearly impossible to resist, and Douglas was quick to take advantage of the opportunities he was offered. He made Jane feel like a protected younger sister.

Next to Douglas was Mary. She was slim, with hair that

was a dark midnight black, yet she had inherited her father's penetrating blue eyes. She was married to a young farmer named Aaron McDonnell. Their farm was only a few miles away and they visited often, bringing with them their two sons, James and Charles.

The last two girls, Jeanette, twenty-two, and Alys, twenty, lived with their parents yet. Jeanette had been married two years to a sailor who had been lost in a shipwreck and she had come home to find a safe harbor in which to draw herself together.

Alys was young, beautiful, and filled with laughter and fun. She did not want to marry, she was having too much fun playing with all the hearts in the villages that surrounded theirs.

Each in his or her own way had made Jane feel she was a welcome member of the family. Jane stretched, yawned, then pushed aside the coverlets and rose. It was early, but she could hear movement in the house that signaled the rising of the family.

She made her ablutions quickly, dressed, and went down the stairs. Margaret was the only one she found in the kitchen, and she welcomed Jane with a quick smile and an offer of a cup of hot strong tea.

"Sit down, lass, and have some tea wi' me before the others come to breakfast."

"Thank you." Jane sat down at the table and Margaret sat down opposite her. There were such obvious questions in Jane's eyes that Margaret had to laugh.

"Have ye not asked me enough questions about the lad yet? Dinna ye get enough answers?"

"I'll never get enough." Jane smiled in response. "I love Owen so much I want to make him a good wife. I want to return to him what he has so unselfishly given to me."

198

"I think, from the light in his eyes when he looks at ye, ye already have, just by sayin' ye'll marry him when he gets back."

"It has been weeks; surely he will be returning soon."

"From what he told us, the journey he planned to make was to be a short trip. I suspect he'll be returnin' quickly. We must begin to prepare for a party. All of our friends will be anxious to meet ye."

"The wedding," Jane said softly.

"Does it frighten ye, child, to marry my Owen?"

"No, oh no, it doesn't frighten me. I . . . I just don't know what kind of bride I'll be with no dowry . . . no wedding gown . . . no family."

Margaret smiled and rose to her feet.

"Come wi' me, child."

Jane rose and followed Margaret up the steps to the attic of the house, where she knelt in front of a large chest. She opened it, pushed aside the wrappings, and drew out a white satin dress. It was beautiful, with layers of old handmade lace at the bottom and at the throat and wrists.

"Ye're much shorter than I, but I believe if we remove one layer of lace, 'twould fit ye well."

"Oh, how lovely," Jane said softly as she took the dress and held it against her, her hands caressing the satin.

"'Twas my mother's, and I married Jamie in it. It would be nice to see my first-born's wife wear it also."

"I am so grateful; it is such an honor. I will wear it with pride and gratitude."

Tears in her eyes, she went to Margaret who held her for a moment and then said in a soft tear-filled voice, "Try it on, child. I should like to see you in it."

Quickly, Jane slipped out of her dress, then lovingly

199

drew the soft gown over her head and let it drop about her. Outside of the length, it fitted her perfectly. Margaret turned back to the chest and withdrew the veil of lace that matched the gown. When Jane put it on, Margaret looked at her and smiled. "Ye'll be a rare treat for the lad. I imagine he'll no be expectin' such a beautiful bride. Shall we keep it our secret?"

"Yes." Jane smiled through her tears. "Thank you . . ."

They embraced each other, then laughed at each other's happy tears.

"I believe we'd best be about makin' breakfast, my girl, or we'll have a lot of hungry people shoutin' for us."

Jane nodded and took off the dress and veil which was put lovingly back into the chest to wait for Owen's return.

They went downstairs together and prepared breakfast. By the time it was ready for the table several hungry mouths were ready for it.

As the days drifted by, Jane, a woman who had never done any physical work in her life, a woman who had been waited on hand and foot since birth, found herself involved in enjoying a whole new way of life.

The MacGregor farm was large, and although they had several young men for hired help, there was still plenty of work in which the family shared equally.

Though unaccustomed to it, Jane threw herself completely into the work and was rewarded by being accepted into the heart of the family.

She worried constantly about Owen's arrival and her preoccupation with it was understood by the entire family. That was the reason Douglas invited her to ride into town with him to see if any ships had arrived—or if there was word of the *Sea Mist*.

Douglas was free with laughter and wit and the trip into town was pleasant for Jane. Feeling his open acceptance of her, she tentatively sought answers to her curiosity about his family.

"Douglas?"

"Aye?"

"Your father, he wasn't always a farmer, was he?"

"What makes ye think that?"

"He . . . he walks, even talks like a man trained in the military."

"Aye, that he was."

"You needn't tell me if you don't want to," she offered, but laughed with him when the twinkle in his eyes denied her words.

"I see na harm in tellin' ye. Aye, me father was a soldier. 'Twas in 1745, me father was just a lad, but his mind and his heart lived with our bonnie Prince Charlie. The clans rose behind him. The Camerons, MacLeans, MacDonalds and MacGregors. Father fought wi' em from the day the prince left France and stepped on Scottish soil to the bloody battle of Culloden. He would ha' fought wi' him till he sat on the throne, but God would na have it that way. I canna tell ye what my father saw that day, but it sent such a sickness through him that when the bonnie prince was defeated, he threw away his arms wi' an oath to never raise 'em again against another man. He set his self to growin' life instead of endin' it. He married my mother who had been his sweetheart since childhood and they set theirselves about raisin' children. Father will na speak of it to this day. He is a farmer and he does na look back on the life before."

"It must have been terrible."

"The battle of Culloden?"

"Yes."

201

"I've only heard stories, but I know the highlanders died by the hundreds."

"And Prince Charlie?"

"We heard only stories to which Father will give no attention. He will na hear any evil against him."

"What did happen to him?"

"He left for France," Douglas said firmly.

"And the men who followed him?"

"No quarter given, they were hunted down and killed. They died by the hundreds. Troops were sent out to hunt down and kill all who had been loyal to the prince. Father escaped barely wi' his life. He and my mother came here, bought the farm, and have lived quietly ever since. Sometimes, I wonder if Father does na still see shadows followin' behind him."

"How terribly frightening it must have been for your mother."

"Aye, but Mother is a fierce strong woman. She would na let Father run wi'out her. She was the strong force that kept my father on an even keel through it all."

"Douglas, your family . . . they must hate the English."

"I would na say"—he chuckled—"that there is any gentle feelin's toward them."

"But . . . I'm English. They do not seem to resent me."

His eyes smiled down into hers. "Well, lass, there's English and then there's English. Ye are the woman our Owen has chosen for wife. We dinna look at ye as English, we look at ye as Owen's. Besides"—he laughed—"when ye wed our Owen, ye'll be a MacGregor. That will begin makin' a scottish lass of ye."

She laughed with him, enjoying the feeling of acceptance and camaraderie he offered her.

When they entered the town, Douglas drove the buggy down the street toward the docks.

"Would ye like to stop in the town and walk about a bit while I go to the dock and ask questions?"

"Oh, Douglas, would you mind if I went with you? I'm so anxious to see about Owen."

He grinned teasingly. "Are ye that anxious for the lad to be comin' back? I thought ye was enjoyin' my unmatchable presence and ye might have forgot Owen for a bit."

She smiled. "I am enjoying you, but I would never forget Owen for a minute."

He sighed as if in helpless defeat. "Leave it to Owen to be findin' the best for hisself and leavin' the rest of us to pine away forever."

"Oh, poor Douglas," she answered in mock sorrow. "I must be lookin' about for a bride for you as soon as possible. You do want to get married, don't you?"

His chuckle broke into a hearty laughter which was joined by hers.

"Dinna rush yeself, lass. I be lookin' about a bit more before I take the step. There's a lot of pretty lasses I hav'na met yet."

"But I do suspect you plan on meeting them?"

"As many as possible, lass, as many as possible."

She was about to answer him again when their buggy turned from the street to the road that led along the docks. Huge high-masted ships sat rocking gently in the harbor. At the sight of one, her face went pale and her eyes widened in recognition.

"What is it?" he questioned.

"The *Pelican*," she whispered softly.

His eyes followed hers to a large ship that sat quietly in the harbor, its sails furled as if it had been there for

203

a while.

"Ye know the ship?"

"It's one of my brother's. Oh, Douglas, he's sent someone for me! He knows where I am." She turned to him, stark fear on her face, and anger grew in him toward a brother who could bring such fear into the eyes of his sister.

"Dinna fash yerself, lass. We'll no let the man put a hand on ye. Ye're Owen's bride, and we'll no let anyone take ye wi'out ye wantin' to go."

He could see the fear still within her. "What will I do? I cannot make any trouble for your family. If Owen is not here, he will make me go back with him."

"Jane, lass." He calmed her with his firm quiet voice. "There is no member of my family tha' would consider defendin' ye a bit o' trouble. Ye belong to Owen and to us. We'll no let ye be hurt by anyone, not even your brother. Believe me, ye'll no be leavin' here unless it's wi' Owen. Come, we'll go home and tell Father. Then we'll plan what's best to do till Owen gets back."

He gave a sharp click of the tongue and slapped the horses' rumps with the reins. Drawing the buggy about in a circle he headed toward home. He was aware of her trembling body beside him and the hysterical tears that hovered on the edge of her long lashes. He would not question her now for fear of breaking her reserve, but he promised to question Owen as soon as he came. It was beyond his belief that a brother could turn his sister into this frightened child by only an indirect contact.

As they crested the hill a mile or so from the farm, Douglas drew the horses to an abrupt halt. Looking at him, Jane saw his clouded eyes and the deep frown on his face. Her eyes followed his and she could see the two horses tied in front of the house.

"It seems we've company," he said softly. "I dinna think I'll be takin' ye home now."

"Oh, Douglas, what can we do?"

"Do? The MacGregors have many friends in the valley. There's no need to be in a dither, lass. I'll be takin ye to a friend's house and ye'll stay there until Owen gets home. As I said before, lass, there's English and English. Those two will na find a welcome anywhere in the valley. If they be searchin' for ye, it'll all be for naught. They'll find no one here to hand ye over to 'em."

Quickly, he turned his horses again and headed away from the farm. In a little over an hour and a half, he drew the buggy to a halt in front of another house that resembled their own. They had no sooner stopped than the door opened. A large man with flame-colored hair and deep blue eyes stepped onto the porch; he was followed by a small dark smiling woman who was obviously his wife.

"Guid day to ye, Douglas. Will ye no step down and visit?"

"Good day, Mr. Campbell," Douglas said as he jumped down and helped Jane alight. He walked up the three steps with Jane's arm tucked in his. He made a short bow to Mrs. Campbell and smiled his best smile.

"Good day, Mrs. Campbell. I would like ye to meet Jane MacIntire, me brother Owen's intended bride."

"Ah." Mrs. Campbell smiled. "'Tis lovely ye are, lass. Owen has chosen well. Will ye no come in and sit? I'll make ya somethin' to refresh ye."

Before she could answer, a young girl appeared in the doorway. It took only one glance to see the girl had eyes only for Douglas. She seemed so withdrawn that for a few minutes Jane could not understand; then it came to her. She thought Douglas was bringing over another girl.

"Good mornin', Anna," Douglas said gently.

"Good mornin', Douglas," came the soft reply, but the girl's eyes never left Jane. Jane could see dismay deep in them as she studied Jane's obviously rich dress and more obvious genteel raising.

"I'm afraid I canna stay long. I have come, Mr. Campbell, to ask ye a favor in the name of Owen and the family."

"Ye need not ask, Douglas. Whatever it is, ye are welcome to anything the MacGregors may need."

"I'll explain as quickly as I can." He went on to explain the necessity of finding a safe place to hide Jane until Owen returned. It was amusing to Jane to see the relief on Anne's face when she heard of Owen's and Jane's planned marriage.

"Ye are welcome in our home for as long as ye care to stay," Lachlan Campbell said, an expression seconded quickly by both his wife and his daughter.

Douglas turned to Jane. "I'll be goin' home now. As soon as I find out what's afoot, I'll be back to tell ye."

"If you hear any news of Owen . . ."

"If I hear anythin' I'll let ye know. Ye'll be in safe hands, lass; dinna be afraid. Owen will come home soon."

"Thank you, Douglas. You are very kind to a stranger."

"Nay, lass,"—he laughed softly—"to a sister."

He brushed a quick kiss on her cheek and in a moment he was back in the buggy. Jane watched until the buggy faded from sight; then she turned about to find all three Campbells waiting silently for her.

"Come, lass," Lachlan said gently. "Come inside and be comfortable. Ye're safe here."

His wife put her arm about Jane's shoulder and the

three of them drew her inside and closed the door firmly against any intrusion.

Douglas pushed the horses to maximum speed, and was surprised to find the two horses still tied in front of his home when he stopped. He cared for the horses and had the buggy put away; then whistling lightly through his teeth, he walked across the wide porch and opened the door. He smiled broadly at family and strangers as all eyes turned toward him.

"'Tis a bonnie day. Mother, I dinna know we was to be expectin' guests."

Before his mother could reply, both men rose from their seats. Douglas could read his parents' faces well; he knew they had denied any knowledge of Jane.

"Douglas MacGregor?"

"Aye, that I am."

"I have warned your parents, and I shall warn you. Your brother is guilty of kidnapping the sister of Jeffrey MacIntire. We believe he brought her here. It would be well for you and your family to turn her over to us peaceably, else we shall have to take more extreme measures."

"Kidnapping!" Douglas laughed. "'Tis not necessary for Owen to kidnap a lass. Most of 'em come wi' him willin' enough."

Nothing in the world angered a Scot more than to be challenged to a fight. Douglas's eyes were cold and only his parents recognized the bubbling anger beneath the quick laugh.

"And what measures did ye have in mind for me?" he questioned softly.

The speaker of the two grew flushed and his shoulders stiffened as he recognized the answering challenge in

Douglas's eyes.

"Jeffrey MacIntire is not a power to be trifled with," he said arrogantly. "He is privy to the king and his power stretches far. I warn you, sir, return his sister and he will consider the matter closed."

"Ach, now," Douglas replied coolly, "I am tremblin' in me boots at the threat of Jeffrey MacIntire." He walked close to the man and stood face-to-face. "I will tell ye what ye can go and say to yer master. You tell him if . . . *if* Owen kidnapped a lass, and I doubt it, for Owen is not of a devious mind like your master must be, he has probably taken the girl to a port somewhere and married her by now, and neither you nor all the power your master has behind him would dare reach out and touch the wife of a MacGregor. There would be a battle your master and his king would remember a long, long time."

"You refuse to return her?"

"I dinna have her, but if I did, I would wait on Owen's word to return her to ye. It seems to me the lass must have been willin' to go, and if she was, I would not be the one to return her where she dinna want to be."

"I will search this house and take her by force if I must, and the authorities will place you under arrest for aiding a criminal."

Now Douglas's eyes sparkled with devilish laughter. "And have ye brought the army of your king along? For ye'll need it if ye plan on searchin' this house wi'out my parents' permission."

Recognizing that his son was near to doing physical harm to the men, James interrupted.

"Nay, Douglas, let them search to their hearts' content. The girl isna here and Owen isna here either. Search . . . then get out of my house before my son and I both lose our tempers."

Both men eyed him with misgivings for it had just occurred to them that the size and obvious strength of James and Douglas were more than they could withstand. As if that was not enough to deter them, Ian chose that moment to arrive.

Faced with three such men, the intruders chose to retreat with as much dignity as they could.

"Father, Mother," Ian questioned, "is something amiss?"

"Nay, son,"—James chuckled—"I believe our guests were just about to search our home."

"Search?" Ian's brows drew together in a formidable frown that hastened Jeffrey's men in their idea to retreat.

"No, I imagine she is not here if you are so willing for a search. But we know he brought her somewhere about here and we do not intend to leave without her."

"Ye would be much wiser to return to Mr. MacIntire and tell him that she could not be found here; then go elsewhere in your search for the lass," Douglas offered. "I wouldna think Owen would be daft enough to bring the girl here. Most likely they are enjoyin' their honeymoon elsewhere. Canna the man accept having a Scot for a brother-in-law, or is it just that his English blood will no accept the fact that his sister chose so?"

"There is no question of marriage; the girl was stolen from her home. She is quite wealthy; are you sure your brother intends marriage . . . or a tidy ransom?"

At these words, all three men drew stiffly erect, then the explosion struck. James did not have to move. Ian, the slow quiet one, grabbed the speaker by the back of his collar and the seat of his pants and ejected him through the front door and down the steps to land unceremoniously in the dust. He was followed closely by his companion as Douglas tossed him heartily from the porch.

"Ye had best mend your manners before ye step foot in my father's house again," Ian said gently. "I'll have no man accusin' any of my family of any kind of shady dealin's."

"We will tell Owen of your accusation as soon as he returns." Douglas laughed. "I'm sure he will be wantin' to meet ye and see to an apology."

The two men rose and literally fled to their horses. The sound of hearty laughter followed them. Once the men were out of sight Ian turned to his brother.

"What have ye done wi' the lass, Douglas?"

"She's at Lachlan Campbell's, safe for a short while. I've a notion Owen will no be long in comin'."

"I dinna like the sound of her brother. What kind of a man is it that treats a sister so?"

"I'll tell ye, Ian. I've no seen so much fear in a lass's face as I did when she set eyes on her brother's ship. The lass is frightened to death of the man."

"Well, we'll hold her safe till Owen comes. Once he has her safely married, the man canna cause her any more grief."

"I hope you're right, Ian, but somehow, I've got the feelin' the man is no the kind ye can get away from. There's somethin' he wants of the girl, and I dinna think he'll let go that easy."

"If she's Owen's wife, we'll protect her," Ian said in his firm steady way. "He'll no be takin' the lass against her will."

"No. I wish Owen would come soon. I dinna understand what is goin' on."

"I've a feelin' he'll be here soon. We must watch Campbell's and see they dinna find her there."

"Aye, I'll ride over tomorrow," Douglas replied

quickly and was rewarded by Ian's quick smile.

"Mind ye, lad, ye'll be there to keep your eye on Jane, not on Anne. I wouldna have anythin' takin' yer mind from your duties."

Douglas chuckled, his good humor renewed, and they walked back into the house together.

The *Sea Mist* leaped through the waves like a ship possessed; her captain paced the quarter-deck in scowling silence. Word of what was happening had gone from first mate to crew like lightning. All of them worked with all their strength to achieve every ounce of speed of which the *Sea Mist* was capable. Yet to Owen it seemed as if they barely moved.

Jane, he thought, if they've put a hand on ye, I'll kill them.

Sleep was something he had not tasted much of in the past few days. With the morning light, they would reach the harbor, and home. Owen's nerves were stretched taut with worry.

He breathed a sigh of relief when the harbor came in sight and brought the *Sea Mist* to dock as quickly as he could. He was surprised to see two men waiting for him on the dock; then it was brought to his attention that the *Pelican* was also docked nearby. It did not take him long to figure out why they waited for him. It was obvious his family had hidden Jane well and they had come to him to find out where she was.

Leaving the *Sea Mist* in the safe hands of his first mate, he strode down the gangplank and proceeded to send someone for a buggy, completely ignoring the two men who walked toward him.

"Captain MacGregor?"

"Aye."

"We are representatives of Lord Jeffrey MacIntire. He knows you have kidnapped his sister and he wishes her returned immediately."

"Why, gentlemen, the man must be mistaken," Owen replied. "I dinna kidnap the girl."

"Do not lie to us, Captain MacGregor. We know you are guilty. Return the woman and there will be no charges pressed. Continue to lie to us and Lord MacIntire will have you hanged for kidnapping."

Being so blatantly accused of lying brought a dark angry scowl to Owen's face.

"I dinna take kindly to bein' named a liar," he said. "I dinna kidnap the girl; but if I had her, I wouldna return her to such a brother."

"You are as stubborn as the rest of your family," one of the men replied stiffly.

"Ah." Owen laughed. "Have ye tangled wi' my brothers? I can see why you might be daft enough to call me a liar. Maybe they rattled your brains enough to make ye foolish. I'll accept the mistake wi' no hard feelin's . . . once."

"Turn the girl over to us, Captain MacGregor, and there will be no more said about it."

"I dinna kidnap the girl," Owen said firmly. "She is na aboard my ship, and since you've obviously been to my home, ye know she is na there. Now, I suggest you leave me be before I become angry and take your insults personally."

"You won't return her?"

"I hav'na got her," Owen said in exasperation.

"But you know where she is?"

"At this moment," Owen said honestly, "I hav'na the slightest idea where the girl is. All I have is the hope she succeeds in gettin' away from the wicked man she calls Brother."

"I would warn you, sir."

"Warn me?"

"Don't harbor the idea of marrying the girl. Her brother will let none of her wealth go to anyone he has not chosen."

"Get ye from my sight, lad," Owen said softly, "before I split ye in two. I am not a man who kidnaps a girl for money. You go back and tell Jeffrey MacIntire he can take all his money and be damned for all I care. I wouldna care to ever see the man again. As for his sister, I do not lie. At this moment I've no idea where she is, but if I did, ye would be the last I would ever tell."

Owen pushed past them, wondering where Jane was at the moment, and if she was afraid or thinking he was not coming.

"We'll be keeping an eye on you, MacGregor," one of the men shouted at his retreating back.

Owen climbed into the buggy, slapped the reins against the horse's rump, and started for home. After a while, he was aware that he was being followed from the dock by the two men.

When he arrived home, he barely had time to step down from the buggy before Douglas, his parents, and the rest of the family were on the porch.

"Owen, Son," his father said. "I'm glad ye've returned so soon."

"Father," he replied; then he swiftly kissed his mother's cheek. "Is Jane safe?"

"Aye, Son, thanks to Douglas. He hid her away before they got to us."

"Where is she, Douglas?"

"She's at Campbell's, but ye canna go there now. It is sure ye've been followed."

"Aye, I have. I'll wait till after dark; then we'll

213

slip out."

"Why not let me visit the two of 'em? 'Twould do me good to feel the cut of their chin wi' me fist."

"Nay, we'll slip away. I want to get married as quickly as possible. After I see Jane we'll arrange it. After that, her brother will na be able to touch her . . . and after that, she and I will go back to England and find out just why he was so damned anxious to marry her off to the man he'd chosen, and why he's so against her marryin' any other. I have a feelin' there's more to this than we know."

"How are ye goin' to arrange the marriage, Owen?" Douglas questioned.

"I've no thought past findin' Jane safe. I'll think about it after she and I talk."

"Then come in," his mother said. "I know ye must be tired and hungry."

They went inside and sat down to a good supper, intending to wait until the sun set and darkness covered their planned movements.

The Campbells sat at supper, too, each of them trying to make Jane worry less and be more comfortable while she was with them.

"I wouldna worry about Owen, child," Lachlan said. "The lad is clever. He'll find a way to ye. Dinna ye fret about that."

"Aye," his wife agreed. "Soon he'll be here and the two of ye will wed. After that, there is nothin' your brother can do to touch ye. Owen and his family are known for protection of their own, and there is na a family in the valley who wouldna help him."

"You are so kind to me." Jane smiled. "I'm so grateful to you."

"Hush, child," Lachlan said. "'Tis an honor to be able

to help ye. Now dinna worry."

"Douglas should come to bring us word soon," Anne offered hopefully.

Jane smiled, and as it always could, her smile captured the hearts of those about her.

The hours drifted by and soon it was time for bed. Although the others retired, Jane could not sleep. She sat by the fire thinking of Owen and how she longed to see him again, to feel the security and the comfort of his strong arms about her. It was only then that she knew she would feel truly safe. Owen . . . Her mind drifted to their days together on the ship. Short and very sweet. She wanted so desperately to hear his strong calm voice telling her all was well.

She rose from her chair, took a shawl from a hook, and wrapped it about her shoulders. Quickly, she unlatched the door and went out, closing it softly behind her. She wanted a breath of air, but she did not want to disturb the family.

The moon was high and golden and a million diamond-bright stars hung in the black velvet sky. A soft breeze ruffled the trees and whispered softly in the night air.

She walked slowly down the path between the house and the barn. There were trees on either side of her, but she was not afraid of shadows. There had been too much real fear in her life for her to fear the dark.

She was caught in the pleasant memories of her meeting with Owen when a sudden muffled sound caused her to stop and listen. It came again. This time she began to feel a light touch of fear. Someone was in the shadows of the trees . . . between her and the house.

Bravely, she wrapped the shawl tighter about her and started back. Surely it was a figment of her imagination, she thought, or an animal.

She walked closer and closer, then froze in her tracks. A man's shadowed form stood between her and the house.

She was so afraid she was almost unable to breathe. Just as she inhaled deeply in preparation for a scream she hoped would rouse the family, a sweetly familiar voice filled her senses.

"Ye are lovelier in the moonlight than any woman has the right to be. Come and welcome me home, lass."

"Owen," she gasped. Then suddenly she was running, running into his open arms, feeling them lift her and crush her to him. She said his name over and over in delirious happiness until his hard hungry mouth found hers and all sound ceased.

# *Thirteen*

He laughed as he stood her back down on her feet, keeping his arms about her. "Wi' such a welcome I should go more often."

"Oh, Owen, the days have been so long. I thought you would never return."

"Ye canna ha' missed me as much as I missed ye, lass," he whispered softly.

Holding her against him with one arm, he caressed her unbound hair and drew her head to his to taste again the warm willing lips. Again and again, his lips touched hers in light kisses until he heard her soft sound of protest. His heart filled with the deepest sense of pleasure when he felt her cling to him, searching for him, pressing herself to him in a need that matched his own.

Reluctantly, he held her a little away from him, knowing if he held her a moment longer nothing could keep him from possessing her, and he loved her too much to make it less than it should be.

"Come, lass, we must talk. There are things that need to be done quickly if we are to go on protecting you from your brother."

He kept one arm about her waist and they walked toward the house.

"Owen, you know the *Pelican* is in port."

"Aye, I've already had a run-in wi' two of 'em; so did

Douglas and Ian. Tossed 'em out of the house." He laughed in remembrance of Douglas's story. "That is how I came about comin' here in the dark; they're still watchin' the house."

"My brother has sent them to bring me home," she said softly, and he could feel the tremble of fear in her body.

"He'll no be takin' ye; by the time they find where ye are, ye'll already be my wife. After that, even though you are not of legal age, it will be too late for him to do anything about it."

"Too late?"

Her innocence of consummated marriage staggered him for a moment. Then he realized her brother had shut her off from the world so thoroughly, she was aware of nothing in a relationship other than what she had read in books. It worried him. Would reality break her spirit, or worse cause her to turn from him in fear? He knew he would tread gently with her for he loved her so much the idea of her fearing him left him shaken. Well, he would cross that bridge when he got to it. For now, he had to find a way to get her safely married to him before her brother's men could interfere.

As they mounted the steps to the porch, a candle was lit within and in a moment, Lachlan Campbell came to the door and peered out. He smiled when he saw Owen.

"I thought I heard voices out here. Welcome back, Owen. Come in, come in."

"Good evenin', Lachlan. I dinna mean to wake the household."

"'Tis naught, lad. We're glad you're home. The lass had been frettin' for ye."

"I'm grateful to ye, Lachlan, for carin' for her. It might have gone hard on ye should her brother's men

218

have found her here. English law would have been on their side."

"English law be damned! I wouldna turn away the lass for any reason, even if yer family hadna asked me; but for the MacGregors I would hide the devil himself from them bloody bastards. . . ."

"No matter, Lachlan. I'm grateful and should ye ever need anything from a MacGregor, ye need only to ask."

"What are your plans now, Owen?"

"Well first I must explain to ye all the problem."

"Set ye down. I'll pour ye a wee drop of refreshment, then ye can go on with yer tale."

Owen, Jane, and Lachlan were seated about the table, and Owen was just about to tell Lachlan all the details when Flora and Anne came to the kitchen door.

"I thought I heard voices," Flora said. "'Tis good to see ye, Owen."

"Thank ye, Flora."

"Come, woman." Lachlan smiled. "Sit wi' us. Owen was about to begin his story."

When everyone was comfortable, Owen began to talk. They did not question him, only listened in silence as he told of Jane's brother. He told them of his virtual imprisonment of Jane all her life and his plans for her future.

"What kind of man would marry his only sister off to such a man?" Flora said in disgust.

"And for money," Lachlan added angrily.

"What are you going to do now, Owen?" Anne asked.

Owen took Jane's hand in his and smiled at her. "'Twill be a difficult thing for you, Jane, love. T' make a weddin' secret and sly seems cruel, but 'tis the only way. We'll marry and I'll take ye on board the *Sea Mist*. By the time we reach England no law will be able to separate us.

Ye can be free to claim what is yours and make your own choices the rest of your life."

"It doesn't matter how we marry, Owen," Jane said softly. "Just so I know I can spend the rest of my life safe with you."

He squeezed her hand, choked by a fierce desire to pull her into his arms and hold her close.

"How do ye plan to do this weddin'?" Lachlan said.

"I'll make the arrangements, and if ye're willin', we'll have the weddin' here. 'Twill have to be done carefully. First I have to find a way to keep our two friends busy. I'm sure Ian and Douglas will think up somethin'."

Lachlan chuckled, and Owen laughed with him. "Aye, I'm sure at least Douglas has some ideas along that line."

"Douglas is very clever," Anne said defensively. "He'll think of some way out of this problem."

"I'm sure ye have faith in the lad, Anne, as we all do." Owen smiled at her blushing face as all eyes turned to her.

"Well, ye find a way to arrange it, Owen, and we'll hold the weddin' here," Lachlan said. "Now, we'll all be goin' back to bed. I'm sure the two of ye have some plans to talk over. Good night to ye, Owen; good night, Jane."

After the rest of their good-nights were quickly said, in a few minutes Owen found himself alone again with Jane. He rose and went to her, and reaching down took her hand and drew her to her feet.

Without a word, he drew her into his arms and held her.

"Jane," he whispered softly against her hair. "I dinna want it to be this way, I would ha' liked to gi' ye the fanciest weddin' and all ye deserve. But it must be, for 'tis the only way I know to hold ye, and I wouldna let them touch ye."

"I know, Owen, I know." She slid her arms about him and rested her head against his broad chest. "I love you so much, Owen, and I appreciate what you are doing for me. You and your family have been so wonderful to me. For the first time in my life, I feel I have a family of my own. I am grateful to you just for that." She tipped her head up to look at him. "And I want to be your wife, Owen. I want to be a good wife. I want you to be as happy as you've made me."

The warm glow of love in her eyes, and the soft feel of her in his arms came near breaching all of Owen's defenses. He took her face in his hands and bent his head to touch her cool sweet lips with his. They softened and parted slightly as she seemed to melt against him. In a moment, the kiss progressed far beyond anything Owen had planned. His tongue, exploring her mouth, felt the receptive searching of hers. He savored the feel of her arms circling his neck and holding him. Her body moved closer, searching for the hard secure feeling of his and the strength of the arms that crushed her to him. He could feel her trembling and knew he was opening doors for her she had not known existed. He held her away from him.

"I'll make the arrangements for the weddin' tomorrow. I'll no be leavin' ye another night," he said firmly. "For now, gi' me one more kiss, lass, and I must be goin'. 'Tis too much for any man to be stayin' under the same roof wi' ye and not be able to . . ." He kissed her again, then turned from her and left. She stood watching the door close behind him. Jane smiled slightly, for all her woman's instincts told her she had found in Owen something rare and special that would make the balance of her life a precious and joyful time. After a while she went back to her bed and to strange yet pleasant dreams of Owen and the future they were to share.

Owen slipped easily back into the house to find Douglas still awake and waiting for him within the darkened interior. They sat and talked for over an hour; then both of them, plans made, found their way to their beds.

It was an uncomfortable night for the two men who kept watch on the MacGregor home, but one of relaxed sleep for all who dwelt within.

The next morning, the MacGregors ate a hearty breakfast; then Owen and Douglas rode slowly into town aware that two men followed not too far behind.

After the men had left, Alys, taking a bundle her mother had carefully wrapped, slipped out the back door, went to the barn, and saddled a horse which she rode, careful that she was not being followed, to the Campbell home. Once there, she gave the bundle to Jane.

"Mother sent this to you and said to be ready tonight. Owen and Douglas will be here with the minister."

Jane took the bundle to her room where she opened it to find the wedding dress, shortened and pressed, with the veil folded neatly on top. Lovingly, she laid it out on the bed and prepared for the long wait for Owen's return. Unknown to Owen, Douglas, or Jane, Ian was preparing a small surprise of his own.

In town, Owen made preparations with the minister and told him where and at what time the wedding would be. Then he and Douglas went outside and stood looking across the street at the two men who were following their every move.

"Douglas," Owen said in a soft amused voice, "shall we take our friends for a wee ride in the hills?"

"Aye, Owen," Douglas chuckled. "I dinna think the

city air is good for their health."

They mounted their horses and rode slowly toward the edge of town, out into the rugged hills that lay between them and home. They traveled slowly not wanting too much distance between them and their followers. The last thing they wanted was for their trail to be lost.

They came to the spot they had chosen before they had left town—a spot where the path narrowed and crested a tree-shaded hill. Their pursuers would have to travel single file between the low hanging trees and brush-bordered pathway.

Once temporarily out of the sight of the two who followed them, Owen and Douglas quickly dismounted, tied their horses out of sight, and went back to the spot of ambush to wait.

The two unsuspecting men fell neatly into the trap. The last thing they expected was to be ambushed, so they rode along slowly.

"We'd best keep these bloody bastards in sight," the first one said. "These Scots are sly and they know this godforsaken land like the back of their hands. There's no telling what they might be up to."

"Well, they have to go to the girl sometime, and when they do, we'll nab 'em. There's a good price on the girl's head, and her brother is mighty anxious to get her back."

"That Owen MacGregor looked to me like he'd put up quite a fight for the girl." The first man spoke with a deep malicious laugh in his voice. "Seems to me he's got hold of a good thing. The girl's rich and she looks like she'd be a right tasty morsel to me."

"Maybe," the second replied, "he's already found out. Think the lucky man's already bedded the wench?"

"Wouldn't be surprised. I would if it were me. I don't think I would give up that pretty thing and her money if I had a chance at her."

Both Owen and Douglas heard the last few remarks as the two unsuspecting men rode beneath the trees in which they waited. Both felt the deep heat of anger at those words. More so, Owen, because the woman he loved was so deeply insulted. It was why he was filled with a fierce desire to do bodily harm to the one who rode beneath him.

They dropped upon the astonished men simultaneously, and after the first yelp of surprise, both men found themselves unhorsed and being bound and gagged by the two they thought were ahead of them.

One glimpse of Owen's anger-filled eyes silenced all protest replacing it with fear as Owen dragged the first one to his feet. This man realized that Owen hovered on the edge of violence and one look at his huge powerful frame washed all resistance from him.

"I dinna believe," Owen said in a deceptively soft voice, "tha' I heard ye say what I thought. I dinna hear ye insult the woman I'm about to marry, now did I?"

The man shook his sweat-covered head negatively and forcefully.

"Good, for I'm goin' to invite ye to the weddin', after which ye'll be spendin' some time thinkin' about yer wicked thoughts and makin' peace wi' yer maker."

The man's face grew even paler at the obvious suggestion that his future might be short. Owen shoved him toward his horse; then he took the man's reins and led his horse behind him. Douglas did the same with the other man and then they continued their journey to the Campbells' for the soon-to-be-performed ceremony.

All of the MacGregors had gathered in the Campbell home by the time Owen and Douglas arrived. Owen's mother and sisters with Flora and Anne were enclosed in the bedroom, while Lachlan and the rest of the men were standing about sharing a drink and talking. When Owen and Douglas came in, they were laughing and pushing the two men ahead of them.

"We've brought a couple of extra guests for the weddin'," Douglas said. "The two gentlemen insisted upon comin' so we thought we'd best make 'em welcome."

Both men were pushed none too gently to chairs, where they sat, too afraid of this gathering of laughing rough-looking Scots to even look as if they were inclined to protest. Drinks were passed about and all except Owen shared freely in them. Owen did not want his wedding night marred because he had been foolish enough to get drunk.

"Where is Jane?" he questioned Lachlan.

"She's safe wi' all the women inside the bedroom. They're helpin' her get ready."

"Helpin' her get ready? How? The lass has nothin' to be gettin' ready."

Lachlan shrugged. "All I know is I was tossed out of my own bedroom. I dinna question Flora when she's in that mood. I just left."

Their laughter was interrupted by the arrival of the minister and soon everything was ready for the arrival of the bride, as was an impatient and nervous Owen who found himself on the receiving end of some very pointed jokes.

It was Ian who went to the door and knocked gently. His mother's face appeared as she opened the door slightly.

"The minister is here, Mother; everything is ready."

"All right, Ian, we'll be right out."

All was prepared. Owen stood beside the minister

watching the bedroom door as if his life depended on it. All the others stood silently about the room until the bedroom door opened. The women came out, each going to her respective place—except Jane. There was a moment of silent, breathless waiting, especially for Owen. Then Jane stepped into the frame of the doorway, her eyes searching the room for the only one . . . Owen.

He felt suddenly as if he could not breathe. Jane's flawless beauty in the beautiful gown caught him completely and thoroughly by surprise. Slowly, she came to him. She stood beside him and gently slid her hand in his.

"Owen?" she said in a soft half-whisper.

"Janie, lass," Owen breathed. "Ye are the loveliest woman I have ever seen. I find it hard to understand my rare luck in yer willingness to marry me."

"I love you, Owen," she said softly. "And I consider the rare luck to be all mine."

She watched Owen's eyes, touched with love, and his smile as he held her hand tightly and they turned to face the minister.

It took less than half an hour for the brief ceremony to be over, a ceremony that Owen barely heard, for he had found it quite difficult to take his eyes from Jane even for a minute.

There was a happy celebration and even their two enforced guests were unbound long enough to eat and—to their surprise—share a drink to the health and well-being of the newly wedded couple.

As Owen and Jane stood talking together, Ian came to them. He clapped Owen on the shoulder and smiled warmly at Jane. "Owen, lad, Douglas and I have a little gift for ye."

"A gift?" Owen said warily, for he knew too well

Douglas's wicked sense of humor, and he suspected that, in this case, Ian might have joined him in some deviltry. The last thing he wanted to happen was anything that might upset Jane on this night.

"Dinna be alarmed, lad." Ian laughed. "Do you know the miller's cabin twixt the two high hills?"

"Aye."

"Well, Douglas and I have repaired and made it ready. 'Twill be easier than spendin' the night in the midst of this crowd."

"Ian."

"'Tis not a joke, Owen. I'm a married man, lad. Dinna ye think I have too much feelin' for the lass to allow any pranks tonight? And dinna worry about our two guests; we'll see that they're kept safe. Tomorrow ye can leave on the *Sea Mist*. By the time ye can get to England safe, we'll let our two friends go. After that there's nothing they or anyone else can do about it."

Jane smiled, and Owen shook Ian's hand in deep gratitude. He had wondered just how he was going to arrange to get Jane away from this crowd.

Owen waited a little longer, until Douglas informed him that the buggy was outside, and within a half-hour, Jane and Owen were riding slowly through the star-kissed night toward their solitary cabin tucked away in the deeply wooded Scottish hills. For a long time, there was no conversation, each suddenly caught in private thoughts.

When they arrived at the cabin, Owen lifted Jane down and walked inside with her. He lit a candle and found the cabin to be exactly as Ian had said it would be. There was only one room with a huge fireplace, a table and chairs in one corner and a huge bed in the other. It had been scrupulously cleaned and the makings for a fire had been

227

laid in the fireplace waiting only for the touch of flame to ignite it. Owen did that first; then he turned to Jane.

"I must care for the horse; I shall be back in a few minutes."

Jane nodded and smiled. Owen left, and she stood looking about the small quiet room, thinking she would be happy to spend the rest of her days here with Owen.

Owen had set the small case she had brought with her just inside the door. Now she took it, placed it on the bed, and opened it. From it she took the things she would need; then she closed the case and put it under the bed. Slowly, she reached up and began to unpin her hair.

Owen whistled lightly through his teeth as he unharnessed the horse and put the buggy away, another habit of his that spoke of his nervousness. Silently, he promised himself he would not rush Jane this night. They would have a whole lifetime to spend together and he did not want this to be a time of regret for Jane.

Mentally forming words in his mind he could use to ease Jane's fears, he walked across the small yard to the porch. When he opened the door he was not in the least prepared for the vision that met him.

She stood across the room from him, her eyes wide and expectant and tinged with no sign of fear. Her unbound dark hair fell about her in thick glossy profusion. The gown she wore was white and very nearly transparent, enough so that his imagination was inflamed by her ghostlike form that could be seen through it. Caught unprepared, he stood in frozen silence staring at her in complete disbelief.

The smile that crossed her face was flickering and gentle; then she walked to him. When she was near enough she reached out and touched his cheek lightly with the palm of her hand. Her eyes sparkled in happiness and she mimicked his Scottish accent. "Did ye think I would ever be afraid of ye, my darling? Dinna ye know that I love ye beyond all else and I feel safe and secure only with ye? I would be your wife, Owen MacGregor, and I will na stand bein' put aside like a child. I'm a woman grown, Owen. . . . I would be your wife." Her voice drifted to a soft whisper. Owen suddenly felt himself overcome with a blazing need for her. With the soft whisper of her name, he held out his arms, and she circled her arms about his neck and lifted her lips for his kiss.

The last thing Jane would ever tell Owen was about the few hours she had spent with his mother, when she had blushingly and hesitantly explained her fears. She also would never tell him of the words his mother had spoken to make things easier for her. She would not tell him for she wanted him to accept her as woman and wife, not a child bride to be protected and sheltered.

She felt the hard strength of his arms as he crushed her to him, felt his heated need of her in the hungry mouth that claimed hers and sent her senses spinning. She had imagined all the things that might happen, but never, in all her dreams, had she imagined the sudden burst of liquid flame that exploded somewhere in the depths of her. It licked through her, turning her world crimson, and leaving her weak yet hungry for the unknown touch of him.

His hands slid into the thick mass of her hair, holding her even closer while his lips traveled from her lips to her closed eyelids, her cheeks and throat. She murmured with pleasure as they seemed to excite every sensation and nerve in her body.

The gown slid from her shoulder as if it had a will of its own as his lips touched her soft skin.

Suddenly, he lifted her in his arms and pressed his lips to the soft rise of her breasts above the gown's neckline.

"Oh, Owen," she whispered as she drew his head even closer. "I love you so very much."

He raised his head and their eyes met, his questioning and hers accepting.

The few steps to the bed were completely unnoticed by either of them. Gently, he stood her on her feet; then he loosened the tie to her gown and it slipped soundlessly to the floor.

He drank in her ivory beauty like a drowning man.

"Janie, love," he whispered. "Ye are the bonniest lass in God's creation and I am filled with love for ye."

With trembling fingers, she began to loosen his shirt, and it did not take him long to aid her. If she was startled by the brawny size of him, she made no sound. He drew her cool, slim body against his hard, heated one, savoring the tingling pleasure of her soft curves pressed against him. His hands strayed down the smooth curve of her back to her hips pressing her more tightly against him as he again bent his head and searched her willing mouth.

Jane was lost in the experience of feeling; she closed her eyes and let herself sink into the sheer joy of Owen's magic touch.

Drawing her with him, he slowly sat on the edge of the bed, then lay back pulling her body across his and allowing his hands the freedom to wander where they would.

Jane no longer needed encouragement for her body was telling her all she needed to know. She searched for him with the same burning need with which he sought her. They were in the grip of a blinding hot passion that made them oblivious to every need but that for each other.

With more control than he would have believed he possessed, Owen sought to lift her to the peak of passion. His hands caressed her and his lips followed them in burning paths across her heated skin until he felt her almost desperate urgency. He rolled to his side drawing her beneath him.

"Janie, love, I wouldna hurt ye," he murmured. He tried to be as gentle as possible; yet still he heard her gasp and felt a shudder ripple through her body. Yet when he tried to draw away, he felt her reach for him. It filled him with joy to know the worst of it was over and he surrendered himself completely to the sheer pleasure of possessing her. All barriers were gone; all reserves had crumbled before their blinding need for each other. She clung to him, lost in the urgent need to draw him within her and hold him forever.

That she called to him in words of love, she did not know; but the words reached his heart and would linger there forever. Now, they moved together, rhythm blending the two as one. Nothing else existed in either's world but the other. She clung to him, velvet arms and legs holding him as he lifted her to a shuddering completion that left them both spent and clinging to one another.

He rolled on his side to take his weight from her, but he held her against him listening as her ragged breathing calmed and her tense body relaxed. Then he raised himself on one elbow and looked down on her. The pale moonlight touched her face and gave it a pale glistening glow. Gently, he brushed a few strands of hair from her sweat-slicked face.

Her eyes were again wide and questioning, but now he could not understand what the questions were. He bent his head and gently brushed her lips with his.

"I love ye, lass," he whispered. "Ye are all I have ever hoped and prayed to find."

He watched her eyes soften and her face clear, and he was grateful he had chosen to say just the right thing to assuage her unsure thoughts.

She reached up and captured his face between her hands.

"All my life I have lived alone and in fear. All my life I have dreamed of but never known love. Now I know love has a name: Owen. I am so grateful I found you. I feel the good Lord has blessed me beyond anything I had ever hoped for."

Her words held him in silence and he could do no more than hold her close in his arms.

"I'm sorry that our time here will be so short, for I would like nothing better than to keep ye all to myself."

"What will we do, Owen?"

"We will go back and claim all that is rightfully yours, and prove to your brother that ye are free of him forever. I only wish there was a way to punish him for all he's responsible for."

"Oh, Owen, I feel sorry for the woman who was foolish enough to marry him. I only hope she came to her senses before the wedding. I would have warned her if I had had the chance. Now I wonder . . ."

Owen became silent, absently letting his hand caress her hair. In fact he was so silent she realized immediately there was something he was holding back.

"Owen?"

"'Tis not a thing I meant to be tellin' ye lass, especially this night, but there's no way out of it. Will ye listen to the story entire before ye judge what I've done?"

"I don't understand, but I will listen."

Owen began to speak, and Jane did not say a word until

he had finished. He told her everything . . . except the name of the pirate. He would leave the choice of that to Morgan. As he suspected, Jane was not exactly pleased with what had happened to Kristen.

"A pirate! Owen, are you telling me you deliberately let a pirate just . . . just take her. I do not believe it."

"Not just a pirate, Jane. He's a man who has a rightful grudge against your brother. In fact he hates him. Since then I have gotten word from him. It seems he and Kristen have fallen in love and she has decided to give up Jeffrey and marry him. He's a wealthy man, Janie, and can take good care of the girl."

"But a pirate . . . ?"

"He's a pirate temporarily. I canna tell ye right now his other name. Ye'll know it one day when he gives me permission to say it. Ye'll understand it all then. Will ye no trust me girl until I'm free to tell ye more?"

"I would trust you with my life, Owen." She laughed. "There is never going to be a question of my love and trust in you. I intend to be proving it to you for the rest of my life. I hope the wind is light and our journey home takes a long time. I find the thought of sailing away with you forever and ever a very pleasing one."

He chuckled and tightened his arms about her, pressing several warm kisses along her throat and shoulder.

"Aye, lass, I find the idea invitin'. Ye'll never know how much I wanted ye the first voyage we made. I intend to see this one is different."

"We must leave tomorrow?"

"Aye, lass. We must be on our way before your brother's men have a chance to do any meddlin'. By the time we get ye home, there'll be no question of our marriage not bein' valid. After that the man can do ye no more harm."

She sighed. "Tomorrow."

"Aye," he said softly. "But tomorrow is tomorrow. There is still tonight. Ye have wakened in me an uncommon great hunger, lass, and ye are the only woman in the world who can satisfy it."

"Then I must do my best to appease your appetite, my beloved husband," she said softly. "For if I ever find you searching out some other way of satisfying it, I shall become violent."

"Nay, lass, there have been those before, but there will be no others after. A man searches until he finds the woman who completes his life. Ye are that for me. I love ye, Janie, and I'll love ye till I die."

"Owen," she whispered as his arms tightened about her and his lips stopped any words or thoughts but of him.

# *Fourteen*

Morgan stood at the window in Jamie Price's study. He held the heavy draperies apart a few inches to watch the man who stood outside the high iron fence that bordered the property. Jamie sat on a long comfortable couch and eyed Morgan in silence.

Morgan's brows were drawn together in a dark scowl; his whole body registered his thoughts to Jamie's quick eye. He dropped the drape and turned around.

"I haven't been able to shake my shadow. He's as tenacious as hell. You were right, Jamie, he is one of Jeffrey's men."

"I told you Jeffrey was suspicious. How much do you think he knows?"

"Nothing, or he wouldn't be having me followed. I certainly have no intention of leading him to Kristen."

"Have you sent word to her?"

"I sent a message."

"She must be one hell of a woman, Morgan, and she must love you a lot to trust you so blindly. You'd better be careful of that kind of love, my friend; if you wound it, it's the kind that can turn to hate."

Morgan sighed, and dropped down into a chair opposite Jamie.

"I didn't plan it this way, Jamie," he said tiredly. "I thought after this much time, it would all be over. I did not plan on falling in love with the girl. It seemed so easy, black and white; a little harassment of Jeffrey, a little money exchanged, and I would let her go. Her husband would have been a little poorer and, at the beginning, I thought they were two of a kind. Now, I find myself caught in a web of lies it's hard to get out of. One way and I lose Kristen, the other way and I lose my life."

"You know what the answer is as well as I do."

"What?"

"Have one of your men bring Kristen home. Depend on her love as much as she must depend on yours. Tell her the truth, and tell her about Charlotte. If she loves you as much as I believe she does, she'll understand; and better yet, she'll never betray you. Marry her and drop all this charade before it costs you Kristen or your life."

"And let Jeffrey go," Morgan replied softly. "Let Charlotte's death go unavenged."

"Damn it, Morgan, I loved Charlotte as much as you did! Yes, I intended to ask her to marry me one day before Jeffrey came on the scene. I loved her, but I know I can do nothing about it. Someday, somehow, Jeff will pay, I believe in that. Sometimes it's the only thing that keeps me going. I went along reluctantly with what you are doing remember."

Morgan nodded.

"If I had known it would do you so much harm, I never would have done it. Leave the balance of your revenge to God. Marry Kristen before you lose her; be happy for a change. Don't you think marrying Kristen from under his nose will cause old Jeffrey a lot of grief? I hear he's deep in debt and since he didn't succeed in marrying his sister off to old Clyde and Kristen has disappeared, he's having a hard time of it. For a man like that to be stripped to poverty is a sweet bit of revenge. He'll suffer a long time that way. What will you gain if you kill him?"

Again Morgan rose to his feet and paced slowly back and forth in front of the fireplace. That Morgan was at war with his emotions was obvious to Jamie, and he wondered if there was something he could say to help Morgan see the disastrous path he was on, or to draw him away from it.

"Morgan?"

Morgan stopped and turned to look at Jamie who said softly, "It's a scale to balance. . . . Is Jeffrey worth the loss of Kristen?"

"No," Morgan replied quietly. "You are right, Jamie, he is not worth the touch of her finger. I guess you've been right all along, you and Jeffrey. But . . . I suppose my guilt was too much to bear."

"That is another thing that I will never understand. I loved Charlotte, but I knew she chose to do what she did. She chose and she is responsible too. Oh," he added quickly, "not as much as Jeffrey, but she bears some of the fault. You, on the other hand, are not responsible for a thing; yet you claim all the guilt. It makes no sense. You have a life, too, Morgan. Don't give it all up to fight a ghost; you'll never win. Let the guilt go."

"I should have stopped her."

"How? For a long time no one even knew what was happening. Neither you, nor anyone, could have stopped her." Jamie laughed. "I've had enough experience trying to stop her hard-headed brother from wrecking his life; just what kind of success do you think you would have had? She had a will of her own. She was in love, and no one this side of heaven could have stopped her."

"I can't let it go just like that, but you are right about one thing. I can no longer punish Kristen for this transgression. I'll do as you suggest. Maybe it is time for some truth. Once she's here, once she's safe . . . I'll tend to Jeffrey."

"Well," Jamie said in exasperation, "one step at a time. Maybe by the time you are happily married and have a babe or so, you'll forget this crazy idea of revenge and get down to living."

"I'll send someone to bring her to London. She can claim she was released since the ransom will already have been paid. I'll try to explain to her and hope she understands."

"Good idea."

"Jamie, every step I take is going to be scrutinized by our friend outside. I think it would be best if we sent someone they are not watching to carry my message."

"Yes, I can get one of the stableboys to go. You write the message; I'll see about the messenger."

Jamie left the room and Morgan sat down at the desk. He thought for a long time about what words he could write; then he picked up the pen and began writing.

He was not quite finished when Jamie came back into the room bringing with him a young boy of about sixteen.

"Won't our friend outside wonder at a stableboy riding one of your best mounts?"

"He'll leave from the back of the stable; our friend needn't see him."

The stableboy looked from one man to the other, not understanding for a minute what was going on.

Morgan finished the letter, folded it, and sealed it in an envelope. Then he handed it to the young lad.

"Tell him where he's to go, Morgan."

"Do you know the coast near Craven?" Morgan asked the boy.

"Yes, sir, me mother has a small farm not far from there."

238

"Just past Craven on the north road there's an inn called 'The Devil's Inn.'"

"Yes, sir, I know it."

"Go there and ask for Jeremy."

"Jeremy who?"

"Just Jeremy. Tell him you have a message for him from me—Morgan Grayfield; he'll understand. There's no answer so you can come directly back."

"Yes, sir."

Morgan took some coins from his pocket and the boy's eyes widened in surprise at receiving an amount of money such as he had never seen in his life.

"It will take you three days going and three coming. See that you and the horse are well fed and cared for. The rest of the money is yours."

"Thank you, sir!" The boy bowed shortly and fled the room as if he were afraid Morgan would have second thoughts about the money.

"You'll be seeing her first . . . before Jeffrey?"

"I'm having Jeremy bring her here first. He'll slip her in and we'll talk; then she can make an official arrival later."

"You know this is the wisest thing you've done since this whole affair started."

"I hope you're right, Jamie; I've got a strange feeling I should finish Jeffrey off, that he's not going to let it go, especially when Morgan Grayfield and Kristen Seaford meet, fall in love, and decide to marry. He's been thwarted once with Owen and Jane. He won't take the loss of Kristen so lightly."

"What can he do? He can have all the questions in the world, but as long as he doesn't have the answers . . ." Jamie shrugged.

"Maybe," Morgan said, mentally shrugging off a vague

tense feeling that something was about to happen, something deadly he had no way of stopping.

"It's going to be a long six days." Jamie smiled. "You'd best keep busy; it will help the time to pass."

"I intend to keep busy."

"Now why does that sound ominous? Just what are you planning on doing?"

"Saving Jeffrey the time and money he spends having me followed. It's time I found out what those two have planned."

"Those two?"

"Leslie Seaford and Jeffrey MacIntire."

Jamie made a sharp aggravated sound. "How do you intend to do that?"

Morgan grinned, and the glow of wicked devilment in his eyes was enough to bring a groan from Jamie.

"I'm going over to Jeffrey's this morning to see if he's heard any word from the elusive pirate and to see if the beautiful Leslie Seaford would like to go for a ride. It's a lovely day and she looks inviting enough for any man to want to share it with her."

"Can't you leave well enough alone for God's sake, Morgan? One slip and those two will make it your last."

Morgan laughed and walked to the door. He opened it and was about to walk out. "Don't worry about me, Mother Hen. I have no intention of getting caught. Take it easy, and when you get word from Jeremy, let me know. In the meantime, I intend to take my shadow on the longest, and if I have my way, the most uncomfortable time in his life."

He waved a jaunty farewell to Jamie and was gone before Jamie could reply.

Morgan considered all Jamie's words while he rode toward the MacIntire estate. He knew Jamie had his best interests at heart; yet he knew he could not let Jeffrey get away with what he had done. He intended to get Kristen out of this entanglement, but he did not intend to let Jeffrey go unpunished.

He dismounted in front of the huge mansion Jeffrey had built. He had to admit it was a rare beauty of a home. Mounting the four steps, he rapped on the door. It was soon opened by a very dignified butler who, recognizing him, escorted him to the study and asked him to wait.

When the door opened, he was surprised to see Leslie instead of Jeffrey.

"Jeffrey will be down in a few minutes, Mr. Grayfield."

"Morgan." He smiled his most charming smile.

"Morgan," she repeated, her voice softly caressing the name. He had to admit she was a damned beautiful woman.

"Is Jeffrey tied up? I'm certainly not adverse to spending some time with a woman as lovely as you."

"He has just returned from seeing to the delivery of the ransom money. I'm afraid he's not in the best of moods."

"Maybe"—he grinned mischievously—"we should find a quieter, more pleasant way to spend the afternoon."

"You have a suggestion?"

"We could go for a nice ride. I know a place where the view of the ocean is magnificent."

"It sounds like a wonderful idea. If you will wait a few minutes, I'll change and be with you."

"I'll wait," he said softly. "Impatiently."

Just as she turned toward the door it opened and Jeffrey walked in.

"Morgan," he said shortly.

It took only one glance to see that Jeffrey was irritated

241

and that his temper was being held in check by force.

"Leslie tells me you've just finished sending off the ransom money. Will it take long to be delivered? I would like to be around when your lovely bride is returned. I'd like to meet her."

"If I can trust that black-hearted pirate to return her at all. For all I know she may be dead already."

"Do you think he's fool enough to do that? A little piracy is one thing, but taking the life of a wealthy woman would bring the whole country down on his head. We should have hope that she'll be safely returned in a day or two."

"He's right, Jeffrey," Leslie agreed. "We must believe my stepdaughter is well. We've sent all the money he has asked for. It certainly was enough to let him live like a king the balance of his life. After Kristen is returned, we'll probably never hear from him again."

"A king's ransom," Jeffrey snarled. "The man wants to break me. Well he won't succeed. He may have taken most of my money, but Kristen's will help me replace it. Then we shall begin an all-out search. I'll have him one day."

"You seem sure of that," Morgan said.

"Morgan, I've always told you, you Grayfields are the only ones I know who can disregard money. But money will put him in my hands, and as soon as Kristen is home, I'll prove it to you."

Morgan remained silent, for he was as conscious of what well-placed money could do as Jeffrey was. He trusted his crew and Jeremy. Yet he was aware of the possibility that a single thread might lead to him. For the first time he was glad he had agreed with Jamie and decided to end it all.

"We were just about to go for a ride, Jeffrey," Leslie

said. "Would you like to come along?"

"No . . . no, I have some things that need attending to. You two go along."

"I must change," Leslie said. "I'll be down in a moment."

She left the room, and Jeffrey spoke again. "Would you like a drink?"

"No, thank you."

Jeffrey went to the table and poured himself a rather large drink of brandy. He gulped it down, then poured another. Morgan watched him closely. He knew in his heart that this man was responsible for the death of his sister; yet he wondered why the knowledge of all he had done did not bring him the satisfaction and peace of mind he sought. The sudden thought struck him that he wanted to kill Jeffrey, yet it frightened him to realize that if he did so, maybe he would still not feel satisfaction; maybe he would not find peace of mind. Then where would his answers be? He shrugged away the thought, not wanting to face it.

"It should only take a day or two for the ransom to be delivered. You should expect her home soon. Will you then be planning the wedding?"

"I don't know. This terrible thing seems to have frightened Kristen. The letter I received when you were here last was from her. I know she wrote it under duress. She says she no longer wants to marry me, that she intends to go home."

"Do you think she will?"

"She has no home to go back to."

"What?"

"As her closest relative, Leslie sold the house to give me some of the money for the ransom. Leslie will talk to her, explain to her that she will be better off here. After a

243

while"—he smiled a soft secretive smile that made Morgan's skin crawl and his anger begin to stir—"I'll convince her she will be happier here married to me."

Morgan used all his control not to fling the knowledge in his face that Kristen was his and would be his forever. At that moment, he allowed all his past hatred to ignite and burn bright. He needed it to help him smother all the other thoughts that had insinuated themselves. He was about to speak again when Leslie returned. In a green velvet riding habit that fit her slim curvaceous body like a glove, and with her golden hair pulled severely back from her face and tied into a chignon at the nape of her neck, she was astonishingly beautiful. Again he wondered what the connection was that held Jeffrey, Leslie, and Kristen together. Did Leslie care for her stepdaughter or was there a motive here that would threaten Kristen? He didn't know, but he intended to try to find it.

"You're sure you don't want to come, Jeffrey?" he said.

"No, you two go, I really have some things to do."

"I'll see you at dinner," Leslie said.

Jeffrey nodded and watched them leave. When the door closed behind them a smile touched his lips.

"Now, buzz around the honey, my elusive bee," he whispered. "And I hope you do not make the mistake of tasting."

It was an enjoyable ride, a ride in which they spoke of everything except the things Morgan wanted to discuss. And pleasant though it was, it left Morgan wondering even more deeply about the elusive Leslie Seaford.

Leslie came back from the ride with her eyes sparkling. When she joined Jeffrey for a drink before dinner, he questioned her.

"Did he say anything to you that might have given you

the idea that he knew more about Kristen's kidnapping than he should?''

''No, he did not mention her at all, which is suspicious itself. I'm Kristen's stepmother; you would think he would have much to say to me.''

''What did he say?''

''Why, Jeffrey.'' She laughed. ''It was a rather romantic little ride. If you must know, he spent a great deal of time complimenting me.''

''Both of us know too much about each other to do anything foolish. We are in this together and there's a fortune to be made. Don't let Morgan's handsome face distract you from what we have to do.''

Leslie's face was unreadable as she looked up at him, but he might have been more careful of what he said and how he treated her if he had known her thoughts. For a germ of an idea had touched her, an idea that did not aim for the same goal as Jeffrey's.

''A handsome face has never distracted me from anything I want,'' she said softly, ''and if I want Morgan Grayfield, I shall have him; but do not ever accuse me of being stupid, Jeffrey for I am certainly as clever as you. If you had carried out your end of this bargain, you would be a widower in control of the Seaford fortune by now. Instead, you have made an enemy and he seems to have the power to take it all away from you.''

''I've paid the ransom, Kristen will be returned, and if Morgan knows anything about this pirate, I'll find that out, for every move he makes is being followed closely. When Kristen is back, we will carry out our plans. Soon, we will be in control together of all we've both ever wanted.''

He drew her into his arms and kissed her, and she responded to his kiss in her well-practiced way, but in her

245

mind was a vision of a tall blue-eyed man who had aroused a possessive hunger in her. She already was beginning to evolve her plan to get what she wanted.

Morgan and Jamie waited for news of Kristen; Jeffrey and Leslie waited for completely different news of her. For three days, Morgan and Leslie had spent most of their waking hours together. It was on the fourth day that they found themselves alone at last. They had gone for a ride in Morgan's buggy. The countryside was bright with late-summer sun. Hobbling the horse, they had walked along the stream. There, they had shared a stolen kiss or two, and there, Leslie's appetite for Morgan had become voracious.

Five days after he had sent the letter to Jeremy, Morgan began to feel the strain of waiting. He could barely stand the hours that must pass before he held Kristen again in his arms. He had dressed for dinner with Leslie and was walking down the stairs of his home. He met his mother on her way up.

"Morgan, you look very nice."

"Thank you, Mother; I'm taking Mrs. Seaford to dinner."

"Morgan . . ." she began hesitantly. Morgan smiled. It was always his mother's way not to interfere in his personal life. She found it difficult to question him; yet he knew something must have upset her or she would not be considering it.

"What is bothering you, Mother?"

"Mrs. Seaford . . . she's not . . . I mean . . . you mentioned a woman you wanted to marry. . . ." she finished lamely.

"You don't really like her, do you, Mother?"

"You know I would never try to tell you who to marry."

"But," he insisted, "you really don't like her?"

"It's not dislike, Morgan; it's just a feeling, a sort of . . ." She shrugged.

"Don't worry, Mother, I've no intention of asking Leslie to marry me and I assure you the girl I plan on bringing here soon is all you'd ever hope for in a daughter-in-law. She's lovely and sweet and I love her very much."

"Then I don't understand. Why these constant days you spend with another woman? Why do you not just bring this lovely mysterious woman here and let us all enjoy a big beautiful wedding. I cannot understand seeing one woman when you plan on marrying another."

"Mother, I ask you and Father to take a lot of things on faith. This is another thing I'm asking you to be patient about without questions. In time, it will all work out, but until the time is right, I cannot explain, nor can I bring her here. I promise you the wait will be worth it. Can I ask you again to just trust me?"

"I have trusted you all of your life." She smiled. "I shan't begin to distrust you now. I will tell you that I am relieved it is not Mrs. Seaford. I cannot even say why. The few times I have met her, she seems pleasant enough; yet I always get a feeling that she is cold within."

"Mother." He laughed. "I have a suspicion you are more right than either of us know. Well, I must be going, I don't want to be late. I have hopes this evening might be enlightening. Good night." He brushed a swift kiss on her cheek and continued on down the steps whistling lightly.

She watched him until the door closed behind him, a puzzled look in her eyes. Morgan had changed since the death of Charlotte and she could not put her finger on what the change was. It worried her, more so because she was helpless to do anything about it.

Again as he had many times before, Morgan was forced to admire Leslie's beauty. It was a wary admiration for he, too, sensed the cold heart that dwelt within.

Tonight she was dressed entirely in deep emerald green and she wore tiny emeralds in her ears and strung on gold threads about her slender throat. Her dress was cut enticingly low to show to advantage her smooth ivory skin. Her hair had been drawn up on her head in a cluster of golden curls. He had to admire her rare beauty, yet his thoughts went to Kristen—Kristen with the laughing eyes and slim sweet body that could drive him to madness. He knew he was safe from the threat of Leslie's charms for he had only to think of her part in the plans for Kristen's future to turn cold.

They left Jeffrey's home and drove in an open carriage to the restaurant where he had made arrangements for their dinner.

Again he was forced to admire Leslie's sophistication and intelligence. He could see why Kristen's father, recently widowed, would fall for her, for she combined beauty with a quick mind. It was quick, he reminded himself, and he was on guard not to make any mistakes.

"This all must be very difficult for you, Leslie."

"You mean Kristen's abduction?"

"Yes. Since your husband died so recently, to have the last of your family kidnapped—"

"Yes, it has been a blow. I am afraid. . . ."

"Afraid of what?"

"Afraid that Jeffrey is dreaming. Kristen will never be returned to us, but if she is . . ."

"Yes?"

248

Leslie's eyes dropped as if it hurt her to say what she was about to say.

"You know how society is. A girl, held by a notorious pirate for weeks . . . alone. . . . She is not of legal age. I feel it will be my duty to send her somewhere where she can be properly cared for. Marriage to Jeffrey would be out of the question. She would be ostracized for a blackened reputation even if it is not her fault. No, I will see that she is cared for. In a convent in France maybe, where scandal could do her no more harm. I'm sure," she said softly, watching his face, "Jeffrey will agree with me. Being so much in the public eye, he cannot afford such gossip."

He kept his face clear of emotion though a dark rage swept through him. He knew now for sure, Jeffrey and Leslie planned on doing away with Kristen completely and most likely sharing Kristen's fortune that would automatically go to Leslie in the event of Kristen's death.

"I'm afraid I will be forced to agree with you. But surely, you will not go with her?"

"I . . . no, I will stay here. I'm sure I can get the proper guardian."

"I'm relieved."

"Oh, why?"

He lifted her glass of champagne and handed it to her; then he took his own and lightly tapped his glass to hers.

"I should be devastated to be robbed of your exciting company. Beauty such as yours should never be locked away behind high stone walls."

She smiled at him, but her quick mind was not fooled for a moment. She still had far to go to win Morgan Grayfield to her side. But she promised herself to do just that. Kristen's money and Morgan Grayfield were two things she wanted, and she had always gotten what she wanted.

After their dinner, Morgan took her to the small ballroom that adjoined the dining room. There they danced and laughed together until late in the evening.

The buggy in which they rode was an open one so that they could enjoy the bright stars and clear night air. Morgan had chosen to drive it himself for he did not want a third party present.

He drove through a small park and stopped the buggy near a softly bubbling fountain. There he helped Leslie alight and they sat on a bench near the fountain.

Neither of them was aware of the small dark buggy that had followed them and now sat in the cover of a stand of trees, its occupants closely watching the two who sat on the bench.

Neither heard the audible gasp from the person inside the dark carriage as they embraced and kissed passionately. Then they stood as the tall handsome man drew the golden-haired woman into his arms. Their kiss was a deep and passionate one and it was obvious to the stunned eyes of the observer that they both intended to enjoy it and much more.

The dark shadow of a man in the small buggy turned to the figure beside him.

"It is him?"

"Yes."

"You have seen enough?"

"Oh, yes," came a quiet reply from the still, shadowed form that sat next to him. "I have seen all I care to see."

"Let me take you home."

"No, I will stay with you a little longer. At least until I have decided what I will do. You do not mind if I stay with you, do you? I have no place else to go yet. I have decisions to make."

"You are talking revenge?"

"Yes . . . revenge."

"You hate them both?"

"Hate," came the soft reply, "is a mild word for what I feel right now. Do not question me for I do not know what I will do yet. I only know that I have the power to destroy and at this moment, I intend to use it. Please, let us go."

The man nodded and eased the small buggy away from the scene.

Morgan dropped his arms and moved away from Leslie. He had tried, but the image of Kristen stood between them and he knew he could not bring himself to make love to the woman who intended to kill her. Any passion he had felt when he kissed her had quickly died. No, he loved Kristen and knowing of Leslie's guilt was enough. He could not betray Kristen's love. Soon, maybe tomorrow, she would be here safe in his arms, and he would tell her the truth. He knew she loved him enough to accept what he had done and the reasons he had had for his actions. He would marry her and they would be happy together. He even made the silent vow to himself that if Kristen wanted it so, he would forget all thoughts of revenge and think only of their life together.

Leslie had enjoyed their evening immensely. She had gloried in Morgan's physical reaction to her and felt it would only be a matter of time until she had eliminated Kristen; then she would have the money and both Morgan and Jeffrey to enjoy.

Morgan rode home slowly after he had taken Leslie home. The only thought that lingered in his mind was that Kristen would soon be with him—Kristen whose magic love could erase all touch of Leslie.

Stabling the horse and buggy, he made his way across

the back lawn of his home. He opened the door and found to his surprise that a light was on and his mother was still up.

"What are you doing up at this hour, Mother? It is nearly two in the morning."

"I've been waiting for you."

"Mother, is something wrong?"

"I don't know yet, you will have to tell me. The messenger said that Jamie told him it was extremely urgent."

She handed him an envelope and he impatiently ripped it open.

Morgan,
    Get over here as quickly as you can. There is a problem and I'm afraid I don't know how to handle it.

"Damn!" Morgan said. "Mother, I'll explain to you later. Right now, I have to get to Jamie's."

"Morgan, at two in the morning! It will be daylight before you get there."

But Morgan was already out the door and running toward the stables. He saddled the one horse he knew had the stamina to carry him to Jamie's without dropping from exhaustion. In a short time he was on the road at a rapid gallop.

Day was breaking when he arrived at Jamie's. The lights still burning in the house told him that Jamie had waited for him the entire night. His heart pounded furiously as tension coiled within him.

Jamie would not have sent the message or stayed up all night if it hadn't been serious.

He opened the door without knocking and found Jamie coming down the stairs. He looked tired and worried.

"Morgan, where in hell have you been?"

"Jamie, what is wrong?" Morgan said quickly ignoring the question.

"Morgan," Jamie began hesitantly, "Jeremy is here."

"Jeremy? Where's Kristen?"

"Morgan—"

"Where's Kristen, Jamie?" Morgan said, but fear of what he would hear was in his voice.

"Come in the study and talk to Jeremy. He can explain better than I."

Morgan followed Jamie into the study to find an even more tired and worried Jeremy.

"Jeremy, what happened? What are you doing here? Didn't you get my message?"

"Aye, sir. I got your message right enough. And I set about doin' what you told me to do."

"Jeremy, get to the point."

"I went to the cabin to bring Kristen here."

"Then where is she?"

"I don't know."

"What do you mean you don't know?"

"She wasn't there. The cabin was empty. I waited for hours and searched the area for miles. There's no sign of her or the boy. They're both gone."

"Where?" Morgan said softly as he sat slowly down in a chair, realizing he had no idea of where or how to look for her.

"I don't know, sir," Jeremy replied miserably. "I only know . . . she's gone."

"Gone," Morgan repeated softly. "Kristen . . . God . . . Kristen."

# Fifteen

Morgan had thought he had taken all things into consideration when he had taken Kristen to the family's hunting lodge. Its seclusion and her lack of transportation, combined with her lack of knowledge of the area and the lack of proximity of any roads that could be called such had made him believe she would be safe until he came for her.

It would have been so except for two things: the capriciousness of fate and a sudden decision by a young man, in a slightly inebriated state, many miles from her.

Christopher Miles was a wealthy friend of Morgan's. The Mileses' mansion was not far from the Grayfields'. He had attended college with Morgan and had shared many happy escapades with him. Although he was not a confidant regarding Morgan's dual personality, he was still considered a friend by Morgan. Christopher had not settled himself to any kind of work and was driving his parents to distraction by his devil-may-care ways, but he was basically a generous, honest, and good-hearted person.

At the moment, having had a little too much to drink was his problem, that and the fact that the boisterous group he was with had challenged his words.

"Come along, Chris." One of them laughed. "You are good with a pistol, but you're not fool enough to do what you just said to prove it."

"Chris, ol' boy." Another joined his laughter. "Consider ol' Lord Godolphin's position. You'd find yourself in a lot of trouble."

Just drunk enough to take offense at their words, Chris straightened as much as his inebriated state would allow. "Are you two suggesting I can't do it?"

"I don't think anyone can do it sober," the first man replied. "And you are far from sober."

"I'm a good enough shot to do it drunk or sober. Would you care to wager on the outcome?"

Now both of his friends became enthusiastic. Betting on the outcome of another of Chris's outlandish pranks was enough to make the situation exciting.

"What do you wager?" the first was quick to ask. Kyle Morton, a drinking friend, was much less of a friend than Chris knew. He was usually the one who maliciously urged Chris to do the things his wicked sense of humor thought up.

The Mortons did not possess nearly the amount of wealth that the Miles family did. Kyle's father had built, and ran exceedingly well, a small chain of stores that catered to the middle class. His money had put Kyle on the edge of the class to which he desired to belong. Yet in his mind, he never felt a secure footing there. Consequently, under the guise of a friend, he urged Chris to drink with him and usually teased and taunted Chris into carrying out some of the outrageous escapades he envisioned.

The second man was Brian DePoint. Brian's family was extremely wealthy, and he was the youngest child of three. At a very early age, he had discovered that he was an unwanted and uncared-for child. An argument between his father and mother had brought this situation to light. Suspicion of an indiscretion had turned the father he nearly worshiped away from him, so he had turned to a destructive life of drinking, gambling, and sexual escapades with women. This life was already beginning to take its toll on him.

"I'm so sure,"—Chris chuckled—"that I'll bet anything you care to name."

"That new stallion you've just purchased?" Kyle said quickly.

"Done," Chris replied. "Come along, gentlemen." The three of them staggered from the club in which they had been drinking all evening. They boarded the Miles carriage which awaited them. The coachman showed no surprise at their destination for he had become inured to Chris's eccentric orders when he was drunk.

They rode to a small cottage that sat in a sparsely populated area. Though there were other houses nearby, this three-room cottage seemed isolated as if it had built up an invisible barrier to any intrusion.

After the driver stopped the carriage in the shadows of a stand of trees that stood across the narrow dirt road, the three of them unsteadily disembarked. Cautioning the reluctant driver to remain hidden, they began what they thought was a stealthy approach to the cottage, proceeding until they were beneath the shade of a large tree that stood no more than thirty feet from the front door.

"He's there," whispered Brian.

"How do you know?" Kyle replied.

"His buggy is parked at the back of the house, there." He pointed. "In that dark area. It's pretty obvious the old bugger plans to spend the night."

Chris chuckled evilly. "I wonder if the old boy is in his nightshirt yet?"

"Better still, I wonder if he beds the girl with his wig on." Brian and Chris laughed softly.

"What do you say we make the bet a little better?" Chris said softly.

"How?" Kyle was quick to grasp anything that might cause Chris some difficulty.

"I'll scare them both out of that place, and in the process I'll cut off a lock of Lord Godolphin's wig as a souvenir."

"Good lord, Chris, are you crazy?" Brian expostulated. "You'll get caught sure as hell."

"Get me a lock of Godolphin's wig, Chris," Kyle said laughingly, "and I'll double the price of your stallion."

"You're on." Chris laughed happily, aware only of the challenge and Brian's wary head-shaking. Slipping a little closer to the house, he picked up a fist-sized stone. Heaving it as hard as he could, he heard it bounce from the door of the cottage and down the steps; then he shouted at the top of his lungs.

"Fire! Get out of the house! Fire!"

In moments, he was rewarded by the door being thrust open and a half-nude woman with flame-colored hair scampering blindly out of the door followed by a man in his late fifties, also in a half-dressed state.

Braced against the tree, Chris held a pistol in his hand. He bent his left elbow and laid the pistol across it. Patiently, he took aim, inhaled, and fired. The ball neatly lifted the wig from the older man's head. He, cursing frantically, desperately ran for the buggy that the girl was already heading out of the drive. He tumbled in and, within minutes, the buggy was out of sight.

The three young men, convulsed in laughter, did not hear the approach of anyone until a voice came to them from the dark.

257

"What in hell is goin' on around here?"

All three choked to quick silence, scampered to their feet, and ran toward their carriage. They scrambled inside falling all over each in their haste.

"Jacob," Chris said, "drive past the house, quick."

Obediently, the carriage swerved and dashed down the road to the front of the small house. Chris leaped from it as it stopped for a minute, snatched up the wig that lay on the ground, and jumped back into the carriage.

The three of them, beside themselves with laughter, were unaware that the unseen man who had called to them was the caretaker for the cottage, and that he had recognized their elaborate and rich carriage as one that belonged to the wealthy Miles family.

Chris thrust the wig into Kyle's lap. "Here's your souvenir, Kyle."

"You are a damned lucky fool, Chris." Kyle laughed. "I'll pay my wager tomorrow. I wonder if old Godolphin has another wig. It would be delightful to see him forced to appear in court tomorrow as bald as a cabbage."

This thought sent them all off into gales of laughter, punctuated by pointed remarks about Lord Godolphin's state of mind and his physical state at being so interrupted in such a delicate situation.

They proceeded to another club where they continued to drink. By the time Chris fell into his bed at home, it was well past three in the morning. He passed out and drifted into happy dreams.

But when his bedroom door was slammed loudly, he came suddenly awake as his father's voice roared, "Christopher Miles! Get up from that bed, you scoundrel."

"Huh?" Chris grunted as he sat erect and gazed at his father's angry face and glaring eyes through a hazy red fog.

There were only two people in Chris's life who could shake his equilibrium and leave him defenseless and speechless. One was his older brother for whom he had the deepest fraternal affection and respect. The other was his very formidable father of whom he stood somewhat in awe.

His respect and love for his father ran to the depths of his soul; yet he always seemed to be a trembling boy in his presence. He had felt absolutely sure no one would know what had happened the night before. What he did not know was that the man who had identified the carriage the night before had been shrewd enough to realize that knowledge and a little well-placed blackmail would turn a small profit for him. In addition, Lord Godolphin's wig had been left forgotten on the floor of the carriage the night before, mute evidence of Chris's guilt.

Blakely Miles held the incriminating wig in his hand and his cold angry gaze caused Chris to gulp back any words he might have said. It was obvious to him that Lord Godolphin knew who the mysterious assailant had been the night before, and with his power in the court, Chris could visualize a number of unpleasant things such as imprisonment or hanging in his immediate future.

"Christopher," his father began in a deceptively soft voice that caused the hair on the back of Chris's neck to rise and created a hollow feeling in the pit of his stomach, "it seems some mysterious person had the audacity to fire a pistol at Lord Godolphin last night."

The evidence of the wig swaying back and forth before him stifled his desire to plead his innocence.

"And," Chris said in a half-whisper, "Lord Godolphin knows who . . ."

"No, he does not . . . but I do, do I not, my Son?"

259

"Father, I'm sorry. I was drinking too much."

"You've been doing that a lot lately, but this time it does not excuse your abominable behavior. I will tolerate your wild ways not one moment longer."

"But if Lord Godolphin doesn't know who . . ."

"I have just paid a tidy sum of money to keep a man silent. He saw and recognized my carriage . . . *my carriage!*" His father's voice raised an octave. "How dare you draw this family into possible scandal by your drunken escapades? This is the very last straw." His father threw the wig into Chris's lap. "Now you will listen to me. I have raised you to the best of my ability. I have tried to give you a sense of responsibility. It seems I have failed. I will pamper you no longer. You will rise from that bed, dress, and pack a few things you will need. As soon as possible, you will leave this house and go to the lodge near Craven. There, you will have one week to think of your past and consider your future. If you decide to continue on the road you are traveling with your drinking and your gambling and your women, then I do not want you ever to return to this house. If you decide to accept the responsibility and honor that the Miles name has always stood for, I shall welcome you back and we will never speak of this matter again. The choice is yours. You have an hour to get you gone."

His father strode to the door and slammed it heartily behind him.

Chris stared at the door blankly for a moment; then his father's words crashed upon him. He knew his father well enough to realize that when he said something, he meant it. If Chris did not leave within the hour he would probably find himself bodily ejected from the house.

Slowly, he rose from the bed. His head pounded abominably and his mouth tasted vile. As if that was not enough misery, his stomach threatened at any moment to evacuate whatever was rolling busily about inside it.

He drew on his clothes, then began to pack a few more things in a small bag. Before he could finish there was a soft rap on the door and it was opened before he could answer. His brother, Blakely Miles, Jr., came in and, closing the door, he leaned against it, his arms folded across his chest and a broad grin on his handsome face.

"In a little trouble again, Chris?"

Chris smiled sheepishly and nodded as he tossed the last of the clothes he was taking into the bag and closed it.

"You didn't have to tell me; I could hear father's bellow in the stables. What in Christ's name did you do?"

Chris told him of the night's escapade, and as he spoke he could see the laughter in his brother's eyes. By the time he got to Lord Godolphin's wig, they were both laughing. Chris's hilarious description of a wigless, half-naked Lord Godolphin tumbling into his carriage with his latest mistress sent them both into gales of convulsive hilarity.

"Maybe," Blake suggested, though almost breathless with laughter, "we should send the wig to his wife. As good citizens, we should send a note to tell her where . . . and how we . . . found it."

"Could you see the old bugger's face when he went home?" Chris replied.

"I can imagine; I've seen his wife's face."

This again sent them into a fit of laughter. They were so involved they did not hear the door open.

Eleanora Miles stood just inside the door and watched with pleasure and amusement as her two sons shared their hearty laughter. When the two of them realized she was there, they both worked to control their laughter.

"Mother," Blake said, "I didn't hear you come in."

"No,"—she smiled—"both of you were too busy sharing some joke. Would you mind sharing it with me?"

"It was nothing, Mother." Chris gulped. "Just an old revived memory."

"Old . . . like last night? Memory . . . such as where your father found Lord Godolphin's wig? Oh, Chris, I'm afraid I haven't seen your father so furious since you stole old Mr. McGuffy's buggy and put it atop his barn. I've heard him roar before, but not like this. He's even told me you will be going away for a few days. What's your punishment this time, young man, and will it curtail some of your atrocious activities?"

Chris filled her in quickly on his father's ultimatum.

"I think he's being quite gentle on you considering what I've heard of Lord Godolphin's discomfort. I expect you to return a little contrite and to request your father's forgiveness. Plus you should give us a solemn promise that this kind of thing will never happen again."

"Yes, Mother," Chris said quietly. "I shall certainly ask Father's forgiveness if he ever lets me near him again."

"Oh,"—her eyes glistened with humor as she turned to go—"he'll forgive you. Do have a safe trip, Chris, and think over your life. It is time you settled down some, Son."

"Yes, Mother."

"Come and kiss me good-by before you go?"

"Of course, Mother." Chris grinned.

Just before Eleanora closed the door she looked back at her sons, her eyes a-twinkle.

"Someday, I shall tell you a few of your father's youthful escapades. It might help you to realize how human he is and how much he loves you."

As she closed the door behind her, Chris and Blake

stared at each other, surprise in their eyes. They had thought of their father as the iron center of their family. It would be enlightening to hear any stories of his past.

"Want me to ride along with you?" Blake asked.

"No, Father wouldn't like it. I'm supposed to think on my own."

"Chris?" Blake began hesitantly.

"What?"

"You know I've never tried bossing you around, but don't you think Father might be right? Don't you think it is time for you to start making a life for yourself?"

"I . . . I don't really intend to do these things, Blake, it's just . . ." He shrugged. "Sometimes, things get out of hand and you find yourself doing things you really don't mean to do."

"If it won't cause you to explode, Chris, I'll give you my opinion."

"And what is that?"

"You're keepin' the wrong company, Chris. Kyle Morton is no friend of yours and Brian is on the road to hell himself. I've heard a few rumors that ol' Kyle has had a lot to say behind your back. He's only trying to blacken your reputation."

"You've never said anything about this before."

"You're a good kid, Chris. I felt you would come to your own senses and see them for what they are. At least this will give you something to think about while you're up there alone."

"Thanks, Blake, I'll think about it."

"Good, now let's get you on your way before Father has a chance to think up something else."

They laughed and left the room. Within an hour, Chris had kissed his mother good-by and started on his way. It took him two days of travel to reach the borders of the

Mileses' hunting estate. He stopped late at night and rose early in the morning.

He stopped for an afternoon meal at a small inn that sat outside the village of Craven. He thought The Devil's Inn had an appropriate name for he felt like a mournful Lucifer expelled from heaven.

By the time he reached the lodge itself it was already nearing nightfall. He stabled his horse and fed him after rubbing him down; then he unlocked the door and went in.

The lodge had not been occupied for several months, so he built a fire in the fireplace to take the chill from the room.

He had brought enough food from the inn to hold him for a day or two, and after a quick snack he put the rest away. Now there was nothing to do . . . but think.

The lodge itself was quite large and very comfortable. There was a small library equipped with a few books but they were excellent selections. He took one and sat by the fire, but he could not concentrate on the words.

With Blake's words in his mind, he relived some of the things he had been doing in the past few months. It did not take him long to realize that Kyle and Brian had really always been there to edge him on and keep him involved even if he tried to wiggle away from anything they suggested.

It alarmed him to realize just how often he had been drunk lately. He also was quick to realize that drinking had usually been the beginning of all his troubles.

Once this train of thought began he started to realize just how very patient his father had really been with him. How often he had paid to keep Chris out of trouble. Despite his thundering and roaring, his father had always stood behind him.

One thought led to another, and he opened his mind to the kind of family and the kind of life he had. He had been given every comfort and the best education his father's money could buy for him. Besides his uproarious extracurricular activities, Chris had been a good student, bright and quick; his professors had found in him a keen intelligent mind.

As each thought created a new one, Chris groaned under a new load of guilt for his childish ways. He searched for the right words to say to his father to show the depth of his feelings and his realization for the need to apologize and assure him that in the future he would be different.

He spent one day walking the forest that surrounded the lodge. It was on that day that he found the path that led to the shore. He sat on the high cliffs overlooking the beach and let the peace and contentment of his new self ease through him.

The following day, he swam in the warm surf exhilarating in the invigorating exercise.

Now his mind was clear. He would go home tomorrow; he would apologize deeply to his father, his mother, and to Blake for having been so blind as to almost lose himself.

Tomorrow, he thought, but before tomorrow could arrive another situation presented itself—a situation for which he was completely unprepared yet one that would bring another surprising change in his life.

He had decided to take a walk along the beach to watch the glory of the sunset. A good way down the sand was a cluster of huge rocks. He had no intention of climbing them, and was about to turn and retrace his steps when a shrill scream came from the other side.

Quickly, he climbed the rocks and looked down.

Facing him to his left was a wall of rock over a hundred feet high. At its base was a stretch of long white beach. It was not this that held his attention, but the extremely beautiful woman who was kneeling beside the quiet still form of a young boy. At a glance he could see the boy was unconscious and that the girl was beside herself with fear for him. Quickly, he climbed down and ran to them. The girl looked up at him first in surprise and then in joy.

"Oh, thank God! Please help me!"

## *Sixteen*

When Morgan left her, Kristen suddenly was overcome by a sense of loss and loneliness. She realized how lonely she had been since her father had died and how much Morgan had filled her life. She knew now that she had never loved Jeffrey. He had been a doorway to a new world, and she would have entered that world without realizing the reasons that motivated her.

She would wait, albeit not patiently, because she had complete faith and trust in Morgan. She thought only of the day he would return. She knew what he was, and she didn't care if he chose to stay where they were. It was enough for her, this beautiful place and Morgan, too.

She walked along the beach in deep thought for a while after Morgan had gone; then remembering that Toby was still there, she made her way back to the cabin.

Toby had been watching for her to reappear, his small face tense and his eyes deep with worry. She was the woman of his beloved captain. He loved her for that and for the new shine she had brought to Morgan's eyes. He also loved Kristen because she was so very beautiful and because she smiled at him in an open way that told him she cared for him.

Toby's near-worship of Morgan went back over three years. Toby, an orphan, had been trapped in an alley by two larger boys who were determined to wring from him the two small coins he had. Frightened and trying his best to fight back, Toby had been losing when Morgan, on the way to his ship, chanced to turn into that same alley.

Toby, on his back but fighting valiantly, saw the two boys lifted from him and held by the collars of their shirts, their feet a good two inches from the ground. They both struggled until Morgan gave each a shaking that made his teeth rattle. Then they realized it was better not to struggle against this tall stranger.

"Don't you boys think the odds are a little uneven?" Morgan asked mildly. He looked down at Toby. "Get to your feet, boy."

Toby scrambled to his feet.

"Tell me what is going on."

Quickly, Toby, who was held spellbound by Morgan's cool blue gaze and amused smile, told him.

"Do you boys want to apologize?"

"Sorry," one said quickly and his mate followed his example. Morgan's laugh broke the stillness as he gave each one another rough shake before he released them. It took them only a second to run from the alley. When they were gone, Morgan squatted on his haunches and looked Toby over closely.

"You will be a little black-and-blue in the morning, but you seem to be all right. Do you live near here?"

"No, sir."

"Where do you live?"

Toby swung his arm to encompass everything. "Anyplace."

"You mean . . ."

"I can take care of myself," he responded belligerently.

"Of course you can," Morgan replied mildly, "but I

was about to offer you some work. If you tell me you would rather stay here . . ."

"No . . . I mean . . . work, sir? Doing what?"

"Cabin boy on my ship."

Toby's eyes grew wide. "I'd like that, sir."

"Then there must be someone to whom I would have to talk. Surely you do not live on the street."

Toby's chin stiffened and his eyes darkened with anger. Morgan's sense of humor was touched, but he retained his cool look.

"I am not a liar. My parents are dead and they wanted to send me to an orphanage. I ran away. I've been living on the street for a long time."

"How long?"

"Over a year."

"That's long enough. What is your name?"

"Toby, sir."

"Toby what?"

Again Toby's eyes grew shuttered and wary. Morgan laughed.

"All right, we'll leave it at that for a while. It's Toby. Come along."

Morgan stood up and walked away and Toby followed his tall figure into a new and bright future he had never expected to find.

Toby stood up when he saw Kristen coming. She smiled and waved and he did not know what he would have done if Kristen had cried, or worse yet, closed herself away from him.

"Toby, I'm sorry. I just wanted a few minutes alone."

"It's all right, Miss Kristen. Are you all right?"

"Yes, Toby, I'm fine. Are you hungry?"

"Yes, ma'am." Toby grinned, for he was almost always

269

hungry. Morgan had suspected this was due to the year when Toby did not know where his next meal was coming from. Morgan also felt that in time Toby's appetite would return to normal.

"Come along, let's eat; then later, we can go for a swim."

Toby agreed and they shared a quiet meal. Later on, before the sun set, they went for a swim; then they sat on the beach in the light of a new full moon and talked.

"Toby, you've known Morgan a long time?"

"No, miss, not really, only a couple of years." He went on to tell her how Morgan had run across him. Kristen laughed.

"You might say Morgan rescued both of us from a bad situation. You don't know anything about his past, where he came from, why he's turned pirate?"

"No, miss," Toby said softly, his eyes intent on Kristen. "All I know is he's good and kind, and I don't care what he is, or what people say about him."

"I don't either, Toby," Kristen said gently. "I love him as you do, and when he comes back, we'll be married. Then we can adopt you to be our son."

"Adopt!" Toby fairly shouted. "You mean I could belong to you and the captain always . . . forever?"

"Yes; of course that will depend on what Morgan has to say, but I would like to, and I'm sure he would also."

"I would be so good," he said in a rush of words. "I would do anythin' you say. I'd never make you sorry, honest."

"I know, Toby, and I'm sure Morgan does too. Shall we go back to the house? I think it is time for you to be in bed."

After they walked back to the house, Kristen tucked Toby securely into bed. Then she went to her bed—a bed that had never felt so empty or so lonely in her life.

The next day brought a surprise to Kristen and to Toby. For Toby it was the moment Kristen decided he should learn to read and write. For Kristen it was when she began to search for equipment with which to begin his lessons.

She checked through the desk in the study, but to her surprise, she found it completely empty. Going from room to room, she looked until she was exasperated. The only place left to look was the huge chest that stood at the foot of her bed.

The lid was so heavy that Toby had to kneel beside her on the floor and help her lift the lid. Inside, there were some clothes piled neatly in one corner, the rest of the space was taken up by boxes of assorted sizes piled one upon the other. A large square picture frame, its picture facing the wall of the chest, stood at the back. Inside the first small box she opened was all the paper she would need; yet she was too curious now to cease searching through the treasure chest. When she opened the second box, she found a bundle of letters neatly tied in a little packet. The handwriting was definitely feminine, and all were addressed to Morgan Grayfield.

At least, she thought, it told her Morgan's last name, a thing he had asked her to trust him about until he returned.

"Do you know anyone named Grayfield, Toby?"

"No, ma'am."

She held the packet of letters in her hand, a desire to open them and read them strong within her. Resolutely, she put them back into the box and returned the box to the chest. The next box she took out had a collection of bright-colored sea shells, large and small, obviously the

271

collection of a child. Toby admired them, so she handed him the box to look through while she went on with her inspection.

There were several more boxes, but now the gilt edge of the portrait drew her attention. She grasped the edge of it and began to slowly ease it from behind the balance of the boxes. Finally, she got it free and turned it over. She gasped and nearly dropped it when she saw the subjects of the portrait. Four people—two women, two men—smiled at her from the canvas. Three she did not know, but the fourth one was definitely Morgan Grayfield. He was younger than the Morgan she knew; yet there was no doubt about who it was. The cool blue eyes still smiled in the same amused mischievous way, and the thick mane of black hair was so familiar she could almost feel it. The older man who stood behind him was obviously his father, for they looked so much alike. She accepted the fact that the older woman must be his mother. These things obvious, she accepted the younger woman as his sister. She had the same thick glossy black hair and startling blue eyes.

Next the elaborate and obviously wealthy clothes they were drew her attention. Jewels adorned the women, undoubtedly expensive jewels.

Everything was so scrambled in her mind. Morgan was a pirate, he had no money, yet the obvious wealth in the picture was unmistakable. Why would he kidnap a woman for money if he had all the money he needed?

"Trust me, Kristen," he had pleaded. She reached for all kinds of possibilities. His family must have lost their wealth, maybe to Jeffrey. Maybe that was another reason Morgan hated him so.

She stood the picture against the chest, determined to ignore all these possibilities and keep her trust in

272

Morgan. As soon as he returned to her, he would be able to explain everything.

"Gather the paper and pens, Toby. We'll begin your lessons now. Maybe by the time Morgan comes back, you will be able to write your name and his . . . whatever it is."

For the following days, they concentrated on Toby's lessons, breaking their tediousness by swimming and exploring the rest of the house and the beach and forests that surrounded it.

One day as they were walking down the path to the beach and, enjoying the breeze and the warm sun, Kristen said, "Toby, we must come back here often to spend some time. It is such a beautiful place."

"I would like that. There's so much to do here, and the cove sure is nice for swimming."

"You like to swim." She laughed. "I do believe you're half-fish and half-boy."

"It's fun," he agreed, "but I like to climb the cliffs, too."

"Cliffs . . . what cliffs?"

"Down the coast a way. They're really only a big pile of rocks," he added hastily, seeing the look of surprise and worry in her eyes. "I can't get hurt down there. Do you want to see them?"

"Yes, I'd like to see them," she replied firmly. "And if they're what I think they are, I don't want to see you there again."

Toby led the way and they went down the beach until they approached a tremendous pile of huge stone boulders. It looked to Kristen as if God had swept up a huge pile of debris, then deposited it there as if to show them that amidst all the beauty of the world, there still existed the hard and dark parts of life.

"It's really not hard to climb. I've been up and down them a lot. Let me show you."

"Toby!" she called to him as he ran toward the huge pile of rocks, but he was already scampering up the sea-washed boulders. She ran to the foot of the craggy rocks and looked up at him, her heart in her throat.

If Toby had been alone, as he often was, there would have been no difficulty, but a little over halfway up, to prove his mastery of climbing, he turned to wave to Kristen.

Neither of them was sure of what happened. Toby's foot slipped and he lost his balance. Kristen screamed as she saw his body begin to tumble. His head struck a rock on his descent and he landed in a crumpled heap at Kristen's feet.

Kristen fell to her knees beside him and rolled him over. His eyes were closed and his pale face drove her nearly to panic as she remembered that the two of them were completely alone and she did not know where to go to find help.

"Toby," she said softly. Gently, she lifted his head and laid it in her lap. Using her skirt, she wiped the blood from his face. Tears filled her eyes and she prayed silently for help. There was no doubt Toby was too heavy for her to carry.

She was about to leave him and go in search of help when she heard a scrambling noise at the top of the rocks and a man's head appeared. Quickly he climbed down beside them.

"Oh, thank God," she cried. "Please help me!"

He came to her side and knelt beside Toby. "What happened?"

"He fell from the rocks."

"I'll carry him; we'll take him to the doctor in the village."

Chris lifted Toby in his arms and with Kristen at his side, they made their way toward Morgan's lodge.

"You're staying at the Grayfields'?"

"Yes."

"You're a relative?"

"No, not exactly."

When they arrived at the lodge, Chris laid Toby on the bed. The fact that he was still unconscious worried him.

"Do you have a buggy here? I can take him into the village."

Kristen felt helpless fear. "There is no buggy . . . no horse even. What will we do?"

For the first time Chris really looked at her. Despite the worry in her gray eyes, she was the most beautiful woman he had ever seen. He stood in profound amazement, wondering how a lovely thing such as she came to be here with no contact with the outside world. The thought that she was Morgan's mistress slipped into his mind, and all he could feel was envy for Morgan's good luck.

"I have a horse, and I'm not that far away. I will go and bring the doctor here. Put some cold cloths on his head while I'm gone. You will be all right, won't you?"

"Yes, I'll be fine. Please hurry."

He left, and running at an easy loping pace, he covered the distance between Morgan's place and his own in an hour. He saddled the horse he had come on and rode the few miles to the village as fast as the horse could carry him. Still, it was over three hours before he got back to the Grayfield lodge with the doctor.

To Kristen, the time seemed endless. She sat by a still-unconscious Toby, putting cool cloths on his head and praying silently for him. During the short time they had spent together a genuine affection had grown between them. She knew how much Toby meant to Morgan and she was frightened that he might die and Morgan would know nothing about it.

The sound of Chris's footsteps across the porch was the most welcome sound she had ever heard. She ran to the door and flung it open before the men could reach it.

"Please hurry, he's still unconscious."

Chris ushered the doctor in. "This is Dr. Menbury."

Kristen smiled, but both men could see she was impatient and frantic with worry about Toby.

"Chris tells me your young friend has had a bad fall. Where is he?"

"Come with me, Doctor. He's here in the bedroom."

Kristen led the way, but the doctor stopped her at the bedroom door. "Let me see him alone for a few minutes, my child."

"Yes, Doctor," she said quietly and reluctantly watched the bedroom door close behind him.

Chris stood watching her, still puzzled by the mystery of her presence at the Grayfield lodge. He, of course, had seen Morgan in the company of Leslie Seaford, and knew they were most likely having an affair, but he could not understand any man hiding away a rare beauty like Kristen.

"Let me introduce myself. I'm Christopher Miles. My family has a place not too far from here."

"I'm grateful you came along when you did. I don't know what I would have done."

It was obvious to Chris that she had no intention of giving him her name or the mysterious reason for her presence here. He would have questioned her more, but he knew Morgan much too well. Morgan's temper was not one with which to tamper. He had crossed its formidable power once and only once. He had promised himself never to do so again.

"There's no need for thanks; I'm just glad I came along when I did. I'm sure the boy will be all right. Children his age have a resilience that's nearly unbelievable—especially boys. I could tell you of the bumps and bruises I've had. You'll see, he'll be fine in a day or so."

"You're very reassuring."

Chris grinned his warmest, most practiced wicked grin which had melted feminine hearts before. He was crestfallen when he saw no response.

Before he could speak again, the bedroom door opened and the doctor came out. Kristen ran to him quickly.

"Doctor?"

"He's all right, child." The doctor smiled. "He has received a nasty knock on the head and he'll have to stay in bed several days . . . but he will be fine."

"Thank you." Kristen sighed with relief. "I'm very grateful you were so near."

"Oh, I've been to the Grayfields' before, especially when young Morgan was growing up. He seemed to have a way of acquiring more bumps and bruises than the average child. I guess it was his curiosity."

Chris chuckled and Kristen was aware of how much better these two people knew the man she loved than she did.

"Anyway, I'm very grateful that you came so quickly. I shall see the account is taken care of immediately."

"Don't worry. Lord Grayfield and I are very old friends. Take care of the boy, keep him down for a few days if you can, and if should you need me, don't hesitate to send young Christopher here for me."

"Thank you, I will."

The doctor nodded and left. Soon the sound of his buggy faded and Kristen faced Chris again, unsure of what to say, yet aware that she could not reveal her real identity to him.

Chris was touched by the mystery that lingered in her eyes. He could hardly control his deep curiosity about her connection to Morgan and just how close it was. He knew one thing for certain: she attracted him as a flame does a moth and he would tread gently, but he would find out just who she was, why she was there, and what her connection was to Morgan.

He sensed at the moment that it would be better if he left, for she kept glancing at the door behind which Toby lay.

"Well, I'll be going now. Do you mind if I come by tomorrow to check on the boy?"

"No, of course I don't mind. Thank you again for your kindness."

"It's all right," he said softly. "I didn't mind at all. In fact, I'm grateful to the powers that be for giving me the opportunity to meet you. I'll see you tomorrow."

She nodded, and Chris left closing the door softly behind him. Immediately Kristen went to Toby's room. He lay quiet, his face pale but his breathing relaxed and easy as if he were in a deep sleep.

She sat down beside him, her mind filled with the need to have Morgan beside her, to hold her and tell her everything was going to be well.

Restlessly, she rose, went to the window, and looked out on the beautiful scene before her; only now she barely saw the beauty.

She turned back to the room, and when she did, her eyes fell on the portrait that still stood braced against the chest. Morgan's blue eyes smiled at her from the canvas; only they seemed to be laughing in wicked pleasure over some mysterious thing. She loved him, yet she shivered suddenly as if a cold wind had blown across her.

"Morgan," she whispered softly, "who are you? What are you?"

The fact that doubt had stealthily crept into her thoughts frightened her and stung her eyes with tears. She buried her face in her hands.

"Oh, Morgan, please hurry and come back to me. I need you so desperately."

These soft words were the only sound in the quietness that surrounded her.

# Seventeen

Toby stirred awake late in the evening, with the worst pain in his head he had ever felt before. He blinked his eyes open to find Kristen seated beside him. For a few minutes, he could not remember what had happened before; then it all came flooding back. He tried to rise only to find Kristen pressing him back on the bed.

"Toby, don't try to get up. The doctor has told me you need to stay in bed a few days. You struck your head on the stones. There's a nasty cut there."

"Doctor," Toby said in panic, for Jeremy's last words were to caution him against any strangers who might happen by. He was to say nothing about who she was or her reasons for being there. Now he felt his stupidity had endangered both Kristen and his beloved captain. This thought brought another. How did she get him to the cabin, and how did she get to a doctor . . . ? "How . . . how did you get me here?"

"Christopher, Christopher Miles. He lives not too far from here, thank heavens. He carried you here and went to bring the doctor."

"He's not coming back, is he?"

"Toby! I'm sure he'll want to find out how you are tomorrow. Not to see him would not only be rude but would demonstrate a definite lack of gratitude to a man who most likely saved your life."

"I'll thank him," Toby said obstinately. "But I don't like him coming here. The captain will be mad. We were supposed to stay hidden."

"I certainly do not intend to tell him who I am or why I'm here. Morgan does not need to worry, Toby; neither do you. You know I would never betray Morgan."

"I know you wouldn't, but I'm afraid for him."

"Don't worry, Toby. I'll see to it that Christopher Miles has no answers to any of his questions. Morgan will be back soon and this will all be over. Now I think it is time for you to eat and then to rest."

Obediently, Toby ate, and before the sun set, he was again asleep. Kristen went for a walk along the beach to unwind from the day's nervous tension. It was two hours later before she returned to the cabin and went to sleep.

Chris was at their door with his most charming smile and a twinkle in his eye. He asked Kristen to go riding with him, but she refused to leave Toby since he was helpless. Toby, who had heard their exchange, intended to stay immobilized as long as possible.

He met Chris's attempt at camaraderie with wary eyes and a cold response that left Chris more curious than ever. Why should the boy be so resentful of his presence when he had saved his life and why should his cold glare begin every time Chris smiled at or spoke to Kristen?

Three days later, days during which Chris had visited regularly, Kristen allowed Toby out of bed—at first only for a short time, but she increased the time daily until Toby passed her critical inspection and she pronounced him well.

Even after he was up and could have been playing on the beach or elsewhere, Toby remained always within calling distance of Kristen. Chris, overcome with irritation at Toby and plagued by deeper and deeper curiosity about Kristen, determined to find the answers to some of his questions. It took him over a week to find the way to do it.

For his lodge Chris's father kept a caretaker, for whom he felt sympathy due to this old man's lack of family and finances. The man kept the house in good repair and tended a small stable in which several horses were kept for friends who came to hunt.

One morning Chris headed for the stable. He planned to ride over to Morgan's lodge and bring an extra horse. Feeling that Kristen had been enclosed in the lodge long enough, he was determined to get her to ride with him. He had not seen her really smile for days.

Just as he reached the stable door, he heard a soft voice from inside. It amused him to think the old man was talking to himself, but after a few more words, he realized he wasn't.

"Ye're a good ol' thing. I'm right proud of ye. They're the prettiest passel of young-uns I've ever seen."

Pushing the stable door open, Chris walked in to find the caretaker, his back to Chris, kneeling on the floor at the entrance to one of the stalls. He walked up behind him and looked over his shoulder. There, in a pile of clean hay, lay a brown-and-white dog with a litter of seven puppies tumbling about her. The caretaker looked up when Chris's shadow fell on him.

"Good mornin', lad."

"Morning. A nice litter of puppies. They yours?"

"Aye, sir, their mother is; as to the father I can't rightly say." He laughed. "She ain't exactly particular who she takes up with. They are a pretty bunch though, aren't they? Guess I'll take 'em to the village. I surely can't keep 'em all here."

"They old enough to be taken from their mother?"

"Aye, sir."

Chris grinned happily. "Saddle one horse; I'll be right back."

Chris ran back to the house and began to search for something to carry a puppy in—a puppy that might be the key to Toby's acceptance. The only thing he could find was one of his mother's sewing baskets. Quickly, he dumped its contents on the bed, and, taking the basket, tucked it under his arm. He ran down the steps and back to the stable; there he found a horse saddled and ready for him.

He went to the litter of puppies, lifted one soft ball of black and white fur, deposited it in the basket, and closed the lid. Mounting, he headed the horse toward the Grayfield lodge, this time with a laugh in his eyes and a soft whistle on his lips.

Kristen and Toby were seated at the table having breakfast. They exchanged glances as they heard the horse approach. Soon they heard Chris's footsteps across the porch and a sharp rap on the door.

"Why don't he go away?" Toby muttered.

"Toby, that's rude. Chris has been very kind to you. He's tried to be your friend."

"No, he's tried to be *your* friend. He don't care what I do or even if I'm here."

"Toby, I don't think that's true."

Another rap interrupted them and Kristen rose and went toward the door.

"The captain ain't gonna like him either," Toby muttered.

Kristen opened the door and smiled at Chris who smiled in return.

"Good morning, my mystery lady with no name." He

laughed. "It is a very beautiful day and I come bearing gifts."

"A gift . . . for me?"

"No . . . a gift for our patient. I hope he's up to handling it."

Toby was, by this time, standing at Kristen's side eying the box suspiciously. The last thing he wanted was to accept a gift from the man he thought was trying to usurp his captain's place in the life of Kristen; yet his boyish curiosity was holding his attention on the basket under Chris's arm.

"What's in it?"

Chris came in, set the basket on the floor, and slowly lifted one corner of the lid. In a few moments, a dark shiny nose appeared, then two large dark eyes. The puppy's shrill little yip went directly to the heart of this little boy who had never really had a possession of his own.

Toby's eyes grew large, and he trembled with the urge to snatch up the quivering little ball of fur that was trying heroically to climb from the basket.

Toby looked from the basket to Chris's smiling face, and then he looked at Kristen. She knew Toby was fighting a battle that was too much for him. She had to assure him he was not disloyal to Morgan.

"It's all right, Toby," she said softly. "Morgan would be the first to understand. Boys and puppies belong together."

"Can . . . can I take him from the basket?" he asked Chris.

"He's yours to do with as you please," Chris replied. "I think the first thing you must do is give him a name."

Toby thought for a long time; then he knelt by the basket and gently lifted the puppy in his arms. He laughed as the enthusiastic puppy wiggled all over and licked his face. "I know what I'll name him!"

"What, Toby?" Kristen smiled, but her smile faded as Toby said jubilantly.

"He's Falcon."

"Falcon?" Chris said. "That's an odd name for a puppy."

Both Toby and Kristen were paralyzed with fear. What if Chris would be able to connect the name Falcon with Morgan. They were silent until Chris spoke again. "Well, Falcon it is. Why don't you find him some food; then take him for a run on the beach."

Toby nodded and went in search of something to feed the puppy. Kristen knew Chris was quick-witted. The last thing she could do now was tell him her name. If she did, it would drop the pieces of the puzzle into his lap, and it wouldn't take him long to figure it out.

Against all her instincts, she would have to create a story he would believe, a story that would divert his mind from any connection with Kristen Seaford, Morgan, a pirate, and a ship named the *Falcon*.

"Would you care for some tea, Chris? How would you like some breakfast?"

"I've not had any breakfast. Yes, I would like some tea and this whole thing isn't fair, you know."

"What whole thing?"

"The fact that you know almost everything there is to know about me, and you won't even tell me your name." He looked into her eyes. "My dear mystery lady," he said softly, "that secrets lurk in those pretty gray eyes? Are you a princess in disguise? What story lies behind that beautiful face?"

"Chris,"—she laughed nervously—"you are making much more of this than really exists. What a romantic you are! There's nothing so exciting or mysterious in my life."

"Then tell me about you. You will never know how many stories I've created about you, or how many sleepless nights you've given me."

"Come and let me make you some breakfast; then we'll take a walk along the beach and I'll tell you about your not-so-mysterious lady."

"That's a bargain. Bring on the food, madam. I've an urge to hear this story as soon as possible."

After they had eaten, Toby insisted that they go to the beach. He ran ahead of them with the puppy tumbling at his heels. Chris walked beside Kristen, more aware of her than he had ever been of any other woman.

They walked slowly along the strip of white sand. Neither of them spoke. Kristen was watching Toby play with the puppy and Chris was content for the moment just to watch her.

Her gold-bronze hair, which she had not had time to style, fell about her in a mass of wayward curls that seemed to pick up each ray of the early sun. He liked the easy way she walked beside him, as if she belonged to this environment. He found himself enjoying her silent presence, the half-smile on her lips, and her clear cool gray eyes that made him warm with pleasure when they turned toward him. They sat on some rocks and watched Toby and Falcon play.

"He's a nice boy," Chris said.

"Yes."

"Is he your brother?"

"No, he's just a friend."

"I don't understand."

"What?"

"Any of this . . . you . . . your young friend who is

very protective of you."

He turned and looked down into her eyes. "I believe you said you'd give me some answers."

"Yes, I did," Kristen replied. She walked a little away from him, for she knew that sometimes her face was a little too easy to read—especially if she was lying, which was an alien thing to her. She used her mother's maiden name and began to weave a story to try to satisfy Chris.

"My name is Jennifer Nelson. I was born and raised in the colonies, in a rather well-to-do family. My parents died and I found myself in the position of being a single woman, alone, with a great deal of money."

"That doesn't seem to be a difficult position," Chris said. "It's almost an enviable one."

"It might have been if I did not have an uncle who was determined to take everything away from me. I am not of age and he thought it best if he were my legal guardian. Naturally I ran away from him. Morgan gave me sanctuary here until I can get my resources together and defend myself."

"I see," Chris said hesitantly. "Jennifer?"

"Yes?"

"Morgan . . . he's just a friend who's offering you protection?"

"Yes," she replied softly, but she froze in suspended shock when she heard his reply.

"I'm glad. I thought he might mean much more to you, and I couldn't bear the thought of him treating you like this while he carries on a blatant affair with the beautiful Leslie Seaford."

She was grateful that she was standing with her back to him, for she could feel the blood drain from her face and she knew her pain must be written there for anyone to see. She tried to gather her wits together.

287

"Who?"

"Her name is Leslie Seaford and I would be the first to admit she is a very beautiful woman. She's the stepmother of Jeffrey MacIntire's future wife. It seems her stepdaughter ran across a pirate on her journey here and was kidnapped. I believe the ransom has been paid so the marriage should be soon. Morgan has taken over Mrs. Seaford's time almost completely; they've been seen just about everywhere together. I imagine it won't be long until they marry also."

She seemed unable to breathe; it was as if all the world about her was suspended in time. Chris's voice faded away and all she could hear was her pounding heart and two names—Leslie Seaford and Morgan Grayfield. All the pieces of an elusive puzzle seemed to fit themselves together—Morgan and Leslie. How clear it was to her. How better to acquire a fortune than for Leslie to rid herself of Kristen's father and for Morgan to eliminate her. He had never intended her to return from this place. The ruthless way he had asked her to trust him, had casually taken all the love she had to give. She pictured Morgan and Leslie together, laughing over her naïveté, over the way he had so easily taken her. She visualized them making their plans together. It was only then that she realized she might be waiting for the return of a man who meant to kill her. Her feelings of love froze within her at the thought of his treachery, and she was left shaken and filled with a deeper fear than she had ever felt before.

"Jennifer?"

At the sound of Chris's voice, she was jolted back to the present. How fortunate, she thought, that fate had put Chris where he was at the one moment when she needed him. A cold dark rage filled her, at Leslie . . . but more so at Morgan, who had deceived and betrayed her.

Resolutely, she brushed the tears from her eyes, composed her face, and straighened her shoulders. Then she turned to face Chris with a smile on her face—a smile he could not read; and for some reason it seemed to startle him.

"Jennifer, have I said something to upset you? You're so pale."

"No, I'm fine, Chris. You were telling me something?"

"I was saying that it's not necessary for you to stay so secluded here. You could come to my home and no one need know you are there. It would certainly be much nicer for you than to be alone like this."

"Oh, Chris." She laughed. "What would your parents think? I've run away with nothing. I've only the few clothes on my back."

"That doesn't matter. I'm sure my mother would be glad to shop for you. Having to care for two boys all her life she'd enjoy shopping for a girl."

"Such an imposition!"

"No! No one in my family would think any such thing. You'd be welcome for as long as you wanted to stay."

"I could send a message to our lawyer. He's a very dear friend of mine. I'm sure he would arrange my finances."

She wanted to run away from here before Morgan could return. She knew she could not bear to face him and know that his words of love were all lies. It was only the thought of Toby that made her hesitate. What would she say to him to make him come along with her without argument? She knew his feelings for Morgan and even though she felt they were built on deceit, she knew he would never think of turning his back on Morgan.

"Give me a day or so to think your offer over. It is extremely kind of you, Chris, and I do appreciate it."

"As long as you'll think about it. I really think it would be best. Think of how close a call you had with Toby's accident. It could have been you, or I could have chosen to walk in another direction. I'd feel so much better if you were among people. I'll even contact Morgan and tell him where you are."

"I must talk to Toby; then . . . then we will talk. I have many things that will have to be explained. Will you have patience with me, Chris?"

"Of course," he said softly. There was no way for Kristen to misread the look in his eyes. That he was rapidly falling in love with her was more than obvious, but love was a painful emotion of which she could not bear to think.

To her relief, Toby chose that minute to interrupt. Breathlessly, he ran to them, the wiggling puppy in his arms.

"Toby, I think we'd best go back and feed you and your friend." Kristen smiled.

"I am hungry," Toby admitted.

"When are you not?" Kristen said as the three of them started back. Kristen deliberately kept silent, knowing Chris would stay for the meal if she invited him, but she needed time alone—time to think, time to make plans. For a deep black anger was slowly taking the place of the pain.

They ate, she and Toby, in silence. He was aware that something troubled her, but his young mind could not grasp the reasons for her troubled eyes.

That night, after she had seen that Toby was safely tucked into bed and was asleep, she sat in front of a low-burning fire and allowed the thoughts she had kept at bay all day to surface and overtake her.

"Morgan," she whispered softly, her voice cracked

with the pain her vision of him caused. She could feel him, the strength of his arms about her, the gentleness of his touch, the magic world his kiss gave her. All this was overcome by her feeling of intense hurt and shame at knowing all those beautiful memories were based on lies, that he had never meant his sweet words of love.

Slowly, she began to draw her thoughts together. Firmly and decisively, she put her memories and pain aside. She would not allow him the satisfaction of success. She would not allow Leslie and Morgan to win. Pride drew the pieces of her life together; pride and anger resolved her thoughts.

She would leave this place: somehow she would create a reason Toby could accept. And when she had found a place of safety, she would write to her lawyer and regain her money. Then her thoughts would turn toward the two who had injured her so . . . Morgan . . . Leslie . . . and revenge.

291

# Eighteen

The night was long and it was nearly dawn before she closed her eyes and drifted into a dream-filled sleep. It was impossible to keep Morgan out of her dreams; he invaded them persistently and she was helpless to keep him and his love at bay.

Mentally and physically exhausted by the time Toby called to her, she reluctantly left her warm comfortable bed to fix breakfast.

No idea had come to her during the night on how to get around Toby's loyalty. Grimly, she decided if it took an outright lie to convince him to go, she would be forced to resort to it.

"Captain should be back pretty soon. He's been gone a lot longer than usual," Toby said as he ate.

Yes, Kristen thought, this time he is too involved with a woman to even remember we are here.

"Maybe he will send a message for us to come to him."

Toby looked up at her, surprise in his face.

"He's never done that before; besides, how would we get there?"

Kristen shrugged. "Maybe he'll send someone to take us to him. No matter how, I imagine if he wants us he will think of a way."

"Yes, I guess so," Toby reluctantly agreed, but doubt was clear in his face.

"Toby, after breakfast you'd best see to your puppy. He needs to be taken outside. Remember, he's not housebroken and you're responsible for any . . . accidents he may have."

"Yes, ma'am."

Kristen stood on the porch and watched boy and puppy run to the beach. Then she went back in and knelt by the chest in which she had found the portrait. It still stood against the edge and as she looked again into Morgan's laughing blue eyes, her determination was renewed. She raised the lid slowly for its weight was nearly too much for her; yet her anger gave her added strength. She rummaged within, looking for something with Morgan's name written on it. She didn't know if Toby would recognize Morgan's handwriting, but she did not want to take the chance. Somewhere in this chest, she thought, there must be something that had been written by Morgan. She was almost ready to give up when she saw another small box. Opening it, she found several more letters, the only difference was that they were addressed to Miss Charlotte Grayfield, and were from Morgan Grayfield.

Hesitantly, she unbound the letters and began to open them and read. As she read, she sensed a deep and sensitive love between brother and sister. He must have been older than she, Kristen thought, for his letters were protective and full of advice as only an older brother's could be. She could not adjust her negative thoughts of Morgan to the gentle man who existed in these letters.

Then she found what she wanted, a short letter that looked like what she wanted.

Charlotte:
I'm sending a friend to pick you up since I'm

involved at the moment. Be a good girl and come along without trouble. It will be worthwhile. See you soon.

Morgan

She took the note to the table and tore from it the top that held Charlotte's name; then she added her name to the top. Satisfied, she put it in the pocket of her dress and waited for Chris to come. She knew he would come soon and she planned on asking for his help.

It was less than an hour before she heard the sounds of his approach. The rap on the door hardly sounded before she opened it.

"Chris, good morning. I've been waiting for you."

"Well, that's an encouraging thought." He smiled. "Could I begin to believe you have been considering my offer?"

"Yes, I've been considering it. But there are many things we have to talk about first, things I would rather Toby did not hear."

"Sounds mysterious."

"No, not mysterious, just important. I'm afraid I will have to ask you to deceive him, and to do it without question."

"Without question?"

Her eyes held his pleadingly. "Chris," she said softly, "it's a matter of life and death. I can only go with you if you will do it my way."

Held by the look in her eyes, he was silent for a moment; then he said quietly, "Then you'll come home with me? Give me a chance to get to know you and for you to know me? You'll stay for a while?"

"Yes."

"Then 'tis done. What is it that you want me to do to

294

deceive the little mite?"

"Tell him that someone gave you this note to give to us, and that we're to come with you and stay at your home until we're sent for."

She handed him the folded note. "And I'm not to read it?"

"No."

"Jennifer—"

"Chris, within a month, I'll explain everything to you . . . everything. You'll understand then. Is that enough for now, Chris? My promise and my gratitude?"

"Yes, I guess it is." He took the note from her hand and put it in his pocket.

They were drinking tea together when Toby returned.

"Good morning, Toby, how is Falcon today?"

"Fine, sir, we had a great run on the beach, but I think Falcon's still a little afraid of the water. The waves got him once and he's been staying away from them since."

Chris laughed. "He's a smart puppy."

"You're here early," Toby said.

"I came directly here because I have to deliver a message to the two of you."

"A message?' Kristen asked innocently.

"Yes, I was told to bring it to you first thing today."

He handed the note to Kristen who opened it and read.

"What does it say?" Toby said. "Read it to me."

"It's from a friend of ours, Toby—the one who is caring for us. He wants us to go with Chris and stay at his home until he can come for us."

Doubt clouded Toby's eyes.

"Toby, this note was written by him. I know you cannot read yet, but do you recognize his writing?"

"I've seen it before."

Kristen handed the note to Toby who recognized

Morgan's handwriting. He had seen Morgan's papers many times.

"We're to go with you . . . where?"

"To my home, where you'll be safe from anyone, and safe from any more accidents that might be worse than the one you had."

"I think we should go, Toby. In the long run it might be the best thing for both of us. You'll be back on ship soon, and I . . . I'll be where I should be, too."

"If you think . . . I guess it's all right."

"I'm sure it will all work out, Toby," she said softly.

"I'll go and bring a buggy back. We can be on our way by lunch. It will only take a couple of days to get home. You'll both find you'll enjoy yourselves there. I'll see to it."

"I'll go get Falcon," Toby said without offering an answer to Chris's words.

He left the room quickly. Kristen, too, felt a surge of pain when the full import of her permanent separation from Morgan struck her.

"I . . . I'll be ready to leave as soon as you get back, Chris. Forgive me, please." She ran to the bedroom door and closed it behind her. Chris stood still in the quiet room. Something was drastically wrong and he had no idea what it was. At that moment his eyes fell to the note that had slipped from Toby's hand and now lay on the floor. He bent down and picked it up. He knew he had promised Jennifer he would not read it, but there had to be an answer to this mystery and he felt the note contained some of the answers to it.

He read the note quickly. At first, it meant nothing to him; then suddenly, the pieces of the puzzle began to fit.

The name Kristen was the first thing that registered. Of course! He remembered that there had been much confusion about the kidnapping of Jeffrey MacIntire's future wife—Kristen Seaford. After that it took him only minutes to realize the significance of the name signed at the bottom. . . . Morgan . . . Morgan . . . Kristen and the fact that she was under his care. There was no reason for Morgan to be hiding her unless he was . . . Captain Black.

There was a decision to be made, and it took him only a few minutes to make it. If Kristen wanted it this way, she must have a reason and he would not betray her secret. Quickly, he folded the note and put it in his pocket. He left the house and returned much later with a buggy. Soon they were on their way to Chris's home where he intended to wipe all trace of Kristen's troubles away and to make her forget any problems she had had before he'd met her, even if one of those troubles were his very close friend, Morgan Grayfield.

They stopped late that night at an inn called the Devil's Inn where they had a late supper. Chris was well aware of Toby's constant surveillance and he suggested Toby share a room with him. That did much to ease Toby's troubled thoughts.

The next morning, they were again on their way.

Chris made the trip for Kristen as easy as he could. Meanwhile he was considering how he would present her to his family. It was his choice to adhere to Kristen's story. She was Jennifer Nelson; she was a wealthy runaway who needed sanctuary from her uncle who was trying to rob her of her inheritance.

He could tell, as they stood outside the front door, that Kristen was extremely nervous. He took her hand and smiled at her.

"Don't forget, Jennifer, you'll find my family will be delighted to have you here and will try to make your stay as comfortable as possible."

True to his word, his parents made her more than welcome, especially his brother. They listened sympathetically to her story, and promised enthusiastically to help her in any way possible.

"If I can just get word to my attorney, I will have the means to acquire a place of my own. Until then, I must stay away from everyone. My . . . uncle must never find where I am."

"You needn't worry, my child," Chris's father said. "I will see that word is sent on the next ship. Until then, let us keep you here as our guest. After these two ruffians,"—he pointed to his sons—"you brighten our home."

Toby and Kristen were given rooms adjoining one another. Kristen was glad, for she had not really had an opportunity to talk to Toby alone. That night, when she was sure the rest of the house was asleep, she went to Toby, not in the least surprised to find him still awake.

"You can't sleep, Toby?"

"No. I don't like this place."

"These people have been very good to us."

"I know, but . . ."

"But what?"

"I don't understand. Why do they keep calling you Jennifer?"

"Because we don't want them to know who I really am. Word might leak out to Jeffrey MacIntire. They're protecting me, Toby, and right now I feel I need protection more than I ever have in my life before."

She counted on Toby's genuine affection for her and was rewarded by his hesitant smile.

"All right, but I hope the captain will be back soon. I don't belong here; I belong on the *Falcon* with Jeremy."

"Maybe . . . maybe I can help you. For now, try to

sleep, and try to be patient . . . please?"

"All right . . . Miss Kristen?"

"Yes?"

"We're . . . we're all still family? You, the captain, Jeremy, and me?"

Unable to answer his question, she bent and kissed him. "I love you, Toby, and I'm sure Jeremy and . . . Morgan do, too. Now, try to sleep. Good night."

"Good night."

He watched her leave the room and close the door behind her. Something was wrong and he didn't know what it was or how to handle it. He was too young to force her to tell him and he had no idea of how or where to find Jeremy or Morgan. He was afraid, and he could not put substance to the shadow of his fear. All he knew was that he would stay with Kristen and keep his eyes open. If Chris and his family were a threat to her he would try his best to protect her.


The next day, Kristen came down to breakfast. Chris's parents were the only two at the table.

"Good morning."

"Good morning." Chris's father rose politely until she was seated.

"Jennifer, I sent your message this morning so that it would be on the first ship out. Your lawyer should receive it within two weeks or so. Before the month is out we should have word from him."

"Mr. Miles, I cannot tell you how very grateful I am for all your help."

"You're quite welcome, my dear. I'm just sorry we couldn't do any more. Your uncle should be brought to the attention of the authorities. It is a dreadful thing for a man to frighten a child like you away from her family and friends."

"No, Mr. Miles, I don't want any more troubles. I just want to contact my lawyer. After that, I'll be able to care for myself."

"Well, you will be staying with us for as long as you like, and if there is anything you need, please don't hesitate to ask."

"Thank you."

Mr. Miles rose, and was about to leave the table when a butler appeared. He carried a silver tray on which rested a white envelope.

"A message has come for you, sir."

Mr. Miles took the message and tore the envelope open. He read rapidly, then smiled at Kristen.

"Jennifer, you said your lawyer was a Mr. Reginald Murkton?"

"Yes."

"Well I'm afraid we've wasted time. He is no longer in the colonies."

"Oh, no! Where is he?"

"Here in London."

"He's here?"

"Yes. It seems he's the Seafords' lawyer, too. You remember we told you about the young Seaford girl who was kidnapped?"

"Yes, I remember."

"Well, it seems he's come to see if he can do anything to help. He has offered an extremely large reward for the girl's return."

"Mr. Miles?"

"Yes?"

"Do you think you could get me an appointment to see him, or better still could someone deliver a letter to him from me?"

300

"But of course. Write the letter and I shall see it is delivered immediately."

Kristen hurried to her room. The thought of the presence of a dear friend, someone who knew her and would understand, someone who cared, almost made her weep in relief.

She wrote the letter quickly, not explaining all the details, but letting Reginald Murkton know she needed him desperately. She also told him the secret of her identity with a request that he keep it to himself, and she asked him if he could come to her at once.

When she returned, she handed the folded note to Mr. Miles, secure in the knowledge that he would never even consider opening it to read its contents.

For the balance of the morning, she was so tense she could hardly control herself. She watched from her bedroom window as the small closed carriage came up the drive, and when Mr. Murkton's arrival was announced, she asked him to be shown to the small sitting room that adjoined her bedroom so that they could talk in private.

When the door closed behind him, he looked at her with a gaze that combined shock and compassion.

"Kristen, my dear child," he said gently. This touch of sympathy and the presence of her one old friend brought tears to her eyes. He held out his arms to her and she ran to him to find herself enclosed in a warm paternal embrace.

An hour later, she stood by the window silently while Reginald sat nearby. As she had begun her story, he was by turns attentive, curious, and angry—especially at the knowledge that Morgan had deceived her then deserted her for a woman he knew was at least an adultress and possibly a murderess.

"It is such a terrible thing to believe. Are you sure

young Christopher is not just a little in love with you and is using your stepmother to turn you against Morgan?"

She turned from the window. "I wish it were so, but to Chris, I am Jennifer Nelson. I have no stepmother named Leslie Seaford, and Morgan is no more than a friend who gave me a place to hide. He has no reason to connect us."

"I'm sorry, child, I still think like an attorney. I still require proof against any man before I condemn him."

"Proof," she said softly; the silent tears in her voice made him realize the depth of the pain she felt. "Must he throw it in my face that I am a naïve fool? A child who trusted. Must I listen to his laughter when he admits how easy it was to use me as part of his revenge. Oh, God, did he hate Jeffrey so much that he could take everything I had to offer and destroy it? I loved him so much, I could not bear it. . . . I could not."

Reginald rose and went to her; he gently laid his hand on her shoulder. "Kristen, will you give him one last chance? Let us, you and I, prove to ourselves, one way or the other, his guilt. If he is guilty, I shall fight with you and help you with whatever you have in mind to do. You know that all you would really have to do is expose him as Captain Black, a pirate. All he has done is enough to see him hang, and I shall press forward your cause. No man can kidnap a prominent wealthy woman such as yourself and go unpunished. Any court would see him hang for what he has done. I'm sure Jeffrey MacIntire would be the first to take advantage of this situation."

"Hang!" she said, alarm clear in her voice. "I . . . I would not like to see any man hang. He has caused no one's death. No, I could not expose him."

"Then," he said gently, "you do still have a doubt in your heart about his guilt."

"Yes, I suppose I do."

"Well," he said softly, "suppose we try to find out. Suppose we give the man the benefit of the doubt until we see his guilt with our own eyes."

She nodded, knowing she sought any means to prove Morgan was innocent of this deceit.

"I shall look into the matter myself. When I find the opportune moment, I will come for you," he said.

Again she nodded, suddenly feeling very tired and afraid.

He patted her arm gently.

"Don't worry, Kristen, my dear, we shall get to the heart of this matter. In the meantime, you are safe. I personally feel that your stepmother is the one behind this. She is a cold and malicious woman who seeks your fortune. I'm waiting now for a letter from America to confirm some of my suspicions. When I heard that you had been abducted, I could do no less than come immediately to do all I could to get you back."

"I do thank you. I'm very grateful for your help and concern."

"You get some rest, and do not despair. Enjoy a few days of solitude here. I'm sure young Chris and his family want you to. They are charming people, and I feel young Chris would be quite willing for you to spend as much time as possible here."

"Chris is a very nice person. He has done a lot for me. I'm very grateful."

"Grateful, hmmm. Well, I must be going. I shall send you word of anything I find out."

"Thank you."

He kissed her cheek, and again patted her arm in a very fatherly fashion; then he was gone, and she was left with her conflicting thoughts. She hated Morgan, yet the thought of his death filled her with terror.

She tried her best to relax and enjoy the Miles family's protection, and they went out of their way to make her as comfortable as possible. Since she convinced them that she had to stay out of sight until her lawyer had arranged things, they confined everything they did to her and to the family.

She often rode with Chris and sometimes with both Chris and Blakely, enjoying their company and the fact that neither of them tried to pry into her thoughts. They sought only to make her laugh and forget the pressures that surrounded her.

A week later, she received a note from Reginald late in the afternoon.

I shall come for you after dinner. I have things to tell you and for you to see. We shall either disprove or confirm our suspicions.

Reginald

She informed the family only that she was going out with her lawyer. Then she waited anxiously for the hours to pass. When she stepped into his closed carriage, she was tense and nervous.

"You have found something?"

"Yes, I'm afraid so."

"Afraid?"

"It seems a lot of what Chris has said is true. Morgan Grayfield has been seeing a great deal of Leslie Seaford. Rumor has it they are having an affair. He is taking her out tonight. We shall see for ourselves." They drove to the Grayfield mansion, and positioned themselves across the road in a spot that would not be obvious, yet from which they could clearly see anyone coming and going.

The door of the mansion opened and Morgan appeared. Her breath caught as a tide of warm emotion washed over her. She could feel his presence from this distance. She watched him walk to the carriage. She remained silent as they followed. When the carriage arrived at its destination, Reginald whispered, "It's the MacIntire mansion."

"How very beautiful it is."

"Yes."

Morgan went to the door and was admitted. In less than half an hour, the door opened again and Morgan reappeared . . . with an exquisitely beautiful Leslie. Again Kristen could feel the dull pain that swept her as she saw Morgan's warm smile and his seemingly affectionate attention to Leslie.

That evening was an agony for Kristen because she thought Morgan and Leslie were sharing romantic hours. But the pain she felt as she watched them, in the shaded path, embrace and kiss passionately, was the worst. Tears blinded her eyes, and she felt as if she were utterly destroyed.

Now she knew. Morgan had hurt her beyond anything she could imagine. All that was left for her was the blackness of her world, and the burning center of it that whispered revenge . . . revenge.

# Nineteen

Morgan paced the floor of Jamie's study while Jeremy and Jamie watched him with worry in their eyes.

"Damn it, she can't just have walked away from there, and where's Toby? He wouldn't have gone without saying anything. You both know the boy. He's entirely too loyal to do that. Something's happened . . . but what? And who did it?"

"I've searched up and down the coast, and all around the area. There's no sign of either of them," Jeremy said.

"Jamie, can I have the use of one of your horses? Mine is exhausted."

"Where are you going?"

"To the lodge. There has to be some trace of her, and there has to be some reason for her to leave. It must be something serious for Toby to agree to leave. I've got to find some trace somehow."

"I'm going with you," Jamie said.

"And so am I," Jeremy quickly added. "If you find a trace you may be needing some help."

"It will take a couple of days to get there," Morgan said. "Jamie, I'll send a message from here to my parents so they won't be alarmed at another of my disappearances. Can you rouse someone to carry it?"

"Immediately," Jamie replied and left the room.

For several minutes, Jeremy and Morgan were silent.

Then Jeremy said softly, "Ye didn't get a chance to tell her who you really were or what you were about?"

"No."

"Maybe she found out on her own, and since ye weren't there to explain, she left."

"No, it couldn't be. Toby wouldn't have gone under such conditions."

"What could have happened?"

"I don't know! Damn it, I don't know, but I intend to find out. People cannot vanish from the face of the earth. Someone knows where they are and I'll turn this whole country upside down until I find them."

"What are ye afraid of, boy?"

"Someone might have happened along; they may have run into some serious difficulties, something they couldn't handle. Neither of them would have left without a word. God pity anyone who might have harmed either of them."

Jamie returned. "The horses are being saddled. I took a chance and wrote a note to your parents. It's on its way. I suggest we do the same. They're packing some food, we won't have to stop except to rest the horses."

"Good! Let's get moving," Morgan said. Within fifteen minutes, the three of them rode into the pale light of early dawn.

They pressed themselves and their horses to the limit of their endurance, and two days later they crossed the boundaries of Grayfield property. Very shortly after, they arrived at the lodge, which to Morgan seemed frighteningly alone and vacant.

He literally ran up the steps and threw open the door. All his senses told him that not only was the house empty, but it had been so for some time.

"Kristen," he murmured softly. He walked from room

to room seeing only traces of the fact that anyone had been there at all. Then he mounted the stairs. As he opened the first bedroom door, he came face-to-face with the family portrait he had long since forgotten. It was obvious Kristen had been searching about and had found it, for it sat facing the door, leaning against the chest whose lid stood open. Panic struck when he began to wonder what other family memories had been packed away here and forgotten, memories that would clearly tell her who and what he was.

He went to the chest and knelt in front of it. He could see the evidence that most of the boxes had been opened. He found the ones that contained the letters and remembered the affectionate correspondence between him and Charlotte anytime he was away. He cursed mildly as he rose knowing that his identity was clear for anyone to see here in this chest of memorabilia.

Now, he knew Kristen knew his name, but it did not account for her leaving, or even how she left. It also did not account for Toby's absence, for he was sure of Toby's affection and knew it would have taken something quite drastic for Toby's loyalty to be breached.

For five days, they searched the entire area for miles about. Morgan refused to think of anything other than finding Kristen, but after the fifth day, when they had covered the area for miles, he had to give up. Twice he had crossed the Miles property, but as fate would have it, each time the caretaker was away. The house, locked and quiet, led Morgan to believe it had no bearing on Kristen's disappearance. Finally, he had to give up the search completely. But he would not rest until he found the reason for her disappearance, until he again held her in his arms and felt the peace and security of her love. It was a morose and quiet group that rode back to London.

Morgan could not sleep and found it difficult to remember to eat. Day by day, his mind was involved only with Kristen, why she had gone, where she had gone, and where she was now. He checked every ship in port and those in nearby ports. He questioned every innkeeper and casual traveler he heard about, but it seemed as if the earth had swallowed up any trace of Kristen and Toby.

There was no way he could search openly. What reason would Lord Morgan Grayfield have to be searching for a woman he was not even supposed to know, a woman who had been kidnapped by a pirate?

One frustration followed another, and one night he wound up so totally drunk that he had to be carried home and put to bed.

He woke the next morning with a foul taste in his mouth and a pounding head that matched the persistent knocking upon his door.

"Come in!" he shouted angrily, then groaned as a wicked pain slashed through his brain. He rolled over and drew the covers over his head.

"Lord Grayfield, sir?" came the soft voice of his valet.

"What is it?" he growled.

"There is someone here to see you, sir."

"Who is it?"

"Capt. Owen MacGregor and his wife, sir."

At first neither the name nor the mention of a wife found its way into Morgan's mind. Then suddenly he pulled the covers down and looked at his valet.

"I'm not sure I heard you right, Michaels. I'm . . . I'm not feeling too well. Who did you say was here?"

"Captain MacGregor, sir."

"And . . . you did say he had his . . . wife with him?"

"Yes, sir. She is quite a lovely lady. I remember Miss MacIntire when she was only a small child."

"Go, Michaels, tell them I'll be down in a few minutes, as soon as I've dressed."

Michaels nodded and quietly left the room. Laboriously, Morgan rose from the bed. He tried to make himself as presentable as possible, a difficult task since he avoided looking in a mirror for he felt that he looked as badly as he felt. Gingerly, he made his way downstairs, and stood at the drawing-room door watching Owen and Jane who stood together by the large French doors, unaware he was watching them. The soft murmurs of their voices came to him.

"Owen."

Both of them turned toward him, and smiled as he walked toward them with both hands outstretched.

"Owen, Jane, it is good to see you two. Congratulations. I'm sorry I did not make it to the wedding."

"It is good to see you, too, Morgan," Jane replied. He was pleased to see all fear was gone from her eyes and she seemed to glow with an inner radiance that could only be labeled happiness. "I've a great deal to thank you for."

"No need for thanks, Jane," he replied as he brushed her cheek with a quick kiss. "You deserve all the happiness you can find."

"Well, I canna speak for Jane, but ye've given me all the happiness a man can hope for," Owen replied, and although he held the smile on his face, he was surprised at the tense, tired look in Morgan's eyes.

"You've had a long trip. You're not planning on leaving here right now?"

"We . . . we are going to see my brother," Jane said quietly.

"Well, you needn't go right now. Why not relax for a while and have dinner with us. Then I'll personally order my buggy and take you there."

310

"That's not necessary, Morgan," Jane said quickly. "I don't want you to go to any more trouble for me."

Morgan grinned, and the humor in his eyes was so obvious that both Jane and Owen smiled back.

"It's no trouble, Jane. I should like very much to be there when you tell your brother that you've married by your own choice and not his."

When Jane did not answer he said, "You're still not afraid of him are you?"

Jane smiled up into Owen's intent eyes. He put his arm about her shoulder and drew her close.

"No, Morgan," she replied softly, "I am no longer afraid of anything, and especially my brother. His days of bringing me fear are over. Now he is just an obstacle I have to surmount. I will claim what our parents left to me, not because we need it—for Owen does not want it— but to prove to him he can no longer take from me what is rightfully mine."

Morgan chuckled. "I'm proud of you, Jane, and now I insist on coming along. I should hate to miss this confrontation."

Morgan sent for a young maid who escorted Jane to a room where she could refresh herself and prepare for dinner. When the door had closed behind her, Owen turned to Morgan, the smile in his eyes gone, replaced by a clouded look of worry. "Morgan, what's gone wrong? Ye look like the devil. What's been goin' on since I've been gone? Did ye and the young lass get married? Surely nothin's happened to her?"

Morgan went to a small table and poured them both a rather stiff drink. Owen was surprised to see that Morgan's hand trembled slightly as he handed him the drink. He was even more shocked to see Morgan gulp his down and reach for another.

"Sit down, Owen. I think it will be better not to be standing when I tell you what this stupid arrogant fool has managed to accomplish," Morgan said bitterly.

Owen sat; he sipped his drink and watched Morgan slump into the chair opposite him. "What is it, Morgan?" he repeated gently.

Morgan leaned forward resting his elbows on his knees. He held the glass of whiskey between his hands and gazed at the amber liquid. Then, in a quiet voice, he began to talk. He could not look at Owen as he spoke; yet he could feel Owen's eyes on him. He continued on until the story was finished and he had told of his agonizing search for Kristen. When he finished speaking he looked up expecting to see Owen's face filled with anger and disgust. Instead he saw compassion and pain.

"Damn it, Owen," he said, "for the first time in my life I don't know what to do or where to turn."

"I canna believe the lass vanished into thin air. Someone must have been there. The only question is who, and why she and Toby would have trusted 'em enough to go wi' 'em. I'll do all I can to help ye, lad. I've a full crew and they can go on makin' an all-out search along the coast. You and I will keep searchin' here. There has to be some word or sign ye may have overlooked. We'll find it together."

"I'm grateful for your help, Owen."

"I dinna want to hear ye say gratitude, Morgan. Ye're responsible for givin' me the best thing in my life. I'll be owin' ye forever for my Jane. Let us be about dinner; then Jane and I can care for the business of her brother. Once that's done, I'll be joinin' the search. We'll find 'em if we have to turn the city inside out."

They finished their drinks, and by that time, Jane returned. The three of them were together talking when

312

Morgan's parents came home. They were surprised to find Owen and Jane there, and even more so to hear that they were married. She was asked many questions which she tried to answer as truthfully as she possibly could. They were shocked to hear of Jane's treatment at the hands of her brother. They were also pleased, from their knowledge of Owen, to know he had put a stop to it. Both of Morgan's parents wanted to go with them to face Jeffrey, but both Owen and Jane said they preferred to meet him first with only Morgan along. And less than an hour later these three found themselves in a carriage heading for the MacIntire mansion.

When the buggy stopped in front of her home, Jane sat for a few minutes and looked at it. That it was extraordinarily beautiful there was no doubt, but for her it held the most intensely painful memories. Before her parents died, she had been a happy child there, but since their deaths, she had lived in fear and misery. Now as she gazed at this house, she felt a sense of peace and release. She would never live in such fear again and she felt a deep gratitude for the fates that had sent her into Owen's arms. She turned to look at him and he smiled, knowing her thoughts as well as she did.

They walked to the door and Owen knocked firmly and forcefully. His behavior made Jane and Morgan aware that Owen intended to put up with no arguments or trouble from Jeffrey MacIntire.

When the door was opened, the butler looked at them coolly for a moment; then he recognized Jane and his face broke into a broad and happy smile.

"Miss Jane! It is so good to see you again. We had feared you would never return."

"Thank you, Charles."

"This place has not been the same without you. There

313

are many here who will be glad to see you back."

"Is my brother home, Charles?"

"Yes, miss."

"Would you tell him"—Jane smiled—"that Mr. and Mrs. Owen MacGregor would like to speak to him?"

"Mrs. . . ." Charles's grin grew even broader as it touched on Owen, taking in his immense size and his quiet determined look. "I should be delighted to inform him, miss, and may I say congratulations. I'm happy to know you are happy and have a new future. As I said before, there are many here who will be overjoyed to know."

Jane chuckled as Charles went rapidly up the steps to take the news to Jeffrey.

"Charles seems to be looking forward to giving Jeffrey the news."

Morgan's laugh answered hers. "He wants to be the first to see the expression on his face when he gets such disappointing news. You've ruined some of his best laid plans, Jane."

"I know."

Before anyone else could speak, a young maid came rapidly down the steps. Her eyes sparkled with happiness and she was smiling. She came straight to Jane.

"Oh, Miss Jane, I'm so happy to see you. We've all been so worried about you since you left. It is good to see you are well."

"I am well, and I want you to meet my husband, Capt. Owen MacGregor. Owen, Marie has been my personal maid and very dear friend for many years. She was the one who helped me the night I left here. I'm grateful to you, Marie."

"As I am," Owen said. "If ye should ever need anything, ye must not hesitate to call on us."

"Thank you, sir, but it was a pleasure to do something for Miss Jane; she was always kind and generous to all of us. She deserves all the happiness she can find after . . ." She hesitated and a fluttering look of fear crossed her face as a heavy foot fell on the steps. Owen was again amazed at the emotions this man created in the people around him.

Jeffrey stood leaning against the mantelpiece in the bedroom of Leslie Seaford. Sipping a glass of wine and smiling at her, he enjoyed her enticing, half-dressed state as she sat before her mirror and brushed her hair. She returned his smile in the mirror. They had just enjoyed a passionate afternoon in the soft warmth of her bed.

"You have had no word of Kristen since the ransom was delivered," she said. "I do not think the man ever intends to return her."

"It is strange. All the times he has attacked my ships, he always, from the accounts I've heard, seemed to be careful not to harm anyone, as if he did not want blood on his hands. I cannot see him killing her."

She rose from the seat and walked toward him, an amused glow in her eyes. "My dear Jeffrey," she said, amusement in her voice, "I really do not believe it is her death he desires. From his description he is a handsome virile man. I'm sure he has already . . . found . . . other ways to amuse himself besides counting her money."

"The bastard!"

"Hardly. He has what he wants; let him keep her. If she never returns, we have the Seaford fortune to spend."

She put her arms about his neck and lightly touched her lips to his, gently caressing his firm mouth with her tongue. He slid his arms about her waist.

315

"Think of it, Jeffrey, you have all the money that would have gone to your sister. Since you have found someone to . . . care for her. You did, didn't you?"

"I imagine, by this time, Jane is safely deposited in the depths of the ocean. They had their orders. When they retrieved her from what she thought was a safe hideaway, they were to make sure she did not survive the journey home. And I still have to find some way to thank our Captain MacGregor. Do not worry, I shall find something special for him, and when I do, he will know who and why."

"In the meantime, I think you should help me to transfer all of Kristen's wealth here, in my name. Then we shall be able to enjoy it most thoroughly."

"First, I am going to my lawyer and my bank today and declare Jane dead. Then all the monies our parents left her will be mine. After that we can see to the transfer of Kristen's money. From now on, my dear Leslie, we will have nothing to worry about."

Her deep throaty chuckle sounded softly in the room as her parted lips accepted his.

He tightened his arms about her and enjoyed the pleasure of her soft willing body in his arms; but only for a few moments, for a knock sounded on the door.

Leslie smiled as she left his arms and he scowled darkly at the door. He waited for Leslie to don a robe, then he snapped a reply as the second knock sounded.

"Come in! Come in!"

The door opened and the butler came in. He was doing his best to contain the real and tremendously joyful pleasure he was feeling at breaking the news of Jane's return to Jeffrey.

Although Jane had been loved and tentatively protected by all the servants, Jeffrey was just as thoroughly hated. It was the servants of their parents who had often stood between Jeffrey and Jane when he was in his most vindictive moods. Quietly and surreptitiously, they had done what they could to ease Jane's pain.

"Well!" Jeffrey said in a cold arrogant voice. "What is it?"

"We have guests, sir."

"Guests?"

"Yes, Lord Grayfield . . . Captain MacGregor and . . ."

"And?"

"Miss Jane has come home, sir."

Both of them stood in stunned silence and gazed at him with dark disbelieving eyes.

"Oh, I'm sorry, sir, I made a mistake."

"What?" Jeffrey said hoarsely.

"It isn't Miss Jane any longer, sir. It's Mrs. MacGregor. It seems she married the captain several weeks ago."

A soft gurgled murmur of restrained fury emanated from Jeffrey, and he saw the amused gleam of contempt in the butler's eyes as he turned away. Charles closed the door softly behind him before he let a grin touch his lips. A glow of triumphant pleasure straightened his shoulders as he walked down the hall.

"Jeffrey!"

"Be quiet," Jeffrey snapped. "Damn. . . . Damn . . ." he muttered. "Those fools will pay for this. How could they have been so stupid as to let her slip through their fingers? I shall see they pay dearly for that mistake."

"It does no good to threaten now. What will you do? You must turn her money over to her if she is married."

"I cannot."

"You've reached into her money already?"

"The baubles and beautiful clothes you like are

317

quite expensive."

"Not to mention your gambling and the deals you've invested in. What are you going to do?"

"For the moment, play along. I shall be a brother who is pleased to have his sister back and overjoyed at her good fortune. Why, I may even go so far as to plan a party to celebrate her safe return."

She chuckled and he smiled in return.

"Now, I shall go down and welcome them back."

He brushed another light kiss across her lips, then left the room. Quickly, Leslie dressed and prepared to go down to join them. It was a performance she did not want to miss, and she wanted to see Morgan Grayfield again.

Jeffrey stood at the top of the steps watching the group that stood unaware below him. Seeing Jane's happy face and hearing the words of welcome from the young maid, so enraged him that he could no longer hesitate. Firmly, he began to descend, aware that all eyes were directed toward him as he started down. He put a smile on his face and walked to meet them.

"Jane," he said as he stopped beside her. "I was afraid I would never see you again. What made you run away without saying a thing to me? I have been quite worried."

But this time Jane possessed enough courage to put aside this pretended brotherly solicitation.

"I'm sorry I ran Jeffrey, but your intention for my future was a thing I could not face."

"My intention was only to make you a good marriage that would protect you and your future. A marriage to a wealthy man is certainly not a bad thing to want for you, is it? I'm sure there are many who would marry you for your wealth."

Both Owen and Morgan stiffened. If he did not know yet that Owen and Jane were married, that was one thing, but if he did, it was an obvious blow to Owen.

"But you see, Jeffrey," she said softly as she slipped her hand into Owen's, "Owen and I are married, very happily married. I am happier now than I've ever been in my life. I wanted you to know. I also wanted you to know that I am no longer the little girl who was so very frightened of you. I am safe and secure and ready to build my own life—a life I expect to spend with Owen. We will take what belongs to me from our parents and we will build our own life."

Jeffrey turned to Owen; his reaction of surprise was expressed only in his facial expression. It might fool Jane, but the cold hard look in his eyes did not escape either Owen or Morgan.

"Married, well I am surprised. But I am pleased." He held out his hand to Owen who could do no less than take it. "Congratulations. Since I was not present at the wedding then I insist on having a party. We must invite all of our friends. After all, it is not every day that a MacIntire marries."

"That is a decision that is up to Jane," Owen said. "But for all intents and purposes, we've already had a wedding party. 'Tis only to inform ye of that and other things that we've come at all."

"What other things?"

"That Jane is safely wed to me, and that I wouldna stand by and let any harm come to her . . . not any harm. We've come home to inform ye of the wedding and to let Jane take what belongs to her."

"Money?" Jeffrey sneered.

"Jeffrey MacIntire," Owen said coldly, his eyes glowing a dangerous icy green, "I will say this only once. I wouldna touch a drop of Jane's money, but I wouldna let it fall into the hands of another. What she does wi' her money is her own affair. But 'tis hers. From what I understand your parents wanted it so."

Jeffrey realized Owen was a formidable foe he could not frighten.

"Her parents," he replied. "Of course, it will take some time to get the affairs in order and turn the money over to her. In the meantime I insist on a party. All the friends she has known before will be anxious to meet you."

Owen turned to Jane with questioning eyes.

"It's all right, Owen. I don't mind. I imagine there are people, friends of our family, who would like to meet you, and I would be proud and pleased to show you off just a little."

"Good, now come in and let me get you a drink. You will be staying here?"

"No," Jane said quickly. "I mean . . ."

"She means," Morgan said, "that I have already asked Owen to be my guest and he has agreed."

"I see," Jeffrey said quietly; yet anger was in his eyes.

"In fact," Morgan went on, "I believe my parents have invited a few friends in tonight to wish the newlyweds well. We'll be expected back soon." Morgan's eyes sparkled with malicious humor. "We only came over because Jane knew you were worried about her and would be most anxious to welcome both her and her husband home."

"Yes," Jeffrey said through gritted teeth. "I am pleased to know you are safe, Jane. I shall call tomorrow and tell you of the plans for the party."

"Good," Morgan replied. "I believe Owen and Jane will be on their way back to Scotland as soon as the money can be transferred."

"I will come over tomorrow," Jeffrey said stiffly, "but

I have warned you it might take some time to get the affairs in order."

"Oh!" Morgan replied mildly. "If you need any help, I'm sure my attorney would be glad to give you any assistance you might need to expedite the matter."

The flush of anger that Jeffrey could hardly contain left him momentarily speechless.

"There isna any problem about Jane's inheritance, is there?" Owen smiled.

"Of course not! Her . . . our parents made it quite clear in their will. Jane, you must understand; it is not a simple matter to do this. You must give me enough time to prepare everything."

"How long, Jeffrey?" she asked, and he was stilled by the firm coolness in her voice. It was obvious Owen's influence had already begun.

"I'm not sure. I suppose a few weeks. In the meantime, as I suggested, we will have a party to welcome you both home. I also want you to meet someone."

"Who?"

"Mrs. Leslie Seaford. She is Kristen's stepmother. It has been quite difficult for us both since Kristen's loss."

"Loss!" Morgan said in a quiet voice. "You've given up searching for her?"

"The ransom has been delivered, quite some time ago. It is obvious, although it brings me great pain to say it, that Kristen is lost to us all. He had no intention of returning her to us from the beginning. I . . . I hate to imagine what has happened to her."

"You think she's dead?"

"Or worse. How does one know what terrible things those villains could have done to her? Especially their leader. That blood-thirsty scoundrel has probably taken the most horrible advantage of her."

"Blood-thirsty!" Morgan echoed, wicked humor again prevalent in his eyes. "I have not heard of him killing anyone. I doubt, since he has killed no man, he would start with a defenseless woman."

"I was certainly not speaking of her death," Jeffrey replied. "I'm afraid it might be worse than that for her. I regret it deeply, but I feel we will never see Kristen again . . . or if we do, it will be under circumstances of such shame that she will never be able to remain in society."

Morgan knew a fury then that matched his misery and despair. Kristen, he thought, my love, where are you now? At that moment, he would have liked nothing better than to feel a sword in his hand, a sword which he would have slid neatly between the ribs of the arrogant man before him.

"In other words," he said in a quiet voice, "if she is found safe, she is no longer fit to be the wife of Jeffrey MacIntire?"

"Well, a MacIntire can hardly marry a . . . girl who has lived with pirates all this time. Society would never accept such a thing."

"I see. Maybe she will choose a path of her own."

"Yes, her stepmother suggested something of the sort the other day. A quiet place, a convent, maybe, where she can feel safe."

"Were you speaking of me, Jeffrey?"

They all looked up as Leslie came down the stairs. Her beauty, as always, captivated all present. Morgan admired it abstractly, for he knew now what was happening. His desperation to find Kristen and save her from their destructive power was so draining that it left him weak and angry.

Leslie was introduced to Owen and Jane and she was told of the marriage and the party Jeffrey planned as if he were the author of both.

Morgan was aware that Owen had been silently contemplating Jeffrey for some time. He knew there were violently active thoughts behind Owen's unreadable face, and he wondered just what they were. His thoughts were interrupted when he heard Jane make excuses so that they could leave. As the three of them turned to the door, Leslie moved away from Jeffrey.

"Morgan, may I speak to you for a moment?" she said. He went to her.

"I have missed you on our rides."

"I'm sorry, I've been quite busy."

"Would you like to come over tomorrow? I have something I must tell you. Jeffrey will be away. It's important."

"Of course, Leslie."

"About one?"

"Yes."

He returned to Jane's side and the three of them left. Once inside the carriage Jane laid her head against Owen's shoulder.

"Oh, I'm glad that is over. I was afraid it would not be so easy."

"I'm not sure of either thing," Owen said.

"What?"

"That it was easy, or that it is over."

"What's on your mind, Owen?" Morgan questioned.

"That I dinna like the man in the first place, that I think he's a devious spider that will sting when ye least expect it. And that there's somethin' a-goin' on between those two that amounts to more than we thought. There

323

was somethin' he said."

Then they became silent and Morgan's thought slipped away.

Kristen, he thought agonizingly, source of love such as I had never known before.

He could still feel her soft warmth against him and the touch of her mouth against his. The longing to reach out and find her captured his mind and soul and his mind was filled with thoughts of her. He could feel her presence as if she were beside him.

Kristen . . . where are you now? he thought. I don't want to lose you, I could not stand it. One sign, one message . . . Kristen . . . my love.

# Twenty

Owen and Morgan sat alone in the library that night, sharing a last drink of brandy. Owen could sense Morgan's anger and pain, for he knew how he would feel if Jane were gone and he had no way to find her.

The firelight flickered across Morgan's face and Owen, who knew him so well, could see the thoughts that lingered in his eyes. He had not spoken for some time, his thoughts entangled in the mystery of where Kristen was at the moment, and why neither she nor Toby had left him any kind of a message.

"What are your plans now, Morgan?"

"It is impossible for Morgan Grayfield to make too many inquiries, but Captain Black may have more outlets."

"Aye, so might Captain MacGregor. I was raised on the sea, Morgan. I probably know more renegades, sea rats, and other sources of information than even Captain Black does. Startin' tomorrow, we'll spread a web, offer a large reward. Ye'll be surprised what some gold can do to loosen some tongues."

"I've got to find them, Owen. I have a feeling she's in trouble, that she might need my help. It is a slight need compared to mine for her. I love her, Owen, I can't lose her."

"Aye," Owen said gently. "I know how ye feel. I will

begin with the mornin' light. I've a few alleys to investigate on me own."

"Jeffrey MacIntire?"

"Aye, it's come to me—what he said that struck a strange note. It's a thing I intend to look into."

"What was it?"

"He kept referrin' to Jane's parents as 'her parents.'"

"I don't understand."

"It's as if they were hers . . . not his."

"You think . . . ?"

"I think that man has more secrets we should know than just his desire to wed a rich girl and marry off his sister. He seems the kind of man to which money and social standin' means everything."

"You've labeled him well. God, Owen, if he's not Jane's . . ."

"Aye . . . he'd want to see her put away safely somewhere or better yet, dead."

"He's an evil that needs to be purged. I wish I could challenge him outright, but he's well protected and I've no reason."

"We need to sit back quietly and do some investigating on our own. Spread about a little money, look into the shadows of his life."

"Yes, we'll do that. But I think it's time Captain Black began a little more harassment. I've managed to make his life uncomfortable on the sea. Now, I think it's time I used other means."

"You have some plans?"

"Tentative ones. I'll work them out. In the meantime, my first priority is to find Kristen."

"Well, we will start in the mornin'."

"Yes."

"I'm going to bed." Owen rose and set his glass aside.

He went to Morgan's side and rested his hand on Morgan's shoulder. "I know how ye love the lass, Morgan. We'll leave no stone unturned to find her. But ye'll be doin' her no good if ye fret yourself until ye lose control. Put aside that brandy and get some rest. Ye've a lot of friends, Morgan, and we'll all be glad to help ye."

Morgan smiled. "Yes, you're right, Owen. I'll be of no help to her like this. Thanks, friend, I'm all right. I'll be going to bed soon."

Owen nodded in satisfaction, and left the room. He climbed the stairs to the bedroom. When he opened the door, he was surprised to see Jane curled up in a chair by the fireplace. She rose as he came into the room.

He stood by the door a few minutes, just absorbing the pale fragile beauty of her. Silhouetted against the glow of the fire, her body was outlined through the thin gown she wore. Her unbound dark hair fell about her, shiny and bright from recent brushing.

"I'm not complainin' about the reception, my love," he said gently, "but why are ye not abed?"

"That bed is too big and too lonely without you, Owen. It's cold. I would have your arms about me to warm it."

He went to her side and looked down into her gold-brown eyes, warm and inviting. Gently, he caressed the softness of her hair; then slowly he drew her into the circle of his arms. He held her silently for a moment, savoring her contentment and the way she clung to him. Her arms encircled his waist and her head rested against his broad chest.

"Oh, Owen you can never know the peace you've given me. Maybe I did not understand myself the need I had for you until we came home and felt secure."

"Janie," he said as he drew her with him to the chair. She curled upon his lap like a contented kitten. "I want

327

to ask ye some questions before my mind gets tangled in the wantin' of ye."

"What questions?"

"What do ye remember of your childhood days and Jeffrey?"

"Fear . . . unhappiness . . . a desire to run away. Is that what you mean?"

"No . . . I mean . . . what are your first memories of your brother?"

For a time she remained silent as she searched backward in time.

"First memory . . . ? It's funny, but I don't remember Jeffrey too well before I was eight or nine. I think he was away a lot. He was often visiting at Aunt Caroline's."

"Tell me about Aunt Caroline."

"Aunt Caroline was my mother's sister. She was a young widow and from what I understood before it was hushed, she was quite wild. One doesn't hear such things when one is eight. After Mother and Father died, I never heard much about Aunt Caroline. In fact," she said slowly, "I don't remember much about Aunt Caroline at all after Jeffrey came home. She must have died also."

He was caressing her hair with one hand while his other began a light exploration that brought a soft murmured sigh from her.

"Where did your Aunt Caroline live?"

"She lived near the Scottish border in a small town called Brawford. I remember, for the only time I ever visited there I was surprised at Aunt Caroline's fine home compared with all the rest of the poor homes about. I even remember Aunt Caroline, for many remarked about how much she looked like mother and how much I looked like the both of them."

"Did Jeffrey ever mention your aunt?"

"No," she said as she sat up and looked down into Owen's eyes. "Owen, why are you asking all these questions?"

The last thing he wanted to do was tell Jane of his suspicions. Instead he put his hands on each side of her face and drew her mouth to his. "Only to know ye better, my love. But it's not important. This is," he said softly as his mouth slanted across hers, forcing her lips apart. Slowly, expertly, he washed from her mind every thought but those of him and the warm flood of love that pulsed through her. Her arms circled his neck and she lay against him.

When his lips released hers there were no words left to be said. Effortlessly, he rose from the chair lifting her with him. His lips traced a path down her slender throat and found the soft valley between her breasts. As she clung to him, he felt the tremble of desire that shook her.

He let her feet slide to the floor, but held her to him with one arm. Sure fingers found the hooks to her gown and released them; it fell unheeded to the floor. She was lost to the magic of the gentle hands that caressed her and drew her firmly against him letting her feel the urgent need that warmed them both.

He took her by the shoulders and held her away from him; then he took two steps backward. He gazed at her pale beauty glowing in the light of the fire. Her cheeks blushed pink, but her eyes held his. Her body, small and slim, held him with its miniature perfection. High, taut breasts that filled the cup of his hand, a tiny waist that curved into slim rounded hips. The dark cloud of her hair framed a face alight with passion. Her half-closed eyes and slightly parted lips spoke eloquently to him of her desire.

He began to throw aside the clothes that restricted him

329

and soon they stood inches from each other, drawn together by a mutual fire that inflamed them.

She, too, gloried in the knowing of him, and in his large muscular body, broad of shoulder, narrow of waist. She could feel the tense strength of him and she submerged herself in it, letting it enfold her like a protective shield.

"Janie, love," he whispered as he reached out and put his hands on her hips, slowly drawing her to him until taut nipples touched the brawny furry chest.

Her slim fingers, touching lightly, slid up his arms. Soft arms encircled his neck and slowly he bent his head and tasted her sweet giving lips. His tongue explored their soft recesses, enticing hers to explore as he did. His mouth escaped her seeking one, to touch her cheeks, eyes, throat, and then the soft rise of her breasts; it captured a tender peak, then slid down to her slim waist. He knelt before her and pressed soft light kisses against the softness of her belly. He heard her gasp in surprised shock as his lips ventured farther and farther discovering the sweet urgent center of her need. He heard her moan softly in pleasure as he drew her even closer. Unaware of anything but him, she caressed his thick hair that tangled waywardly in her fingers.

He rose slowly and lifted her in his arms, holding her close against him. She rested her head on his shoulder and pressed her warm lips to the pulse that beat wildly in his neck. A few quick steps took him to the bed. He did not lay her on it, but let himself fall back against it carrying her with him. Her long silken hair fell about him as his hunger exploded into a consuming fire, and his lips again sought hers.

Her world careened out of control. There was nothing in existence but Owen. Her heart sang Owen, and her body sought his with every sense she possessed. Words of love and encouragement were whispered softly. And she felt the strength of him as he turned, pulling her beneath him.

He could bear the sweet agony of his need no longer, and he buried himself deep within her as a soft groan told her of his deep pleasure.

Her flame-engulfed body rose to meet his, and her hands slid from the heavy muscles of his shoulders, down the curve of his back until they rested on his hips urging him to seek the very depths of her. And seek he did, his body moving with slow powerful strokes until it nearly drove her to madness. The world seemed to spin in a kaleidoscope of colors and warmth as they surrendered joyously to one another in a blazing fiery completion that left them weak and clinging to one another as if there were nothing beyond them.

She nestled against him, and they lay entwined until they could bring their thoughts and their breathing into some semblance of control.

His earlier questions had completely left his mind so their whispered words before they slept were only of their love for each other and of their plans for a future together.

If the night was a deep joy and pleasure for Owen and Jane, it was the complete opposite for Morgan. It was a hell. He mounted the stairs with the brandy bottle and an empty glass. He poured a drink and sipped it while he prepared for bed. But sleep was not to be so easy.

He lay on his back and looked up at the ceiling. In his mind, gray clouded eyes appeared in the mist of an ethereal face . . . Kristen. She smiled, and her golden hair blossomed about her. She laughed and her breeze-touched hair blew in whispery strands across her face.

331

Her soft, moist inviting lips called to him.

Bed was impossible. He rose, poured another drink, and stood by the window. He drew the curtains aside and looked out. Gray-white clouds passed along a dark sky. The moon sent pale beams of light to touch them. In the mist of the clouds she came again. This time she stood before him, his Kristen from the island in the outlandishly seductive costume he had forced on her. Her feet were bare and her unbound hair drifted about her. She wavered and faded before him. "Morgan." Her lips whispered his name. His hand clenched the curtain as he saw tears streak her face. She seemed to be calling for him in desperation. Sweat touched his brow and the hand with which he held the glass gripped it until his knuckles were white.

A multitude of thoughts crowded his mind. They had both been swimming and drowned. No! his mind screamed. But following came other even more unwelcome thoughts. The worst of all was that they had chosen to go away with someone else. It burned into his mind and he spoke aloud without even realizing it.

"You're mine, Kristen, and I'll find you wherever you are. You're mine and no one walking the face of this earth will take you away from me. I'll find you . . . I'll find you."

Several miles away, in the Miles mansion, Kristen, too, stood by a window looking out into the mist-shrouded night. Sleep was impossible, for it opened the door to unwelcome dreams of Morgan, dreams she did not have the strength to resist. In these dreams she was again in the warmth and safety of his arms, accepting the magic touch of his lips on hers, experiencing a need she could not face. The only word that always surfaced in her mind escaped her lips in a soft whisper as warm tears slipped unheeded down her cheeks. "Why, Morgan . . . why?"

Two others were awake in these dark midnight hours. In the library of Jeffrey's home, he and Leslie sat in conversation.

"It is obvious the situation with Kristen is no longer our problem," Jeffrey said. "You can see he has no intention of ever sending her back. I would be the first to admit the man has excellent taste. She was a lush little piece."

"May he enjoy her for a long, long time." Leslie smiled as she raised her glass to him.

Jeffrey chuckled and went to her. Bending forward, he braced both hands on the arms of her chair and kissed her firmly and lingeringly.

When he lifted his lips from hers, she looked at him closely.

"But something else is wrong; what is it Jeffrey?"

"Owen MacGregor."

"Ummm. What do you intend to do about him?"

"I certainly am not going to hand over all that belongs to Jane to him. Once I have him out of the way, Jane will again be in my control."

"You mean to kill him?"

"Of course; what other path would you suggest?"

"How?"

"Leave that to me. I'll arrange for the departure of one Owen MacGregor . . . soon. I did not work all these years to get complete control of Jane to have this renegade sea captain spoil all my plans."

He walked to the fireplace and stood contemplating the glowing embers.

"No," he said softly, "I shall eliminate Captain

MacGregor. When I do, Jane will understand my anger. She will pay dearly for her attempt to stop me. That spoiled bitch will never stand in my way again."

"You intend to do away with her, too?" Leslie asked softly.

"In time, but not before I show her who is master here. They thought to cut me away; they thought to leave her everything. Well it will be mine, and she will taste a touch of revenge that will crush her."

"They?"

He looked at her startled. "What?"

"You said they . . . who are they?"

Before the words were out of her mouth she regretted them. Never before had she seen such a cold look of intense hatred in Jeffrey's eyes. He came to her and grasped her arm. With a quick jerk, he pulled her from the chair and bound her against him in a grip that almost crushed her. She gasped and looked up into his eyes. For the first time in her life, Leslie Seaford had met her match; for the first time in her life, she felt the light touch of fear.

"Do not interfere in my affairs, Leslie, my love," he said in a deceptively soft voice. "Leave this to me. Soon we will possess both fortunes, a wealth you cannot even imagine. Until then, do not meddle; it might prove to be unhealthy."

She had to calm him. While her mind calculated ways to find out what intense secret this man held, she smiled seductively and, twining her arms about his neck, molded her body to his.

"Jeffrey, let us forget Jane and all the others for tonight. I'll not pry again. I know how well you will care for all the ah . . . matters. For tonight, let us just enjoy each other."

She drew his head down to hers and kissed him. His mouth began to warm and to possess hers so she let herself enjoy him. It was well for her peace of mind that she could not read his thoughts, for they had touched lightly on the value of Leslie and how long he would need her to complete his plans. He knew then that Leslie Seaford was an expendable commodity. She alone knew the most about him, and Jeffrey MacIntire was not one to leave an unbound end that could unravel his secrets.

Owen lay still, listening to Jane's slow even breathing. Then gently, he eased himself from the bed. He went to the desk and took paper from it. Then he sat down, took the quill in his hand, dipped it into the ink, and began to write a letter that he would send to his family in Scotland. He thought carefully of his words as he looked across the room at the slim form of his beloved Jane beneath the covers and at her dark hair spread over his pillow. Setting his thoughts in order, he began to write.

An hour later, satisfied with what he had done, he folded the paper, applied hot wax, and impressed in it a seal from a ring he wore. He knew his brothers would recognize this seal and honor immediately his call for help.

The fire had burned low by the time he was finished and he was thoroughly chilled. He went back to the bed and slid beneath the covers. Jane stirred and came half-awake.

"Owen," she whispered. "You've been up. You're cold."

He chuckled as he drew her warmth into his arms and lightly tasted her warm lips. "Aye, I'm cold, lass," he whispered as he began to caress her. "Warm me, my love. Warm me as only ye can."

And together they fled again to their own quiet sanctuary of peace and love.

Jeremy had returned to the Devil's Inn to wait for any word of Morgan's plans. He sat nursing a tankard of ale and musing on the unwelcome thought that they had somehow overlooked something in their search for Kristen. He felt that the lodge still held some trace, some find thread of evidence that would tell, not only where she had gone . . . but why.

He finally found his way to bed, but in his mind was the determined thought that he would return the following morning and search again for some elusive clue that might reunite Morgan and Kristen. How well he could read the misery in his captain's eyes, and feel the need that existed in him to find the woman he loved and to seek the reason why she had run from him.

Morning found him rising with the sun, and on his way back to the lodge on the horse he had borrowed. He arrived at the lodge, tied his horse, and began a thorough search that netted him no results, yet it left him with the tense expectant feeling that he was missing something right under his nose.

Finally, after hours of searching, he gave up and sat on the porch. Then he thought of the Mileses' lodge and decided as a last resort to ride there and look it over again.

He did so, and when he arrived at the Miles lodge, he thought it was as deserted as Morgan's had been, but after he had been there a few minutes, he heard a door at the back of the house slam and heavy footsteps cross the floor to the door where he stood. Both Jeremy and the caretaker were surprised to see one another.

"Eh, what are ye doin' here? This is private property. 'Tis the Mileses' huntin' lodge. Ye're trespassin'."

336

"I'm sorry, I didn't mean to trespass. I'm searchin' for someone."

"Who be ye searchin' for?"

"A young girl, pretty, gold hair and gray eyes. She was stayin' at the Grayfields'. Have ye seen any sign of her or of any strangers here about?"

"Aye, that might be the girl that young Christopher found, the one he got the doctor for."

"Doctor?" Jeremy said in alarm. "Was the girl hurt? Is she all right? Where is she?"

"Nay, the girl wasn't hurt. 'Twas the lad was with her. It seems he had an accident, fell from the rocks and nearly split his head."

"Is he dead?"

"Nay, young Christopher had the doctor for him. They got him on his feet all right. Then young Chris took them home with him."

"Took them home?" Jeremy said softly. "They've been right under our noses all along. I don't understand. Why didn't she leave word of where they was goin'? I'll have to go find Morgan at once."

"What?"

"Never mind. I thank ye, ye've been most helpful."

Jeremy left at once and returned to the inn where he made arrangements to keep the horse a few more days. After he ate, he had some food prepared and began the long journey to Jamie Price's home, from where he could safely send for Morgan.

To his distress he found that Jamie was away and he had to wait an impatient day until Jamie returned.

Jamie was surprised to see him there.

"Jeremy, what's wrong? Has Morgan decided to sail again? I suppose he wants an alibi from me."

"Nay, sir, 'tain't that. I've found the girl. We've got to

337

send word to Morgan."

"Found her! Kristen Seaford! Good Lord, man, you couldn't have done anything better for Morgan. Where did you find her? What did we overlook?"

Jeremy told him quickly about Toby's accident, and about Christopher Miles's sending for a doctor. Then he told him that Christopher had taken Kristen and Toby with him back to his home. With a puzzled look on his face, Jamie sat slowly down in a chair and voiced the questions that had been uppermost in Jeremy's mind.

"I don't understand, Jeremy."

"Nay, neither do I."

"Why, if Chris knows who she is, didn't he send word to the authorities? There's certainly been enough news spread about her kidnapping."

"Aye."

"And why didn't Kristen send word to Morgan about where she and Toby were?"

"I don't understand," Jeremy said, "but I think we're wastin' our time thinkin' about it. We should send word to Morgan right away. When he comes I'm sure he'll find the answers."

"You're right, Jeremy. I'll send word at once. Stay and I'll get you something to eat and drink. You'll need all your strength when Morgan gets here."

"Aye." Jeremy chuckled. "I'm afraid there'll be a lot of questions and answers, but at least he'll be relieved to know she's alive and safe."

Morgan had tried intermittently to sleep, but had failed dismally. When he did go down to breakfast, he had reached a stage of near exhaustion. He had shaved carefully and dressed, and his try at appearing natural might have fooled any gaze other than his mother's.

His thoughts seemed to be far away, as in truth they were. Owen was also quick to understand why. He could see the questions in Morgan's mother's eyes, and he took the first opportunity to take her aside and speak to her.

"Owen, what problem is on his mind that distresses him so?"

"I canna answer your questions wi'out betrayin' his confidence. I can only tell ye that ye would do the lad more good by keepin' silent and trustin' him. Morgan is a man who knows how to settle his own problems. When he decides to act, he will. Until then, we have to stand by and make it easier for him."

She smiled at him and rested her hand on his arm.

"I'll ask no questions, Owen, but I must tell you that I am grateful my son has the friends he has."

"Thank ye. 'Tis an honor to be friend to a man who has been so good to me. I've found him to be dependable and I wouldna betray his trust."

She reached up and kissed him lightly on the cheek.

"And neither will I. Thank you, Owen."

She walked away and Owen smiled, watching her, knowing no matter how she worried, she would ask Morgan no questions until he chose to come to her and tell her the truth.

He went back to the breakfast room to find Morgan alone.

"Where is Jane?"

"Mother has taken her off somewhere to discuss fashion or whatever it is that women discuss when they're together."

Owen sat down opposite Morgan and poured himself another cup of hot tea. While he did so he studied Morgan's face.

"What are ye plannin', Morgan?"

339

"I've gotten a message today."

"What?"

"It seems Jeffrey is getting brave. Since I let his last ship get by without touching it, it seems he thinks I'm satisfied with the ransom money."

"What's he up to?"

"Sending another ship out."

"And Captain Black sails again?"

"That's right."

"What about finding Kristen?"

"I'm doing everything I can. I've sent out word to a lot of ears. If she's in this area anywhere, I'll find her. In the meantime, I have no intention of letting Jeffrey recoup his losses. I intend to keep him off balance."

"I wouldna mind sailin' wi' Captain Black one time."

"What would Jane think of that?"

"Ye dinna understand the lass, Morgan. She's no so weak as ye seem to think, or for that matter, as her brother seems to think. The girl has got iron under that soft skin. She would be the first to tell me to go."

"Then you are welcome to come along."

"When is it to be?"

"Jeffrey's ship leaves dock next Monday morning. The *Falcon* will be waiting for him. We have three days before we leave here. I intend to use them to search for Kristen. There's no way a woman and a child can have vanished. Someone, somewhere has seen or heard something. I'll find that someone if it takes the rest of my life."

"Why do ye seem like a man who's ridin' himself wi' guilt?"

"It seems I've done the same thing to the two people I love the most. First, I let Charlotte die when she needed me; then I left Kristen alone when I should have stayed with her. Whatever has happened to her is my fault."

"She loves ye, lad. She'd be the last to be blamin' ye if somethin' went wrong."

Morgan slammed his hand down on the table and rose to his feet.

"Damn it, Owen! I cannot understand it. Surely if she had been found, word would have circulated by now. I'm sure old Jeff would be the first to say something just to gloat."

"'Tis beyond me to give ye any aid, Morgan. I've no thought in me mind of what could have happened. I only know whatever it was, it happened to the both of 'em at the same time. If it had been foul play, we would have known by now."

Morgan sighed and dropped back down in his seat.

"I tell myself that. I tell myself he's safe; she's well somewhere. But I cannot erase her face from my mind. I see her crying, calling to me for help, help I am powerless to give."

"Stop it, Morgan, before ye drive yerself mad. We'll keep up hope. We'll try to believe that the lack of news is good. It means no one has done them harm or we would have found traces of it."

Morgan was about to speak again when the butler appeared.

"Lord Grayfield?"

"Yes," Morgan replied.

"There is a letter for you, sir. Lord Jamie Price has sent a man. I have asked him to wait in case there might be a reply."

Before he could finish speaking, both Morgan and Owen were out of their seats and on their way to the entrance hall. There, they found a young stableboy who stood, hat in hand, in wide-eyed, open-mouthed awe at the beauty of the house in which he stood.

341

"You've a message for me?" Morgan said.

"Yes, sir," the boy mumbled and began to fumble through his pockets in search of the message. Morgan held his impatience in check with superhuman effort, for he felt the need to grasp the boy and rip his clothes in search of the letter.

Finally, when Morgan's nerves could no longer stand the strain, the boy found it, drew it slowly from his pocket, and handed it to Morgan who literally snatched it and tore it open.

Jamie did not want to mention Kristen's name for fear the message might find its way into the wrong hands.

Dear Morgan,
    I've found word of what you search for. Come as soon as you can.

                                                    Jamie

Morgan took a coin and flipped it to the boy who grasped it, then, in profound shock, stared at such an enormous sum.

"Send to the stables and have my horse saddled," Morgan told the butler. And when butler and boy were gone, he turned to Owen.

"Jamie's found word of Kristen."

"I'm goin' wi' ye."

"No, I don't have time. I'll be back as fast as I can. In the meantime, explain our plans to Jane."

"Aye. Hurry back, Morgan. We're all worried."

"I know, Owen, thanks. See you soon."

Owen watched as the door closed behind Morgan. He had thought of something Morgan had not. Jamie had said he had word. He did not say if it was good or bad. Owen began to worry about what would happen if it was bad.

Morgan covered the distance between his and Jamie's house faster than he ever had before. In front of the house he jumped down from his horse and ran to the door. He did not bother to knock, but threw the door open and shouted for Jamie.

Jamie appeared quickly accompanied by Jeremy.

"Jeremy?" Morgan said questioningly.

"Yes," Jamie answered. "We know where Kristen is. Jeremy found her. We just don't understand why she is where she is and why there's so much silence about it."

"Where is she, Jamie?"

"In the Mileses' mansion. It seems she's a guest of Christopher Miles."

"Chris . . . how?"

"We don't know," Jamie answered, "but . . ." He went on to explain the use of a new name.

"Jamie," Morgan replied, "we'll soon find out. There's some explaining to do on all sides. It's about time we began."

In a few minutes, he was gone, leaving Jeremy and Jamie gazing after him in complete surprise.

# Twenty-One

When Morgan left for Jamie's, Owen returned to their room to find Jane there. She smiled at him as he entered. Scattered about her was evidence that she had been trying on and discarding pieces of clothing. Lifting a rather flimsy bit of sheer material from a chair, he sat down and ran his fingers over it.

"What's this?"

"A nightgown Morgan's mother gave me. It's . . . it's a little revealing."

At that remark he chuckled aloud and beckoned her to come to him. When she stood by his chair, he reached up, took her by the waist, and brought her down on his lap.

"Ye're right; I dinna prefer the material. I'm more inclined to prefer ye as ye were last night . . . wi'out the interference of cloth between us."

She laughed, threw her arms about his neck, and pressed several soft light kisses across his face. He took immediate advantage and enclosed her in a warm embrace as their kisses slowed, became more lingering, and soon more passionate.

"Ah, Janie," he said as she rested her head on his shoulder. "Findin' ye has been my greatest blessin'."

They sat for a few minutes in contented silence; then the thought of what she had been doing occurred to him.

"'Tis daft I am for not seein'," he muttered.

344

"Seeing?" she questioned.

"I've been draggin' ye about wi'out a stitch of clothes to call your own. Here ye are, my wife, borrowin' clothes."

"Owen, I have more clothes than I will ever need. Clothes, jewels, furs, and all material things that have never made me happy."

"But ye dinna have any now."

"Everything I own is in Jeffrey's home."

"Then we'll go and get them."

"Owen."

"I canna abide that man keepin' anything that belongs to ye. Get yerself ready. We will take the buggy and go get what you need for now and warn your brother that we are sendin' someone for the balance."

Jane rose from his lap.

"There are some things I valued. A locket that belonged to my mother, some letters and papers she left . . . pictures, some other personal things my mother left."

"Then that is what we'll get today. You get ready and I'll go down to see about the buggy."

Obediently, Jane set about making ready while Owen went down. In a few minutes, she came down the stairs. Seeing Owen smile as she approached, she was amazed at how safe and secure she felt, and how much more courage she had acquired since she had put her hand in Owen's and said the words that made them husband and wife.

When the buggy stopped, Owen stepped down and helped Jane; then they walked to the door. Owen's knock was answered by the butler who smiled and welcomed them in.

Jeffrey was sent for and Owen grew coldly angry at the

arrogant way he tried to treat Jane.

"Mother's jewelry? Really Jane, I'm sure it was meant to be an heirloom, to be left in the family as this house was."

"I do not want it all, Jeffrey. I only want what mother left me personally. The rest you can keep."

Jeffrey shrugged, satisfied he would be keeping most of it, and it took all of Owen's will power not to strike him. In fact, the urge to beat him to a pulp nearly overcame him. It was Jane's cool hand in his that brought him back to reality. She had already become able to read her husband's face and emotions quite well.

"I'm afraid you will have to excuse me. I've some business to attend to. I'm sure you will be able to find everything you need, Jane."

"Yes, Jeffrey," Jane replied, "and I assure you I shall take only what belongs to me."

Jeffrey gave a slight bow to them both, then was gone.

"Damned arrogant bastard," Owen muttered.

"Don't worry, Owen, he didn't bother me. I only want what is mine. He is welcome to anything else. Come, let's go up. I'll show you where I have lived all my life, and my few good memories."

They climbed the stairs together, and when Jane opened the door of her old room, Owen walked in.

He would have known the room was Jane's even if she had not told him. Her presence permeated its every corner. This was a room that spoke of a gentle introspective person . . . and a lonely person. The walls were a pale gold color. Here and there, a small tasteful painting or etching was hung. The soft white ruffled curtains at the windows matched the ruffled spread and canopy of the bed. The floor glowed with a feeling of warmth in the shine of the wax. It was obvious Jane had

346

spent much time reading, for there was an over-abundance of books.

"'Tis a beautiful room, Jane. In this house, it surprises me a little."

"It was always my sanctuary. When anything was too much for me, I ran here."

He went to her and lifted her hand to his lips.

"Ye needn't run again, Janie . . . except to me."

He watched the sparkle of tears touch her eyes, tears she hastily brushed away as she turned from him. She went to kneel by a chest. When she opened it, she took from it a bundle of letters and a small wooden box. These she handed to Owen. Then she packed some of her clothes and shoes in a case. These she set by the door, and having done so, she went to her dressing table and opened a rather large jewel box. Owen was aghast at the amount of jewelry it contained.

"Jeffrey used to let me wear them when he wanted to impress someone . . . or when he decided to auction me off to the highest bidder."

"Jane."

"It's all right, Owen, there are only a few things here I want. The rest carry only bad memories and I don't want them."

She lifted an oval locket from the box.

"Mother specifically said this was my very own and I should never part with it. It had been given to her when she and my father met and fell in love. I've never worn it, really. I guess I've been saving it for a special time."

She put the locket in the pocket of her dress and turned to Owen.

"Is this all ye'll need for now? It does not seem like much."

"I can make a list of the clothes I need and have Marie

pack them and send them over. This is all I really want now."

Owen nodded. He handed the small box to her and lifted the larger one. They returned to the carriage after Jane had given instructions to Marie about the balance of her things. Then they returned to Morgan's.

When Morgan got back, he exchanged some light conversation with his family and with Jane, then he took Owen aside. Quickly he explained what Jamie had told him.

"This is beyond my understandin', Morgan. Why did she no leave ye a message of some sort? And Toby, the lad worships the ground ye walk on. He wouldna go wi'out a reason."

"Well, I can't see the Mileses holding them prisoner. She has to be there of her own free will."

"There have to be some circumstances. Even if she found out who ye were, she would have had the sense to wait and talk to ye. No, there has to be a reason stronger than that. I dinna believe the lass is foolish or turns her love off and on so easy."

"Well, I have to find out. I have to have her back, Owen."

"Do ye need my help?"

"Not for the moment; first I have to find a way to get to Toby. I want to talk to him."

"How are ye goin' to do that?"

"Tonight, I'll do some searching, find out exactly what is going on."

"If ye need me, just let me know."

"I'll do that, Owen, thanks."

Morgan remained much to himself the rest of the day thinking over the situation and trying to justify ways in his mind to understand why Kristen would turn from him. It was nearing midnight when he dressed in dark clothes, went to the stable, and saddled a horse. Then he rode to the Mileses' house staying off the main path. He circled the grounds until he came to the back wall. There he tied his horse and made his way, using the shadows of the trees for cover until he stood a few feet from the veranda that circled the back of the house. Most of the windows were dark and he was sure everyone was reasonably settled for the night.

The house had an upper veranda that also circled it. From this, French doors opened into each bedroom. He made his way up the veranda steps knowing he would have to try each room before he found either Kristen or Toby.

He stopped before he reached the first. It was still lighted and he could hear the voices of Mr. and Mrs. Miles. Quietly, he passed it and went on to the next.

Trying to remember, from all the times he had been invited to this house, where the guest rooms were, he passed the next two for he knew one was Chris's and the other was his brother's. At the following one, he stopped. The door stood ajar, and the room was dark. Gently, he pushed the door open enough to slip through. Once inside he stood still and listened. He was satisfied to hear the soft evening breathing of someone who slept.

Slowly, he moved to the side of the bed. It took a few minutes for his eyes to become accustomed to the darkened room so he could make out the form in the bed . . . Toby. He bent forward, laid his hand firmly over Toby's mouth, and gripped his shoulder.

"Toby," he whispered.

Toby jerked to awareness and began to fight the hands that held him.

349

"Shhh, Toby, be quiet," came the familiar voice.

The boy stopped fighting and Morgan removed his hand.

"Captain?"

"Yes, Toby."

He could hear Toby's audible sigh of relief.

"I knew you'd come, sir, I knew it. I kept tellin' Miss Kristen it wouldn't be too long. Did you come to get us, sir?"

"I came back to the cabin to get you both, Toby, but you were gone. Why didn't you leave some kind of message for me and why did you leave when I gave you express orders to watch and stay put until I came?"

"Huh?" Toby said, dumfounded at his words. "We only went because your message told us to."

"Message? Toby, I sent no message."

"What do you mean? I saw your name on the bottom of the note. Miss Kristen has been teachin' me to read. I could read your name clear; I've seen it on enough papers on your desk."

"It wasn't sent by me, Toby. Get up and lock your door; then light a candle, we have some talking to do."

Toby leaped to follow his commands while Morgan sat on the edge of the bed. He could find no answers for what Toby had told him and he had a vague premonition he was going to like the balance of the story even less.

Toby came back to the bed with the lighted candle in his hand. He placed it on the table and sat down beside Morgan.

"Are you all right, Toby?"

"Yes, sir, I'm fine. Miss Kristen, she takes good care of me. Only I surely missed you and Jeremy and the *Falcon*. I'm glad you're back. Are you goin' to take me and Miss Kristen with you now?"

350

"Right now, Toby, I'd like to know everything that happened from the time I left you until now."

"Yes, sir," Toby replied, and quickly he launched into his story. Morgan sat in silence. It was true, he thought miserably; he did not like the balance of the story. He was about to speak when Toby told him how Kristen has cautioned him to call her Jennifer while they were here.

"Whoa, boy, back up a step. Jennifer?"

"Yes, sir, you see nobody here knows who she really is. We're supposed to keep it a secret."

"Toby, this is getting darker and darker. Why didn't Kristen leave me a message without Chris knowing? I'm sure she wanted to get you to a doctor, but she could have left a note. And who told you I left a message?"

"I told you, sir, Miss Kristen was teachin' me to read. I read your name myself. But . . . about Miss Kristen . . . she'll be mad at me if I say, but . . ."

"But what, Toby?"

"After you left, when she found the things in the chest, she knew who you really were. . . . That was all right; then something happened one day after Mr. Miles was there. I don't know what. I only know that she cried a lot at night when she thought I couldn't hear and even sometimes in the day. She was real sad, and she went and looked at your picture a lot."

"Cried? But she never said anything?"

"No, sir, but I got my suspicions."

"What?"

"That Mr. Christopher, he likes Miss Kristen a lot. I think he said somethin' to upset her. She only started cryin' after that day when he came and talked to her."

"Toby, I want you to do two things for me."

"What?"

"I want you to tell me where Kristen's room is; then I want you to get dressed. I'll take you with me."

"What about Falcon?"

"The *Falcon*'s where she usually is."

"No, sir, my puppy. Mr. Christopher gave him to me. I named him Falcon after our ship. Can I take him with me?"

"I see," Morgan said softly. "The way to a boy's heart."

"What?"

"Never mind. You can take the puppy with you. Where is he?"

"Downstairs, sir. Miss Kristen said he couldn't stay all night in my bedroom until he gets some manners."

"Damn," Morgan muttered.

"Sir?"

"I can't have you running all over the house. You stay here; I'll see Kristen first."

"You can't, sir."

"Why?"

"She ain't here tonight."

"Where is she?"

"She went with Mr. Christopher and a couple of their friends. They went sailing up the coast and visiting. They won't be back until tomorrow."

Morgan rose to his feet. All his plans had been completely destroyed and he knew no more now than he had when he came.

"Well, Toby, tell me where her room is."

"It's the one right next to mine. On the balcony you could be there in a couple of steps."

"All right, now, can you keep a secret, Toby?"

"Yes, sir, you know I can."

"I mean a secret from everyone . . . including Kristen?"

"You mean I can't tell Miss Kristen?"

"No one, Toby, no one. My life depends on it."

Morgan could see the determined glow in Toby's eyes and the lift of his chin. He knew then his secret was safe with Toby.

"Yes, sir, I can keep a secret. I won't tell anyone."

"All right, now, as far as anyone knows, I've never been here. You go back to sleep and I'll see you soon."

"You're comin' back? I mean . . . you ain't goin' to leave me here for good . . . or Miss Kristen? I don't like the way Mr. Christopher smiles at her all the time. He wants to keep her here for good."

"Now listen, Toby, you understand this," Morgan said gently. "Miss Kristen belongs to me, and you are part of my family. I don't intend for us to be separated. I'll come back and the next time you both will be leaving with me."

"Yes, sir." Toby smiled. He watched Morgan walk to the door, smile, wave a quick good-by and leave.

"I knew he wouldn't leave me," he whispered to himself. "I knew it."

He blew out the candle, lay back on the bed, and drifted off into a dream-filled sleep in which he, Morgan, Jeremy, and Kristen sailed on the *Falcon* to their own special island where they lived happily together.

Morgan, his mind on Toby's story, made his way across the dark lawn to his horse and began the ride home. So many things did not make sense. Number one, what had Chris said to Kristen to make her cry then decide to leave with him? Two, why did she leave no message for him? Three, if she knew who he was, why didn't she try to contact him? And . . . last, why Jennifer—why not say who she really was? One thing was certain in his mind. He intended to return the next night; he intended to take Kristen with him, and no one, not even Chris Miles was going to stand in his way.

He went home, and late that night told Owen all that had happened.

"I will say this business makes no sense. That girl was on board my ship for some time before ye took her. She's not the devious, twistin' kind. I dinna understand this at all."

"Well, don't worry. By this time tomorrow night we'll have all the answers we need. We'll also have Kristen and Toby back with us where they belong."

"What about young Chris Miles?"

"Chris is an old friend." Though Morgan grinned, his eyes were dangerously cool. "But Chris will have to be taught a lesson. He can't go about taking what belongs to another."

"And about Jeffrey's ship?"

"I'll take care of it. Once I get Kristen and Toby away safe. Then we'll settle all accounts with Jeffrey . . . and with Leslie Seaford. Somehow she's in this with him. I get the strange feeling we only know part of a story, and I've a feeling Leslie knows more about it than anyone. Anyway, first things first, and the top priority is Kristen. I find it very difficult to successfully accomplish much more until I have her back. I have to know what happened and only she can tell me. And . . ."

"And ye love her so much ye find it hard to go on wi'out her. I understand. Good luck, Morgan. I wish ye both well."

"Thanks, Owen. Good night."

"Good night."

Owen watched Morgan climb the stairs. Inside he knew Morgan was taut and near the point of explosion, and he wondered what would happen should Kristen have changed her mind and refuse to go with Morgan. It was a choice he knew Morgan would never be able to accept.

Morgan, too, as he sought escape in sleep, could not push the thought of Kristen and Chris Miles out of his mind.

It was a good thing he did not know all that had transpired between Chris and Kristen. If he had, he would have left the security of his bed and gone after Chris, sword in hand.

Chris loved Kristen. There was no doubt in his mind. In fact, the only thought in his mind was to erase all trace of Morgan from her thoughts without her knowing what was being done. She had no idea that the note she had used to entice Toby was in his possession. He read it again and again. He was aware of what and who Morgan was. He had been a friend of Chris's for a long time and Chris knew he could never reveal his double identity.

He also knew now that he had touched a very sensitive spot in Kristen when he had spoken of Morgan and Leslie Seaford. It did not take long for him to take advantage of the situation; yet soon he found that it had gotten beyond his control. He had used it more than he had planned to, had found himself inventing assignations and a wild passionate love affair that did not exist. He realized he had gone too far on the day he asked her to come with him and his new friends to sail up the coast and eventually stop at his aunt and uncle's elaborate home that sat on the high cliffs overlooking a beautiful stretch of beach. He remembered the day well, it was only a few days since

355

he had brought her there.

She had wanted to stay in seclusion for a while, she had said, using the excuse that she was still afraid of her uncle finding her. But he knew it was Morgan and Jeffrey MacIntire from whom she ran, and he intended to keep it so until she ran into his arms where he would keep her.

Early morning found Chris and Kristen walking among the trees on the broad green lawn behind the house. She had been so involved in her thoughts that she did not hear him approach, and he was annoyed to think that she was thinking of Morgan.

"Good morning, Jennifer," he called, and watched her turn, recognize him, and then smile.

"Good morning, Chris."

"How are you feeling this morning?"

"Quite well, thank you. I didn't see you at dinner last night, Chris."

"Oh, I was out with some friends. By the way, I saw some really interesting people."

"Oh, who?"

"Well, let me see. The Duke and Duchess of Brent, Captain and Mrs. Bradly Whipply—you know, he's the big naval hero."

She nodded.

"And of course the lovers of the season." He laughed.

"Lovers?"

"Oh, yes, Morgan Grayfield and Leslie Seaford. It seems they're seen everywhere together and rumor has it he sees even more of her in private than in public."

He watched the color drain from her face, saw her turn away so he would not see the start of tears in her clouded gray eyes.

He continued to walk beside her and talked of other things until she regained her composure.

"Jennifer?"

"Yes?"

"I've an invitation to come up the coast and visit my aunt and uncle. It would only be an overnight trip. My aunt would be more than pleased to meet you."

"Oh, Chris, how do you know that?" She laughed.

"I believe," he replied with a chuckle, "that the rumor has gotten to her that her wild nephew has finally met the girl of his dreams. She wants you to come. . . . I do, too. Come along, Jennifer—one day. You'll enjoy it."

"Chris . . ."

"Jennifer, I'll not say one word to you that you do not want to hear, at least not now. You have my word as a gentleman. It's just a day of freedom you can relax and enjoy. Come on."

"All right, I'll go. But what about Toby?"

"He'll be well taken care of here, and you know there's no way to separate him and that puppy. We'll be back before he misses us."

"All right."

"Good, I'll go make the arrangements. We'll leave this afternoon. Right after lunch. Can you be ready?"

"I'll try."

He smiled at her and walked away feeling a sense of triumph. He knew his words about Morgan had hurt her, maybe turned her away from him, and he intended to be around when she needed a strong shoulder to cry on.

After Chris left her, Kristen found a quiet bench in the middle of the garden and sat. She could still feel the sting of Chris's words about Morgan. She knew now that all of Morgan's professions of love had been a game. She felt herself burn with shame to realize he had so brutally used her emotions, played upon them, and then forgot her in the arms of a woman she knew as an enemy.

357

Bitterly, her mind sought ways of revenge. At that moment, she was possessed with a burning desire to see Morgan Grayfield dead. She also knew she had it in her power to do just that. With Kristen Seaford's return, with her tale that Lord Morgan Grayfield was also Captain Black, his fate would be sealed. Why then, she questioned herself, did she not do just that? Why did she not just hand him over to the authorities? She knew the answer before the question was even fully formed. Because she could not erase him from her mind, her heart, her dreams. She had to wait until she felt strong enough to face him, until she could control the need that lingered below her calm exterior.

Maybe, she thought, Chris might be the answer. She knew Chris was in love with her, just as she knew she felt nothing for him but gratitude and friendship. Yet maybe in time she might be able to repair the damage Morgan had done and face a new life.

She went to Toby and explained to him where she was going.

"I'll not be gone long, Toby, just until tomorrow. Please keep Falcon out of mischief. Remember we are guests here."

"Yes, miss, I'll remember. Falcon's a good dog. He won't get in any trouble."

"Good, and remember to study your lessons. I expect you to be able to read at least two whole pages by the time I return."

"Two!" He groaned.

"Two," she said firmly. Then she laughed at the disgust on his face and bent to kiss him. He watched her walk away, thinking how pretty she was and how beautiful it would be when she and the captain were married and had adopted him as their own son. The thought of them for his very own parents made him quiver with joy. It would be good when Morgan came, for he could erase the dark gray clouds from Kristen's eyes, and she would laugh again as she had on the island, instead of crying herself to sleep at night as he had heard her do often of late.

The trip to visit Chris's aunt was a happy one. Despite how she felt within, Kristen enjoyed it. She especially enjoyed meeting Chris's Aunt Elspeth, a rather buoyant-spirited woman, and surprisingly frank. She was tall and elegant, and her direct gaze seemed to pierce Kristen to the depths of her heart. When they were alone for a few minutes walking in the garden the older woman turned to Kristen.

"Do you love my nephew?"

"I . . . why I . . ."

"Well, do you, girl?" she said more gently.

"I don't know."

"Then you do not love him."

"Why?"

"Because,"—the older woman laughed as she tucked Kristen's arm in hers and continued to walk—"if you loved him you would not be unsure. Jennifer—may I call you Jennifer?"

"Yes, I'd be pleased."

"Jennifer, my nephew is an affectionate scalawag. And I love him dearly. I suppose I helped to spoil him so atrociously, but I want him to be happy and to marry and have children. I want the woman he marries to be happy, too. One must never marry for any reason other than love." Again she turned to Kristen. "Do you understand me, child?"

359

Kristen nodded.

"Never marry a man for any other reason than that you find happiness with him and only with him."

Immediately Kristen's thoughts leaped to Morgan.

"I see," the older woman said softly. "Follow your heart, child. You'll be happy no other way."

Before Kristen could answer, they were joined by others and the opportunity to talk with Elspeth did not come about again. Yet she felt Elspeth's eyes upon her often.

It was a quiet Kristen who returned to the Mileses' home the next day. She was bound in her thoughts on the decision she would make. She helped Toby with his lessons and went through the day the best she could. That night, she went to her room, the decision firm in her mind. She would go to Morgan, face him with the truth. She would tell him that he had nothing to fear from her for she had no intention of turning him over to the authorities. The only thing she wanted was for him to let Toby come with her. She would return to the colonies, give Toby a good education, and resume her life as if he had never entered it.

She went into her room and closed and locked the door behind her. There was one candle lit on her dressing table and one on the stand by her bed. It cast the room into deep shadows.

Tiredly, she removed her dress and petticoats. Clad only in a sheer flimsy shift she sat down at her dressing table and loosened her hair. As it fell about her, she took her brush and began to brush it. She let her mind drift to what she would say to Morgan and what he would reply. Her mind was so deep in thoughts of him that she must have been looking at his reflection in her mirror several minutes before she realized it was not a dream and that the blue eyes that held hers in the mirror were his. She spun about and looked up at him.

"Morgan!" she gasped.

"You are as beautiful as I remembered, my love," he said softly as he reached for her. "Come, let me see if my mind still remembers your sweetness. Come, welcome me home, love."

# Twenty-Two

Morgan went through the next day on the edge of his nerves. He waited impatiently for night to fall, trying not to think that she was with Chris. He knew Chris's happy-go-lucky charm for women, had in fact seen it work quite often. He built visions in his mind of Chris and Kristen together, then firmly discarded them. He would try to remember only her profession of love for him, try to think only of their future together.

Magical pictures appeared in the mists of his mind. Kristen, laughing in the surf of their island with her wind-blown hair flowing about her. Kristen, in his arms with her warm giving love enfolding him. Kristen, offering him all she possessed in the world to keep him close to her. Kristen, Kristen, Kristen, were the only thoughts that his mind could contain. She was like the echo of a haunting melody that lingered always beneath the surface of his mind, a song he would forever sing, the music of love that would wake him in the morning and lull him to sleep at night. He would see her every moment in their future. By the end of the day, he was obsessed with only one thought: to get to her as soon as possible and finally to put an end to their charade. After that, they could spend the balance of their lives together.

The last rays of the sun found him already preparing himself to leave. But he knew he would have to wait for quite a while yet, for he did not want to take the chance of the Miles family finding him there. So he saddled his horse and rode slowly, arriving at the Miles mansion long before they were abed. He tied his horse beneath a tree, well-concealed from any eyes that might be watching from the house. Then he sat and settled himself to wait.

With infinite patience, he watched the house as one by one the downstairs lights flickered out. Now, only the bedrooms were lit. He kept his eyes on Kristen's room. One by one, the bedroom lights went out. Kristen's was the only one still glowing and he wondered what thoughts kept her awake.

He rose, and began working his way toward the house, his dark-clad body only another shadow among the trees. As he stood in the dark area beyond Kristen's door and watched her, his heart beat a harsh tattoo when she began to disrobe. Her dress was cast on a chair, and her many ruffled petticoats followed. He could see her slim golden body through the flimsy shift she wore and every sense he owned remembered the velvet feel of her skin beneath his hands, her cool rounded body pressed against his.

She sat at the dressing table, unbound her golden tresses, and let them fall about her in a thick mass of curls. Slowly she lifted the brush and began to run it through her hair. He could see the preoccupied look in her eyes and knew by her introspective gaze that her thoughts were a long way away.

He wanted desperately to take her in his arms, to feel her thick silken hair on his fingers and to taste the warm sweet taste of those lips. On silent feet, he moved across the floor and stood behind her. Still her eyes, filled with faraway thoughts, did not register his presence. He held her eyes with his, and suddenly, she sensed his presence. Her eyes widened in recognition and the startled sound of his name burst from her as she spun about on the seat to face him.

"Morgan!"

"You're as beautiful as I remembered, my love. Come, let me see if my mind still remembers your sweetness. Come, welcome me home, love."

He was prepared for many reactions, for her to cry or to throw herself into his arms. He was not prepared for what did happen. Her eyes went from shock to pure rage. He stood still, amazed as her cheeks flushed and her body quivered with barely controlled indignation. He could not understand what was transpiring before his eyes.

"Kristen?"

Kristen again felt the deep wash of shame course through her. How dare he, she thought, how dare he use me so shamelessly, walk away leaving me to sit helpless and alone, then return and expect me to fall on him?

"Kristen?" he repeated and took a step nearer. He reached out to touch her and bright stars flashed before his eyes as she slapped him across the face with all the strength she had.

"Get out of here! Leave me alone! What do you want with me now, Lord Morgan Grayfield—another romp in bed? Are you bored with your current love? Do you need a little variety to add to your life?"

Stunned, he could only stare at her for a moment.

"Kristen, what the hell are you talking about? I've come for an explanation. You owe me one for running off and leaving me no word."

"I . . . I owe! You conceited monster. Did you think you could play me for a fool forever? Did you think I would never find out? Oh, God, Morgan, just how naïve and stupid to you think I am?"

"Find out what? That I'm Lord Morgan Grayfield instead of Captain Black? Does that mean so much to you?"

"I wouldn't care if you were the devil himself. Take your name, and everything else and leave. I will try my best to forget I've ever known you, to erase you from my mind as you seem to have been able to erase me."

"I've never erased a moment I've shared with you."

"Liar!"

"I may have lied to you about some things, but never about that."

She stood silent for a moment realizing she wanted to give him a chance to deny Leslie, to tell her about Leslie and make her believe what she had seen and heard was not true.

"Tell me, Morgan," she said softly, "tell me what is the truth?"

"The truth is that I love you. That I've been doing all I can to work out our future."

"And how did you plan to do that, by keeping me safely locked away until you received my ransom? Until you had completed your revenge on Jeffrey for the death of your sister, Charlotte?"

He started, and his face drew into a dark scowl.

"What do you know of Charlotte? Who told you, Chris Miles?"

"Yes, Chris Miles, and I know that you feel Jeffrey was responsible for Charlotte's death. You wanted revenge, you wanted to make Jeffrey pay. So you chose me. I had done nothing to you, yet you took me, pretended to love me, made me ... oh ..." She sobbed, her breath catching in her throat. She turned away from him. He stood in silence, feeling the pain that emanated from her, seeing her slumped shoulders. Desperately he wanted to

365

reach out to her, to take her in his arms, to hold her and tell her that nothing more could harm them, that their love was strong enough to keep them safe forever.

She remained still, waiting for him to complete the story, to tell her about Leslie, to explain it away and end her fears. That was all it would take . . . but in the next few words, he condemned himself.

"All right, Kristen, yes, I did all that, and for the motives you say. Only you do not know all. I kidnapped you, not for ransom, but for revenge. But I didn't count on falling in love with you. All that was between us is truth. I love you. I left you to find a way so that we could stay together without the truth of my identity being known. That is all that is a lie between us."

"There is nothing else . . . nothing you have forgotten?"

"No, I've told you all that has happened. I came back for you and you were gone. What made you leave?"

She turned to him. Now she seemed to have a cold control over herself. She looked at him through frigid eyes.

"Tell me about Leslie Seaford. Tell me about my stepmother, my beautiful stepmother. The one you conspired with to rid her of me."

What registered in his eyes as absolute shock looked to her anguished heart as fear . . . fear and guilt.

"How do you know about Leslie? What wild stories are you believing now? There is nothing between us. Anything you might have heard are lies, Kristen, believe me."

"Believe me, Kristen; trust me, Kristen. Stay in my little cabin, Kristen, and be a good girl until I go and find what Leslie wants me to do with you."

"That's not true."

"Isn't it?"

"No!"

"I don't believe you. I believe what I saw with my own eyes." Tears started in her eyes, tears that angered her for she did not want him to know the pain that nearly crushed her at the memory. "You . . . you and my beautiful stepmother. I saw you together. Saw you kiss her, hold her. I knew the truth then. The Seaford money and Leslie, too. All you had to do was to get rid of me and that fell in well with your plans of revenge against Jeffrey. You could accomplish everything all at one time. How it must have amused you," she choked. "To have made me fall in love with you, to have made me give myself to you so easily. Did you laugh at the stupid little girl who fell so easily into your bed?"

"Have you said all you want to say? Can a condemned man have a word to say in his defense?"

"I don't care anymore, Morgan. I don't care."

"Now who lies?" he said softly.

She turned from him and ran to the door, but he was there first to put himself between her and escape.

"Who lies, Kristen? Was what you told me on the island lies? I don't think so. I think you have seen something your jealousy does not understand, something that is not true. I think you loved me then, and you love me now." His voice ended in a whisper as he began to move toward her. Slowly, she backed away, seeing his intent clear in his eyes.

"Morgan, leave me alone."

"I can't, my love," he said gently. "You are as much a part of me as my soul. I cannot chance losing either."

Aware of his warm gaze enfolding her, she continued to back away from him, trying to reach the open windows.

"Forget it, Kristen." He chuckled. "I can get there before you."

"What do you want from me? Is my pride not enough? Haven't you done enough to me? Go, Morgan, or I shall scream and bring the whole household down upon you."

"But I don't think you will."

"So arrogant! I will see you hang as a pirate!" She knew the words were false bravado as soon as they were spoken. Worse yet, she knew that he knew it also for she saw his wicked smile gleam in the candlelight. Fear struck her then, fear that if he touched her, held her, kissed her, she would not be able to withstand his intoxicating hold over her senses.

She leaped toward the bed; landing on it she rolled across. But he anticipated her move, and she came to her feet on the other side to find herself enclosed in iron-hard arms, crushed firmly against a chest that felt to her as solid as oak. He held her immobile even though she struggled valiantly. Realizing her strength was no match for his, she suddenly became motionless. Firmly, she lifted her chin and glared defiantly into his eyes. She would remain cold and unfeeling; that, she thought, would be her only defense. Her resolve was nearly shattered when she heard his warm chuckle as he brushed her ear with his lips.

"Shall we see who is lying, my love?" He pressed a feather-light kiss on her rigid lips, then on her eyelids and cheeks, and again he brushed an ear. He let his lips touch again and again the slim column of her throat. She gasped and began to writhe in his arms, desperate to break his hold before the dam of her emotions broke before his attack. Her struggling only made him more physically aware of her slim near-naked body in his arms, and soon she could feel the hard strength of him against her.

He held her with one arm and slid his other hand through her hair. Grasping it firmly, he drew her head back until she was forced to look up into his eyes. There she saw the blazing heat in his gaze as he slowly bent his head and caught her mouth with his. She moaned softly and struggled, but it was as if she were a child in his grip. His mouth ravaged hers, forcing her lips apart, seeking with his tongue the sweet taste of her.

Somewhere in the depths of her being a relentless flame burst into full glow. It coursed through her, leaving her weak and shaken in its path. She knew she could not withstand the onslaught of his passion and the uncontrollable flame it built within her.

"No . . . Morgan, no . . ." she moaned and she renewed her struggle to get him to release her.

"Kristen," he whispered as his lips touched hers again and again. "You tell me. Tell me you do not feel as I do. Tell me and I'll let you go. Tell me you do not feel as I do. Convince me you do not want me as badly as I want you. No matter what the barriers, this is ours and you cannot deny it."

"I hate you," she choked.

"No, Kristen, that's one lie that won't stand." He held her immobile. "Look at me!"

She refused, trying to turn away her tear-filled eyes from his searching ones. Relentlessly, he held her head firmly.

"Look at me!"

She raised her eyes to meet his and the warmth of his gaze reached out and held her as it always could. She knew she was possessed now, and always would be.

"Morgan, set me free. Don't play with me. Let me go. I won't tell anyone who you are. You can have Leslie or any other woman you want."

"You damned little fool," he said gently as his arms tightened about her. "I want no other woman than you. I cannot set you free for it would be separating part of myself. Whatever your . . . informants have been telling you, it is not so. There is not now, nor has there ever been a conspiracy between Leslie Seaford and I. I kidnapped you because I wanted to get back at Jeffrey. I admit that, but Kristen, I love you. I have loved you I think from the moment I saw you in Owen's cabin. So beautiful and so angry. I want you, Kristen, only you. And if you will stop lying to yourself and to me, you will admit that what I'm saying is true. Tell me now that you do not love me."

She reached for words, words that could deny what he said, words that would let him know of the pain and misery she felt when she saw him and Leslie together. But she was choked to silence by his intense blue gaze that had the ability to look into her soul. For no matter how much she felt that he was lying about Leslie, she loved him still and she could not deny it.

"You cannot," he said gently. "Because you know as well as I that you love me. I won't let anything or anyone separate us, Kristen."

Slowly, he bent his head to touch his lips to hers. His arms still held her bound against him and she could not move. She tried in vain to hold back the flood of emotion that swept her up and carried her away. She tried to resist the firm insistent mouth that ravaged hers with calm deliberation. The battle was over, all her defenses were shattered, all her resistance melted by his passionate assault. When his arms loosened their hold, when her arms crept about his neck, she did not know. His hands slid down the curve of her waist and rested on her slim hips drawing her tight against him.

Slowly, he released her lips and they stood, caught in the magic that would always hold them. His eyes smiled into hers.

"I would explain everything to you now," he whispered, his voice touched with controlled urgency, "but I have been long without you, love. I can bear the strain no longer."

His voice ceased as he bent and lifted her in his arms. His lips traced a gentle pattern on her heated skin, touching lightly on the soft rounded curve of her breast. She clung to him as he crossed the few steps to the bed where he lay her gently against the pillows. Then he stood and looked down on her.

The soft glow of the candles touched both the spun gold of her hair and the bright glow of love in her clear gray eyes. The seductive glow of her creamy skin and her expectant trembling held his rapt attention. She was now as she had been the first time they had lain together. And he wanted her more at this moment than he had then. As he tossed aside his clothes, he mused on the fact that he would probably want her more every day of their lives.

When he lay beside her, he drew her cool body against his. With expert fingers, he did away with the last flimsy barrier between them. He took her face between his hands and began to touch her cheeks, eyelids, and forehead with gentle kisses. He slid his hands into the silken mass of her hair and with a soft groan of pleasure he caught her mouth with his in a searing kiss that crushed forever any remaining thought of resistance. Her lips parted in sweet giving acceptance of the broiling heat of his passion. Tongues explored, caressed, sought the depths of their mutual need.

His hands caressed her, familiarized themselves with her sweet smooth curves. He wanted this moment to

371

linger in both their minds as the best time they had ever shared together. Aware of how close he had come to losing her, he was filled with a violent need to draw her close and bind her to him for now and always.

He rested on one elbow and gazed down on her slim loveliness. With tender sensitivity, he brushed the wayward strands of hair from her face, letting his fingers trace a line down the side of her cheek to her throat. Her soft skin sent a tingle through the tips of his fingers. He continued this gentle touch, from the pulsing heat at the hollow of her throat to the soft rise of a rose-tipped breast. He captured one breast in his hand and caressed it gently while his thumb touched its passion-hardened nipple. Then slowly, he bent forward and let his tongue trace a circular pattern about the nipple. Hearing her soft murmur of pleasure, he captured it in his mouth, sucking gently . . . feeling her body tremble.

Once he tasted, he sought more. His lips found the gentle curve beneath her breasts making her gasp as pinpoints of ecstasy followed each tender touch. He held her slim hips in his hands as he continued to trace heated kisses across the flat plain of her belly.

She writhed in his hands, her body searching for the source of this extreme pleasure. Gently, he slid his hand down one silken hip to her knee, then up the soft inner flesh of her thighs, pressing slightly to part her trembling legs. Then his lips continued their search, touching her soft skin with nibbling kisses that drove her to distraction.

"Morgan," she moaned as her body twisted in urgent desire. An agony of need surged through her and she expressed it with her voice and body. But he continued his gentle search of her sensitive places until she quivered beneath him and her breath was coming in ragged sobbing gasps.

Her hands had been searching for him as his had for her. Enjoying the feel of the hard rigid muscles beneath his smooth taut skin, the breadth of his shoulder, the slimness of his hips, and her lips, too, touched his skin in a burning path that exploded sensations through him like a thundering storm.

He rose above her, gazing in rapt wonder at the sensuous beauty that called to him. In a moment of both agony and ecstasy he sheathed himself in the deepest depths of her, and with a feeling of wonder and deepest pleasure felt her twine herself about him. They could hold back no longer. He whispered soft words of love as he slid his hands beneath her and blended the two of them into the one they would always be.

Their gentle slow movements accelerated to those of burning abandoned passion, and neither of them knew anything existed in their world but each other. Up, up they climbed to the pinnacle of desire, then down, down they tumbled into the cauldron of molten love.

They clung to each other, wordless in the face of the explosive passion they had shared. He rolled on his back drawing her with him. Tenderly he brushed her sweat-slicked brow with his fingers.

"Kristen, if I had never known you, I would never have lived; and if I had lost you, I would have ceased to live. Never doubt again you are part of my body and my soul and I shall never let you escape."

She rose on one elbow and looked down on him, feeling his gaze, warm with completed love, wash over her like a warm wave.

"Tell me, Morgan."

"What, love?" he questioned gently as he slid one hand through her hair, toying with it.

"All the things I should have been told at the beginning. All the secrets you've held away from me. I want to be part of you in every way, not just the good part."

"What good part?" He chuckled wickedly.

"Morgan, be serious."

"I am, love." He laughed. "I tend to agree with you. This certainly is the good part."

"Are you going to tell me?" she threatened. "Or must I keep you here until you do?"

"Such a threat!" He laughed. "I think I can hold out for a while, say fifty or sixty years."

She smiled and bent forward, brushing his lips with hers, and letting her fingers lightly caress his skin.

"If you don't talk to me, Morgan Grayfield, this will be the last night of your life."

He laughed and drew her back into his arms. Then he began his story with Charlotte. She remained silent throughout, but her mind was filled with understanding for all he had done, and with disgust and anger toward Jeffrey.

"Morgan?"

"What?"

"What about you and Leslie? What is between you?"

"Nothing, absolutely nothing. I will admit that I intentionally started it out to be more. I was going to find out what was going on by getting close to her."

"What stopped you?"

"You."

"I . . . how? I wasn't even around."

"Oh, yes you were," he said softly. "You have been here since the moment I found you. You will always be here, a shadow that lives within me and holds my heart. If I reached for her, you were there between us. If I kissed her, it was your lips I desired to taste. I knew it would never work that first night in the park. From then on, I knew it was useless to even think of another woman. But after that, I found you gone. You will never know how lonely and lost I have felt until tonight."

"Yes, Morgan, I do. I felt the same lost lonely feeling when I thought you had left me, had turned from me to another."

He smiled, drew her back into his arms, and held her close. Then he said softly, "Kristen, what does Chris Miles mean to you?"

"He's a friend, Morgan."

"That's all?"

"Yes, that's all."

"Does he know anything about me?"

"Of course not, Morgan! He doesn't even know who I am. He thinks my name is Jennifer Nelson and that I'm running away from a lecherous old uncle who is trying to steal my inheritance."

"I wonder."

"What do you wonder?"

"I wonder if he's in love with you. No," he added. "I'm sure he is. How could a reasonable man not be? Kristen, I think it's time you reappeared in society, where you can meet, fall in love with, and marry Lord Morgan Grayfield—who, by the way, is madly in love with you right now."

"What do you want me to do?"

"Do you have the courage to tell them the truth? If you do, then tell them at once. Then we can take it from there. I want to meet you, sweep you off your feet, and marry you before Jeffrey knows what is going on."

"And then you'll put Jeffrey in your past and we can live the balance of our lives without fear?"

375

Morgan eased from the bed and began to dress.

"Morgan?"

"Don't, Kristen. Let it rest as it is. We'll take one step at a time. First I want our marriage."

She rose from the bed, panic squeezing her heart into a tight ball. Unaware even of her own nakedness, she went to him.

"Morgan, I must know. I asked you once on the island if you loved me and if our love was enough for you. Now, I ask you again. Is it, Morgan? Can you let go of this need for revenge, this hatred? Can our love be enough?"

"Kristen, I want our love to be a separate thing from all this. I'm sorry for all the grief it has caused you. It will never involve you again."

"How can you say that?"

"I do love you, Kristen. I want to marry you."

"Why?"

"What do you mean, why?" he said as he donned his shirt and jacket; but his eyes refused to meet hers again.

"Is it only because you love me that you want to marry me?"

"That's a stupid question. What other reason could there be?"

"Two, Chris Miles and Jeffrey MacIntire."

He laughed and shrugged.

"Ridiculous!"

"Is it?"

"Kristen." He reached for her, sliding his arms about her. He kissed her lightly. "Forget everything else except the fact that we love each other and that is our way of being together without identifying Captain Black."

She looked up into his eyes and all her intuition told her something was wrong.

"You . . . you don't want Captain Black identified

because you intend him to sail again, don't you? Don't you?"

He dropped his arms and went to sit on a chair to draw on his boots.

"Chris Miles may be in love with me, but I don't love him. That doesn't worry you, but Jeffrey MacIntire does. You do intend for the *Falcon* to sail again, don't you? You do intend for Captain Black to strike again and again until they catch you and hang you."

"Are you telling me you don't want to marry me?"

"You know I'm not. You know I love you. I love you enough to want you to get rid of all this deceit, the lies and pain, and live a happy life with me."

He went to her then and took hold of her shoulders. He gave her a gentle shake.

"Yes, it makes me furious that Chris lied to you about me, led you to believe I was having an affair with Leslie. I have my own thoughts about that and I'll straighten it out with Chris one day soon."

He reached over, lifted a blanket from the bed and wrapped it about her.

"You distract me, love," he whispered gently. "Kristen, you have to understand. I want you beside me as my wife. I want that more than anything else I've ever wanted. But I've got a debt to pay, an obligation to keep. I can't let Charlotte's murder go unavenged. I have no way of fighting Jeffrey except as Captain Black. He's powerful, but his wealth lies on the sea, and I, with the *Falcon*, intend to see that he loses everything. Don't leave me, love. Stay with me until this is over and I promise you I'll spend the rest of my life trying to make you happy."

"No! Morgan, please. Are you blind with this thing? Can you not see it will kill you? He will laugh when they

377

hang you!"

"He'll have to catch me first."

"He will! He will. Oh, Morgan." She threw herself into his arms. "I will tell them who I am tomorrow. I will meet and be happy to marry Lord Morgan Grayfield. But you must choose too. I could not bear thinking about you when you were gone; I could not bear thinking you dead or captured or facing a hanging. No, you must choose me . . . or your revenge."

"Kristen, don't be a fool."

"I'm not. I'm a woman in love and I want the man I love to be with me, to hold me. I want to live with you, laugh with you, bear your children."

"And I want to be with you. You must understand."

"Why must I understand hatred and revenge when I want only to share your love?"

"Damn it, Kristen, will you be reasonable?"

"I am. It is a reasonable thing to ask you to put an end to revenge."

"And leave Jeffrey free to enjoy life while Charlotte is dead? No! I cannot."

"Morgan, we can find some way together. Leave Jeffrey to the law and to God. Please, Morgan." Tears choked her voice. "I would die if I were to lose you again."

He held her against him.

"Don't cry, love. We'll talk of this further, but first, you must be free of all this. Will you tell the Mileses tomorrow?"

"Yes, I'll tell them."

"Damn, I just thought of another difficulty."

"What?"

"Once they know who you are, once your story is out, Leslie and Jeffrey will insist you live there."

"I'm not afraid of either of them."

"Well, it won't be for long. Morgan Grayfield will come calling soon and often."

"Then . . . ?"

"Shhh, love," he whispered as he silenced her with a warm passionate kiss. "We'll cross all our bridges when we get to them. For now, go back to bed and get some sleep. I must leave here before the temptation to stay becomes too much for me."

He dropped the blanket to the floor and lifted her in his arms. He placed her on the bed and covered her with a blanket, but not before he took one last opportunity to caress her silken skin once again.

"You are much too warm and inviting. I look forward to the nights when I have you safe in my own bed where nothing can interfere—to nights when you are mine alone. Rest well, love, and remember that I love you very much. I shall be seeing you soon."

"How soon, Morgan? How soon?"

He grinned and bent over her, kissing her most thoroughly.

"Will you continue to leave your windows unlocked? If you do, I have a feeling you will have a visitor again tomorrow night."

"I'm afraid," she whispered, "I am most forgetful when it comes to locks. I'm sure if an intruder does come in the night, he will find the doors open to him."

"I shall check to find out," he whispered. She watched as he walked to the window and turned. He grinned, waved a jaunty farewell, and, in a moment, he was gone.

Kristen pulled the covers about her for suddenly the whole room seemed chilled and empty.

She thought of all that Morgan had told her. Of course, she felt the pain he must have felt at Charlotte's death, pain for her and for his parents. Yet, she knew it would be nothing to what she would feel if he were captured as a pirate and hung.

She would do as Morgan asked; yet she would try everything she could to stop him from the road he was determined to follow.

She rolled on her side and held in her arms the pillow that still carried the impression of his head. She thought of the anger and need for revenge she had felt for him when she believed Leslie was his mistress. She understood how Morgan must feel, yet she knew she had to find a way to stop him. As she drifted off to sleep, she wondered if her love for him would be enough to change his path.

Morgan rode home possessed of a sureness of purpose, determined that all would work as he planned and both Kristen and revenge would be his. Morgan's was the vanity of all humans who do not take into consideration the capriciousness of fate. It was to twist and turn and lead both him and Kristen down a different road from that either of them had planned to take.

# *Twenty-Three*

Kristen stirred awake, and before she opened her eyes, she missed Morgan's presence at her side. She lay still, allowing her thoughts to surround him and hold him close to her. Soon, she thought, there would be no more waking alone. Soon, she would be with him and there would be no ghostlike Morgan who came and went in the dark shadows of her life, but a material Morgan who would stand at her side for all the world to see.

Vividly, she remembered the night before and the wild taste of him as he touched her senses the way no other could. She remembered the plans they had made together. With determination, she swung her legs over the edge of the bed and rose. Quickly, she made preparations to go down to face the Miles family and tell them the truth of who she was. Then she would ask Chris to take her to confront Jeffrey and Leslie. She knew one thing that she was going to make very clear to both of them. She had no thought of conforming to what they wanted in her life. She was no longer a little girl who could be twisted to their mold; no longer a lonely girl, but a woman who had tasted the strength and giving of love and one who had every intention of filling the balance of her life with nothing less. Of course, her stepmother and Jeffrey would try to make her feel shame or guilt for what had happened to her—Morgan had warned her of their intentions—but she would not fall into that trap. No, she would hold her head up proudly and wait for the moment she and Morgan would be together forever.

Reluctantly, she thought of Chris. She knew he was in love with her, and she did not want to hurt him, but she was past the time that she would mold her life to others' needs. When the time came and Morgan had claimed her, she would tell him that she could not come to him without love. She remembered his Aunt Elspeth's words and knew that wise old woman had read her well, had known she was in love with someone else, and had told her that she should listen to her heart.

Preparations made, she gave herself one last look in the mirror. Satisfied that she looked calm enough to handle the situation, she turned to the door. But before she got to it, there was a rap on it that she recognized. She and Toby had arranged a signal knock, mostly because this secretive conspiritorial behavior appealed to Toby and seemed to draw them closer together. Already in the back of her mind, she thought of herself and Morgan as Toby's parents. She knew he worshiped Morgan, and felt he was nurturing a deep abiding love in his small heart for her also.

"Come in, Toby," she said quietly, not wanting her voice to carry farther than his ears.

Quickly he came inside and closed the door behind him.

"Mornin', Kristen." He grinned.

"Good morning."

"Will we be goin' ridin' this mornin'?"

Toby had not been well-acquainted with horses and besides teaching him to read and write Kristen had decided he should learn to ride.

"Why?" had been his first question. In his mind there

would be no use for him to learn to ride a horse when he would most probably spend his life on the sea as he thought Morgan would.

"Because a gentleman should know."

"But I ain't no gentleman and I probably won't ever be."

"Toby," she had replied gently, "Morgan is a gentleman, and it would please him very much to see you get a good education, too. You would not want to disappoint him, would you?" she had added in a calm reasonable voice. That was exactly the right note to strike with Toby, for there was no dearer aim in his life than to do everything in his power to please Morgan.

So they had begun his riding lessons. Now they were an important part of his day.

"No, we can't this morning, Toby. There is something very important I have to do."

"What?"

"Toby, come sit beside me."

Obediently, he came and sat beside her, his eyes filled with questions.

"Toby, Morgan came here last night," she whispered.

"He did! But . . ."

"But what?"

"Nuthin'."

"Toby, what were you going to say?"

"I can't. I promised," he replied worriedly.

It took her only moments to realize that Morgan had already visited him and sworn him to silence. She did not want to put pressure on the deep loyalty he felt for Morgan.

"Anyway, I am going down and tell the Mileses the truth. . . . Well, at least part of the truth. I will tell them who I am. Then, as Kristen Seaford, I will be free to marry Lord Morgan Grayfield and"—she smiled—"we would then be able to adopt you. In a matter of a few months, we will be a family. You, Morgan, and me. Would you like that?"

She watched the happiness leap to his eyes, and saw them fill with tears he manfully tried to suppress.

"Yes." He gulped. "I really would."

"Then let's go down to breakfast. It is time we get things started."

He leaped to his feet and together they went down the stairs. The muffled sound of voices told them that all the Mileses were already around the breakfast table. She and Toby walked into the room and all eyes turned to them.

All three men rose as Kristen entered, but it was Toby who insisted on holding her chair for her, bringing a twinkle of amusement to the Mileses' eyes by his defiant look. He was prepared to do battle to care for his soon-to-be mother.

"Good morning, Mr. and Mrs. Miles." Kristen smiled. "Blake, Chris, 'tis a lovely day."

They all acknowledged her greeting.

When their plates had been set in front of them and the servant had retreated to the kitchen, when everyone seemed to be settled for a relaxed quiet breakfast, Kristen took hold of her nerves and said firmly, "Now that we are all together, I have something of the utmost urgency to tell you."

"Jennifer," Chris said quickly, "is something wrong?"

"That is the first thing that is wrong, Chris." She took a deep breath. Then added in a quiet voice, "You see, my name is not Jennifer Nelson. . . . It is Kristen Seaford."

Blake, Jr. whistled softly. "The heiress who was supposed to marry Jeffrey MacIntire and was kidnapped by pirates?"

"Yes," Kristen replied softly.

"Kristen Seaford," Chris repeated numbly, wondering why she had suddenly made the decision to tell them. There was a deeper reason behind the move than she intended them to know and he was determined to discover what it was.

"Why in heaven's name did you keep it a secret all this time?" Blake said.

"I . . . I was frightened. I needed time to collect my thoughts. I needed time to be alone."

"And that is when I found you," Chris said gently.

"Yes."

"There's no need for you to be frightened of anything, child," Mr. Miles said firmly. "There is no one who would see anything wrong in wanting some time alone. Do you want us to return you to your future husband? I'm sure he must be beside himself with worry about you."

"I want to go to the MacIntires'," she said quietly, "but it is not to be his wife. I have no intention of marrying Jeffrey MacIntire now, or in the future."

Chris's heart leaped, and he wanted to shout for joy. Maybe, he thought, he had been in some way responsible for her change of mind. Perhaps, after a while, after a long and intense courtship she would forget about Jeffrey, Morgan, or anyone else but him.

The family was filled with questions and she answered them as best she could in a way that would not endanger Morgan. She had been taken, she said, to an island, where she had been left alone in a small cabin while the pirate ship had sat in the harbor to guard her. When the ransom had been paid, she had been taken to a spot on the coast where she had had the good fortune to run across Morgan. He had wanted to take her home immediately, but she had begged for time so he had given her the use of his hunting lodge for as long as she wanted it. He had left Toby, the son of a friend of his, to keep her company. She had been doing well until Toby was injured.

"And that's when I came along," Chris added.

"Yes, a piece of good fortune for which I will always be grateful," Kristen said.

Chris's eyes glowed with the emotion he felt for Kristen, and his brother Blake was pleased until he looked closely at Kristen. He knew immediately that no matter what Chris felt for Kristen, what she felt was affectionate gratitude and nothing more. It pained him to realize that Chris was on a collision course with heartbreak. And there was nothing he or anyone else could do to stop him.

"Would you like just to send word of your whereabouts and stay with us? We would be delighted to have you as a guest for as long as you would care to stay," Mrs. Miles said.

"No, I must go and speak to him personally. He and my stepmother will be surprised. I thank you for such consideration."

"Keep in mind that the offer is always open," Blake said. "If you want to come back, merely send a message; one of us will come for you."

"Thank you. My lawyer has transferred some of my funds here. Eventually, I shall find a place of my own. Right now, my life is very unsettled. I have many things to take care of in the next few weeks, but I shall be back to thank you more properly for all you have done for me."

Again, she was assured by the entire family that she was most welcome. Chris wanted to take her to Jeffrey's, but in the end, the entire family accompanied her.

When the buggy stopped in front of Jeffrey's

magnificent home, Kristen sat for a moment and looked at it. If it had not been for the intervention of Captain Black, she would have been married by now and mistress of this house. However, she felt nothing but pleasure in the fact that she was making her first step toward Morgan.

They were ushered into the library by a surprised butler, whose eyes widened in shock when he found out who she was.

"Wh . . . who?" he asked.

"Tell Mr. MacIntire and Mrs. Seaford that Miss Kristen Seaford is here," Kristen said quietly. The man disappeared and Chris's and Blake's lips twitched in an effort to keep their amusement under control.

The butler went up the stairs and knocked lightly on Jeffrey's door. Jeffrey was sitting at his desk, papers scattered about him; he was working out his plans for transferring all Kristen's funds to Leslie's name and making an official announcement that Kristen Seaford was permanently lost—killed by an elusive pirate named Captain Black. He hoped it would finally put a price on Captain Black's head that would tempt someone to betray him.

"Yes," he called sharply, angry at the interruption. The door opened and the butler came in.

"Well," Jeffrey said impatiently. "What is it?"

"There are guests, sir, who would like to speak to you."

"Guests? I'm not expecting anyone and Mrs. Seaford is out. Who is it?"

"Mr. and Mrs. Miles, their sons, Mr. Blake and Mr. Christopher, and . . . Miss Kristen Seaford."

He was pleased to watch the color drain from Jeffrey's face, and to see the hand that held the papers tremble.

"Who?" he gasped.

"Mr. and Mrs.—"

"Damn it, I know you said the Miles family, but you also said . . ."

"Miss Kristen Seaford. She's waiting with them, sir."

"Kristen," Jeffrey whispered softly. Then his eyes caught the wicked glow of amusement in the butler's eyes. He stiffened and said coldly, "Tell them I'll be down in a few minutes, and get them some refreshments."

"Yes, sir," the butler said softly and turned and left the room.

Jeffrey sat staring at the closed door for a full ten minutes; emotions rolled over him one after another—disbelief, hot anger, followed by a few minutes of stern self-control. Somehow, Kristen had escaped or been released by Captain Black. After this much time, he had been sure she was either dead or in such abject shame and misery over what had happened to her, she had chosen not to return. Just when he and Leslie had everything well planned out, the two women they had thought to be rid of, both turned up safe and well. He could see all his plans begin to disintegrate. Then he grasped control of himself. It would take a great deal to stop Jeffrey MacIntire from getting what he wanted.

He rose and went to the door. Leaving the room he strode down the hall. As he was descending the wide staircase, from the library, he heard the muffled sound of voices and soft laughter . . . Kristen's laughter. At that moment he could have strangled her with his bare hands. Instead, he formed his face into a warm smile and walked into the room.

"Kristen, my dear," he said, concern and anxiety in his well-practiced voice. He went to her and would have taken her in his arms, but she took a step backward. She smiled, trying her best to control her disgust and anger at this man. She did not want her rejection to be too obvious so she held out her hand to him and he took it in both of his.

"It is so good to see you are safe and well. I have been distraught with worry over you these past weeks. My poor dear Kristen, what you must have been put through." He bent forward and kissed her on the cheek, feeling her resistance even to that. Someone or something had altered the hold he had had over her when he left America. He would have to work with patience and care to revive her feelings for him.

Kristen was irritated at being referred to as poor Kristen, and she resented his subtle reference to her terrible experiences.

"Thank you, Jeffrey."

Jeffrey greeted the Mileses warmly, but with a questioning look as to how Kristen had come to be with them. Quickly Chris explained the situation.

"Morgan!" Jeffrey exclaimed with irritation. "But if he knew who you were, he should have returned you to me instead of hiding you away."

"I lied about who I was," Kristen said calmly. "I wanted some time alone to think so I told him my name was Jennifer Nelson. It was quite kind of him to give me sanctuary. It gave me time to do a lot of thinking."

"Yes," Jeffrey said stiffly. "Morgan Grayfield, always the gentleman. Kristen, you should have sent me some message. I have been worried to death over you. My days and nights have been filled with thoughts of you, and all the terrible things that were . . . might have been happening."

Again his suggestion that she had been severely compromised angered her. She was about to answer when the door opened and Leslie came in.

"Jeffrey, dear, I—" She stopped dead in her tracks and her eyes widened in absolute shock. At that moment, Kristen surmised just how much time Jeffrey had spent missing her.

"Leslie," Kristen said softly, "I'm glad to see you are here. I know how anxious you must have been also."

She had to give Leslie credit for drawing herself under rigid control. Quickly, her expression changed into one of pity and solicitude.

"I admit it has been a terrible shock. After all the terrible stories we've heard about this pirate, we did not expect to see you look so . . . so . . . recovered."

So Leslie and Jeffrey had joined forces on the idea of promoting common gossip about her—that Kristen had been used, abused, and then discarded. Kristen's anger was held in stern control, but it was not the same with the entire Miles family. That indignation showed plainly in all their eyes, while those of Chris and Blake expressed complete rage, did not go unnoticed by either Leslie or Jeffrey.

"We have returned Kristen here at her own request," Chris said coldly. "But she is assured she is most welcome to return to our home at any time. I'm sure she understands that no one in this city would misunderstand her circumstances while we are her protectors." His emphasis on the words *we* and *protectors* brought a flush to Jeffrey's face and a cold piercing look to Leslie's eyes.

"Of course, no one misunderstands. Now that she is home we must go on with the plans for the wedding. The sooner she and Jeffrey are married, the quieter the gossips will become."

"I'm sorry to disappoint you—again Leslie," Kristen

390

replied, "but I have no intention of marrying Jeffrey soon; in fact not even in the distant future. I'm going to find a place of my own to live and then enjoy the money Father left me. I have time to think of marriage at a later date, when I've decided just whom I want to marry."

Leslie was so furious at having their plans thwarted she would have gladly killed Kristen where she stood. It was Jeffrey who intervened before Leslie could reply.

"You are upset now, Kristen. Let me take you to a room where you can make yourself comfortable. We'll talk after you've had some time to adjust yourself to being home. After a while, you will be more adjusted and everything will work out for us. You are just in time to attend a party I'm giving for my sister Jane and her new husband, Owen MacGregor. It will be a good way for you to meet all our friends."

"Thank you, Jeffrey," she said, but he could read her eyes clearly and knew she did not intend to go any further in their relationship. He cursed Captain Black and renewed his vow to see him dead.

"I cannot wait to see Owen again. I'm grateful to him for the consideration he showed when he first came for me."

"Well, the party will be magnificent, and I cannot wait to show them the most beautiful woman in the city."

Kristen smiled in acknowledgement of the compliment.

"Come, Kristen," Leslie said, "I'll take you to your room. My dressmaker can begin at once to make your dress for the party."

Kristen thanked the Miles family and was grateful for their insistence that they wanted her to come visit them as often as she could.

"You will save me a few dances at the party?" Chris

391

said. "I'm sure once you've been viewed by all the local swains it will be difficult to get near you."

"Chris." She laughed. "You are very special and there will be dances whenever you choose."

"Watch, madam." He grinned. "I might choose to have them all."

"No, Brother," Blake said. "Didn't Mother and Father always try to teach us to share?"

They all laughed, even Leslie, whose dislike for Kristen increased.

When the Mileses had gone Leslie took Kristen upstairs to her room.

"I'll send for the dressmaker. Obviously she must start with essentials. You look . . ." She shrugged. "But then you always liked to run around at home like a hoyden. I'll see you at dinner."

She closed the door behind her and Kristen stood looking at it. One thing was certain. She could hardly wait for Morgan to come and take her from this place for good. She wondered how it would be if she had to face living here with these people for the rest of her life without Morgan. It was a thought she quickly shook off for she could not bear to picture such an existence.

For three days, she saw no sign of Morgan. Chris and Blake came to call often, and Leslie and Jeffrey did see that she was fitted with a complete new wardrobe including a beautiful gown for the party.

On the morning of the day before the party, having gone riding, she returned and went to her room to change. She brushed her hair and coiled it in a thick rope at the nape of her neck. Slipping into a casual cotton dress, she prepared to go down to find something light for lunch when she was interrupted by a light rap on the door.

392

"Come in," she called. A young maid came in.

"Miss Seaford, Mrs. Seaford has asked you to come down to the library. There is someone there who would like to meet you."

"Who is it?"

"Lord Grayfield, miss."

Kristen's heart leaped, and she smiled. "Tell them I'll be there immediately."

"Yes, miss."

The young maid left, and Kristen, giving a soft contented laugh, whirled about in an explosion of happiness. In a moment, she left the room and ran lightly down the stairs. From the library, she could hear the deep, warm, and very welcome sound of Morgan's voice . . . and Leslie's.

"Of course, it must have been a most terrible time for Kristen. I shudder to think . . ."

"I'm sure none of what you think occurred."

Morgan's soft amused voice came. "The man has a reputation for ravaging ships . . . not women."

Kristen opened the door and walked in. It was the most difficult feat of her life not to run directly to his arms and feel them close safely about her.

Tall and handsome, he stood near the fireplace. His smile welcomed her as did the deep flicker of warmth in his eyes.

"Well," he said softly, "whom do I meet today, Jennifer Nelson or Kristen Seaford?"

"Kristen Seaford." She smiled. "And I do apologize for deceiving you. I felt it necessary at the time."

"Kristen," Leslie said sweetly, "I have just reminded Morgan about the party. We would be quite disappointed if he did not attend."

"Oh, yes, Lord Grayfeld . . ."

"Morgan," Morgan interrupted.

"Morgan," she repeated. "It will give me another chance to thank you for saving me."

"Saving you?" Morgan grinned. "I was just assuring your stepmother that it was not what she imagined."

"Oh, but it was," Kristen replied; the wicked glow of devilment in her eyes reflected his. "The man was an arrogant selfish beast."

"Really, now, I've heard stories that he was a gentleman. Handsome and considerate."

"Oh, no, you've heard wrong," Kristen said innocently. "He was ugly."

"Ugly?"

"Quite . . . deformed, an evil-looking man with a bad temper."

"Really?" Morgan questioned, but Kristen could read the glow in his eyes as a promise to repay her insults at his first opportunity.

"Well, I'm glad to see you are well, and I look forward to a dance at the party."

"Of course, could I deny the man who so gallantly saved me from a fate worse than death?" Kristen said softly.

"Well, I must go. It was nice to see you again, Kristen, and I must say that I like your new name even more than the other."

"Thank you."

"I'll walk you to the door, Morgan," Leslie purred as she slipped her arm through his. Kristen watched them leave wondering why she suddenly felt the urge to scratch Leslie's eyes out.

She spent the day having a final fitting for the gown she would wear to the party and shopping with Leslie. She bought some perfume and a few other accessories she might need. When they were in town, Kristen took the opportunity, while Leslie was being fitted, to go across the street and see Reginald Murkton. They walked for a while and he assured her that he would let her know as soon as the correspondence came from America about the transfer of her money.

"Until then, my child, I would like to provide you with anything you might need. You can repay me later."

"Thank you, I do not like taking anything from Jeffrey MacIntire. I don't understand how I could have thought of marrying that man in the first place."

"Well, you soon will be free of him. I think I might have found a nice place to rent. You will approve, I'm sure. After the party I will take you to see it."

"Good, I will feel much better when I'm on my own."

"A lot better," he answered gently. "And a lot safer?"

"Yes . . . a lot safer."

"Take care of yourself, child; you'll be out of there soon."

"I'm grateful to you for all you've done."

"I know, child. I loved your father too much to let anything happen to you. You have friends, remember."

"I will." She kissed his cheek and left to rejoin Leslie.

The next night, she dressed with the most elaborate care she had ever taken. Her red-gold hair was drawn to the top of her head in a mass of ringlets with fringes of curls framing her face and slender neck. Her dress was a deep emerald green. It was cut daringly low. The slenderness of its tight waist was accentuated by a voluminous skirt. She wore a string of pearls about her neck and pearl earrings.

She put the last touch of perfume behind each ear then surveyed herself in the mirror. Satisfied, and anxious to see Morgan again, she left her room and went down the stairs.

Jeffrey was the one who awaited her at the bottom of the stairs. She was late in coming down and Leslie and Jeffrey had been there long before her. She watched Jeffrey's face as she descended and wondered why she had not noticed his lust-filled look before. He seemed to undress her as she walked down and her skin crawled with aversion. It intensified her need for Morgan.

"You are absolutely beautiful, Kristen," he said.

"Thank you, Jeffrey."

"Come, I want to introduce you to all my friends," He took her hand and tucked it under his arm in a possessive way that irritated her, and they walked together into the breathlessly beautiful ballroom.

The music, combined with the bright colorful display of beautiful gowns and sparkling jewels excited Kristen, who had never experienced this brilliant world. She watched the dancers whirl about the floor and her body swayed a little to the sound and beat of the music.

The first people he led her to were Owen and Jane. She greeted Owen with happy enthusiasm, and he was overjoyed to see her again.

"Ye are bonnier now than ye were then; 'tis a magic way ye have of growin' bonnier every day."

"And you are a true Scot with a compliment always on the tip of your tongue." She laughed. "I have missed you, Owen."

"Aye, our partin' company was rather sudden. Ye are well, lass?"

"Yes, Owen, very well." She turned to Jane. "And you could be no other than Owen's Jane. You are as beautiful as he said you were. I feel almost as if I know you; Owen talked of you so much."

"Yes, I'm Jane." Jane laughed. "And I have heard

almost as much about you. I'm sorry for all the problems you have had. Please come and see me soon; we must talk and become friends."

"I would like that. I know so few people here."

"Oh, that's right, you were born in America."

"Yes."

"Then I insist we talk soon. We have such different backgrounds it should be interesting to share them."

Kristen was about to reply when Jeffrey interrupted by taking her hand; and with a smile, he insisted she share the first dance with him. Owen was the only one to wonder if Jeffrey had another reason for wanting to separate the two women . . . a reason like not wanting them to share any memories, thoughts, or ideas.

"I want to show you off." Jeffrey laughed. "And what better way than on the dance floor."

Without another word, and with no chance for her to protest, Jeffrey swung her out onto the floor. She had to admit that despite the fact that she would have preferred another partner, she enjoyed the dance.

When it was over, she stood with Jeffrey and Leslie by the food-laden table sipping a glass of champagne. The music began to play a soft low waltz, and before Jeffrey could speak, a deep voice came from behind her that set her a-tremble. She spun about to look up into a pair of humorous blue eyes.

"I promise I shan't step on your toes," he said in a warm voice.

"What?"

"I asked if I could have the pleasure of the next dance, Miss Seaford, if"—he looked at Jeffrey—"Jeffrey doesn't mind."

"I'd love to," Kristen said quickly before Jeffrey could voice any opposition.

Morgan took Kristen's hand in his and led her to the edge of the floor. When she turned to him the intense warmth of his gaze lfited her and held her.

"Hello, love," he whispered as he reached for her. "It's been too long since I've held you. Even dancing is better than just living with thoughts of you."

"Morgan," she murmured softly as his arm slid about her and he swung her onto the floor.

She smiled up at him, feeling the strength of his grip. "You were waiting for me?"

"The room has been very dim until you came. In fact I was growing impatient, about to come up and get you."

"Morgan, you wouldn't dare!"

He laughed and drew her closer in his arms. "I must say, love, you look ravishing, but still . . ."

"Still what?"

"I'm rather fond of the gypsy who played in the surf on my island." His eyes became serious and his voice softened. "I love you, Kristen, and before too long, I want to take you back to my island."

"My dream," she whispered.

"Our dream," he corrected.

They whirled about the floor, unaware that they made such a beautiful couple that most of the other dancers had stopped to watch. The tall handsome man and the slender golden-haired girl in his arms seemed to belong to each other. Almost all the people admired the two . . . almost.

For Chris felt a deep burning jealousy. He knew without doubt that Kristen was in love with Morgan and he with her. He also knew that Morgan was the pirate, Captain Black, and that to be rid of him he need only open his mouth and make the information known. Leslie and Jeffrey stood together, neither knowing the circumstances, but aware that there was something alive and flowing between the two.

"The Grayfield charm still works well," Jeffrey murmured angrily.

"I would do my best to keep those two separated." Leslie smiled maliciously. "You might find another fortune snatched out of your grasp."

"Leslie, for Christ's sake, shut up. Sometimes you talk just a little too much."

The dance came to an end and Kristen reluctantly left Morgan's arms to be escorted back to Jeffrey's side.

For the rest of the evening, she was swarmed by young swains who wanted an introduction and a dance with the beautiful newcomer. She could see Morgan's eyes on her often, and they seemed amused and pleased that she was having such a good time.

However, Kristen's beautiful evening was not to have such a good ending. Jeffrey escorted her to her room and his mood seemed to her to be much less than pleased.

"Kristen," he began at her door, "we have had a great deal of disastrous luck that has seemed to separate us somehow. I would like very much to change that. I would like to start again, for my dearest desire is to marry you. I know it has been hard for you, captured by this blackguard, held for so long. But I'll put an end to all the gossip and hard fortune for you if you'll let me."

His voice expressed sympathy for her whispered-about situation, but his eyes, denied what his lips were saying as they twisted into her; yet she kept her face serene.

"I'm sorry, Jeffrey. I know what a great honor you do me, trying to save my blemished reputation, but I would not take advantage of your kind heart. I must have more time to recover from my . . . ordeal. Soon I will have a house of my own. Then maybe, when I have lived down the whispers, I will be able to consider your offer. For tonight, I cannot. Good night."

She went in, and closed the door behind her before he could answer.

Inside, she stood leaning against the door suppressing laughter at Jeffrey's stunned face. The room was dark, and a wide path of moonlight lay across the floor from the open French doors. The room was quiet, and yet she knew. All her senses tingled with expectancy. Morgan was there.

She could not see him, yet she knew with every sense she possessed that he was near. She walked into the path of the moonlight, and, feeling the presence of him, a surge of warmth washed over her. She smiled, aware of the fact that he didn't think she knew he was watching her.

Slowly, she reached behind her for the laces to her dress, released them, and let the dress fall to the floor in a soft rustle of silk. Her petticoats followed slowly as did the other pieces of clothing she wore. She stood in the moonlight and lifted her arms to unbind her hair and let it fall about her in a tangled mass. She ran her fingers through it sensuously and a warm throaty chuckle came from her as she heard his voice, soft, warm, and caressing.

"You are a little witch, my love." He stepped from the shadows near her and she laughed as strong arms lifted her against him and his hard searching mouth claimed hers in a searing possessive kiss.

"You knew I was here?" he whispered as his hands gently caressed her slim waist and hips.

"I knew," she replied. "I will always know when you are near. I can feel you with my heart. I wanted you, Morgan; I shall always want you."

"It was quite a performance, my love. You look like the goddess Aphrodite bathed in gold moonlight. 'Twould have stormed the senses of the most resolute man, and I assure you I enjoyed every moment of it."

Gently, he drew her against him. His lips played with hers softly and with an expertise that set the blood coursing through her veins. Her arms slid up about his neck, and as she molded her body against his, she sighed with pleasure at the tingling glow that built deep within her and bubbled through her body like molten lava.

"God, Kristen," he murmured, "I have no thoughts but you. I eat, sleep, and drink your beauty. I could no more have stayed away from you tonight than I could have flown."

It was then the real fact of his presence came to her.

"Morgan, how did you get in here? It's so dangerous. What if someone had seen you?"

He laughed, and bending slightly, swung her up into his arms and carried her to the bed, where he unceremoniously dumped her in the center and stood back enjoying her tumbled beauty. Then he began to remove his clothes.

"The tree outside your window was made for climbing, and your open window was too much of an invitation to ignore."

"But you must be careful. You must be gone before daylight makes it impossible."

He lay beside her on the bed and drew her against him, crushing her in his arms while his lips again began to explore her willing ones.

"There are many hours between now and morning, hours I do not intend to let go to waste. Lying in my lonely bed at home with dreams of you here is too much to ask. Soon, love, I'll not have to leave you."

"Oh, Morgan," she whispered as his arms enclosed her and his lips planted abandoned kisses along her throat and shoulders. "I find it so hard to wait."

"And I find it an agony. But do not worry, love, Lord Morgan Grayfield intends to court you and wed you before anyone realizes what is happening."

"Morgan, what are your plans toward Leslie and Jeffrey? Will you put them out of our lives, forget them, let us live happily together? It's over, isn't it, this pirate thing? I could not bear it if anything happened to you now. My life would end."

The last thing Morgan wanted was to upset her or to have her thoughts on what he might be planning on doing. Urgently, he kissed her again and again until she clung to him and returned his kiss with a blinding passion. Her mind and body knew nothing but Morgan, Morgan who could draw from the very depths of her soul all the giving love she possessed. She was joyfully lost in their mounting passion, lost and never wanting to find her way back.

The dark sky reluctantly began to lose its hold on the night. A pale gray border was lining the horizon with the first touch of day when Morgan began to slip quietly from the bed. Kristen stirred at the absence of his warmth and murmured his name as she reached for him.

"I've got to go, love," he whispered as she nestled against him. "I hate to leave, but I must."

He held her for a moment letting his hands lightly caress the warmth of her smooth skin, enjoying again the intense pleasure he felt knowing her need matched his.

"There's no help for it, love, I've got to get out of here."

He turned to her, looking into her sleepy gray eyes. He slid his hands through the tangled mass of her hair and brushed a light kiss across her lips, before sliding from the bed and dressing rapidly. Then he went back to her side and sat for a moment. Lifting her hand he placed a kiss in the center of her palm.

"Keep this," he said gently. "I shall want it returned soon."

"I will multiply it over and over if you will tell me when you will return," she whispered.

"Tomorrow night. I can stay away no longer than that." Again he bent to kiss her, then he rose and went to the window. Having made sure that no one was moving about yet and the area was empty, he turned, smiled, waved a jaunty salute to Kristen, and in a moment he was gone so silently and so quickly that to Kristen it seemed to happen in the blink of an eye.

She sighed and curled up, drawing his pillow into her arms to hold. She knew now that nothing in her life could be complete or whole without Morgan. She closed her eyes and allowed the dreams to come. Dreams of the day she and Morgan would be together forever.

# Twenty-Four

Douglas MacGregor rode slowly toward his brother Ian's home. In his pocket he carried Owen's letter which he had read several times. He tied his horse and went to the door. Before he could rap on it, it was swung open and a little girl stood before him, a wide smile on her pretty face and the sparkle of affection in her eyes.

"I saw ye comin', Uncle Douglas, from over the hill. I've been watchin' ye."

"Flora, me darlin', come and gi' yer uncle a kiss. 'Tis awhile since I've seen ye. Ye've grown an inch taller since I've seen ye last and ye're even prettier than before."

With a little half-laugh, half-giggle, she raised her arms to Douglas who lifted her up, swinging her high in the air. He caught her to him and kissed her soundly. Then, still holding her in his arms, he walked into the house and closed the door behind him.

"Where is yer mother, Flora?"

"She'll be here in a minute, Uncle Douglas. She has just carried fresh water to Father."

"Would ye do me a favor, Flora?"

"Oh, yes, Uncle Douglas." She smiled brightly, for Douglas was one of her very favorite people and she would consider doing anything he asked.

"Run out and tell yer father to come back wi' yer

404

mother. I've a letter from Uncle Owen and 'tis important for him to read."

He stood her on her feet and watched with pleasure as she ran lightly out the back door.

Douglas sat down and took the letter from his pocket. He opened it and scanned again the words he already knew.

Before long, the sound of heavy approaching footsteps accompanied by lighter ones told him Ian was there. The back door opened and Ian came in.

"Douglas, Flora has told me ye wanted to see me about a letter from Owen. Is there somethin' amiss?"

"Aye, Ian, there is. 'Tis better ye read the letter than for me to try to explain it."

He handed the letter to Ian who sat down on a stool by the fireplace and began to read. Douglas watched him, but could not read any expression on his face. He smiled—Ian, always the strong quiet one, but always dependable. If Owen had reached out for quiet strength and happy adventurism, he had chosen the right two to call upon.

"Well, what do ye think, Ian?"

Ian looked up at him and smiled. "I think that if Owen needs our help 'twould be best if we be about findin' what he needs to know."

"Today?"

"Aye, why put it off? Sophia," he said as he turned to his wife, "would ye be good enough to pack us enough for a few days? Douglas and I are goin' down to Brawford to dig up some information Owen needs for Jane's safety."

"Aye, Ian," she said softly and went about the house doing as he had requested. There was a quiet love between these two that Douglas could sense every time he walked into their home. It was an intangible thing that

405

he could only feel, without being able to name one definite act that revealed it.

Douglas sat down in a chair opposite Ian, and Flora promptly found a comfortable place on his lap. To her pleasure, he absently caressed her long hair while he spoke to her father.

"What will we be doin' first, Ian?"

"First we go to Brawford, then we find Caroline Stewart and begin to search about in her past as best we can. From the way Owen sounds he suspects that this woman is Jeffrey's mother. We'll have to find out if she was married to or consortin' wi anyone. Then we'll try to discover where Jeffrey was born and how he came to be raised by the MacIntires as Jane's brother. If we can prove they are not brother and sister, if we can prove Jeffrey is not a MacIntire, then we will have all the proof Jane will need to be sole heir to the MacIntire estate. She will be free of all her so-called brother's claims on her."

"Do ye know, I sensed it the first time I realized the lass was so uncommonly afraid of her brother. 'Tis unnatural for a brother to treat a sister as he did. I have a feelin' we will surely find out it is true and that that sweet lass could no be a sister to that man."

"Aye, I've felt the same. We'll do the best we can and hope it is enough for Owen to be able to rid Jane of her brother."

Sophia came to Ian's side and he smiled up at her. The man and child who sat opposite them were warmed by the obvious affection these two had for each other.

"Everything is ready, Ian."

Ian stood and slid his arms about her waist.

"Sophia, I would like ye to take the lass and go to my mother."

"But, Ian, there is much to do here."

"Aye, I know there is," he said softly as he smiled into her warm eyes, "but I will feel better knowin' ye and the child are safe. I wouldna be worryin' about ye. Will ye no do as I ask ye, lass, for my own peace of mind?"

"Yes, Ian, if ye wish it so. I shall go as soon as ye leave. I must prepare a few things first."

"Before 'tis dark?"

"Aye, my worrisome husband." She laughed. "Before 'tis dark. I promise ye me and Flora will share supper wi' yer family."

He chuckled, drew her closer to him, and kissed her with deep and open passion.

Ian and Douglas set out on their journey to Brawford which was over four days' ride away. They stopped at night only when it was too dark to go on, and rose before the dawn each morning to be on their way.

The town of Brawford was rather large and much busier than usual. They found themselves accommodations in an inn not too far from the edge of town for they did not know exactly how long it would take them to find out what Owen wanted to know.

They made themselves comfortable, then went down to the main room ostensibly to get a meal, but more to listen to the gossip and pick up whatever news might exist.

They made a point of striking up a conversation with several people and an hour later they were enjoying a last drink with two men whose positions and loose tongues might make it worthwhile.

"'Tis a fair-sized town ye have," Douglas said. "It seems t' be leapin' wi' life."

"Aye, 'tis that. We are proud of it. Did ye know it was here that the bonnie prince stayed wi' half his army on the way to Culloden."

"Ye'd no be jestin' wi' me?" Douglas laughed.

"Nay, 'tis not a jest. The bonnie prince and one of his best, Lord George Murray, slept in this very inn."

Douglas was about to speak again when he noticed Ian's intent gaze on the man. Something in the man's words had caught Ian's deepest interest. Douglas held what he was going to say in check and waited for Ian to speak.

"'Tis an excitin' thought, I should ha liked to be here. Did he stay in the town long?"

"Both times."

"Both?"

"Comin' . . . and goin'," the man grinned.

"Just how long did he stay?"

"Comin'? Well, let me see. 'Twas well onto six months he was here; then goin' nearly three."

"Six months," Ian said gently. He leaned forward and in a very conspiritorial tone said, "I imagine it was a fine time for the people here. The prince has the reputation of being a man of ah . . . deep female appreciation. I'll wager it set the women's hearts a-twitter knowin' the prince was here. I can just imagine they threw themselves at his feet."

"Aye." The man laughed. "He certainly had no trouble wi' 'em, tha's for sure."

"But knowin' the prince's discriminating taste, I'll wager there was one lass bonnier than all the rest. One that held him just a little longer than the others?"

The man thought for some time; then he and the other man shook their heads negatively in unison.

"Nay, there was na anyone special. The prince was free wi' his lovin'."

Disappointment registered in Ian's face only to be quickly replaced by a look of deeper interest when the second man spoke.

"Aye, the prince spread his lovin' about well, but it certainly was na the same wi' his friend the lieutenant general."

"The lieutenant general? Who . . ."

"George Murray, or should I say Lord George Murray. Do ye know the name?"

"Who doesna know the Lord George Murray? He was probably the wealthiest, most important lord in all Scotland next to the prince. Wasna the man killed sometime later?"

"Aye, that he was. 'Twas sad, he was a bonnie lad, was well-liked here about. The people would have been glad to hide him here after Culloden and protect him, but no, his loyalties lay wi' his prince and follow him he did . . . to his death."

"Ye were speakin' of a woman?"

"A woman? . . . Oh, aye . . . a woman. But not just any woman. She were the bonniest lass for miles around. There wasna anyone who dinna love her and that included all the able-bodied men about."

"Would her name have been Caroline Stewart?"

"Na."

Again Ian felt disappointment, for he felt he had the answers all straight in his mind.

"It wasna Mrs. Stewart . . . it was her young ward, Isabel Maclean."

"Isabel Maclean?"

"Aye, she was the ward of Mrs. Stewart. Word has it that she was some sort of royalty herself but no man ever knew the truth of it."

"What else do ye know of Isabel Maclean and Lord Murray."

"Nothin'. Most everyone's attention was on the

prince. I expect there's no one about knows what happened atwixt those two except that they were taken wi' one another. Often ye would see them ridin' out together. Handsome couple they was. She wi' her black hair and fair skin and he so tall and dark. Aye, a handsome couple they was, but no one knows wha happened wi' 'em."

"Ye're wrong there," the second man added.

"Wrong?"

"Wrong. There was one would know the whole story, but she's na goin' to speak on the subject."

"Who, who is it?" Ian asked quickly.

"Lady Caroline's maid, ol' Miss Warriston."

"Where do we find this Miss Warriston?" Ian asked quickly.

"She's still livin' in the house at the other end of the town, the one Lady Stewart left to her when she died. But she'll no tell ya a thing about either woman. She's ferociously loyal to both of 'em and she'll no say anythin' about 'em to strangers."

"Will ye describe the house to me? I'll be willin' to take my chances. It's of the utmost importance to someone close to both the women under her care," Ian said quietly.

"Aye. 'Tis at the far end of the town, a small stone house wi' a stone fence about it. It sets a little apart from most. Ye canna miss it. But mind ye, she'll be no talkin' to ye."

"I thank ye for yer information," Ian said as he rose and tossed a few coins on the table. Douglas rose and stood beside him.

"Ye have given a great deal of aid to both women and to another whose very life might be dependin' on what we find out."

The men both nodded, not sure of what they had done, yet having the strange feeling that what they had done was right. They watched the two tall strong men walk away.

Ian and Douglas walked through the damp cobbled streets of Brawford. It did not take them long to find the small stone house they had been looking for.

They stood outside for a few minutes looking at the house.

"Strange, to find the answers to Jane's troubles in this little stone house. Maybe they were right. Maybe she'll no tell us anything," Douglas said.

"Well," Ian said, "we'll never know until we try."

They walked to the heavy wooden door and knocked.

The woman who answered it was a small woman with a face that spoke of many years of hardship and work. Her eyes were a shrewd brown that studied them both closely.

"Miss Warriston?" Ian said.

"Aye, that I be. And who might ye be?"

"My name is Ian MacGregor and this is my brother Douglas. We have come a fair piece to speak wi' ye. Might we come in? 'Tis best to keep our conversation personal."

"Ye'll be tellin' me what ye want to converse wi' me about or ye'll no step through my door," she said firmly and Douglas would have laughed except Ian cast him a silencing look.

"We would speak to ye," Ian said in a soft voice that would not carry far, "of Isabel Maclean and Lord Murray."

The woman became still, her guarded eyes studying Ian closely.

"And why would I be talkin' to ye of anyone? I dinna know any more than any other in the town. Go and ask

411

your questions somewhere else."

"We would also speak to ye," Ian added in a whisper, "of a child who might be the heir to a fortune and the key to solving a great problem."

Again she stood assessing Ian; then she stepped aside and motioned for them to come in. They did, and she looked carefully about her before she closed the door and latched it.

The house was small, yet quite comfortable. It was easy to see that the woman was an immaculate housekeeper.

"Sit ye down, I'll pour ye some tea."

Both men sat, neither wanting tea, yet prepared to humor the woman until they got the information they needed.

As she poured the tea and gave a cup to each of them, Ian noticed quickly that her hand trembled. She sat opposite them.

"Now, ye will tell me who ye are and why ye are here. I shall decide if your questions need answerin'."

Douglas watched as Ian began to talk. Her eyes never left his as he spoke. Ian told the entire story.

The old woman sighed.

"I told Lady Caroline there would be trouble over this, but she was always the one for laughin' and havin' fun and enjoyin' the gentlemen. I told her that young thing was too sweet and shy a lass to be alone wi' him."

"Him?" Ian asked.

"Lord Murray. Oh, I admit the handsome lad was taken wi' the lass, and why not, she was the prettiest thing about."

"Miss Warriston will you tell me exactly what happened?" Ian said.

412

"All right, ye know that the prince was here for some time."

Ian nodded.

"He met Lady Caroline. She was a beauty, and she was laughter and forgettin' for the prince. But her ward, Isabel, was a sweet shy child. Then she met and tumbled head over heels for Lord Murray who was the prince's right arm. They spent all their spare time together; then the army moved to Culloden. A great battle was fought, but our Prince Charlie was beaten. Then the lass came to Lady Caroline and told her . . . she was pregnant."

"What happened then?"

"I don't rightly know. From then on, Lady Caroline kept everythin' secret. I know the army came back through, I know that Lord Murray came again, but I dinna know what happened in that."

"What happened to Lady Caroline?"

"She kept her secret. When she died, she took it wi' her."

"What happened to Isabel?"

"That I dinna know either. I only know when she left here, she was pregnant wi' Lord Murray's child, and Lord Murray had died after the battle of Culloden. He came here once after the battle and we got word of his death later."

"And this is all ye know?" Ian said.

"Aye, I wish I knew more. Isabel was a sweet lovin' lass and I would have liked to care for her and to know what the child was."

"Aye," Douglas said, "and so would we."

The woman rose from her chair.

"There is na more I can tell ye."

"I'm grateful for what ye have said. I have only one

thing to ask ye," Ian said.

"What?"

"Where did the lass attend church?"

"Church?"

"Aye."

"The small one ye passed on your way here."

"Thank ye, ye've been most helpful. If I find word of the child, I shall make a point of sendin' word to ye."

"Thank ye," she answered softly and the soft shine of grateful tears touched her eyes.

Once outside, Douglas turned to Ian. "Well, we dinna know any more now than we did before."

"Nay, lad, we know all we need to know."

"I dinna understand."

"I'll tell ye what I believe."

"What?"

"I believe Isabel Maclean married Lord George Murray, and that a child was born to 'em. A child that must have been Jeffrey MacIntire. But that raises another problem."

"What?"

"If Jeffrey is Lord George Murray's child why would he have to have Jane's money? Murray was a wealthy man. Why would Jeffrey want to get rid of Jane? Why not claim his own inheritance?"

"Where do we find that answer?"

"In the church. First we find out if there is a record of the marriage . . . then of the child's birth. At least then, we'll know the child's sex."

They went to the church, but were soon disappointed for no record existed there, either of the marriage or the child's baptism. Again on the street, they stood and talked.

"Now what?" Douglas asked.

"There are many churches, in this town and in the ones surrounding it. We were fools to think it would be performed so close to home."

"Where and how do we begin?"

"Lady Isabel and Lord Murray rode often. It has to be close enough for them to ride there and back in less than a day. We begin now and try every town in riding distance until we find it."

Two days later they found the church they sought. With Ian's and Douglas's quick tongues, it did not take them long to find some of the records they wanted.

"He married the lass," the minister told them. "I performed the ceremony. But they left here and I never saw them again. I have no record of the child's birth. I asked Lady Caroline one day and she told me what had become of the record of the child's birth."

"And where did she say it was?"

"Why, she sent it to Mr. and Mrs. MacIntire who were her only relatives. They were to care for the child. Ye must ask them where the records are and what they say."

Both Douglas and Ian were taken by surprise by this.

"May we have a copy of the marriage certificate? We want to make sure the child gets all that is coming to it . . . whatever that is," Douglas said.

With the copy in their possession, they left. Starting their trip home immediately, they tried to make their plans on the way home.

"I just don't understand," Douglas said. "If the records were sent to the MacIntires, then Jeffrey would know. If it were he, then the greedy bastard would have claimed the money. If it were Jane, he would have destroyed both of them a long, long time ago."

"We must go and give this information to Owen," Ian said. "The lad will know what to do about it."

"Aye, 'tis the best thing. God, can ye imagine being the heir to the Murray fortune?"

"I canna see Jeffrey lettin' it slip through his fingers."

"I think we'd better move fast."

"I've a feelin' Owen isna safe either. If someone wants that much money, he is surely not going to let Owen come between him and it. Let us get home, lad. I must tell Sophia, then we'll be on our way to see Owen and gi' him this little gift of mystery."

They returned home where Ian made sure Sophia remained at his parents' home with Flora. Quickly, he told her the entire story, for there had never been a secret between them.

Before they made preparations to leave, their mother questioned them closely. They told her all they knew.

"Poor Jane," she said. "The lass is such a sweet child. She is a good woman for our Owen. I dinna believe that Jane is the kind of woman to which that kind of fortune and life would mean much. I dinna believe it would matter to her what type of ancestry she has. If her brother wants the fortune, and it were hers, I imagine she would give it to him."

"Mother!" Ian said.

"What, what did I say?"

"Ye've said the very reason for all this."

"What?"

"Jeffrey doesna have the proof either way. Of course he wants the money, but he canna prove it either way, that he is the child or Jane is. I will wager my soul that the MacIntires knew what Jeffrey was and somehow hid the evidence. I'll also wager they left clues somehow for whoever would come lookin'."

"Ian, do you know what you are implyin'?"

"Aye, that someone murdered the MacIntires."

"You are also implyin' that Jane could. . . . She is a sweet lovin' child."

"Nay, Mother, I wasna implyin' that, but I will agree with ye she is a sweet child, and she may have been used somehow. Anyway, I intend to go at once and tell Owen what we know. Maybe he can reach back into Jane's past and find out the truth."

"Yes, Ian, go at once. I hate to think that both Jane's and Owen's lives are in danger."

Ian and Douglas left at once and made the trip as rapidly as they possibly could. Both Owen and Jane were more than delighted to see them, and Morgan, after their explanations, was almost more than pleased at the information they brought. Owen had cautioned Ian and Douglas not to tell Jane the circumstances under which they were there. He did not want her put into any more danger than she already was.

It was only after Jane was asleep that he and his brothers and Morgan sat over drinks and talked.

"No one knows whether the child was male or female?" Morgan asked.

"The only evidence on that was sent to the MacIntires a long time ago. What they have done with it is the mystery," Ian answered.

"The secret is somewhere in Jane's past," Owen said. "It is a past she doesna seem to remember too much of. I must go gently wi' her. I dinna want her to be hurt by her past life any more than she has been. I will do it slowly and maybe I will get her to remember something solid on which we can begin our search."

"Maybe I can be of some help," Morgan said.

"You, how?" Owen replied.

"Well not necessarily me, but maybe Kristen. Kristen

417

and Jane have one thing in common . . . Jeffrey Mac-
Intire. If they talk, become friends, maybe Kristen can
touch this hidden well of information and find us the key
to this mystery."

"Aye, Jane was very upset when she thought Kristen
was about to marry Jeffrey." Owen grinned. "She was
also very upset when she found out I had let her
deliberately be taken by a pirate."

"She knows?" Morgan said in surprise.

"Who you are, no. I told her everything else but that.
One day you can tell her the rest of the story."

"Yes, in the meantime there is the matter of another
ship of Jeffrey's. It has finally gotten its orders to sail."

"And I go with you," Owen said.

"I have changed my plans, Owen. It is best that you do
not go. It is much more important that we find out what
Jane knows. It is the one way we can effectively stop
Jeffrey. All of this must be brought out into the light
where we can see it clearly. There is still something that
eludes us, something that we have to find before Jeffrey
decides it would be worth it to finish the game by
eliminating the participants."

"Kill Jane," Owen said. "He could have done that a
long time ago, before she ever met me."

"No, Owen, he might just decide that you are one of
his bigger problems. Especially if he found out Ian and
Douglas have been searching about in the past. He might
just think you are a little too dangerous."

"Aye," Owen said thoughtfully. "I'll be very careful
from now on."

"And ye'll no be goin' anywhere wi'out one of us,"
Douglas said.

"I dinna need a keeper. You two had best be goin'
home before he gets suspicious."

Both Ian and Douglas smilingly shook their heads negatively and Morgan chuckled.

"Give up, Owen. You've got bodyguards whether you want them or not."

"Aye . . . stubborn," Owen grunted. "When does the *Falcon* set sail again?"

"As soon as my informant sends me word. I must tell you three: a few months ago, I thought I stood alone against the world. Now the four of us will put an end to this and see Jane and Kristen happy and free of their problems. Then we can all begin to build a new future."

Owen nodded, but his eyes were saddened by the fact that Morgan still held a touch of the same hatred for Jeffrey. He hoped Morgan would never be faced with a choice, for he knew just how badly Morgan wanted to see Jeffrey MacIntire dead.

# Twenty-Five

Owen lay still, listening for what it was that had wakened him. When he had left his brothers and Morgan, he had gone upstairs where he had subtly tried to question Jane about her past.

It was a difficult thing, for it seemed to upset Jane to try to remember. For some reason, Jane had blocked out of her mind all knowledge of the years before she was eight. Questions about Jeffrey not only made her tense and nervous, but brought no results.

Now he lay listening as the sound repeated itself. Jane was moaning softly in her sleep. Owen's questions had opened doors in her dreams that she could not face in the day. She tossed restlessly and whimpered softly like a lost child. Owen drew her into his arms and whispered comfortingly to her.

Still she seemed to be fighting something. She began to resist Owen's hold.

"No . . . no . . . Mama! Mama! Don't go!"

Owen held her, yet she fought him with an almost desperate battle.

"I won't go," she cried. "You can't make me. I won't go. Mama, please don't go . . . don't go!"

She was sobbing now and her slim body twisted in his arms in a feverish attempt to escape him.

"Janie! Janie!" Owen called to her as he held her body

close to him rocking her gently as one would a frightened child.

She shuddered suddenly, then became still and Owen knew she was awake.

"Owen?" she said softly.

"Ye were dreamin' love," he whispered against her hair. "'Twas a nightmare. Ye were fightin' something."

She seemed to have control over herself now so Owen rose and lit a candle. He set it on the stand by the bed, then he again lay beside her and drew her against him. She looked up into his eyes.

"Can ye remember it, lass? What were ye fightin' so hard. What distresses ye so?"

"I don't know," she answered. "It is gone."

"Ye called out to your mother, askin' her not to go, claimin' ye wasna goin' to go somewhere. Can ye na remember any of it, love?"

"No. . . . Oh, Owen it makes my head ache so. I can't remember." She sobbed as she laid her head against him. Her slim body trembled in his arms. He did not want to upset her anymore, and the headache she'd spoken of had recurred every time he had questioned her about her past. Obviously she had experienced some terrible event in her childhood that had created a block in her mind. It was a dark area in which her mind did not want to wander. He did not want to press her for fear it would do her more harm than good. In time, he thought, with love and care, he would reach back into her past and unlock the door that held her prisoner. For now, he would love her and hold her and keep her safe from the arm that reached from the darkness to touch her.

"'Tis all right, love," he whispered as he brushed her lips lightly with his. "There is nothin' more important in our life than lovin' each other. Dinna worry anymore, love."

Her slim arms circled his neck and she clung to him as if desperate to hold on to the solid rock of her world.

"Oh, Owen, I love you so. Hold me . . . love me."

Willingly, he crushed her to him and his mouth took hers in a possessive all-consuming kiss that took her thoughts and centered them on him and his blazing need of her and nothing else.

His hands caressed and warmed her and his lips drove her to the wild abandoned passion she felt only with Owen. She surrendered to the gentleness of his love.

Afterward, when she slept again, curled contentedly against him, he caressed her hair thoughtfully and wondered what secret lay in the shadows of her mind. It was obviously much too painful for her to bear. He would do nothing in this world to cause her any pain, but he was determined to find out somehow the source of these shadows and free her from the past. He was sure that Jeffrey had had a strong part in the unhappiness she'd suffered, and he would wait and watch for every clue that might give him a ray of light into the darkness.

The next morning they rose and dressed for breakfast. At the table they enjoyed a relaxed easy meal enlivened by Douglas's sense of humor. He made Jane laugh and Owen and the others were captivated viewers of the pleasant and cheerful disposition she had when she was relaxed and happy.

A message was brought by the butler to Jane who opened it and read it. Then she said to Owen, "Would you mind, Owen, if I went riding with Kristen this morning? I have many things I would like to talk to her about. I asked her the night of the party and she has sent a note to tell me she is free today."

"Nay, love, go. 'Twill do ye good to get out and enjoy such a beautiful day."

"And you, what will you be doing?"

"I have to go into town. I've a few things to be carin' for. Go and enjoy yourself."

She rose, walked around the table, and brushed a kiss on his cheek. "Thank you, Owen, I'll see you at dinner."

"Take care, love." He laughed. "I wouldna have a bruised wife from bein' tossed from a horse."

"Owen!" She laughed as she blushed. "I'll have you know I'm an excellent rider. I've ridden since I was a very little child. I remember Mother and I . . ." Her voice stopped and she looked at him blankly as if the memory had flashed and gone.

"Went riding often?" he added softly.

"I . . . I don't remember," she began painfully, tears starting in her eyes.

Owen rose quickly and put his arms about her.

"Dinna think of it, love. Go and enjoy the day." Again her hesitant smile, then she nodded and walked away, his troubled eyes following her.

"She canna remember a thing?" Ian questioned.

"Not from the time she was eight or nine. I would give my life to know what happened before that that has frightened her so."

"Time, Owen," Morgan said. "Time and your love will open the doors and answer all of your questions . . . maybe some of mine also."

"What are your plans for today, Morgan?"

"I'm riding up to Jamie's. I'll send messages from there. We'll get the *Falcon* ready to sail again."

Before Owen could answer, Morgan's parents entered the room. All talk of the *Falcon* and Captain Black were thoroughly silenced for the time being.

"What are your plans, Owen?" Douglas said.

"I'm goin' to talk to a man named John Preston; he's an attorney."

"Wasn't he . . ." Morgan began.

"Yes, he used to be the MacIntires' attorney. When they . . . died, Jeffrey took all the affairs into his hands. I've an appointment to see him."

"I'll go with ye," Douglas said and the words were echoed by Ian in a moment.

"I will have the two of ye following me about like bloodhounds," Owen said in irritation. "There's enough things for each of us to do. I dinna need a bodyguard. I'm a man grown now. I dinna still stumble over me own feet. We must each be about the search or we'll never find what we need."

"What do ye want us to do, Owen?" Ian questioned.

"Dig into Jeffrey's past. From the time he was a child till now. 'Tis best to know all about your enemy if you're goin' to do battle wi' him."

"Aye, Owen," Ian said, but Douglas remained very quiet.

"Well, I must be goin'. My appointment is early and I'll see you at dinner."

Owen rose and left and Morgan laughed as he saw Ian and Douglas exchange a silent look of understanding. Douglas nodded, smiled, and rose to follow his brother.

"Ian," Morgan said, and Ian chuckled softly.

"There are times Owen can be uncommonly stubborn. At such times, 'tis best to humor him . . . then take care of him wi'out him knowin'."

Morgan smiled and his parents laughed, knowing the feeling of the deep love a brother had for a brother . . . or a brother for a sister.

\* \* \*

424

Owen rode slowly to the office of John Preston where he was quickly ushered into Mr. Preston's office.

John Preston was a man of about sixty. He was tall and very distinguished-looking. He held out his hand to Owen immediately, and Owen took it, John's clear dark eyes holding his.

"Good morning, Captain MacGregor."

"Good morning," Owen replied as he took his hand in a strong grip. "'Tis good of ye to see me so early. I know ye are a busy man."

"I am never too busy to speak to Jane MacIntire's husband. What can I do for you?"

"Ye were attorney for the MacIntires for some time?"

"Yes, I was."

"Can ye tell me why you no longer are?"

John's eyes searched Owen's; then he smiled. "You have no love for your new brother-in-law," he said gently. Owen grinned.

"Nay, that I don't, and I've a feelin' ye dinna have much either."

"I cannot abide the man. When the MacIntires died, I was happy to hand all his business back to him. The only thing I regretted was Jane, but there was nothing I could do about it. He had every legal right."

"'Tis not his business I'm interested in. As far as I'm concerned, he's welcome to anything . . . as long as it does not rightfully belong to Jane."

"What can I help you with, Captain MacGregor?"

"Owen."

"Owen," he repeated, "and call me John. I've a feeling we're going to be friends. Now as to my question, what can I help you with?"

Owen began to explain the loss of Jane's past and the suspicions he had as to Jeffrey's part in this. "'Tis an uncommon thing for a brother to treat a sister so."

"You're right. And I would agree with you—if they were brother and sister."

"What?"

"They're not brother and sister."

"Which one does not belong to the MacIntires?"

"Neither of them."

Owen was stunned. "I dinna understand."

"It's simple, the MacIntires adopted both Jeffrey and Jane."

"Then you know their parents?" Owen said hopefully.

"I'm sorry. I've no idea who the parents of either of them are. I only know that neither of them belonged to the MacIntires by birth."

"My God, this doesna clear matters, it only makes them worse. Can you tell me how Jeffrey and Jane stood in regard to their inheritance?"

"Let me tell you what I think, Owen. I think the MacIntires were being paid to care for both children, paid quite well, enough to make them well off but not rich. They left the home and a substantial sum to be divided between the two, but it was not great wealth and because of the way Jeffrey's handled it, I've a suspicion there's not much left . . . for either of them."

"Ye mean ye think he's already taken Jane's?"

"I think so; I think he's desperate for money."

"That explains his need to marry Kristen Seaford."

"Yes."

"And . . . possibly tells us why he might have killed Morgan's sister. The Grayfields are not the type to hand over their wealth to the likes of Jeffrey MacIntire, and Kristen had no family except a stepmother who wouldna have done a thing to protect her from Jeffrey."

"I hate to think of that sweet girl being killed, but I for

one would not have put it past Jeffrey. Yet he's got a lot of power and protection. There's no way to prove it."

"Well, I'll not let it drop here. I'll find out the truth. I'll also find out what he's done to Jane to wipe out her childhood and leave her wi' nothin' but tears and nightmares."

"If I can help in any way, please do not hesitate to call on me. I liked the MacIntires and I liked Jane."

"Thank you, I'll remember."

Owen stood, and they shook hands again before he left the lawyer's office. While he was in town, he intended to go and shop for something for Jane, a wedding present he had never had the chance to buy before. He walked through the streets of town slowly, going from shop to shop, unaware of the shadowed figure that followed him.

Finally he found what he wanted, a ring of rare beauty made of delicate entwined bands of gold. On its top was a small cluster of diamonds surrounded by three glittery emeralds.

"I will bring my wife for the ring to be fitted," he told the jeweler. "In the meantime," he added as he took out of his pocket a purse in which coins clinked heartily, "keep it safe." He gave half of the coins to the jeweler.

"Yes, sir." The man beamed. "We shall cut it to fit at your convenience, sir."

"Thank you," Owen replied. He left his name and address, and the man recognized the address immediately.

"You are guests of the Grayfields?"

"Aye."

"It will be a pleasure to take care of this for you, sir. If you will bring your wife tomorrow we will fit it perfectly."

"Thank you."

Owen left the shop and started down the street. It was then that he decided to take a shortcut to go back to his carriage. He turned down a dark narrow alley. His boots clicked sharply against the cobbled stones. Douglas was far behind him so that Owen would not notice he was being followed. He hated to think of Owen's anger if he spotted him. He turned into the alley when Owen was only a few feet from the far exit.

Owen was walking slowly, his mind on the facts that John Preston had given him. All his thoughts were clouded by this new mystery and he was so engrossed in his thoughts that he didn't hear the muffled footsteps that sounded beside him, and did not sense the danger until it was almost too late. He spun about and saw a ray of light glitter off a raised knife. He tried to defend himself but he had been caught so off balance his move was ineffectual. The knife rose and fell, but not where it had been intended to fall or Owen's life would have been over. It struck him high in the shoulder. Owen felt a searing hot pain then he grasped the arm as it raised to strike again.

From the loss of freely flowing blood, Owen could feel himself weakening. He could hear the panting breath of his assailant and felt his powerful body as it continued to do battle with him. Instinctively, he knew this man was not robbing him but planned murder, just as he was sure he knew who was behind it . . . Jeffrey MacIntire. He was losing his control and a deep black fog began to press down on him. Just as he began to lose consciousness, he heard a loud shout, felt himself released, and dropped to the damp cobbled stones.

Douglas saw the dark shadow leap from the darkness, saw the knife quickly rise and fall, and with a sickening feeling knew he could not reach them before the knife could find its mark again. He gave a loud shout and ran toward Owen, hoping to startle his assailant enough to stop him for a moment. He did. The man dropped his hold of Owen and ran, and with the heat of tears in his eyes, Douglas saw Owen fall. He reached his side praying to himself Owen was not dead. He turned him over, feeling a hot sticky substance on his hands that he knew was Owen's blood.

"Owen," he panted. "Owen, for God's sake tell me ye're not dead . . . Owen." He tried to feel through Owen's bulky cloak and breathed a ragged sigh of relief when his hand, pressed against Owen's chest, felt a heavy steady heartbeat. He could have cried for joy as he bent forward and heard Owen's ragged breathing. Owen began to regain consciousness then. He could hear Douglas's voice as if it came from a distance and there was a thick heavy buzzing in his ears. It took him a few minutes to realize just who was bending above him and whose voice was half-sobbing, half-pleading for him to be all right.

"Douglas," he gasped.

"Owen, how bad are ye hurt? Can ye make it to the carriage if I help you?"

"I'll try. 'Tis my shoulder. Help me up."

Supporting most of his weight, Douglas helped him stagger to his feet. He knew Owen was injured badly or he would not have leaned so heavily on him. Staggering under Owen's weight, he made his way to the carriage. Once he had Owen in, he unbuttoned his shirt to see the wound. It was a deep nasty cut high on the shoulder and Douglas was afraid something important might have been severed. To him there seemed to be an extreme amount of blood. He staunched the flow with his and Owen's handkerchiefs, but that did not do much good. Then he took the reins and began the race for home.

He was grateful that Jane was still gone for the amount of blood on Owen's clothes would have frightened her to death.

They put Owen to bed and sent for the doctor, who arrived within the hour. He stitched the wound closed and bound it after it had been washed and cleaned. By that time, Owen was awake. He was pale and shaken but in control of himself. And, Ian and Douglas thought with relief, he would soon be well.

"''Tis a good thing Douglas and I decided he should follow ye," Ian said. "Or your body would have been found in that alley after a long time. Someone intended for you to die and I imagine we all can guess who."

The three brothers were alone in Owen's bedroom.

"Aye, it was sure not robbery. He could have had my purse easy enough. No, I'm sure I'm gettin' close to somethin' and he wants me out of the way. He needs to have his hold over Jane back again before she remembers things he does not want her to remember."

Kristen and Jane sat in a small park, their horses tied nearby. Finding a deep rapport and an easy friendship developing, they had been talking for some time. Kristen would tell no one, not even Jane, about Morgan's double identity, and the one subject that Jane stayed away from was the mysterious pirate in Kristen's life. Owen had told her Kristen loved him, and she was delighted that Kristen had chosen not to marry Jeffrey.

"Kristen, you will not be staying with Jeffrey and Leslie much longer, will you?"

"No, my money is here now, and Mr. Murkton is looking around for the right house. Soon I'll be in my own home."

"Then what will you do?"

"Do?"

"Kristen . . . you would never reconsider marrying Jeffrey would you?"

"No, Jane . . . I . . . I don't want to upset you, but I could never marry Jeffrey, not after . . ."

"After you have found out that Jeffrey is a cold unfeeling man who wanted to marry you for your fortune."

"Yes, that and . . ."

"And you've met and fallen in love with someone else."

"Yes."

"I hope everything works out well for you, Kristen. I hope you're happy. You deserve it after all you've been through."

"Thank you, Jane. Someday I'll tell you about him. Until then, I have to keep it a secret. Do you mind?"

"Of course not."

Jane was looking out to sea, a faraway look in her eyes. Suddenly she shivered as if a frozen hand squeezed around her heart.

"Owen," she whispered.

"What?"

"Oh, Kristen, I must go home. I feel as if something is wrong. Do you mind?"

They mounted their horses and rode to the edge of the bridle path where they separated. Jane arrived home at the moment the doctor was climbing into his buggy. The need for a doctor left her frightened.

"Dr. Morton?" she said when she rode up beside him.

"Now, Jane, don't get upset," he began.

"Who . . . who needed a doctor?"

"Owen."

"I knew. . . . What happened?" she said in a choked voice.

"Someone took a knife to him."

"Oh, God," she moaned softly. She slid down from her horse and ran into the house and up the steps. She flung open the bedroom door and ran across the room.

"Owen," she cried as she sat down beside him and took his hand in both of hers, pressing it to her lips. Ian and Douglas slipped quietly from the room, leaving Owen to explain it any way he saw fit.

"Now, Janie, love, don't get so frightened. I'm well. Someone just decided my purse looked too invitin' to be let go. He tried to take it and I fought wi 'im. I'm afraid he got the best of it." He laughed and she could see it hurt him. She looked at him with her gold-brown eyes serious.

"Owen, we will not lie to each other anymore. Jeffrey tried to have you killed. You know it and so do I. Owen, let's go back to Scotland. I don't want Jeffrey's money. The only thing I want in this world is you. Owen, let's go away from here. Nothing in this world is worth your life. I . . . I should die if you were to leave me now. I could not face the world without you."

The tears on her cheeks hurt him many times more than the knife had done, yet they stiffened his anger and determination to find the answers. He had to catch Jeffrey, for if he wasn't around, he did not want Jeffrey to be either. He had to find out the answer to this mystery that surrounded Jane's past before it killed both him and the woman he loved beyond anything else in the world. He reached up and brushed a tear from her cheek.

"Lie beside me, love."

"I'll hurt you."

"Na if you be on my good side."

She came around the other side of the bed and climbed up on it. His arm encircled her, and she sighed as she nestled against him.

"'Twill be all right, Janie, love," he whispered. "Everything will be all right."

"I love you, Owen," she said softly. His arm tightened.

"I know love . . . I know. We'll find our way out of all this and then I'll take ye home where ye'll never be touched by such evil again."


Kristen went back to Jeffrey's house. She found Leslie in the front sitting room.

"Where have you been, Kristen?" she asked in her arrogant voice. This time Kristen allowed her irritation to surface.

"I'm not a child, Leslie, and I am not in your power any longer. What I do"—she paused—"is none of your business."

Leslie smiled, which was a surprise to Kristen, for she had always reacted with anger before.

"Where's Toby?" Kristen asked.

"Out of my sight. The little ignorant ruffian with his papers and books. One would think he could conquer the world. He'll be nothing but a common sailor all his life."

Kristen's dislike for Leslie grew in intensity.

"He'll not be. Toby is bright. He'll grow into a good and decent man and I intend to see he gets all the education he needs to do what he wants . . . no matter what it is."

"You'll be wasting your father's money on that little piece of salvage the sea has tossed up. What a waste of money."

"I don't consider it so," she answered coldly. "Where is he?"

433

"In his room I suppose. I told him to stay out of everybody's way."

Kristen bit her tongue to keep a sharp angry remark inside. Soon she and Toby would be gone from here. She ran lightly up the stairs to her room. She opened the door to see Toby, engrossed in a book she had given him, lying on his belly in front of the fireplace. She smiled to see the light of happy love in his eyes when she walked in.

"Toby, I see you've been reading. Why are you upstairs, why not in the library?"

"I don't want to be down there. I don't like her and I don't like him either. I can see why the captain hates him so much."

"Toby!"

"Well, I do."

"Well, let's forget them both for now. I want to hear how well you read, and then I'm going to teach you to play cards and then chess."

He was delighted and they spent a happy afternoon together. She knew it irritated Jeffrey and Leslie to have Toby at their table, so she shared her dinner with him in her room. Later that night, she went to his room to make sure he was tucked in comfortably, then she went back to her room to spend another lonely night thinking of Morgan and how very much she needed him.

She had had the maid light a small fire which sent a warm glow about the room. She dressed for bed, then brushed her hair. But when the difficult time came, she knew she could not just go to that huge bed and go to sleep.

She walked out on the stone balcony that circled the house. Standing by the rail, she looked out over the moon-touched gardens of Jeffrey's home.

Then, again, as always happened, she sensed his

presence before she saw him. She gave a small half-laugh as his arms came about her and she leaned against him in the sheer joyous pleasure of the strength that would always be her support.

"What were you thinking about?" he said softly. "You were so far away."

"I was no farther away than your arms, no farther away than your love. I always think of you." She turned to face him. "I am so glad you are here, Morgan; the days and nights are so long and so frightening when you are away. I love you, my very dear Captain Pirate."

She heard his warm laugh as his arms lifted her against him and his mouth claimed hers.

"And I love you, Kristen, very, very much."

"Morgan, how long must this pretense continue?"

"Not much longer, love," he said. He told her what Owen's brothers had discovered and that if they found proof, Jeffrey would be exposed and it would be all over.

"Morgan, that means you no longer have to sail as Captain Black again. You do not have to take the chance of being discovered and hung for piracy."

He released her and leaned against the rail looking out over the garden. "It will only be once more, Kristen."

"What do you mean?"

"He has a ship sailing again."

"And Captain Black intends to strike?"

"Maybe for the last time."

"Anytime could be your last time. If you are caught and hung, what of me? What am I to do without you? Morgan, please if you are not afraid of danger to yourself think of me. I could not bear it, not to lose you now when I have just found you."

He gathered her into his arms and kissed her into temporary silence.

435

"Kristen, I promise you. This is the last time. If what Owen thinks is true, I will have revenge on Jeffrey MacIntire."

"Revenge! Is that all you can think of? I have asked you before. Is our love not enough?"

"If it were not, I would never consider stopping. This one last time, love, and we will find a way to marry." Before she could speak he again bent his head to touch her lips with his. His arms slid about her and crushed her to him in a grip of intense hunger that only seemed to increase each time he was near her.

"I'll stop, Kristen; after this time there will be no more sailing for Captain Black. I will repaint and refinish the *Falcon* and use it as part of our shipping business. Captain Black will return to being Lord Morgan Grayfield. He will marry the most beautiful woman in London and set about raising children. One day, you and I will go back to our island and spend some time remembering the beauty we found there."

"Oh, Morgan, I pray for that day," she said softly.

Morgan bent and lifted her in his arms. His warm lips touched the smooth skin of her throat and she sighed contentedly. He carried her into the flame-lit room, to the bed they shared with such joy. They sought again to renew and relive their always wild and tumultuous love.

Neither of them was aware of the surroundings; and neither was aware of the dark figure that detached itself from the depths of the shadows not far from where they had stood and made its way down the veranda to enter a room and close the door behind it.

The figure made its way across the dark room to the hall, down it, and down the stairs to the library where Jeffrey MacIntire sat.

When a knock sounded on the door, Jeffrey called out.

"Come in."

The figure entered and closed the door. Jeffrey looked up and smiled.

"Well?"

"Well, I have found something I know you will be overjoyed to hear."

"What is it?"

"I know who your nemesis, Captain Black, is."

Jeffrey smiled broadly and leaned back in his chair. Then he said softly, "Well, my dear, Leslie, just who is our pirate?"

"Lord Morgan Grayfield."

Jeffrey sat up, his smile fading. "You are joking?"

"No."

"How do you know?"

"It seems Captain Black and Kristen Seaford are very much in love. In fact . . . he is with her now. I overheard them on the balcony talking. He told her that he intends to take your next ship. Then he intends to marry Kristen."

Jeffrey's face grew red from his contained anger.

"I shall go up and have him taken right now."

"All that will prove is that Kristen and Morgan are having an affair. That is not a hanging offense as you and I well know. That does not brand him a pirate, and being caught in a compromising position will not hang him. No, that is not the way."

"I will see him dead."

"We need only to prepare our ship to greet Captain Black properly. We need only catch him in the act of piracy. Then he would have no way out. That will take care of one of your problems. If Kristen is in love with him, I'm sure a little pressure on your part will convince her that marrying you would be better than seeing her lover hang."

"Quite good, my dear," he said softly. "And I have arranged to have Owen MacGregor . . . removed."

"So . . . it is only a matter of time until we have all we wanted."

"Yes," he said softly. "It might surprise you, Leslie, just how much is in the balance." Something in his voice touched a note that wakened suspicion in Leslie, a Leslie who was always aware when something was slipping beyond her control.

"Jeffrey," she began softly, "I have committed murder to throw Kristen into your arms. We both know that. And if anything were to go wrong you think I might be eliminated by that. You're wrong. You have committed murder also."

He looked at her in surprise.

"Did you think I did not know? Do you think I do not know all the shadows in your life? I know that you killed your own parents. That is why you will be very careful with me. I would not like to think you were not willing to share all the wealth with me."

"Leslie, I agreed to share everything that we could get. When Kristen and I are married, when she's . . . gone, we will share the Seaford fortune. When Jane is taken care of we will share her wealth. What more do you want?"

"Nothing. Just keep what I said in mind."

He rose and came around his desk and went to her. He put his arms about her and she smiled up at him. Here were two who were exactly alike. They could kill calmly and without regret. They understood each other completely. Yet they stimulated each other, like a heady wine that excites the passions deep within.

She laughed softly as she molded herself against him

and he echoed her sound of pleasure as he kissed her hungrily and very thoroughly.

In the pale gray light of early dawn Morgan kissed Kristen lightly while she slept; then he silently left the room. He made his way across the garden and rode home in a buoyant mood.

He did not know that Jeffrey stood at a window and watched him go. He watched him with a slight smile on his face.

"Captain Black." He chuckled softly and the sound reached Leslie who lay on the bed behind him. "Soon, you will sail on your last journey."

# Twenty-Six

Jeffrey sent word to the captain of the *Night Star*, asking him to come to his house before he set sail. He made plans while he waited for the skipper to come.

Capt. Ezekiel Lambert had captained the *Night Star* for over three years. He was a tall slim man in his late fifties. His hair, white as snow, was matched by a full white mustache and beard. He was tanned and his eyes had a permanent slight squint from looking into the sun.

Originally, he had worked for Amos MacIntire, and had been a good friend. When Amos had died, while Ezekiel was at sea, it had come as a surprise for Amos had always been in good health. Ezekiel had not known then what his future might be. But Jeffrey had assured him that he was to have a position as captain of the *Night Star* until he chose to retire. Ezekiel knew that Jeffrey's ships had been harassed by a pirate named Captain Black, but he had never run across him himself. Of course, he had heard gossip as to why Captain Black attacked only Jeffrey's ships, but he had discounted it as just that, gossip.

His position as captain had been very lucrative, and often he had been rewarded for bringing his ship in ahead of schedule.

He treated the men under him reasonably well, exercising hard discipline and rewarding work done well.

As he headed his carriage toward Jeffrey's home, he wondered just what was behind this sudden call. His ship would be ready to leave on the next day's tide. He realized it must be important for Jeffrey to call him in person. Any other time, he could have just sent a message.

He dismounted the carriage, went up the steps, and rapped sharply on the door. A young maid, who had seen Ezekiel there many times before, opened it.

"Captain Lambert, Mr. MacIntire is expecting you. Will you come with me please?"

She led him to Jeffrey's study door where she rapped lightly.

"Come in."

She opened the door and entered. "Captain Lambert is here, sir."

"Good, send him in please."

The maid smiled at the captain and stepped aside to let him pass; then she left closing the door behind her.

"Captain Lambert." Jeffrey smiled as he rose from his chair and extended his hand. "Thank you for coming so quickly."

"Your message said it was important."

"Yes, it is. Sit down and let me give you a drink. I have a surprise for you."

Ezekiel sat in the chair opposite Jeffrey's desk and accepted the glass of brandy Jeffrey poured for him. He took a sip, appreciating the excellence of the brandy as he appreciated all the other signs of wealth that surrounded them.

"You are ready to leave on the morning tide?"

"Yes, I am."

"Good."

"There is no change in plans then?"

"Not connected with the time you leave."

441

"There is something you want me to do?"

"Yes, I have one small change in your plans."

"And what is that?"

"I want you to leave here on schedule, but I want you to make one stop you had not planned on."

"Oh, where?"

"About twenty miles up the coast where you will find some men waiting for you. I will give you a map as to their location. You will land at night, board them, and put them in the hold where they will not be seen."

"I will do whatever you say, Mr. MacIntire, but may I ask why?"

"Of course you can, Ezekiel, these men will be well armed, for you see, you are about to be attacked by Captain Black."

"The pirate! He intends to attack my ship!"

"He does, and this time I intend to catch him."

"The bloody nerve of that man is remarkable," Ezekiel said angrily.

"Well, we will not have to worry about him again if you do as I say and carry out my plan to the letter."

"I shall do so, sir. It will be a pleasure to help you capture this scoundrel. Attack my ship! Really, sir, it will be a distinct pleasure."

"Thank you." Jeffrey smiled as he rose and extended his hand to the captain. "I assure you that you and your men will be well rewarded."

"Most generous, sir. I thank you."

Jeffrey watched the captain leave, sure for the first time that he would be able to take from his path two barriers . . . one, the freedom for his ships to move without interference from Captain Black; and two, a path to the Seaford money, for if Kristen were again left alone, with no one to defend her, it would not be long before

Jeffrey took advantage of that.

Jeffrey and Leslie celebrated that night as he told her of the plans he had made. They were delighted, but their enjoyment would have been spoiled if they had been apprised of an occurrence in a tavern a few miles away.

Chris Miles was to be faced with a dilemma that he found more difficult than any other he was to face in his life.

He had asked Kristen to go to dinner with him, but she had delicately refused. She did not want Chris to harbor any false hopes that she might return his love.

Chris, at loose ends, decided to have a drink and look up a pretty barmaid who worked at a nearby tavern. She would be most willing to help him forget all other thoughts, at least temporarily.

He went to the tavern and sat at a table alone for a while, nursing a tense feeling of anger at Morgan for his ability to hold Kristen's thoughts even though Chris had done as much as he could to destroy his memory.

After a drink or two he was able to get the barmaid's eye and motioned to her to come over. She was quite willing, for she had fond memories of Chris and some delightful nights she had spent with him.

"Hello, Chris." She smiled as she sat down opposite him. "It's been a long time since I've seen you. Your friends have been around a lot."

"I've been pretty busy, Netta."

"Too busy to come see an old friend?" She pouted. He stood and went to her side of the table and slid down on the bench beside her. Putting his arm about her waist, he brushed her bare shoulder with a kiss.

"You know I'm never too busy for you," he whispered.

443

She laughed throatily as she leaned against him and allowed his wandering hands to rediscover familiar territory. After a few moments, she pushed him a little away from her.

"Chris, I still have to work. Will you wait a couple of hours until I'm off?"

"Wild horses couldn't drag me away." He laughed. His hands again moved toward her, but she giggled and pushed him more firmly away.

"Later, Chris, later," she whispered. "Don't go away, please."

She got up and went about her work continuing to cast a look toward him now and then to make sure he was still there.

Chris was about to launch himself into his third tankard of ale when the door opened and another young sailor came in. Recognizing him as someone he had drunk with before, he hailed the sailor who grinned and came toward him.

"Hello, Chris."

"Hello, Jack, I didn't know you were in port. I thought the *Night Star* was still at sea."

"No," Jack grinned. "The big boss called the captain to his house today; we got orders to leave tomorrow mornin'."

"Good, let me buy you a drink."

"Thanks."

Chris waved Netta over and ordered a drink for Jack. When she put it in front of him, Chris dropped a gold coin between the valley of her voluptuous breasts and winked at her.

"What is your destination, Jack?" he said as his attention turned back to the sailor whose eyes were glued to Netta's swaying hips.

"Huh?" Jack said as Chris repeated the question. "Oh, first up the coast a ways. In fact we're being reinforced. We're picking up a bunch of armed men up there. By God, our ship will be able to take on a whole foreign navy before we're through."

"What for?"

Jack chuckled. "Seems the ol' man has some sort of spy." He bent forward and said conspiratorially, "We're gonna catch ourselves a pirate."

A tingle of alarm moved through Chris, but he remained smiling.

"What pirate? I didn't know there were any in these waters."

"You mean you ain't heard of Captain Black?"

"Well, yes, I've heard of him, but it seems to me he's given up. He hasn't touched a ship in a long while."

"Well, he's gonna grab this one . . . or he's gonna try to. He's gonna get one hell of a surprise when he does. It will be the last time he tries. We, my friend, are gonna trap us a pirate, and I know for a fact ol' MacIntire is gonna make sure he hangs for it."

Chris drank from his tankard, his mind spinning. It was obvious to him Morgan planned to sail again as Captain Black. He remained still as his thoughts twisted and turned within him. If Morgan was caught, he would be hung. . . . Kristen would be free. And who would she turn to as a friend? In one blow he would rid himself of Morgan and have Kristen.

Morgan and he had been friends, were still friends. He remembered how many times it had been Morgan who had shared his escapades in college. He had drunk, laughed, and often chased women with Morgan.

Dragging his mind from Morgan he let it rest on Kristen, and that promptly made matters worse. No matter how much he loved her, wanted her, he knew she loved Morgan. He also knew if Morgan were dead because of him he would never be able to look into her beautiful gray eyes without knowing he could have prevented it.

Jack's attention had wandered again toward Netta who moved with agile grace between the tables.

"Jack."

"What?"

"I have to go someplace. I was supposed to have supper with Netta. Do you think you could . . . ?"

"Entertain the lady?" Jack grinned happily. "I'd be more than happy to help you out of your great difficulty, friend."

Chris laughed. "Funny, I just knew you'd be glad to make a sacrifice for a friend. You look like the type."

"I'll console her in her hour of need," Jack said as Chris rose to leave.

Chris rode rapidly toward Jeffrey MacIntire's, trying to console himself over what he knew would be the loss of Kristen.

He was ushered into the MacIntire living room where he found Leslie, Jeffrey, and Kristen, who was sitting away from the others reading with Toby. Jeffrey rose when he came in and it was an effort for Chris to shake his hand and be civil.

"Good evening, Chris, what are you doing here?"

"If you two would excuse us just for a moment, I have something very important to say to Kristen."

Kristen and Toby both looked toward him in surprise; then before Jeffrey could answer, Kristen rose and came to Chris's side.

"Chris, is something wrong?" she asked.

"No, Kristen." He tried to smile his calmest and best smile. "I just have something I'd like to ask you. Could we take a walk in the garden?"

"Of course," she replied.

She tucked her hand under Chris's arm and they walked toward the French doors as three pairs of eyes followed them.

"Well," Jeffrey said snidely, "it looks like our smitten young swain intends to propose. Too bad it will never happen. I really don't consider him much competition."

Toby's eyes flashed in anger.

"Miss Kristen ain't gonna marry nobody now. We're gonna have a house of our own. And she don't need anybody tellin' her what to do."

He glared at them, then ran from the room and up the stairs. They could hear the slam of his door.

"Impudent little upstart. When I get that little piece married to me, he's the first thing I intend to get rid of. I'll dump him back into the sea where she found him."

Chris stood in the garden with Kristen, searching for a way to tell her what he knew so that she would believe him.

"Kristen, do you remember the day I found you on the beach?"

"Of course, Chris. How could I forget? You were a lifesaver for me."

"Well, do you remember the note you had me give Toby, the one we used to get him to come along with us?"

"Yes . . . Chris, what's wrong?"

Slowly, he took the note from his pocket. He had been carrying it with him since the day he'd found it. He watched her as her eyes registered shock and then the realization of what he must know.

"Chris . . . I . . ."

"Kristen, listen. . . . I only showed you this note to make you understand I could have turned Morgan in any

447

time I wanted to."

"Why didn't you, Chris?" she asked softly.

"I guess, because I'm in love with you, have been since we met. I don't want to see you get hurt, and I love you enough to give you up. I want to see you happy, Kristen."

"You came here to tell me something, Chris?"

"Yes, Morgan's in danger."

"Danger, what kind of danger?"

Rapidly, he explained how he had come by the information and all the details he knew. Her face went white and he reached for her, thinking she was going to faint.

"I'm all right," she said. Determinedly she looked at him. "We have got to stop him."

"I'll go to him now," Chris answered.

"No, he'll never believe you. I'll go with you."

"Kristen!"

"Chris, make your excuses and leave. Go around to the back of the house. I'll meet you at the stable. Hurry, Chris! We have to get to him before he makes this fatal mistake."

Before he could say another word, she was walking away, and he had to run to catch up with her.

Inside he made rapid excuses which he could hardly remember, and left. Kristen, too, began to think of a way to get free immediately.

"Where's Toby?"

"The little ruffian was insulting and then went to bed," Leslie replied. "Really, Kristen, how can you bear that uncivilized brat?"

"Toby is a wonderful child, Leslie," she replied coldly, "and someday I intend to adopt him. If you will excuse me I think I shall go and see if he's all right."

She left Jeffrey and Leslie glaring after her and ran up

the steps. She went immediately to Toby. Rapidly she explained everything and saw the fear leap into his eyes.

"I'm going to him now, Toby. I shall beg him if I have to, but one way or another I will warn him and prevent him from falling into Jeffrey's trap."

"He would . . . he would hang the captain?" Toby gasped, disbelief in his face.

"Oh, yes, Toby," Kristen said softly. "He would be delighted to see him hang."

"You can stop him?" he asked hopefully.

"I shall try my best, Toby," she replied and kissed his cheek. "Now remain quiet. I'll be back as soon as I can."

He nodded. Kristen smiled and held him close for a moment; then she kissed his cheek again and said softly, "Don't worry, Toby, I'll tell him how we feel. Maybe our love will be the thing to stop him."

Kristen left Toby's room and ran to hers. Quickly, she changed her clothes into a riding skirt and blouse. She pulled on her boots and blew out all her candles. Going to the French doors, she slipped out, closing them quietly behind her. She ran lightly down the steps into the garden. She had to look about before she found Chris in the shadows. Together they ran to the stables where Chris saddled two horses without waking the stable hands. They wanted no one to know they had gone. Chris had to admire Kristen's horsemanship as she bent low over the horse's neck and urged her steed to a speed that Chris had difficulty matching.

When they came to Morgan's home, they tied their horses in front and ran to the door. Impatiently, Chris knocked loudly.

When the butler answered the door he looked at them in surprise.

"Miss Seaford, Mr. Miles!"

449

"Is Morgan here?" Kristen asked.

"No, miss, he's not at home."

Kristen's face drained of color and she reached for Chris's hand.

"Where has he gone?" Chris said as he squeezed Kristen's hand to give her courage.

"He has gone to see Lord Jamie Price, sir. It seems Lord Price is quite ill and has sent for Lord Grayfield to do some business for him."

"Where is Captain MacGregor?" she asked, praying that Jane and Owen were at home.

"He's abed, miss. The doctor said he was not to get up for a few days."

"Doctor!" she repeated in alarm.

"Yes, miss. The captain was attacked by a footpad in town. He took a nasty cut with a blade. His brother Douglas brought him home."

"I have to see him just for a moment."

The butler seemed hesitant to disturb Owen, and Kristen was about to rush past him when Douglas came down the stairs. She ran to him and as quickly as possible explained the situation.

"If anyone knows how to find Morgan before 'tis too late, 'tis Owen. Come wi' me. He'll no be appreciatin' it if we dinna tell him."

They went to Owen's room and after a light rap, Douglas walked in with Kristen and Chris behind him. Jane was seated by Owen's bed, his hand in both of hers and they were quietly talking. Owen looked up in surprise and Jane stood.

"Douglas, Kristen, is something wrong?" she asked.

Knowing she could keep Morgan's identity a secret no longer Kristen ran to the side of the bed.

"Owen," she began, "you must tell me where Morgan

450

hides the *Falcon*. I've got to get to him before he sails. Jeffrey has set a trap for him and he is on his way. Owen, we've got to stop him!"

"*Falcon*," Jane repeated, a small frown on her brow; then suddenly her eyes flew to Owen whose face was grim. "The *Falcon* . . . Morgan is . . . ?"

"Captain Black," Owen supplied. "What kind of a trap?"

Quickly Chris filled him in on all that he knew. "We've got to get to the *Falcon* before Morgan sails. It's a death trap."

Owen sat up and swung his legs over the edge of the bed. He reached for his clothes that were hung across a nearby chair.

"Owen, you cannot think of getting up. You will reopen your wound," Jane cried.

"Nay, love, I'm bound tight as a drum. 'Twill na hurt me. I am only a little weak. Help me like a good girl."

"I will not!" she cried, tears on her face. "I will not help you kill yourself."

He reached out and took her trembling hand in his and drew her close to him.

"Jane, love, a man's life hangs in the balance. A man who's responsible for us findin' each other. The only man who's had the courage to fight your brother. Will ye have me lie here and nurse a small hurt while he gives up his life? Will we be able to live wi' each other and our consciences if we let him hang? I'm the only one who knows where the *Falcon* is right now except Jamie Price and they'll no have time to get to him. I'm also the only one who has a ship ready to sail, the only ship, I might add, that has a ghost of a chance of reachin' the *Falcon* before it has time to leave its harbor. Do ye no understand, love, 'tis a thing I have to do?"

451

IIis voice dropped to a gentle whisper and he raised her hand to his lips and kissed it tenderly.

"Oh, Owen," she whispered softly, "you will not let anything happen to you?"

"Nay, love, I'm safe on the *Sea Mist*. We'll find Morgan before he leaves and all this will be a tempest in a teacup. I'll be home before half of tomorrow is over. Now, help me."

Jane helped him dress and Douglas and Chris helped him down the stairs. Before they could reach the door, Ian's voice called from the top of the steps.

"Owen, where in God's name do ye think ye're goin' in yer condition? Are ye insane, man? Ye'll kill yerself."

"'Tis no good to argue wi'me, Ian, and I've no time to explain. I've got to go."

Ian came down the steps rapidly and stopped at Owen's side.

"Ye'll be no goin' anywhere wi'out me, lad. Come along, ye can explain on the way. I imagine it is a good story and I wouldna miss it for the world."

Owen grinned at his brother's angry concern and nodded. They sent for a carriage and gave the driver orders to get to the harbor as fast as he could.

It was a trip Owen would never forget. He winced often as he was jostled about, and he kept to himself the fact that he could feel a trickle of warm blood beneath his coat.

He had to have help to disembark from the carriage and to get up the gangplank. Once there, he gave crisp commands and soon the sails filled and the *Sea Mist* left the harbor.

She picked up the strong sea current, and flew across the waves.

Time flew just as rapidly and its pace affected the

nerves of all aboard the *Sea Mist* for their thoughts were concentrated on the ship and the man they sought.

Owen stayed on the quarter-deck drawing all the speed he could from the *Sea Mist*. Ian, Douglas, and Chris stayed beside him. They watched the full sails, watched the lift and fall of the ship as she cut gracefully through the waves. But most of all they kept a close eye on Owen who stood still and silent.

Kristen sat in Owen's cabin, remembering her first trip on the *Sea Mist*. She remembered the crash of the huge oak door as it flew open and her first view of the man who was to possess her completely. Each scene unfolded before her. Her anger, their battle, the island, and the rare and beautiful day they had found each other.

She prayed silently that they would reach Morgan before the *Falcon* set sail, for along with her pleasant memories came the image of Jeffrey and what he would be capable of doing to Morgan if he fell into this trap.

The hours drifted by; a full moon rose and lit the crests of the waves that broke about the bow of the *Sea Mist*.

It was nearing two in the morning when Owen turned to Douglas.

"Go down and tell Kristen to come on deck. We should be nearin' the small cove where Morgan hides the *Falcon*."

Douglas went below immediately and rapped lightly on her door. It was opened so quickly that he knew Kristen had been waiting.

"Ye've no been able to get any rest, lass?"

"Oh, Douglas, I cannot rest until I know he is safe. When I see the sails of the *Falcon* everything will be all right."

"Owen has sent word ye are to come on deck. We'll be reachin' the cove where the *Falcon*'s hid soon."

Kristen threw her cloak about her shoulders and she and Douglas went on deck. The five of them stood, silent, and watched the span of sea ahead of them.

They circled an outcropping of rocks and entered the small cove. Kristen's sob caught in her throat. Owen spat out a pain-filled curse that was echoed by his brothers. The cove was empty.

"Owen!"

"'Tis too late. The *Falcon*'s gone."

"Owen," Kristen cried, "what can we do?"

"There is nothing we can do here. But we can return home and face Jeffrey with this."

"He'll simply say he knows nothing," Ian said calmly. "Nay, we must go home and wait."

"Wait?" Kristen said miserably. "Wait for him to invite us to Morgan's hanging?"

"Well, lass, I've been givin' this a lot of thought in the past few hours. I will admit Jeffrey would like nothin' better than to hang Morgan, but knowin' the man like I do now, I'll wager he tries to use Morgan before he does him in."

"Use? How?"

"Lass, he's wanted your fortune all this time. It wouldna surprise me if he did not try to get some of it from ye in return for Morgan."

"I would pay it gladly! He can have every shilling I own if he will return Morgan."

"Kristen," Ian said softly, "ye dinna really think that Jeffrey will let Morgan go? He will take your money if ye offer it, but in the long run he will see Morgan disgraced and hung to soothe his ego. Nay, he willna let the man live if he can, but we might be able to use the time in between to free Morgan. Is your entire fortune worth the chance, lass?"

"Yes!" Kristen said without hesitation. Ian smiled.

"Then we'll go home and remain silent. The time will come when ye must face Jeffrey. Ye will offer him all ye possess. In the meantime we will be doin' all we can to free the man. Do ye have the courage, lass?"

"I love him, Ian," she said softly, "and I will give Jeffrey anything he demands, for there is nothing of value in my life if Morgan is gone."

The *Sea Mist* turned about and headed back to London harbor to wait for whatever Jeffrey had in mind. It would be a long dark wait for Kristen Seaford.

# Twenty-Seven

Morgan stood on the quarter-deck of the *Falcon* with Jeremy beside him. He was annoyed with the emotions he felt at the moment—annoyed and frustrated.

Each time the *Falcon* had set sail he had been elated. Filled with a sense of adventure, he had known he was doing something to relieve the pain he carried deep within him. Now he was faced with another emotion, the knowledge that he no longer felt the easing of pain and the fulfillment that previous strikes at Jeffrey had brought him. Now he felt a need for Kristen and the warmth of the love she so freely gave him.

For the first time since Charlotte's death, he realized that most of his hatred had done more to hurt him than to hurt Jeffrey. He began to remember Jeffrey's constant and consistent admonitions. He knew now he had chosen this way because of guilt, and for the first time he looked his guilt in the face and recognized it for what it was.

He thought of what he had put Kristen through. Kristen, the only good thing that had happened to him since the whole affair had begun.

He thought of her anxiety at his going to sea again as Captain Black. He realized this had only been one last gesture, one blow more at Jeffrey. Yet he knew it was unnecessary, for marriage of Owen and Jane, and his planned wedding to Kristen would effectively stop all the plans Jeffrey might have.

"Jeremy."

"Aye, sir."

"When this trip is over, I want you to take the *Falcon* and repaint and refit her. Then you will bring her into London harbor with a new name and a new future."

He watched the pale moonlight flicker over Jeremy's broad smile.

"That pleases you, Jeremy?"

"Aye, sir, that it does. 'Tis good to know you've finally understood the girl means more to you than all your thoughts of revenge. I've got a feelin', sir, that time and fate will be what takes care of Jeffrey MacIntire. You'll not regret what you're doin'. The girl will make you happy and that's somethin' you haven't been since your sister died."

"I imagine you're right, Jeremy. Maybe I should have listened to you in the first place but . . ."

"But the hurt was too much, and the guilt you never deserved ate at your soul until you had to do somethin' to ease your own pain."

"It is still difficult to accept the fact that he will get away with murder. She loved and trusted him. It is not fair."

"There are many things that happen in the world that are not fair. But often I have seen fate turn about and do the punishin' itself. When you dwell on hate, Morgan, it has a way of twistin' the finest soul into a knot it cannot unravel."

"Well, maybe I'll be able to unravel this now. With Kristen's help, I'll be able to put the past to rest."

"She's a beautiful woman, and"—he chuckled—"I don't know why, but she seems filled with love for you. You'd be a fool to let it slip away."

Morgan laughed. "Speaking of things slipping away, we'd best watch. It's nearing dawn and we should cross the *Night Star*'s path just after the sun comes up."

"You're sure you still want to do this? There is time yet to change your mind. If you're going to lay Captain Black to rest, why not now?"

Morgan hesitated. It would be so easy to forget the *Night Star* and Jeffrey. He could turn about now and no one would ever know how close the *Falcon* had come to striking again. Then he shook his head negatively.

"No, Jeremy, I cannot resist one last touch. I want to give him something to worry about every time he sends out a ship in the future. He'll always be looking over his shoulder to see if Captain Black is behind him. If nothing else, it should decrease some of the fortune he values so highly."

They laughed together, unaware that the decision he had just made would come close to costing him Kristen . . . and his own life.

The *Falcon* leaped through the gentle sea, a thing of rare beauty. It covered the miles that separated them from the *Night Star* rapidly, and the *Night Star* with its cargo of armed soldiers, waited like a spider in the center of its web for the unsuspecting prey to come. For the first time since Morgan had built her, the *Falcon* was to be prey instead of the predator.

Morgan had chosen to come at the *Night Star* from the rising sun so the *Falcon* would not be spotted until it was nearly upon them.

The captain of the *Night Star* set about a pretense of trying to escape. Reluctantly he admired Morgan's skill as the *Falcon* closed in, agilely cutting off every attempt at escape.

When he felt he had put up enough resistance, the

captain struck his colors, lowered his sails, and awaited the boarding of his ship by the man who would soon be his prisoner.

When Morgan swung on board the *Night Star* with his men behind him, another token fight was put up. His men subdued the men on deck and Morgan faced Ezekiel.

"Captain Black." Ezekiel smiled. "I knew one day I should run across your path."

"Captain." Morgan bowed slightly toward him. "I'm sorry for this inconvenience, but my men will be going below to dispose of your cargo."

Ezekiel shrugged. "What can I say, Captain, we are in your power. You will not harm my men or my ship?"

"No, my fight is not with you; it is with your owner. I would suggest you sail with a different line in the future. The next time I strike I may not be as merciful."

"Captain Black, may I invite you to my cabin for a drink before you leave us?"

Morgan laughed and shrugged eloquently. "All my men are here," Ezekiel added. "I'm sure there is no danger to yours."

Morgan's eyes glinted with dangerous humor at the jibe at his courage.

"Of course, Captain, I'd be delighted." He turned to Jeremy. "Leave a few men to guard these and take the rest below. Destroy the cargo as usual. I'll meet you back on deck."

"Aye, sir," Jeremy said. The procedure was not new to him. It was the same thing he had done many times before. Morgan went with the captain and Jeremy ordered his men below. He went with them to make sure Morgan's orders were carried out exactly. They were laughing and joking among themselves when they went into the dark hold. The laughter faded from their lips as several lanterns were suddenly lit and they stared at the number of men there and at the guns pointed at them.

"Morgan," Jeremy groaned, for he knew immediately of the trap they had just fallen into.

Ezekiel closed his cabin door behind himself and Morgan. He walked to his desk and poured two drinks, one of which he handed to Morgan who lifted it in a toast.

"Here's to a captain with some common sense," he said. "Why do you not join the Grayfield lines? I should hate to see your beautiful ship sunk."

Ezekiel laughed and raised his glass. "Thank you, Captain, I may consider that, but for now I have another toast for you."

He raised his glass and clinked it lightly against Morgan's.

"To the capture," he said softly, "of the elusive Captain Black and his ghost ship, the *Falcon*."

Morgan stood perfectly still, his smile fading as what Ezekiel's words meant came through to him. He set the glass on the edge of the desk and went to the door. He jerked it open and looked at the two armed men who prevented him from leaving. Slowly, he closed the door and turned back to Ezekiel, a grin on his face. He leaned against the closed door and folded his arms.

"A trap," he stated softly.

"Just that, Captain . . . a trap."

"Set by Jeffrey MacIntire."

"Yes."

"My men?"

"They are already confined. The *Falcon* has been boarded, and is now in tow. You are my prisoner and your career as a pirate is over."

"I see."

"Do you, Captain?"

"That you intend to take me back and face a trial, possibly to hang."

"Oh, but you are wrong, Captain. Mr. MacIntire does not want to do that . . . just yet. He has other plans for you, plans that will net him a much greater profit."

"May I ask what those plans entail?"

"It's not for me to say. Mr. MacIntire will tell you soon enough."

"I see."

"No, again I say you don't. You see, your men will be taken back for trial, your ship will be confiscated . . . but you . . . you will vanish, never to be seen again. You will have no trial, you will not have the chance to slip away. You will face your fate alone and no one will ever know what happened to the infamous Captain Black."

Morgan looked at Ezekiel and knew he spoke the truth. Slowly, he walked back to the desk, picked up his drink, raised it in a silent toast to the captain, and drank it. Then he sat down in the chair and waited for Ezekiel to tell him of his fate. His smile hid his thoughts for the only thing on his mind at the moment was the fate of his men, and what Kristen would do when he did not return.

Morgan was held in the captain's cabin without being able to speak to Jeremy or any of his men. A full day passed and he paced the floor as the shadows of the night fell. He could not sleep for visions of Kristen filled his mind. Anger at himself clouded his thoughts, but the possibility of what might happen to Kristen, who was left without his protection, sent him into a frenzy.

When he watched the sun come up from the window of the captain's cabin, he realized that the ship was sitting still in the water, and that they were near a spot on the coast that seemed to be isolated.

He turned when he heard the lock click, and the door

opened admitting the captain and two of his men. Both men were well-armed and Morgan knew there as no chance of escape. Ezekiel smiled, for he, too, knew Morgan would never consider leaving his men to face their fate alone.

"Good morning, Captain."

"You are about to leave us, Captain."

"Oh? Just where am I going?"

Ezekiel chuckled. "To meet a very dear friend of yours who is most anxious to see you again."

Ezekiel waved toward the door. Morgan walked out with the two armed men behind him. They went on deck, a deck that held only Ezekiel's men.

"Captain," Ezekiel said, "you will climb into the longboat and four of my . . . well-armed men will row you ashore to a prechosen place."

"And if I refuse?"

Ezekiel smiled. "If you refuse my men are ordered to shoot one of your men every ten minutes until you do as you are told."

Morgan glared at him, knowing he spoke the truth and knowing he knew that Morgan would never willingly sacrifice the life of one of his men for his.

Morgan went to the longboat and sat while two men rowed and the other two kept him under guard.

On shore, ahead of the men, he walked up the beach for a quarter of a mile; then they forced him to climb up a large grassy hill. At the crest, he stopped. Ahead of him, less than a mile away stood a large square stone edifice. It was a cold gray-looking building and Morgan, nudged relentlessly from behind, began to walk toward it.

They stopped in front of a huge door that looked strong enough to withstand the force of a small army, and Morgan was shoved inside. He found himself in a large square room with one window placed high over his head. The walls of stone were moist and cold. The only furniture was a wooden bench and a small square table. There was straw on the floor, thick and dirty, and, Morgan surmised, containing vermin of unmentionable types.

The men who were with him refused to answer his questions, or to speak to him in any way. On the table they left a basket that he imagined contained food. Some candles lay beside it.

The door closed behind the men and he heard a heavy bolt slide home. He lit one of the candles, throwing an eerie light over the room. Looking in the basket he found one loaf of hard dark bread and a container of tepid water. Slowly, he sat down. Try as he might to consider his situation, the only thought that lived vividly in his mind was one: Kristen . . . Kristen . . . Kristen.

Again the sun faded and pale beams of moonlight streaked through the one small window. Morgan had surveyed his prison well, there was no possible means of escape.

He must have slept for a while because the next thing he knew the door was being unlocked. It swung in and brilliant sunlight flooded the room. Morgan squinted at its brightness and gazed at the cloaked shadowed figure that filled the doorway.

"Well, well," came the familiar cold arrogant voice. "So we have finally clipped the *Falcon*'s wings, eh Morgan, old friend?"

"Old enemy, you mean Jeffrey." Morgan smiled. "I'm careful of the friends I choose."

"You are in no position to antagonize me, Morgan."

"Will it make any difference? I mean"—Morgan laughed—"if I tell you I think you are part of the slimiest

463

scum of the earth, will it change what you plan on doing?"

"It might," Jeffrey said in a soft malicious voice, "change the way I treat Toby and Kristen."

Morgan started toward him; the urge to feel his hands about Jeffrey's throat overwhelmed him. Before he could reach Jeffrey, two huge shadowed forms appeared in the doorway behind him. Jeffrey's tanting chuckle drew Morgan up short. He would not give Jeffrey the satisfaction of trying to attack him and being stopped by his two bodyguards.

"Very wise," Jeffrey said. "Now go and sit down. You and I have something to discuss."

His anger boiling within him, Morgan returned to his bench and sat down. "I see nothing we have to discuss."

"I thought you might be interested in the fate I've planned . . . for you, for Kristen . . . for myself."

"Kristen has nothing to do with us. You know she has no intention of marrying you."

"Now, Morgan," Jeffrey chided. "The girl is very much in love with you."

Morgan watched him, but remained silent.

"And because of that love, she will go to any lengths to save your life. I would suggest she would even go so far as to marry me, thereby signing over her entire fortune to me. I will keep her as my wife for as long as it amuses me, then"—he shrugged—"my unfortunate wife will meet with a fatal accident."

"Like my sister's suicide?" Morgan asked softly.

"Charlotte was an impossible child who threatened the fortune I intend to have. She got in my way, as her unfortunate brother has done. I eliminated her . . . and I shall eliminate you—when you have served your purpose."

Morgan's anger threatened to choke him and his hands twisted from his urgent need to kill. It was a need so deep and so strong that perspiration beaded his brow as he tried to control it.

"She was carrying your child, you animal; is there no thought in your black heart for that?"

"Another unfortunate accident. Charlotte was a very passionate woman. I sometimes forgot my goals when we were together. If she had listened to me instead of being unreasonable, the child would have been done away with and she might be alive today."

This was more than Morgan could bear. He leaped at Jeffrey and felt his hands close about his throat. He squeezed, hearing Jeffrey's shout. The two men grabbed him, but it took all their efforts to release his hold.

Brutally, they threw him on the floor and dragged his arms behind him, tying them tightly with rope. Then they lifted him and roughly thrust him down on the bench again.

"Bastard," Jeffrey gasped as he loosened his cravat and sucked in a deep breath. "I shall remember that when I have your woman beneath me. She shall pay and pay well for that."

He went to Morgan and struck him across the face; then he reached behind him and drew the ring with the Grayfield crest on it from his finger.

"I'm sure this will be evidence enough that I hold you."

He stood up. Both the men went toward Morgan to release him.

"No, leave him tied. It will do him good to understand he is completely at my mercy." Jeffrey walked to the door. "*Au revoir*, Captain. Maybe I'll be back before you starve to death; maybe I'll send someone to release

465

you . . . maybe."

Morgan could still hear Jeffrey's triumphant laugh as he walked out and closed the door behind him. He closed his eyes when he heard the final sound, the bolt sliding home. It brought the heat of frustrated tears to his eyes; these were accompanied by an all-consuming hatred for Jeffrey MacIntire.

After a few minutes, he began to look about for a way to release himself. Before his agonized eyes he could see Charlotte's face, pale and sea-washed in death. It glimmered and faded and there instead was Kristen, her eyes closed in death. He began to methodically scrape the rope back and forth across the edge of the bench.

Kristen stood at the rail as the *Sea Mist* reached harbor. She had never felt so defeated and frightened in her life. Ian came up beside her and stood without speaking. He heard the quiet choking sob she made as she tried to hold back her tears. He put his arm about her and drew her head against his chest.

"'Tis better to cry, lass," he said gently.

She leaned against him and allowed the tears to fall. "Oh, Ian, they'll kill him. Jeffrey will see he hangs."

"Nay, lass, not before he makes another attempt to get what he wants. He'll use Morgan before he kills him."

"What will we do?"

"Have ye the courage, lass, to just wait and pray?"

"I'll wait, and pray you are right."

Ian nodded and held her to comfort her.

By the time the ship was docked it was obvious to all of them that Owen was rapidly losing strength. They found his shoulder soaked with fresh blood, and hustled him into a carriage to take him home as rapidly as possible. By the time he was home, he needed the aid of Ian, Douglas, and Chris to get to his bed. Jane held her tears in check, covering them with tense anger as she berated Owen for reopening the wound. Owen lay still while she ministered to him. By the time she was done, he was asleep from exhaustion and loss of blood.

Ian, Douglas, and Kristen stood before the large fireplace in silence. There were no words to be said that would have any effect on the situation. Jane came into the room.

"Jane?" Douglas questioned.

"He's asleep, Douglas."

"'Tis good," Ian said. "He needs the sleep to mend him."

"Kristen, would you like to stay here with me?" Jane said.

"No, Jane, thank you. I must go back. I must be there in case Jeffrey . . . in case there is any word of Morgan."

"I'll take you home," Chris said.

Kristen nodded and slowly walked from the room with Chris while the others watched with sympathetic eyes.

Ian and Douglas sat before the fire. Jane was about to go back up to Owen when their words stopped her.

"There is still a great mystery here to be solved, Ian," Douglas said.

"Aye, I canna get any reasonin' to it. If the child of Isabel and George Murray were Jeffrey, surely there would be no need for this. And if it were Jane . . . I dinna believe he would have let her live this long."

Standing at the bottom of the stairs, she looked back into the room where they sat, unaware their words carried to her.

They did not see the stark pallor of her face or her trembling hand that rested on the stair rail. Their words echoed in her mind and she felt as if a thick black hand

467

had closed around her throat. A sharp piercing pain in her head almost made her cry out. "Isabel . . . Murray . . . Murray." The words echoed in her mind, a dark threatening shadow from the past. She could not remember. All she knew was they brought blackness and pain . . . pain. She did not want to reach for the past, for it would only hurt. Owen, she needed Owen, to hold the pain at bay, to tell her everything would be all right.

Staggering under the excruciating pain in her head and the weakness in her body she made her way up the steps and into their room.

Owen lay on the bed in a semisleep. He had fought sleep for one reason only, Jane was not beside him and he did not want to rest until she lay with him. He lifted his head a little from the pillow when she came in. He was about to speak when he saw the candlelight flicker across her face. He had never seen such fear in anyone else's face in his life.

He sat up in the bed and watched her. She was panting slightly and her hand rested against the rapid rise and fall of her breasts, as if she could not get her breath. He rose and slowly made his way to her.

Owen had never taken into consideration the effect his huge dark form would have on her. With the candlelight behind him, to Jane, he looked like an immense faceless form. He stopped in his tracks as she whimpered like a lost child.

"I'll remember," she gasped, fear trembling in her voice. "Please, I don't want to go . . . please. I'm not Jane Murray . . . I'm not Jane Murray . . . I'm not Jane Murray."

She kept repeating the four words over and over like a chant. She sounded to Owen like a child repeating a verse she had been told to remember.

He could feel the agony emanating from her and knew

he would drive her over the brink if he went to her. Instead, he backed away a few steps and spoke in a gentle voice.

"Ye dinna have to go this time, Jane," he said and watched her visually relax. "But ye must tell me all the lesson ye have learned."

A rattled sigh came from her and he was amazed at the fact that she did not seem to know where she was or who he was. Her eyes were wide and sightless as if they were looking within instead of outward.

"I'll remember," she chanted softly in a faraway little girl's voice. "I am not Jane Murray, I'm Jane MacIntire. . . . I am not Jane Murray, I'm Jane MacIntire. You're my brother, Jeffrey . . . you're my brother. I'll be good, Jeffrey, I'll be good. Please . . ." She whimpered. "Don't take me there anymore. I'll be good."

Feeling her hurt, he wanted to take her in his arms and comfort her. He took a step toward her and regretted his carelessness immediately. She drew herself together and sheer terror washed over her face.

"No, Jeffrey, please," she moaned. "I'll be good. I'll do what you tell me. I'll remember. Please!"

He backed away again for he was terrified that another step would drive her into the darkness. He had to find a way to reach her, but he was utterly lost as to how. Desperately, he spoke softly to her.

"Go to bed, Jane, you can sleep now."

He waited breathlessly to see what she would do.

Obediently, she walked to the bed and lay down. In a few moments, she fell into a deep sleep. Even that, to him, seemed less than natural.

He went about the room and lit every candle he could find, brightening the room until it looked like day. Then he went to Jane's side, sat down beside her, and gently took her hand in his. With his other hand, he brushed away the tears on her cheek. At that moment he would have most happily killed Jeffrey MacIntire.

He knew he had to reach inside her mind and open the doors behind which the darkness lay, but at that moment, he did not have the faintest notion how.

He had lit the candles because he did not want Jane to waken to a dark room and find his large dark form bending over her. It might be enough to drive her beyond where he could reach.

"Jane," he said softly, watching her stir as his voice reached her. "Jane, love."

Her eyes opened and this time he saw reason in their depths. He also saw that she was disoriented and could not understand why she was in bed and he was not.

"Owen?" She looked at him in surprise. "What are you doing up, and . . . how did I get in bed with my clothes on?"

"Ye dinna know yerself when ye lay down."

Her eyes darkened as the import of his words came to her. It was another of those vacant unremembered times that seemed to plague her. Those and the dark nightmares were frightening things. She started to get up, but he gently pressed her back on the bed.

"Janie, 'tis time for us to talk."

"Talk . . . ? Of what? Owen, I'm very tired."

He held her hand tightly.

"Janie, love, ye know my love for you is a strong thing."

"I know, Owen."

"'Tis strong enough to support the both of us, strong enough to help ye wi' whatever is troublin' ye."

"I don't know what you're talking about, Owen," she said, but now her eyes avoided his and he felt her hand grip his tighter.

"Janie, ye must rid yerself of this black thing in yer

mind. 'Twill be better to bring it out into the open where we can face it together."

"Owen," she said softly, "my head hurts. Can we not talk of this some other time. I do not feel well."

"Nay, Janie." He held her hand tight. "We will go back into this darkness together. When we have faced it, when we have defeated it, ye will find all the nightmares and the headaches will be gone. Walk wi' me, Jane. Let me be the strength ye lean on. We can do it together. Wash away the fear so ye can be free the rest of your life."

"I . . . I'm afraid, Owen," she said in a choked voice.

"Of what, Janie?"

"I don't know."

"That is the problem, Janie. Ye know, in the back of yer mind; ye just canna face it."

"What . . . what do you want me to do?"

His hands now gripped both of hers and his eyes held hers in a commanding gaze that would not free her.

"Remember, Janie," he said softly. "Think back through all the years. Ye do not remember yer . . . brother before ye were eight or nine years old. But ye knew him before that. I'm here to help ye, Janie, hold on to me and let yer mind go back to those childhood years. Do ye remember yer mother or father?"

"No . . . I . . . my father, I never knew him."

"Yer mother?"

"Pretty . . . I remember . . . she was so pretty."

"She went away and left you."

"No!"

"She went away, Janie."

"No, she did not go away. They came and took her."

"Who? Who came and took her?"

"Owen I don't want to remember!"

"Ye must, Janie. Ye have to be free of this."

"It . . . it was night. Mother had just put me to bed.

471

She read to me . . . she always read to me. She loved me, Owen; I know she loved me."

"Of course she loved ye, Janie; how could she not? Now, tell me, who came for her?"

"I . . . I don't understand."

"What . . . what don't you understand?"

"It . . . Jeffrey came with them. But he couldn't, he's my brother, he couldn't come with them he was already there . . . but it seems . . ."

"He's no yer brother, Janie. He wasna livin' wi' ye, Janie. Tell me what yer mother looked like."

"It's so confusing, Owen. She seems one way then the other. Her hair was black like mine and yet, sometimes it's brown. I . . ."

"Mrs. MacIntire . . . she had brown hair?"

"Yes, but why do I feel my mother's hair was black?"

"Because it was. Mrs. MacIntire was not yer mother, Janie, nor was she Jeffrey's mother. She raised the both of ye from the time ye were eight or nine. How much older is Jeffrey?"

"About ten years."

"Then he was eighteen when ye came to the MacIntires'."

"Oh, Owen . . . I remember. Mother always seemed so . . . so frightened. It was especially so one night just before she put me to bed. She told me . . . 'Jane . . . I've put the papers away. They are your only protection. You must never tell anyone where they are.' It was just after that that they came. I remember they seemed so large. They dragged Mother away. . . . She was crying. I was so frightened. I called out to her, 'Mother don't go! Don't leave me! Don't leave me!' But she was gone and only Jeffrey was there. He picked me up and took me— No! No! I don't want to remember! It hurts! I don't want to remember!"

"Janie!" he said firmly and gripped her hands in an even tighter hold. "Ye must go on; the pain will go away. Get it out and the pain will go away!"

"He wrapped me in a blanket and took me to a carriage. We went . . . I don't know where it was. I only know I was afraid. It was a big room . . . dark. All made of stone. I remember, there was only one window and there was straw all over the floor. He put me in there and he went away and locked the door. Owen . . ." Her voice cracked in terror. "It is so dark, and there are crawling things. I cried, I screamed, I begged someone to come . . . Mother!" Her voice ended on a note of pure agony as her nails tore into his hands. Owen clung to her. He could physically feel her terror and what a small eight-year-old girl must have gone through. Her voice was a barely perceptible whisper as she went on. "I was there so long . . . so long. And then he came back. He asked me where the papers were. I was so afraid. I did not know what he wanted. He said . . . he said I had to learn my lessons well. Then . . . then, he hit me. He hit me again and again, and he kept saying, 'You are not Jane Murray, you are Jane MacIntire. You are not Jane Murray, you are Jane MacIntire.' Everything is black. All I remember after that is that I was in the MacIntire house."

"How old were you?"

She looked at him blankly. "Nearly ten."

"Good God," he whispered. "Over a year."

He brushed the perspiration from her face and bent to kiss her cheek gently. Then he said in a very quiet voice, "Janie . . . where are the papers your mother hid for you?"

A slow smile, a smile of anger, of revenge, of escape touched her lips.

"I never told him, I never told him. All this time he's been waiting and watching, but I hid them, I hid them."

473

"Where, Janie . . . tell me where?"

"I . . . I don't remember."

"You do remember. This is not Jeffrey; it's Owen. It's Owen, love; tell me. Where are they?"

"In the box, the little box."

His mind raced to think of what box she meant, then he remembered the box Jane had brought from Jeffrey's house the day they had returned for her things. He went across the room and lifted it from the dresser. He returned to the bed, opened it, and dumped the contents on the bed. There were a number of miscellaneous things in the box, but there were no papers.

"Janie, there are no papers here. Jeffrey couldna have found them or he wouldna be searchin' yet. Janie, for God's sake, love, do ye know where the papers are?"

"My mother was very clever," Jane said with a sly smile. "She knew he was evil; she knew he would find the box one day. But he didn't know the secret. . . . Janie knows the secret, but Mother says not to tell nobody . . . nobody. . . . He will kill me if I tell him the secret."

Her mind still wandered in that dark shadowed place carrying her secret. He had to find the papers if he were to save Jane from Jeffrey . . . and from madness. He went back to her and sat down beside her. Again, he took her hands in his. He watched clouded suspicion darken her eyes, and he knew she was balanced precariously between the black shadow of madness and his love. He had to swing the balance.

He lifted one of her hands and pressed his lips against it. Fear that he had pushed her beyond what her mind could bear held him.

"Janie, love," he whispered. "I dinna care anything about the papers or what they might tell me about your past. I care only for you. Listen to me, Janie. We'll go home, back to Scotland, where the sea is gentle and the grass is green. Ye'll find peace there and no one will ever touch you again, I swear. I love ye, Janie, I love ye more than anything in the world."

"You don't want the papers?"

"Nay, lass, I dinna want anythin' but to have ye well and safe."

She gazed at him and he saw recognition begin to glow in the fire-flecked depths of her eyes.

"Owen," she said softly.

The touch of rationality in her voice held him.

"I love you, too, Owen. Maybe I can trust you with the secret. I can't trust anyone else, you know?"

"I know, lass, but dinna worry. We'll go home soon. You can get well and we will forget Jeffrey MacIntire ever existed."

"The key," she whispered, "is locked away."

"Locked away?"

She nodded. He had to move aside as she sat up and slid off the bed. She walked to the closet where their clothes hung, and he was sure now that he had pushed her to the edge of insanity.

She fumbled about among her dresses until she found the one she wanted. Then she reached into the pocket of the dress and withdrew the gold locket. She held it up by the chain and it glittered in the glow of the candlelight.

He did not rush to her as he wanted to for he knew suspicion still lingered. Instead he stood by the bed and smiled at her.

"Do ye want to give me your secret, Janie?"

She stood watching him for a few moments; then all suspicion seemed to melt away, and the old familiar look of love reappeared.

"Of course, Owen. There is no one else in the world I can trust except you. You're the only one who has ever given me love."

He breathed a sigh of relief so deep it was painful; then he went to her, put his arms about her waist and rocked her gently against him.

"I do love you, Janie," he breathed, "more than my life."

They stood for a moment feeling only the need to hold and comfort each other. Then she stepped back and handed the locket to him.

He opened the locket and found two pictures, one, a handsome man, and the other a beautiful woman who looked enough like Jane to have been a twin.

"Your parents?"

"Yes."

"I don't understand. You said there was a key here."

"Yes." She reached out and took the locket from him. She snapped the locket shut, then twisted it between her fingers until the back slid open. There, in a small compartment, lay a thin sliver of gold about an inch and a half long. One end was smooth and the other was shaped like a small key. She lifted it out and went to the box. Turning the box over she showed him a small hole. Into this, she inserted the key and turned it.

From the side of the box, a small drawer slid out. In this lay a packet of papers. Jane withdrew them and without any hesitation handed them over to Owen. He knew then that all the shadows between them were gone and she trusted him completely.

Owen took the packet and sat on a chair by the fireplace. Jane sat at his feet prepared to answer any questions he might have.

Owen opened the letters and began to read.

# *Twenty-Eight*

Kristen had cried all the tears she had. She stood by the window looking out at the moonlit lawn. She had made her decisions and waited only for day to break to carry them out. She had waited . . . waited until she could bear the waiting no longer, but still she had no word from Jeffrey. Now she could stand the tension no longer.

Dawn began to break as she stood and watched. She remembered the day she and Morgan had stood on the island's cliffs and watched the sun come up. It had been one of the sweetest moments they had ever shared, and she clung desperately to the poignant memory.

She began to dress and prepare to go, her mind still on Morgan. She would beg if it were necessary, offer Jeffrey any amount of money he wanted, anything he wanted if he would only give Morgan his freedom and bury the secret of Captain Black.

She had been so distraught when she had come home with Owen that Jane had insisted she stay with them for a few days. She had tried her best to be patient as Ian had cautioned her, but she could wait no longer. The agony of suspense was too great; the idea of not knowing if Morgan was dead or alive, if he was wounded, if he needed her, was beyond her control.

She planned on slipping out before anyone in the

house knew she was gone. She knew they would either try to stop her or that one, or several of them, would insist on going along.

When she had donned her riding habit she examined herself in the mirror. She was pale, and dark shadows smudged her eyes. She had carelessly braided her hair and wrapped it about her head. She drew on gloves and left the room, closing the door softly behind her. Tiptoeing down the hall and the stairs, she made her way to the front door and slipped out.

She made her way across the lawn and the garden to the stable where, without waking the stable boy, she saddled a horse herself.

She kicked the horse into motion, enjoying the heavy feel of its strong muscles beneath her and the freedom of movement as she bent low against his neck and urged him to faster and faster flight. After a while she slowed his pace and let him rest.

She thought she had prepared everything in her mind, and that she would be ready for whatever Jeffrey MacIntire might say. He would make excuses, perhaps claim he did not know where Morgan was, but she would know he was lying.

When she arrived at the house, she was surprised to see lights aglow in one window. It was much too early for anyone to be up—anyone except Jeffrey. She tied her horse and walked across the stone veranda, her heels making a sharp clicking sound in the early-morning air. Outside the doors she stopped for a second, hearing the soft murmur of voices from the lighted room. It took her only a few minutes to identify the voices she heard . . . Leslie's and Jeffrey's. She opened the door and stepped inside. If she thought she was going to take either of them by surprise she was mistaken. Her eyes met Jeffrey's

478

across the room and he smiled. His smile was one of superiority and deep satisfaction.

"Good morning, Kristen. Your timing is excellent. I have just been telling Leslie we should be able to expect you soon. You did come alone?"

She nodded.

"That was wise of you, my dear. Should you have brought your friends, or should they have caused me any inconvenience it would have cost your lover his life."

"I must talk to you, Jeffrey," she said.

"Of course you must. I have been looking forward to this conversation."

Kristen walked to him trying her best to keep her control, and to ignore the arrogant pleased look in Leslie's eyes.

"Where is he?"

"Who, Morgan or Captain Black?" he asked innocently; then he laughed. "I must say he gave us quite a chase. And all this time we were so worried about our poor little Kristen being abused by a vicious pirate and here they were," he jibed, "lovers all this time on their own little island."

"What are you going to do, Jeffrey?"

"Do?" Jeffrey asked softly. "Why, Kristen my dear, I'm going to see to it personally that my dear old friend Morgan Grayfield hangs by the neck until he is very, very dead and can cause me no more trouble."

"Please, Jeffrey," she said softly, ignoring Leslie's look of triumph. "Let me talk to you first before you do anything."

"Talk to me about what, Kristen? I have caught a pirate red-handed. It is my duty to see he is hanged for his crimes."

"The Grayfields are not exactly unimportant people.

479

They will put a stop to this."

"Oh, Kristen." Jeffrey laughed. "Do you not know that I have enough friends in court that I can have him hung before the Grayfields even know he has been captured?"

"Don't hang him!" Kristen cried.

"What?"

"Don't hang him. He has done you no real harm. A few cargoes. The cost can be repaid to you. My kidnapping . . . Jeffrey it did you no harm."

"No harm! He interfered in my plans, he made my life quite uncomfortable, he kidnapped the woman I was to marry. No, I'm afraid, my dear, I see no other alternative but to hang him."

"I'll give you another alternative."

"Oh, what is that?"

"I'll give you everything I have. Every shilling my father left to me. All you have to do is let Morgan go and forget Captain Black ever sailed. He will never sail again. I'm no fool, Jeffrey; it is my fortune you were after. It is my fortune you can have. All I ask is Morgan's freedom in return."

"I see," Jeffrey replied, and for the first time, Kristen could not read the look in his eyes. "You would give up a fortune, everything you own, for Morgan's freedom?"

"I love him," she said simply. "Were it to cost my own life I would give it freely if it meant his freedom."

Honest and unselfish love was a thing that neither Leslie nor Jeffrey understood. "I'm afraid that seems too easy. You would give your fortune up now only to have Morgan and his friends fight to get it returned to you. No, I cannot take that chance. I'm afraid I would feel much safer if Morgan were dead . . . unless . . ."

"Unless?" she asked hopefully. Her heart skipped a

beat and Leslie smiled to see her snatch so quickly at the dangled bait.

"Unless you were to complete the plans we made before the untimely entrance of Morgan Grayfield."

"Wh . . . what?"

"Why, how simple, Kristen. Do you find it difficult to understand? I will make it quite plain to you." His voice changed from taunting laughter to cold clipped words. "You will marry me the day after tomorrow. If you do, Morgan will be released . . . after the wedding. If you do not, he will be dead in the same amount of time."

"Morgan was right," Kristen said softly. "You really are a cold heartless beast. You want my money; it is all you have ever wanted. Why should you want to marry me?"

"I'll tell you why." He smiled. "To make sure Morgan understands that he is completely and undeniably defeated."

Kristen turned from him. The fiery anger in her threatened to consume her and she could not jeopardize Morgan's life by doing something foolish.

"I want to see him," she said quietly.

This was the last thing that Leslie and Jeffrey thought she would say. They looked at each other in surprise. She turned back to face them.

"After all your deceit and lies, do you really believe I will just accept your words? You want my money, you shall have it. You want me to marry you, that I will do, too . . . but not until I see him."

"Impossible. You will concede to my wishes or he shall die, that is my final ultimatum."

"Then hear me, Jeffrey MacIntire. I will not marry you. I will not sign any papers that will give you access to any of my money, and you can do what you will. I will never surrender anything to you in any way until I see Morgan, until I know for sure he is alive."

"The stupid bitch is as stubborn as her father," Leslie snarled, and Kristen turned to face her.

"My father finally knew you for what you are. It was a wise thing that he did not leave all his money to you. How long have the two of you planned all this?"

"For a long time, Kristen, and don't think you know so very much. There are many things you will never know until it's too late."

"Leslie!" Jeffrey snapped. He turned his angry flashing eyes toward Kristen who refused to flinch from them.

"I want to see him," she said in firm hard terms, "or I will die before you see one shilling of my money. Believe me, Jeffrey, for if I have to, I will kill myself and leave every bit of the money to Owen and Jane. Believe me," she finished softly, and at that moment Jeffrey did believe every word she said.

"All right, if you want to see him we shall go right now. I have no intention of letting you return with an armed force. If it is not now, it will not be at all."

"Now is fine," she said.

"Leslie, you stay here in case some questions are asked. You need only tell them that I'm away on business and you have not seen a sign of Kristen today."

Leslie nodded, her hate-filled eyes still on Kristen.

Jeffrey came to Kristen's side and reached to take her arm. Quickly, she snatched it away. She could not bear the thought of him touching her. He shrugged and smiled and led the way to the door. She followed, her heart thudding fiercely at the thought that she would at least see Morgan one more time before her life was over, for it would be over if Morgan were gone.

They led her horse to the stable and she stood aside while he harnessed a pair of horses to a buggy. While he was busy she cast her eyes about for some weapon she might be able to slip to Morgan. Her eyes fell on a knife that was used to cut leather, but it hung on the wall. Slowly, she worked her way toward it. Quickly, she took it down, lifted her skirt, and slid it down into the side of her high boot. Not a moment too soon, for Jeffrey turned to her.

"Come along, we've a long ride ahead of us, but first . . ." He took a scarf from his pocket and covered her eyes. "It is best for you not to see where we're going."

She climbed into the buggy and he climbed up beside her. Taking the reins he slapped them against the horses' rumps and they were on their way.

They did not speak to each other during the entire drive. To Kristen, the ride seemed to take hours. In fact, it was nearly noon before they started down the half-hidden dirt road that led along the rocky cliffs to the stone prison where Jeffrey had left Morgan . . . two days before. He did not expect Morgan to be in excellent health when they arrived, but he did not care. He would not have much longer to live anyway. He took the scarf from her eyes and Kristen's eyes widened as the stopped in front of the stone edifice. Jeffrey tried to help her down from the buggy, but again she resisted any attempt by him to touch her. They walked together to the door and Jeffrey took the key from his pocket and handed it to Jeffrey; then he took a pistol from his pocket.

"You will unlock the door and go in. You have half an hour. If you do not come out then"—he smiled—"I shall come in and shoot him immediately."

"I shall come out."

"Good. It would be quite unwise for you to attempt anything foolish." He pointed. "There on that knoll are two armed men. If I should signal them, Morgan . . . and you would be at their mercy. They should enjoy caring for both of you."

She nodded; then she put the key in the lock and turned it.

"Now, give me the key."

Obediently, she handed him the key; then she turned back to the door and pushed. It took all her strength to open it enough to slip in; then she shoved it shut. In the near-dark room it was impossible to tell who had entered. Morgan, who had finally sawed through his bonds, sat on the hard bench and watched the dark figure approach. He did not want anyone to know he was free . . . unless the person was within his reach. He was prepared for many things, but not for the sound of Kristen's voice calling to him from the darkness.

"Morgan?"

He nearly leaped to his feet as the soft sound of her voice came to him. She saw his dark figure rise and in a moment she was in his arms and he was crushing her against him.

"Morgan . . . Morgan," she cried. "We came to warn you; we found out about the trap, but you were already gone. Oh, Morgan, I was so frightened. Are you all right? Are you hurt?"

"Shhh, love," he whispered. "Don't be frightened. I'm fine; just let me hold you."

Her arms came up about his neck and his lips found hers in a hungry kiss that told her just how shaken he was. He took hold of her shoulders and drew her with him to where the window's ray of light would touch her face. She could see the strain in his eyes; yet his blue gaze was tender as he looked at her. He reached out and laid his hand against the side of her face.

"So beautiful," he murmured. "I've had your face in my mind. I've held it close to me. It was as if you were here."

Tears slid down her cheeks as he slowly bent his head and touched her lips in a feather-light kiss. Their lips blended for a moment; then, as if he could not bear it, he again reached out and drew her slim body against his. She clung desperately, knowing his questions were not far behind; she was right.

"Who is with you Kristen, Owen? Douglas? Ian? How did you find me?"

She was silent just a little too long. He took hold of her shoulders and held her a little away from him. The truth was there in her clouded gray eyes for him to see.

"Kristen . . . talk to me. Tell me I'm wrong."

"Morgan . . ."

"That sadistic bastard! Kristen." He gave her shoulders a shake. "Jeffrey brought you here. He brought you here?"

"I asked him, Morgan. I had to see you; I had to know you were well."

Suspicion held him. In a moment, he knew why she was saying these words.

"Why, Kristen? Tell me why. What has he told you?"

"I love you, Morgan," she sobbed as she clung to him. "I love you. I would not see you dead."

"What lying promises did he make you?"

"He'll set you free."

"For what price?"

"All my money."

He held her against him, caressing her hair with one hand; then when she could bear the silence no longer he spoke quietly. "That isn't all, is it, love?"

"Morgan . . ."

"He wants you."

"I don't care! Morgan, you cannot die. I, too, would stop living."

"I care. Do you honestly believe he will ever let me go? He knows I would come for him and kill him if he touched you. No, he cannot let me go, and you cannot marry him, Kristen."

"I have to take what chance we might have, Morgan. I will marry him the day I see him set you free."

"No!"

She reached up and took his face between her hands.

"I will marry him the day he sets you free. I know you are angry and hurt, and I know you don't believe him; I do not either. But I'm not a fool, Morgan. I will have to see you free; then, he can have the money if he wants it. There is nothing I would not give for your life."

"Once you see I am free, you could refuse to go through with the marriage."

"He is no fool either. He will take precautions."

"Damn it, Kristen, I cannot let you. Do you think I could live and know he's holding you, touching you? I could not stand it. I would kill him."

She again put her arms about his neck and pressed herself close to him. She was aware that Jeffrey was listening at the door. Her lips close to his ear, she whispered, "Morgan, there is a knife in my boot. You must take it. Somehow you must get free. He will kill you."

Relief flooded him, she had been acting out a part obviously for some listener's benefit.

He drew her with him to the hard bench. Sitting down, he drew her down on his lap. His hands began a gentle adventure. They passed by the handle of the knife and caressed a silken thigh while his lips brushed hers.

Slowly, his hand slid back down to the handle of the knife and slid it from her boot. He tucked it under the bench, then continued to caress her while he lost himself in the sweet magic of her kiss.

The rattle of the door being slid open forced them both to their feet. Jeffrey stood just inside the door, his pistol pointed at them.

"Your time is up, Kristen. Come here."

He smiled at the fury in Morgan's face as Kristen left Morgan and walked to his side. Deliberately, Jeffrey slid his arms about Kristen's waist letting his hand rest possessively on her hip.

"Go ahead, Morgan." He chuckled. "If you did get to me, my two armed men would take care of both of you. You, they would quickly kill, but her . . . I think they would enjoy her for a long, long time. Go ahead, Morgan . . . try."

He would never know how close Morgan came. If it had not been for Kristen, he would have leaped at Jeffrey, pistol or no, and beat the life from him.

Again Jeffrey laughed as he dragged Kristen with him until they stood outside. Then he pulled the door shut and locked it.

Morgan heard the carriage depart. He bent down and took the knife from its hiding place. Sweet, Kristen. She knew Morgan's time was limited once she had said the words to Jeffrey that would make her his wife. He grinned; all that stood between him and Kristen were foot-thick stone walls, a huge oak door, and two armed men; and all he had was a knife.

Kristen rode beside Jeffrey, again in silence. She was

aware that their position was very nearly impossible. If they took Morgan from that place and tried to kill him he would at least be able to defend himself. If he did get free all the marriage vows in the world, all the armed men, any precaution Jeffrey had taken would be for naught. He would come for Kristen. If he did not get free, then Kristen did not care for her future, for without Morgan, there was none.

Jeffrey had covered her eyes again. He had taken the precaution to prevent her from seeing where she was going, but he had not considered her senses. She listened for any familiar sound and concentrated on the scent and feel of the place about her. Besides this, she made a point of asking Jeffrey the time for she wanted to judge the distance they had gone.

When they had returned to Jeffrey's, he made clear what his plans would be.

"I will make the arrangements for Morgan's freedom and our marriage in a way that will satisfy you. We will be married the day after tomorrow. In the meantime, I will prepare the papers for the transfer of your money."

He reached out and grasped her chin in his hand, forcing her to look at him.

"I intend to enjoy you for some time, Kristen. Don't try anything foolish. I should hate to see Morgan's life be the price you pay."

"You keep your word, I'll keep mine," she said as she pushed his hand away. She left the buggy, went to the stable, retrieved her horse, and rode back to Morgan's. It was important now to talk to Chris, Ian, and Douglas. They had to see if they could find Morgan before Jeffrey sent someone to kill him.

# *Twenty-Nine*

Kristen crossed the lawn to the house and was greeted by a jumble of voices as she entered. Owen, whom she did not expect to see up at all, was seated in a large chair. She could tell his wound had been freshly bound for she could see the bandage beneath his shirt. Jane was seated next to him, her worried gaze on Owen's face. To Kristen, she, too, seemed pale and distraught.

All eyes turned toward her when she entered, and the same sense of relief seemed to wash over all of them at the same time.

"Where have ye been, lass?" Ian questioned gently. "We have been beside ourselves with worry when we found you were gone."

"Aye, I was ready to tear Jeffrey's place apart lookin' for ye," Douglas added. "'Tis the only other place I could think of to look."

"I went to see him," she said defensively.

"Ye went to see him!" Owen repeated. "'Tis like a tasty fly walkin' into the spider's web."

"Owen, we knew Jeffrey had captured Morgan."

"Ye dinna mean to tell me he admitted to havin' Morgan hid away somewhere," Owen said in surprise. "'Tis the last thing I'd expect him to do."

"Yes, he admitted he had Morgan. He said he was going to have him hung."

"The Grayfields would never let that happen."

"I said the same thing. He laughed. He said he'd have him hung before they even knew he was captured."

"Kristen," Ian said quietly. She looked at him, feeling his deep intent gaze read her accurately. "Tell us what happened. I've a feeling there is more we should know."

"Yes, Ian, you are right. He not only told me he had Morgan . . . he took me to see him."

"Took ye," Douglas replied. "Where?"

"I don't know."

"What do you mean you don't know?"

"Douglas," Ian said sharply, "the lass is frightened enough; don't shout at her."

"I'm sorry, I didn't mean to shout, Kristen. I just canna understand."

"He covered my eyes. I could not see where I was going."

"How was Morgan?" Ian asked.

"Oh, Ian, he's being held in a terrible place. It's dark and cold. It's all made of stone, and it . . . it smells. There must be evil things in there. It is such a horrible place to be. A large thick door, and one window so high it barely gives light."

Owen's startled eyes turned to Jane whose face had gone even whiter than it had been. He reached over and took her hand.

"I'm all right, Owen." She looked at him, distress in her eyes. "It must be the same place. It is a place he must enjoy using. If it is, we must somehow help him for it is a terrible, terrible place to be."

"Owen?" Kristen questioned; hope filled her eyes. "Do you know where it is?"

"No," Owen replied. "But the kind of a place it is is well-known to Jane. She spent some time there . . . as a child."

"A child," Kristen gasped. "That horrid place!"

"Aye, sit down, Kristen, there is a long story that we must tell ye. Then Douglas and Ian are goin' to do some more investigatin'. When we face Jeffrey MacIntire, we want to have all the evidence we need to hang him."

Slowly Kristen sat down and waited for Owen to continue.

"I always thought that there was a reason behind Jeffrey's doin's that we dinna know," he began. "The first time I met him he slipped when he was referrin' to the MacIntires. I sent Ian and Douglas to investigate." He went on to tell her what Ian and Douglas had discovered. "I thought that it must have been Jane who was Isabel's child—and George Murray's. But it left me wonderin' why Jeffrey did not just rid himself of her. Then I wondered if Jeffrey was Isabel's child. Together Jane and I found some of the reasons. We found Jane's proof of birth. We also found some letters that told us where we could find all the proof we need. It seems in the end, that Isabel dinna trust Caroline either. She left the proof wi someone she did trust, and left that name hidden wi' Janie's papers. Ian and Douglas will be talkin' wi 'em to see if we can get that proof. 'Tis the only way to stop him. Unless we find that, and where Morgan is being held, there is na more we can do."

"What must we do, Owen?" Kristen asked. "I can't let Jeffrey kill Morgan. You know he will. We must stop him."

"Aye, that we must, but we must use our heads. Jeffrey is no fool. Nay, to catch him we have to have proof of all the crimes we suspect him of. We must show no signs right now that anythin' has changed. Ye say the weddin' is to be day after tomorrow?"

"Yes."

"Ye also say ye know the timin', how long it took ye to get to the prison?"

"Yes, Jeffrey rested the horses three times, and it took over four hours."

"Four hours," Owen mused. "Wi' restin' the horses tha many times, it would still be better than three hours. What else do ye remember?"

"The sea breeze, Owen." She smiled. "Have we not enjoyed the salty taste of it? I could feel the breeze in my hair and taste the salt on my lips when we were nearly there."

"Ye are a clever lass."

"It was rocky, Owen. You could hear the horses' hoofs on the ground. I'd say, with the breeze, that we were near some rocky cliff."

"Yes," Jane said as she rose to her feet.

"Jane," Owen said worriedly, "we'll find it; ye dinna have to push yerself."

"It's a thing you've given me the courage to face, Owen, and I must do so. I can help put an end to Jeffrey and his evil."

"Maybe if we put what is remembered together we can begin a search," Douglas said.

"'Twill take a day-and-night search, but if we could find Morgan before the time is up then he wouldna have any hold on ye," Ian replied.

"Douglas," Owen said firmly, "get ye to the stable and saddle a horse. Go and fetch Chris Miles and his brother Blake. We must scatter in all directions if we are goin' to succeed."

Douglas nodded and in a few minutes, he was gone. It was not long before they heard the receding clatter of hoofbeats.

"What are yer plans, Owen?" Ian questioned.

"You and Douglas are to go and get the proof we need. It will be pushin' yerselves til ye drop, but ye have a name. Ye must get back with the proof in less than three days."

"And what will ye be doin' in the meantime?"

"Chris, Blake, and I will split up and cover as much of the coast as we can in a search for the place they're holdin' Morgan. We have got to get him free."

"Owen, no!" Jane said anxiously. "You are not fit to be riding."

"'Tis my shoulder hurt, Jane." Owen chuckled. "Not my nether parts. I can ride. It is a thing that has to be done. Morgan's life depends on us."

"I will go with you, Owen," Kristen said.

"No, you and Jane have a much more important job to do."

"What?"

"Ye are to keep Jeffrey and his mistress from being suspicious. If ye can delay the hour of the weddin' it would give us a wee bit more time."

"I will delay it until the very last second. I still cannot see how he will arrange proof that Morgan is free."

"Dinna doubt the man. His mind works in devious ways. He'll find a way."

They waited for Chris, Blake, and Douglas to return, and filled them in on what each of them was supposed to do. Chris and Blake agreed to help, but while Owen was explaining, Chris's eyes never left Kristen's face. When they began to carry out their plans, Kristen walked to Chris's horse with him.

"I'm grateful for your help Chris," she said.

He looked down into her eyes and knew with finality she would never be his. All he could see in their crystal gray depths was gratitude.

"I hope we find him, Kristen. I want you to know I'll do my very best. Don't worry, we'll find a way to stop Jeffrey."

"Thank you, Chris," she said softly. Standing on tiptoe, she placed her hands on his chest and kissed him lightly. For a moment, he held her against him, her eyes locked with his.

"I will say it," he whispered softly. "Even though I know you don't return it, I love you, Kristen. If ever you need me you know you need only call."

"I know, Chris. I only wish . . ."

"No, it's all right, Kristen. Just remember you will always have a friend if you need one."

She smiled through her tears and again he bent to brush her lips with his, knowing it was for the last time. Then he mounted. Joined by Blake and Owen, she watched him ride away.

When they reached the main road, Owen pulled his horse to a halt. Chris and Blake stopped beside him.

"Chris, ye take the north; Blake, ye go south, then come up the coast. I shall start on the coast here and ride down to meet ye. Remember the description of the place we're lookin' for. It's on the cliffs, and it's all made of stone. If ye run across it, mind ye that it is well-guarded. The last thing we want is for another of us to be caught. Remember also to ride four hours, but rest your horses three times for fifteen minutes each."

Both Blake and Chris agreed, and a few minutes later, Owen watched them ride away from him. Silently, he prayed one of them would run across this secret prison, for he was sure it was Morgan's one and only hope.

Blake took his gold watch from his pocket and checked the time; then he continued to ride until he could hear the sound of the sea.

The coast in this area was pounded by a violent sea. Hugh gray rocks extended far out into the ocean. A strip of rather rough beach was bordered by cliffs. Working slowly, and remembering to rest his horse every hour for fifteen minutes, he rode the cliffs checking closely every turn, every path; but at the end of four hours, he knew he was defeated. The stone prison in which Morgan was being held was not on this area of the coast. Reluctantly, he started back to his rendezvous with Owen.

Owen, too, made an exhaustive and very thorough search of the area, but was just as disappointed as Blake.

At the rendezvous point he built a fire on a strip of sandy beach and waited for the return of Chris and Blake, hoping one of them had had better results than he.

Chris rode slowly, letting his horse pick his way while he watched for any path that might be hidden from the casual viewer.

He rode an hour this way; then he stopped, checked his watch and waited the allotted fifteen minutes. Mounting again, he went on with his slow methodical search. Ride . . . rest . . . ride . . . rest again. He repeated the procedure three times. The hope that he would find any trace of the secret hiding place began to fade. He felt he might have missed some half-hidden path, some sign that would have led him to Morgan. In his mind, he felt the pain Kristen would feel if they came back without success.

He reached the end of the four-hour ride, and sat his horse, motionless, as he considered turning back.

Then, looking up the coastline, in grim determination, he continued on. He would go another hour, he promised himself; after which, if he saw no sign, he would return to the rendezvous point.

His head began to ache from the tenseness of his search and the fear that it was useless. Time went on, ten minutes, twenty, thirty, forty. The hour was nearly over.

Ahead of him the cliffs seemed to be grading downward. A dirt path, barely wide enough for a buggy to maneuver turned off and wound downward. He followed it to a sandy beach and rode along slowly. Ahead of him was a large grass- and boulder-covered knoll. Anyone on the other side of it, would surely see him coming.

Dismounting, he took a pistol from a holster he carried on the back of his saddle. Then slowly, in a half-crouched position, he made his way to the top of the hill. His heart nearly leaped into his throat and he wanted to shout for joy when he peered over the edge of the knoll and saw the huge stone building that sat between him and the sea. He was facing the door, and he remembered that Kristen had said there was a window. It must be on the side facing the sea, he thought, for there was no window to be seen on the two sides he could see.

Now he remembered that Kristen had said there were supposed to be two guards. He would have to find them before he could be effective in releasing Morgan. One of them had to have a key, for he knew they had been given orders as to what to do with Morgan, and they would have to open the door to do it.

His eyes scanned the area slowly and methodically, but nearly a half-hour of constant watching passed before he saw the first sign of movement that located the place from which the two guards kept their vigil.

With extreme caution, he began to work his way around so that he could come up behind them.

With nerve-wracking slowness, he made a wide circle, keeping as close to the ground as he could. He could not afford a mistake now. He would have one chance to take them by surprise. If he alerted them, it would be two armed men against one and he was reasonably sure how that would work out.

After an exasperating amount of time, he worked himself into a position from which he could watch the two guards. He was amazed at their immense size and vowed silently that he would be extra careful. Meeting even one of them in hand-to-hand combat was a thing he could not even consider.

Slowly, ever so slowly, he worked his way toward them, keeping himself well hidden as he did. When he was within hearing range, he rested for a moment. His body wet with sweat and his muscles aching from the unaccustomed activity, he lay and listened to them talk while he recovered his strength.

Their discussion was on everything from wine to women and Chris lay still, amused at their words. He wondered, if Morgan's life were not in the balance, and if he had thought to bring along enough bullets, just how much havoc he could have caused them from his vantage point.

He considered several ideas, but discarded them. He even considered going back to get Owen and Blake, but that would take at least six or seven hours and he did not know what might happen in between. They might receive word to take Morgan from here. In that case, all their efforts would have been for nothing and they would be ineffective in stopping whatever plans Jeffrey might have made for the disposal of Morgan.

His breathing under control, his tired body relaxed, Chris again began to move toward the two men.

Owen sat by the low-burning fire and nursed the sharp piercing pain that ran from his shoulder down the length of his arm. To keep his mind away from it, he thought of Jane and what she had gone through as a child. It amazed

497

him that she was the sweet loving woman she was after such treatment.

Time ticked by, and he began to wonder where Chris and Blake were. They both had already had enough time to search their area and return.

He stood up and let his eyes scan the north stretch of beach. . . . No sign of Chris. Then he turned southward and was rewarded by seeing, some distance away, a dark form that he soon recognized as Blake.

When Blake joined him by the fire, he slid down from his horse and his first words were for Chris.

"Where's Chris?"

"He's no returned yet; in fact, I dinna see any sign of him. Ye dinna think the lad would do anythin' foolish should he find the place?"

Blake chuckled. "Chris is an unpredictable boy, but he is not stupid. He would not go up against a force that was too big for him to handle, and he would certainly not jeopardize Morgan's life by doing something foolish."

"Then we must sit and wait awhile longer," Owen replied. He eased himself to the ground and Blake could see he was in considerable pain.

"Owen, let me check your shoulder. I don't want to see that wound reopened."

"'Tis all right. I just checked it; it's not opened again. 'Tis only a twinge."

Blake sat down beside him, but he still was certain Owen was suffering much more than he would ever admit.

"Owen, while we wait would you mind filling me in on what is happening?"

Owen looked at Blake in surprise; then he smiled. "Ye've been helpin' wi'out knowin' why. Aye, set back, lad. I'll tell ye a story that will shake ye. Ye'll see why so many carry an uncommon hatred for Jeffrey MacIntire."

Owen talked for a long time, explaining to Blake all he knew of Jane's and Jeffrey's past and what Jeffrey had been responsible for.

"My God," Blake said, shock clear on his face. "How could a man treat a child so? He must have no heart, no feelings at all. And Jane, she is so kind and so beautiful. It's hard to see how she survived at all."

"He doesna have a mite of human feelings," Owen replied. "'Twas much to my satisfaction to find the two of 'em were na brother and sister. 'Twould suit me t' kill the man wi' my bare hands."

"You are wise, Owen, to wait until we've had a chance to free Morgan and to get all the proof we need. From what I can tell, Jeffrey has enough influence that if we're not careful, he might slip through our fingers."

"Aye, I dinna intend for him to get away. He'll pay the piper for the dance."

"Owen, maybe we had best start looking for Chris."

"He has been gone an uncommonly long time. I hope the lad dinna try to take justice into his own hands. It might cost us Morgan's life if he did. I know that Chris feels he has a very strong reason to do Jeffrey in."

"You mean because he's in love with Kristen?"

"Aye."

"You don't think for a minute that Chris would willingly sacrifice Morgan's life?" Blake said, his brow furrowed in anger.

"Nay, lad." Owen laughed. "That thought dinna cross my mind. I just felt maybe he might be angry enough to try to free him."

"We'd best be going," Blake replied.

They put out the small fire about which they had been sitting. Blake resaddled both horses and he and Owen mounted and headed up the beach to begin their search for Chris.

They rode in silence, their minds occupied by what Chris could possibly have found, and . . . what he had decided to do about it.

When they had covered three-quarters of the distance from where they were to where Chris was supposed to stop, Blake suddenly reined his horse to an abrupt halt.

"What's wrong?" Owen said quickly. Blake pointed ahead of them and Owen's gaze followed his.

A rider was coming in their direction. He was moving at a rapid speed. Owen could not make out the rider, but his talent in the saddle was a thing he had to admire.

"It's Chris," Blake said positively.

"How can ye tell from here?"

"I've raced against him and lost too often not to know that rider. It's Chris all right, and something must be very wrong. He would not press a horse like that unless it were absolutely necessary."

They spurred their horses forward and within half an hour they met on a strip of rocky beach. Chris drew his lathered horse up short.

"Chris, what is wrong?" Blake said.

"Yer far past your appointed place," Owen said.

"I know, Owen, but I had found nothing; yet I felt I should go just a little farther."

"Was it rewarding?"

"Yes, and no."

"What do ye mean, yea and no?"

"I found the place . . . that prison where Jeffrey was having Morgan held. It's a monstrous place. There were two guards there."

"Ye dinna do anything?"

"I took care of them both, they're tied well and are waiting for us. Maybe you'll be able to make more sense of all this for I can't understand it."

500

"What is it you can't understand?" Blake said. "If you've found the place and disposed of the guards, then Morgan must be on his way home."

"No, Blake, this is what I can't understand."

"Explain, Chris, please?"

"I spotted the guards. I made my way to them without their having any idea I was there. I took them by surprise and despite their very nasty protests, I forced them to go and unlock the door where Morgan was being held. I don't know who was more surprised—them or me."

"Surprised at what?" Owen questioned.

"Morgan was gone."

"What?"

"It is an impossible thing for me to believe. Walls a foot thick, a door so strong it would have taken ten men to break it down. One window at least fifteen feet from the floor. No weapons . . . and Morgan was gone."

"Impossible," Blake said.

"That's what the two jailers said. He never came out past them. No one came in. The door was still locked . . . but damn it, Blake, Morgan was gone."

"Now, Chris, for God's sake, the man is clever, but he can't vanish through walls."

"I suggest the two of you come back with me. You can question the guards and look the place over. Then you can explain to me just why the place looks very, very empty."

An hour and a half later found them all completely puzzled. They had questioned the guards and found them frightened, but both swore that no man had entered or left the building. Yet Owen, Chris, and Blake stood in the center of the large room and looked about a completely deserted prison.

# Thirty

Ian got down from his horse. He felt stiff and sore and was thoroughly exhausted. Douglas felt the same for they had ridden nearly day and night. They stood together now and looked at the house.

"Ye are sure it's the right one, Ian?"

"Aye, I'm sure. 'Tis the only one that fits the description."

The house that sat before them was an imposing one. In the village it was the largest and obviously the richest one in the area. They walked to the door. Ian knocked upon it several times. In a few minutes a girl appeared. She smiled brightly at them.

"Yes, sirs?"

"We would like to speak to Sir Bruce Fitzroy," Ian said pleasantly, but the girl's eyes had already flickered toward Douglas whose eye for a pretty girl had not dimmed with his exhaustion.

He smiled his most charming smile and said gently, "'Tis very important, lass; in fact, 'tis a matter of life and death. Could ye no let us come in and explain to ye?"

She smiled and stepped aside to let them come in, and Ian wondered if they would have gotten inside so easily if Douglas had not been there.

"If ye will tell me your names, sirs, I shall tell Sir Fitzroy ye are here."

"He willna recognize the names," Ian said. "Would ye just tell him that we are here on behalf of the child of Isabel Maclean and George Murray."

"Aye, sir, I shall tell him. If ye will follow me, I shall make ye comfortable in the sitting room." Her words may have been for both of them, but her eyes and bright sunny smile were definitely for Douglas who did not hesitate to return them.

They barely had time to sit down in the sitting room when they heard firm footsteps approaching. The man who came into the room was more imposing than the house he had built. He was tall and broad of shoulder, with a strength that seemed to come through as an unseeable force. His hair, black as midnight despite his nearly sixty years, was in deep contrast to his piercing blue eyes.

They both stood without even thinking, for Bruce Fitzroy had a presence that would raise men to their feet anywhere.

"Sir Fitzroy," Ian said. He offered his hand and it was taken in a grasp that nearly crushed his fingers.

"Aye, that I am. And who be ye gentlemen who come to me brandishin' such names about?"

"My name is Ian MacGregor and this is my brother, Douglas."

"Ye are MacGregors? Ye would no be the sons of James MacGregor?"

"Aye, sir that we are. Do ye know our father?"

"Know him; I fought wi' him. Shoulder to shoulder all the way to Culloden and back. Jamie was a man to stand with. He is well?"

"Aye, sir." Douglas smiled. "He is well."

"And your bonnie mother?"

"Well, also, Sir Fitzroy."

"Ah, she was the bravest, bonniest lass ever. I would ha fought your father tooth and nail for her except I knew her heart would always be wi' Jamie."

Both Ian and Douglas were pleased at this turn of events for it made the whole matter easier.

"The lass told me a strange thing; that the two of ye are here for a purpose that surprises me."

"Surprises you, sir?" Douglas said.

"It is a thing of the past I never expected to hear about again. When Lord George Murray died, I returned to find his wife. Caroline had taken her away. It took me some time to find her. When I did, she had a strange story to tell me, a story I did not quite believe. I began to look into it myself."

"Ye found the answers to all the questions?" Ian said softly.

"Aye, I found all the answers, kept all the records. But ye see, the MacIntires were good people. I thought the child was best kept wi' em. For if the wrong people knew, the child would have been a prize for any greedy relative to use. I told Isabel I would keep her story and her child safe. Is there something ye would tell me to change my thinkin' on the matter?"

"Aye, sir," Ian replied. "We have a very strange story to tell ye, and 'tis a story we hope will convince ye to give us your records and your facts."

"Sit ye down. Let me get ye a wee drop of whiskey. Then ye must tell me all you know. I am not sayin' I shall turn the papers over to ye, but I may just go wi' ye to see for myself."

They sipped their whiskey while Ian and Douglas explained all they knew. Fitzroy listened without interrupting. When they finally finished, he sighed deeply. "I would no ha thought it would come to this. I shall go and gather my papers and records, and some letters I have. I believe you will be surprised at what they contain."

He left a puzzled Ian and Douglas and was gone for some time. When he returned, he carried with him a box. He sat down and handed the box to Ian.

"Read what is within; 'twill answer most all of your questions. It will also tell ye a story that will startle ye. After what ye have told me, I canna believe I am partly responsible for all that has happened."

Ian opened the box and took out the papers and letters. He handed half of them to Douglas and both of them began to read.

They were mesmerized with disbelief at the truths contained in the papers before them.

"Sir Fitzroy, this is a terrible injustice, and has been the cause of much evil and grief."

"Aye, lad, I can see that now. I can only say that I dinna do anythin' about it because I thought the child was safe and everythin' was for the best. I dinna know so much tragedy could occur."

"Will ye give us these papers to prove the legitimacy of the Murray heir?"

"That is not all I will do. I would go wi' ye to see the child for myself. Maybe to ask pardon for all the grief and pain."

Both Ian's and Douglas's horses were in a state of exhaustion. Sir Fitzroy had a closed carriage made ready and they began their journey.

As they talked through the hours on the way home, Ian and Douglas were seething with the need to see injustice righted and a punishment put on evil.

Jane sat in front of the low-burning fire. She was

watching Kristen who seemed to be daydreaming.

"Morgan?" Jane said softly.

"Yes, I cannot bear the thought of him being in a place such as you have described."

"It is a terrible place, but soon he will be set free. I know how it feels to be set free, Kristen. But the love you have for Morgan is strong, like the love Owen has given me. It is the only thing that can reach beyond anything else."

"Jane, after all you have been through, I wonder that you are not filled with hate and anger at the man who made you suffer so."

"I would feel that. I did feel that. But that kind of emotion cannot live long when it has to make room for love. I have Owen. I have peace and love. Jeffrey is welcome to anything else he wants. He's welcome to the money if that is what he needs. The money and my sympathy, for he has never known love, not love of any kind. That is a terrible cold place to live, more terrible and more cold than where Morgan is now."

"You understand so well, Jane. I only pray that Chris and the others find Morgan so I can tell him again how much I love him."

"They will find him, but in the meantime we must make our plans. They have been gone for a day and a night. It means we have only hours before you are to be married. We must think up a reason to lengthen the time."

"I have tried, but I don't know what I can say or do that will not arouse Jeffrey's suspicions and anger. If we fail, he may kill Morgan before anyone can get to him."

"We will not fail."

"I hope you are right, Jane. The thought of being married to Jeffrey, of letting him . . . It makes me ill."

Jane smiled, then she rose and went to Kristen. "We will pray that they find Morgan first. We will also pray that Ian and Douglas get back in time. But just in case . . . in case Jeffrey tries to force you into the marriage, you"—she chuckled—"will become very, very ill."

"Ill?"

"Very."

Kristen began to smile. "Why, Jane, I might even faint right there at the altar."

"I wouldn't be surprised."

"Jeffrey will not accept that for long."

"No, but maybe just long enough for them to return with enough evidence to hang Jeffrey."

"I hope you are right, Jane," Kristen mused. She rose from her chair and walked to the window. She gazed out with unseeing eyes while her thoughts went out to Morgan.

Wherever you are, my darling, she thought, have faith, we will be together. We will.

Owen and Chris and Blake approached the house. They rode slowly now, not only because they were so very tired, but because they dreaded facing Kristen with the news—or lack of news—they carried.

They had discussed the situation over and over again, but still could not come up with a logical answer. Over and over again, they faced the fact of an empty locked room from which an unarmed man had completely vanished.

They left their horses at the stable and walked across the lawn to the house. Both Jane and Kristen had been watching for them. Kristen turned from the window from which she had been watching and flung open the door. Her smile faded as she saw their faces.

507

"Owen!" she said in a thin trembling voice.

Jane ran to Owen and he slid his good arm about her. She was distressed at the tired lines etched on his face and the smudges of dark shadows under his eyes. She also had a suspicion, from the way his arm was held at his side, that his wound was causing him a great deal of trouble.

"Your arm, Owen?" Jane said softly. "You are in pain?"

"Nay, lass, 'tis all right. Chris rebandaged it this morning."

"Owen, please," Kristen said softly, "did you get Morgan free of that terrible place?"

"Nay, lass," Owen said tiredly as he sagged into a chair. Jane dropped beside him and held one of his hands in hers.

"We dinna get him out . . . because he wasna there."

"Wasn't there?" Kristen said in alarm.

Chris went to Kristen and took one of her hands in his. Slowly, he began to explain what had happened. Miserably he watched her eyes fill with tears.

"Then you don't know where he is?"

"No, Kristen, we don't."

"Jeffrey could have had him taken from there."

"What about the guards? They saw no one."

"But maybe he sent men who didn't think to tell the guards."

"I can't accept that," Chris said angrily.

"But I must; I can take no chances with Morgan's life. To get what he wants he must prove to me Morgan is alive."

"He can't do that."

"How do you know?"

"It . . . it just can't be," Chris said lamely.

"I am going to see Jeffrey," she replied firmly. "I must find out if he has taken Morgan from that place. If he has, and has set him free, I will agree to the wedding and the signing over of my money. I have no choice. I will not let Morgan die."

There was a heavy silence in the room as Kristen turned and left, for none of them had the answers as to where Morgan was.

Kristen changed into her riding clothes and rode to Jeffrey's home. She would not let anyone accompany her.

When she was ushered into Jeffrey's study, he looked at her with amusement. "Is this anxiety, my dear? Are you coming to tell me you will marry me sooner?"

"Hardly," she said coolly.

"Then to what do I owe this visit?"

Before she could answer a knock sounded on the door and a young maid came in bearing an envelope.

"A message has just come for you, sir."

Jeffrey took the envelope and smiled at Kristen. "Do you mind?"

"No," she replied.

He tore open the envelope and she watched his unreadable face for any sign that the message might be about Morgan. His eyes did not show a touch of emotion as he folded the paper and put it in his pocket.

"Well, well, my dear, it seems some of your friends have been doing some independent searching. It also seems they have found one of my most secret places. Too bad I had already removed our mutual friend."

"Morgan?"

"Yes, Morgan. This makes a slight change in our plans."

"The marriage?"

509

"You can forget it. I no longer desire to have you as my wife. No, there is something I want even more . . . and I want it now."

"What do you want?"

"You will sign over what money you have to me . . . now. Then you will do one other thing, and I shall accompany you. Jane has some papers in her possession that belong to me. I want them. It is then and only then that I will take you to Morgan."

"I cannot ask Jane for anything. She need not sacrifice anything for Morgan's life."

"You do not know Jane as well as I know her. The papers she has now will not be more valuable to her than a life. It is a thing I should have thought of a long time ago, except I was not sure she knew herself where they were. Now, since the interference of her husband, she is remembering too much. I want those papers. You can go and tell her. I will meet you on board my ship the *Pelican*. When you give me the papers I want, I will release Morgan and be gone."

"How can I trust you?"

"You do not have a choice." He smiled. "I alone know where Morgan is. If you want to see him again, you will do as I say. I intend to leave on the midnight tide. I suggest you hurry for I will leave without them, and you, my dear, will never know where Morgan's body is for I assure you if I have to leave without those papers, Morgan will be dead."

Kristen had no choice. She would not take the chance that Jeffrey's threat was not true. Morgan's life hung in the balance and the cost was too high to pay.

"I'll do as you say."

"Good, go back to Jane and take the papers she has and bring them and your own to the *Pelican* before midnight.

I caution you, do not let anyone come with you. If I see anyone, I will leave and take Morgan's fate with me."

"I'll come alone and bring what you want. But I will caution you also, Jeffrey MacIntire: if anything happens to Morgan, I will join forces with all my friends and we will find a way to pay you back."

"Don't threaten me, Kristen. Just do as you are told. You'd best hurry. You do not have much time. You can barely make it now if you hurry."

She realized the truth of this and without another word, she spun about and ran to her horse.

When she arrived at Morgan's home, she found the entire family waiting for her. Morgan's parents had finally been told of Morgan's double identity and the fate that had befallen him.

Chris had retrieved Toby who had left Jeffrey's home, filled with worry about Kristen, and had attempted to walk to Morgan's. The boy sat on a couch between Morgan's mother and Jane. Morgan's father sat opposite them. A pale Owen slowly paced the floor. Chris and Blake, too, remained silent while Kristen told them all of Jeffrey's ultimatum. She ended her story by telling Jane and Owen that she knew it was a great sacrifice for them to make and she would understand if Jane chose not to make it.

"All those papers have ever given me are grief and pain," Jane said. "It was his search for them that nearly destroyed my life. I will give them to him gladly if it will bring Morgan back."

Owen smiled at Jane for he had known from the beginning what Jane would do.

"I canna see him settin' Morgan free," Owen said. "The man is filled wi' too much hate. I will go wi' ye when ye take them to him."

511

"No, Owen, if he sees anyone else he will go without the papers and Morgan's life will go with him. We cannot take that chance."

"Something rings wrong here," Blake said.

"What, Blake?" Chris questioned, for he had a deep respect for Blake's level-headed logic.

"First, I can't figure out why Jeffrey's guards would not be told of Morgan's transfer; then there are his sudden thoughts about forgetting the wedding and going away. It sounds to me like Jeffrey is on the run."

"The only thing that would make him take flight would be Morgan's escape. But we know he couldn't have. We walked through that door. We know it was locked. No one could have gotten out of there."

"We cannot guess, or suppose; I do not have the time. I am going up and write out the agreement to let all my money be turned over to Jeffrey. When that is done, I shall leave. I must, if I am to reach the docks in time."

"When you are ready to leave, I will give you my papers also," Jane replied.

"I'm grateful to you, Jane," Kristen said.

"You need not be, Kristen. Morgan is responsible for the only good thing that ever happened to me. There is no amount of money that can be as valuable as what I have."

"Thank you," Kristen said. She left the room and climbed the stairs. There she made out a paper that would entitle Jeffrey MacIntire to everything she owned in the world. Strangely, she felt no sadness at its loss. All she could think of was Morgan's safety.

When she came back down the stairs, it was already becoming dusk. She would have to ride rapidly to get to Jeffrey's ship before midnight.

Jane handed a small packet of papers to Kristen and they all stood quietly, each mind touched by helpless misery as they watched her ride away.

When they returned to the firelit room, it seemed strangely cold and empty.

"Owen, we must follow her," Blake said.

"Aye, but we've got to give her a little time to get ahead. I've already given orders to have our horses saddled. I've a feeling both Kristen and Morgan will need our help."

Owen, Blake, and Chris prepared to leave, to follow Kristen, to try to protect her from whatever devious plan Jeffrey might have in mind.

But when Owen opened the door to go saddle the horses, he was startled to find a very tired Ian and Douglas, accompanied by another man, on the doorstep.

"Ian . . . Douglas."

"Come back inside, Owen," Ian said. "We have something to tell ye of utmost importance."

Owen watched as they walked in; then he closed the door behind him. He would hear what they had found, then he would set out to finish their mission.


Jeffrey watched Kristen leave; then his face twisted into a mask of raging hatred. Taking the steps two at a time he burst into Leslie's room.

"Pack some things at once," he said.

"Jeffrey, what has gone wrong?"

"So damned many things that it is hard to start telling you. We're leaving tonight on the *Pelican*."

"Leaving, why?"

"Because . . . Morgan Grayfield has escaped."

Her face went pale. "Escaped! That is impossible. No one could escape from that fortress."

"No! Well I received a note from the man I sent to move him. He found the guards tied and the place empty.

The guards had a very strange tale to tell." He went on to explain to her how Owen and the others had made the guards open the door only to find the place empty.

"Then . . . then we've lost everything."

"Don't be a fool, Leslie. Do you think I will let all that slip through my fingers?"

"What can we do? How can I prove I'm . . . ?"

"Listen to me," he said firmly. Then he began to explain to her all that had transpired between him and Kristen. "The papers we get from her will be the only things recognized in court. You will have Kristen's money, and we will have the Murray name, power, and wealth. Then neither Morgan nor anyone else will be able to touch us. From here, my dear, it is only a short jump to all we've ever wanted. Do not give up so easily. By midnight, we will leave with all the proof in our pockets. Now, go and pack. I want to be on board the *Pelican* and ready to sail when my little pigeon gets there."

"Jeffrey, you intend . . ."

"To take her with me." He laughed. "Of course. How else do you expect me to keep Morgan at bay? This time I will take precautions. No one will ever find her. Morgan will be helpless as long as he thinks we hold her."

"And just how long will you hold her before you kill her?"

"As long as she pleases me, my dear." He chuckled. "As long as she pleases me."

Leslie laughed with him; then they went to their rooms and began to pack.

Jeffrey sent for a buggy, loaded the baggage, and he and Leslie left for the harbor. They had their baggage placed aboard and they went to Jeffrey's cabin to await Kristen's coming.

The soft sound of the ship's bell told Jeffrey it was

midnight at the same time a knock sounded on his cabin door. Leslie smiled and he spoke quietly.

"I suggest you leave us alone while I break the news to my lovely little conquest that not only is she never to see Morgan again, but this night I shall share her charms."

The man who stood at the door was a disgustingly dirty sailor, his body bent and misshapen from God only knew what unfortunate accident from his sordid past. One eye was missing and over it was an extremely dirty patch.

"What do you want?" Jeffrey said.

"There a gal who says she's here to see ya. Should I bring her down?"

"Yes, imbecile," Jeffrey snarled. "And make it quick. Then, as soon as she is aboard have the captain hoist sail. I want to be on my way immediately."

"Aye, aye, sir," the man mumbled and turned away.

Within a few minutes, Kristen slipped across the threshold and closed the door behind her. She took the packet of papers and letters and handed them to Jeffrey.

"Here are the papers you wanted."

"Jane's also?"

"Yes, Jane's also. Where is Morgan?"

Jeffrey could feel the imperceptible lift of the ship and he knew they were underway. There was no escape for Kristen now. He rose and walked to her. Standing near enough to inhale the perfume she wore, he said softly, "Morgan escaped a few days ago, but that won't do him any good. For now, I hold the one thing he values most. He can do nothing, Kristen, my sweet. I have your money, the Murray name and power . . . and I have you."

515

## Thirty-One

Owen was as stunned as the others when Sir Fitzroy explained to them the real source from which all their problems had started. Sir Fitzroy told the story carefully and slowly.

"It all began wi' Prince Charlie's attempt at the throne. Lord George Murray was his lieutenant general, and his right arm. The prince dinna move anywhere wi'out him. George Murray was also close friends with Mr. and Mrs. MacIntire. The battles were going badly . . . very badly. Then they moved toward Culloden. Prince Charlie took his men toward Culloden by way of Brawford. They stopped in Brawford and remained there for six months. Caroline Stewart was a woman who enjoyed all social affairs . . . and men. Prince Charlie was enamored of her for a while; then, as always, his passions cooled. He wasna one for clingin' to one woman too long. Of course, he found out that Caroline was somewhat older than he, and that dinna excite him much. He also found out that Caroline had a daughter, about seven, whose father was unknown—I imagine even to Caroline, who was somewhat free wi' her favors. Caroline also had a young ward, a Lady Isabel Maclean. If ye'll remember back a little further ye'll find Sir Robert Maclean who died durin' the first uprisin'. His wife was already dead. To Isabel, he left a fortune so vast I canna begin to tell ye.

516

It was this fortune Caroline had her eye on."

"Caroline's daughter," Owen asked quietly, "what was that child's name?"

Fitzroy smiled. "Her name was Leslie ... Leslie Stewart."

"Leslie," Jane gasped.

"Aye, and I'll tell ye about their plans."

"Go on, Sir Fitzroy."

"Young Isabel, a sweet-natured, good lass, met and fell in love wi' Sir George Murray. He loved her, too. I remember, I was present the day he married the lass. He knew she was wi' child the day he wed her. He loved the girl beyond reason and he knew they would be leavin' Brawford soon. He also knew, as the brilliant officer he was, that Culloden might be the battle he wouldna return from."

"But he did return," Ian said.

"Aye, he did. Long enough to tell Isabel what to be afraid of, and what to do about it."

"What did she do?" Jane questioned.

"Lord Murray told her of friends of his, friends who would protect her. He also gave her papers that would give the child all the wealth he had should he not come back. He gave me copies of these papers also and I put them away for safekeeping."

"And then Lord Murray followed his prince to his death," Owen said.

"Aye. I came back to the village two days later and found the lass had already been told of her husband's death. She became frightened and fled.

"I couldna find any sign of them. 'Twas as if the earth seemed to have swallowed them up. In fact, I dinna find a trace until over seven years later. 'Twas by accident and consistent goin' through all those papers that I ran across

517

the name and location of Sir George's friends. I started out for their home, but . . . I arrived too late."

"Too late?" Ian questioned.

"I shall have to take ye back in time again. It seems Caroline thirsted for all this wealth that would soon belong to Isabel's child. She thought up a plan by which she could take it. Ye see, no one knew of Isabel's child yet, so Caroline thought that if she took the one and substituted the other everythin' would be hers. 'Twas there she made her fatal mistake."

"She chose an accomplice younger and by far more evil than she," Owen stated quietly.

"Aye, Caroline had a maid, a slovenly wench, who had a son of about eighteen—a man of no morals, no feelings, no compassion, who readily agreed to carry out Caroline's plans. But she dinna know he was formin' plans of his own. With no thought at all, he got all the evidence he wanted and then . . . he got rid of Caroline."

"Would I be safe in sayin'," Owen said, "that this man's name was Jeffrey?"

"Ye would. Now," Fitzroy continued. "Jeffrey knew what he wanted; he just dinna know where the papers were that he needed for proof. He decided to force them from Isabel. But Isabel had already sent word to the MacIntires. She wanted them to come for her daughter, Jane, to keep her safe."

"Oh, God," Jane whispered softly, as tears slipped down her cheeks. She mourned quietly for the brave mother she had never known.

"Jeffrey came one night, knowin' he did not have long before the MacIntires came for the girl. He had Isabel dragged from her home, separated from her daughter, and when she wouldna tell him what he wanted to know . . . he had her killed."

518

Jane sobbed aloud; a feeling of pain ripped through her as unwanted memories again appeared. Owen went to her and held her close to him.

"Please," she said softly, as she clung to Owen. "Go on."

"Then he turned on the child. He took ye from your safety, Jane, and tried to frighten ye enough to tell him where the papers were, but ye were so frightened it must have blocked out all memories from your mind. Ye couldna remember. The MacIntires came and Jeffrey performed an act that convinced them he was a lovin' guardian of the girl, so the MacIntires took home the boy and girl and eventually adopted both. Now we have Jane and Jeffrey MacIntire."

"The story doesna end there?" Douglas said.

"Nay, lad, it doesna. As the years went by Jeffrey embedded a fear in Jane that drove her near to insanity, but he couldna find the papers. He convinced the girl, in the terror of her mind, that she wasna Jane Murray, she was Jane MacIntire—his sister. He waited only for the day he would find the papers. Then he would kill Jane, substitute Leslie, and they would share wealth of which one can only dream. But the MacIntires became suspicious, and he did away wi' 'em.

"He and Leslie grew up holding their evil plans and watching Jane grow into a rare sweet beauty. Then Jeffrey devised another way. He would wed Jane to a monster of a man who had agreed to share the wealth wi' Leslie and Jeffrey if he could have Jane. Thank God for Owen who saved her from that fate. Jeffrey, by this time, and wi' help from Leslie, had squandered all the MacIntire wealth. They needed money. So, Leslie, a beauty wi' a heart as dark as night, met, seduced, and married one James Seaford. She thought he would leave his money to her. But when he died, he left it all to Kristen Seaford, his daughter. I dinna know how she did it, but Leslie convinced James Seaford that Jeffrey MacIntire would be a good husband for Kristen. They needed her money to continue their plans. As you know, Kristen agreed and started here.

"That's when all Jeffrey's plans went wrong. Jane ran away, met and married Owen, and Kristen was kidnapped by a pirate on her way here."

"And this is where we are," Owen said. "Kristen is on her way to Jeffrey wi' all the proof he'll need to make Leslie the heir to the two fortunes of Maclean and Murray."

"He doesna have all he needs. I have George Murray's letter and Isabel's letters to the MacIntires. When the lass returns, we will turn the tables on Jeffrey MacIntire."

"But he doesna know that," Owen said, and suddenly his face grew stark. "Good God, the man doesna intend that she *is* to return. Somehow he suspects Morgan might be free; he'll take the lass wi' 'em to hold as hostage."

"We've got to stop him, Owen," Ian said.

"Aye, we must go to the docks before that ship can sail. 'Tis obvious now. Jeffrey is on the run, and he intends to take his protection along!"

No one felt the exhaustion from their continual searches as they rode toward the docks. Each of them prayed silently they would arrive before the *Pelican* left. Combined now, they would defeat Jeffrey's plans.

But their prayers were not to be answered, for when they arrived at the edge of the dock, the *Pelican* was a small receding shape on the horizon. It was a silent group that watched it disappear. Owen turned to them.

"It will probably be in vain, but if ye would join me on

the *Sea Mist* we will try to follow them."

They agreed, although they knew the attempt would be unsuccessful. For all intents and purposes, Jeffrey and the *Pelican* were gone, and so was Kristen, the evidence she had, and all chances of protecting her.

They went to the *Sea Mist*, but preparations had to be made; men had to be roused from sleep. Time . . . time slipped by them and they knew they were defeated. Nothing and no one could save Kristen now.

Owen was about to give the order to sail when one of his sailors approached him.

"What is it, Rob?" Owen questioned.

"There's a man on the dock, sir. He says it is important, a matter of life and death; he must talk to you before you sail."

Owen nodded, and followed the sailor to the top of the gangplank. Below him on the dock, stood a man he had never seen before.

"I'm Captain MacGregor," he said. "Ye wanted to talk to me?"

"Yes, Captain, will you come down here? What I have to say is for your ears only."

Owen and the sailor exchanged glances. Owen had already been a victim of Jeffrey's treachery and he had no intention of being one again.

"If ye must speak to me, come aboard," Owen replied. At least on board the *Sea Mist* the man would not be able to get away should he attack Owen.

It was difficult to see anything but the man's shadowed form, but a soft mild chuckle reached him on the cool evening breeze.

"There is no need to hurry, Captain MacGregor; you will not be sailing this night."

"Whatever ye have to say, come aboard and say it. I've

no time to bandy words about wi' ye."

Again the soft laugh reached him and sent a prickle of annoyance through him. He was about to turn away in anger when the man's voice came again.

"I tell you, Captain, you have no need to sail. The black bird has flown."

At these words Owen stiffened, then he smiled. He turned to Rob.

"Go below, tell the others we will not be sailin'."

The sailor nodded and left. Owen walked down the gangplank and stood by his silent nocturnal visitor.

"Now," he said quietly, "ye have a message for me?"

"Yes, I do." The man reached in his pocket and took from it a small folded piece of paper which he handed to Owen. Owen put it in his pocket.

"How long ago?" he questioned.

"Before the *Pelican*."

"Then ye are right. The *Sea Mist* dinna need to sail. I thank ye for deliverin' the message. Ye have done a great service to many people this night."

"I have returned a large favor by doing a small one. The one for whom I delivered this message has been owed a debt by me for a long, long time. It's my pleasure to do it. Good night, Captain MacGregor."

"Good night. Canna I at least have your name?"

"I would prefer it this way. It's a name all would recognize and I would rather keep it to myself."

"Aye," Owen said quietly. "I thank ye again. God go wi' ye."

"Thank you, Captain, and again . . . have a good night, for there is no need to worry anymore."

The man faded from sight as silently as he had come. Owen watched after him for a while; then he turned and walked back up the gangplank. Immediately he was met by the others who were very upset at the orders not to sail.

"Owen," Douglas said, "yer lettin' the man go. He'll no be leavin' a trail for us to follow."

"Are ye daft, man?" Ian said. "If ye dinna leave now, ye've lost the one slim chance we ever had of sightin' his sails."

"We aren't sailin'," Owen said quietly.

"What!" Chris and Blake said in unison.

"We are no sailin'," Owen repeated mildly.

It was Ian who caught the glint of amusement in Owen's eyes. He smiled and leaned against the rail. Then he spoke and all the others grew silent.

"Owen, have ye had some news that might change our plans?"

All eyes turned to Owen and he grinned.

"If ye will accompany me to my cabin where we can get some light, we will read the message I've received just a few minutes ago."

It took no more encouragement to get them all to move rapidly to Owen's cabin. Once there, he closed the door behind him. The room was silent as he took the folded paper from his pocket, opened it, and read.

His face brightened; his eyes took on their old gleam of laughter. He began to chuckle, then he threw back his head and roared.

Ian took the note from his hand and scanned it quickly, then he, too, smiled in pleasure.

"Read it, Ian"—Douglas grinned—"so the rest of us can share Owen's obvious pleasure."

"Owen," Ian read obediently. "Do not worry. A friend is with her and the *Falcon* is not far behind. This time he will pay in full for all he has done. Keep the home fires burning. We will return home soon to celebrate the end of this affair and a new future. Captain Black."

"Morgan is alive!" Douglas exclaimed.

"Well, that man has some explainin' to do," Owen said. "I want to know how he got out of that prison."

"Aye." Ian laughed. "And what he's been doin' since, leavin' us to wait and worry."

"'Tis like him," Owen replied. "To appear just when ye need him. I wonder who's on board the *Pelican* to protect Kristen and how he got Jeremy, his crew, and the *Falcon* safely away wi'out the authorities holdin' him. The man's got a lot of explainin' to do."

"Let us go home and tell Jane and Morgan's parents, they must be frantic wonderin' if we got here in time to keep Kristen from bein' taken by Jeffrey," Ian said.

They returned to Morgan's house. At first the Grayfields and Jane were convinced they had been too late.

"Morgan and Kristen are both lost," Jane said. "Jeffrey will make them pay for trying to keep him from accomplishing his nefarious scheme. Oh, I wish I had never seen that man. I wish I had been born a nobody to poor parents; at least I would not be responsible for the deaths of two such friends."

Owen went to her and put his arm about her shoulders. He laughed as he said, "And would ye cheat me out of the pleasure of knowin' ye and havin' ye for my wife, love? I'm grateful to whatever fates carried ye in my direction. Besides, ye shouldna be leapin' to conclusions. The game is far from over. Morgan Grayfield and Captain Black are very much alive. At this moment the *Falcon* is stalking the *Pelican*. This is one quarry that willna escape Captain Black."

"Owen?" she cried.

"Aye, lass, Morgan and the *Falcon* are on Jeffrey's trail

524

and I'll wager he willna escape what is due him this time."

They pressed him for explanations, and asked question after question until everything was understood.

"There is proof of everything except Leslie Seaford's guilt. She can claim she knew nothing about what Jeffrey was doing. After all she is not too many years older than Jane. She can claim she was a child at the time and Jeffrey is the one who is carrier of the sole guilt," Ian said. They were all stunned when they realized this was true. There was no definite proof that Leslie had helped Jeffrey in his attempt to steal the Murray fortune. Ian was about to speak again when another voice came from the doorway. They all turned to see Reginald Murkton standing there, with another man beside him.

"You need not worry about the fate of Leslie Seaford."

"Reginald," Morgan's father said. Quickly he explained to everyone what place Reginald Murkton held in Kristen's life.

"I have overheard what you have been talking about. I'm sorry to have made it seem as though I was eavesdropping, but I needed to know the details about Leslie Seaford's part in all this."

"Come in, Mr. Murkton," Owen said. "If you will have a seat, we will be glad to answer any of your questions."

"Thank you."

Reginald Murkton sat down, the man accompanying him sitting stiffly beside him.

"You need not tell me who the gentleman is sitting across from me." Reginald smiled. "There is no man who does not recognize Sir Fitzroy."

"Thank ye, sir." Fitzroy laughed. "I am very flattered. I must say, sir, that your reputation as a lawyer has preceded you. Who," he repeated gently, "does not recognize Reginald Murkton?"

"Mr. Murkton," Douglas said, "you have come to us wi' some purpose in mind, have ye not?"

"Yes, young man, I did. It is the same purpose for which I stood and listened to your conversations before I made my presence known."

"Would ye mind tellin' us what is on your mind and how our two purposes combine?" Owen said. "I for one wouldna like to see Leslie get away scot-free after all that Jeffrey and she have done to make Jane and Kristen suffer."

"I've listened to what you have said about all that Jane has been through. I sympathize completely with the misery she has experienced. I also know that Kristen has suffered a great deal, maybe more than even she knows. Let me begin by introducing you to this gentleman beside me. Randolph Duplett. He is a young assistant of mine. When I left America, it was because I had many clues and some evidence to the fact that Kristen's father, James, was most foully murdered. I did not take the time to gather all the evidence for I was afraid Kristen was here in this country and without friends, but I had enough evidence to permit me to come and be with her while the balance was accumulated. Now, gentlemen, we have final and convincing proof that James was murdered. He was poisoned by his wife, Leslie Seaford. When I knew that Kristen was to inherit the entire estate, I, too, doubted. But now that I know all the reasons behind it, I know why she murdered James. She was part of Jeffrey's plans, a most willing part I might add. No, Leslie will not go scot-free, for I intend that she should be punished to the limit of the law for the premeditated and cold-blooded murder of James Seaford. . . . Yes, gentlemen . . . she will not go free."

"Poor Kristen," Jane murmured.

"Yes, it will be a difficult thing; but now, since I know about her and Morgan, I feel that she will have all the help she needs to survive this tragedy and make a new and exciting life."

"'Tis a thing that we will make happen both for Kristen and for Jane if"—he chuckled—"we survive the waitin' on word from Morgan."

"Morgan." Chris chuckled. "Always the unpredictable, always doing what you least expect him to do. Who in God's name would ever think he was a pirate?"

"Yes." Blake grinned. "And talkin' to Jeffrey cool as a cucumber all the time."

"I just thought of something, Blake," Chris said.

"What?"

"Being Captain Black can still get Morgan hung."

"You're crazy."

"Am I? I think Captain Black will catch Jeffrey . . . but with all Jeffrey's sailors as witnesses . . . who's to deny that the pirate captain and Morgan Grayfield are the same?"

"My God," Owen muttered.

"Aye," Ian said. "If Captain Black catches Jeffrey, if the *Falcon* attacks the *Pelican* . . . Morgan will be hangin' himself."

"Well I don't believe for a minute that this situation is one that Morgan has not already considered. I, for one, intend to have complete faith in him. He has done things we did not think possible, like getting out of that prison. He is responsible for bringing Owen and me, who were world's apart, together. I'll not give up my faith in him now. He loves Kristen. He'll find his way to get her free." Everyone blinked as quiet subdued little Jane stood facing them, her cheeks flushed and the bright glow of anger in her eyes.

It was Owen who first regained his sense of humor. He laughed and went to Jane and took her in his arms.

"Aye, Janie, lass, we willna lose faith in him now, and if worse comes to worse we'll defend him wi' our lives. In this room, from attorney to a man who wields power in the court, from his parents to the sweetest lass who ever defended a man, there is no one who wouldna do everythin' to protect him. I'm wi' ye, lass, for I dinna think I have the courage to ever be agin' ye."

They all laughed together, but privately everyone in the room wondered if, indeed, Morgan had considered his attack on the *Pelican* might be fatal to him. It might be the one chance Jeffrey needed to rid himself of the curse of Captain Black for all time. It also might mean that Morgan would pay with his life and Kristen would be in his power forever, as would the papers that had belonged to Jane. For the first time it came to them all. . . . Jeffrey might still win.

# Thirty-Two

Holding the knife in his hand, Morgan sat on the edge of the hard bench. He smiled at Kristen's efforts to release him from an impregnable prison with a knife. He lay back on the bench. Putting the knife beside him, he folded his hands behind his head. He lay still, searching . . . searching for some way he could do something.

His eyes slowly scanned his prison . . . the walls of rough-cut stones, the heavy door that he had already checked for its resistance to any kind of force. No matter where his mind turned, he met a solid barrier.

Restlessly, he rose from the bed and walked to the walls. He reached out and touched them. They had been built of huge rough-cut stones, some of which had sharp, ragged edges. Some of these stones protruded several inches from the wall. He ran his fingers between them and noticed something strange. The grainy substance that held the stones together seemed to be deeply grooved. The reason for this suddenly came to him.

He went back to the wall opposite the one that held the high-placed window. For several minutes, he stood and searched out every groove. After a few minutes, the gleam of his smile reappeared, followed by the soft chuckle of Captain Black.

He took the knife and tucked it into his belt. Then he took off his boots and tucked them also into the back of his belt. Moving slowly, letting his toes and fingers find the worn grooves, he began to climb the wall.

He reached the top and grasped the bars of the window to hold himself in place while he checked to see if what he thought had happened really had. He smiled again. It was as he thought it was. The bars of the window, placed inside, had left a wide ledge on the outside. This edge had been graded inward. Rain had fallen over the years, rolled inward, and lay in pools about the area where the bars joined the stone. Once the water had been there long enough, it had eroded its way down the grooves that held the walls together. He took hold of another bar and began, with all the force of a strong muscled arm, to move it back and forth. He could have shouted with joy when the bottom piece of the bar moved freely.

He reached for the knife. Holding on with one hand, his feet dug into the rocks, he began to dig about the bottom of the bar.

Perspiration rolled down his face as he worked slowly and laboriously. Two thoughts plagued him: how deep were the bars imbedded? And if he did get one free and got on the outer edge, what would he face? How high would the drop be? Despite these problems, he continued to work at the base of the bar.

Over an hour had passed. The arm that braced his weight felt as if it were being pulled from its socket. His feet, cut by the ragged stones, clung tenaciously to the wall. The hand that wielded the knife was so badly cramped he could barely stand it; yet he continued to work.

Then suddenly, his knife slipped under the bar. It was free. Gently, he wiggled it loose. He did not want to lose it for his ever-present malicious sense of humor had thought of a way to temporarily frustrate anyone who came in to find him. He fully intended to replace the bar as if it had never been touched. Gripping the knife between his teeth; with both hands, he pulled himself up. He wedged the loose bar against the frame of the window, then slowly wiggled his body out onto the wide outer ledge. There he could sit comfortably while he surveyed the area about him. On doing so, he received another shock.

The building had been built at the top, and on the very edge of a cliff—a cliff over a hundred feet high . . . a hundred feet straight down to the turbulent ocean below him. Add to that distance the height of the building itself and he sat over a hundred and twenty feet from the water—water, whose depth he did not know; water that showed no sign of the rocks that might linger just below its surface.

Morgan had never been a coward, but the idea of a leap from this height caused his stomach to flutter. Resolutely, he returned to his plan. He braced the bar back in the groove from which it had come. Then he slowly gathered the grainy damp substance he had loosened and refilled the hole. Firmly he patted this down about the bar. When he was finished it looked as if it had never been touched.

Now he turned to face the most dangerous challenge he had ever faced in his life: the leap to either freedom . . . or death.

He sat for a moment gathering his thoughts. He could not afford the loss of his boots. Being a strong swimmer, he knew the added weight would not be enough to stop him. He drew his boots back on. Then he stood on the edge of the wide ledge, feeling the salty sea breeze touch his hot sweaty skin. He took the knife between his teeth. He inhaled deeply, bent his knees slightly, then leaped outward and plummeted down to the blue sea beneath him.

He cut the water clean and plunged into its depths, down, down, down. Then he arched his body and began his search for the surface, grateful that his favorite lady, Mother Ocean, had given him safety from the depths of her heart.

He thrust with all his strength, for his lungs burned like fire and he felt as if they were about to explode. Up, up.

God, he thought, will I be able to reach the surface? Then he burst into the bright warm sunlight. He was panting from the exhaustion of the past two hours, and almost overcome with relief. He was free! Now he had to find out where Kristen was, and just how far he was from home and how he could get there fast. He knew he had to get to shore and rest even if it were only for a short time. He did not know where he was, but he knew he did not have too much time to find out.

Thoughts of Kristen and Jeffrey together set him into a paroxysm of anger that shook him so thoroughly he trembled. He would find them, and if Jeffrey had touched her . . . just touched her . . .

To him it seemed miles to the small outcropping of sand less than two hundred yards away. When he reached it, he was beyond exhaustion. He dragged himself up on the sand and lay, letting the sun touch him with its healing power.

Over an hour he lay so, until he felt his strength begin to return. Then he rolled over on his back and let the sun's heat penetrate him.

In a few minutes, he rose to his feet and started away from the gray colossus of stone that had very nearly cost him his life.

He knew that if he followed the beach, he would find no help, and since at the moment a horse and directions were his soul thought, he left the area of the beach as soon as he could find a path that would take him up the cliffs and inland where he would find inhabitants.

He felt as though he had been walking for a long time. He broke into a gentle loping run that covered a great deal of distance, then lapsed into walking again. In a little over two hours, he spotted a house ahead. Again he broke into a run and closed the distance between himself and it.

As he approached the thatch-roofed farmhouse, it looked deserted, and it was. The members of the family had all gone to a fair that was being held in a nearby village. He pushed open the door and stepped inside. After a quick look about he found some food and ate ravenously. It had been a long time since he had eaten the loaf of bread Jeffrey had left him.

He sat at a small table, and for the first time since his escape, he gave some serious thought to his future plans.

It was barely dusk when he left the house and made his way to a small stable where he found two horses of unmentionable age and untold wear and tear.

"Beggars can't be choosers," he muttered as he led one of the horses outside. Without benefit of saddle, he mounted and headed toward the south. Somewhere in that direction lay home . . . and Kristen.

He rode for over two hours before familiar ground told him where he was. Now that he knew where he was going he kicked the horse into the fastest gait it could achieve.

He headed directly to Jeffrey's since he knew he had to see Kristen somehow. He hid the horse well, then crept through the shadows. He intended to go directly to Kristen's room, but he had to go past Jeffrey's then Leslie's first. He could see Leslie standing in her lighted room, and was about to slip past when the door opened and Jeffrey walked in.

Rage swept through him, but the words Jeffrey spoke held him in his hiding place and made him want to listen to the balance of what was being said. Jeffrey was telling Leslie to pack at once and explaining that he intended to take Kristen with him as a hostage.

He listened to every word they said, and as they spoke a new plan began to form in his mind. A slow smile touched his lips and in a few minutes, he slipped away.

The first thing Morgan did was to consider the disguise he would use to do what he wanted to do. For the things he was planning were not only going to rid the world of Jeffrey MacIntire and Leslie Seaford and right an injustice of many years, they also were going to see the permanent demise of a pirate named Captain Black.

Morgan made his way to the dock where the *Falcon* was being held. There was only one guard who watched the ship, and there was a guard at the door of a makeshift jail not far away on the dock.

Moving like a dark ghost, it did not take Morgan long to silence the guard at the jail, and to slip in, and release Jeremy and the rest of his crew.

Jeremy could not believe what he saw when Morgan bent over him and cautioned him to silence.

"Morgan," he whispered, "I thought he might have killed you. What happened?"

Quickly Morgan filled him in; then he gave Jeremy precise orders. He slipped away as silently as he had come. Jeremy and the crew overcame the guard at the ship without a sound. They boarded the *Falcon* and soon its sleek dark form moved slowly away from the dock to the mouth of the harbor. There, in the deep shadows near the coast, it waited for the ship that would soon be coming.

Morgan made his way to the home of a very good friend who owed him a debt; he knew this man would do him a favor. After his friend had overcome his shock at seeing Morgan's disreputable state, he agreed to carry a message. At a precise time, he would deliver it.

"Remember," Morgan cautioned, "Owen MacGregor, and only if he attempts to take the *Sea Mist* and pursue the *Pelican.*"

"I'll remember." His friend laughed. "Where will you be?"

"Me?" Morgan chuckled. "I'm going to take a ride on the *Pelican*. It is time I put an end to this situation, and it's time I took back what belongs to me."

"Don't worry, Morgan, if the *Sea Mist* tries to leave, I'll see to it Owen gets the message."

"Thanks." Morgan turned to leave. "I'll not forget this," he said firmly.

"Be careful," his friend said, but the doorway was already empty by the time the words were spoken.

Now came the final preparations. Morgan made his way to the *Pelican*. Before he slipped aboard, he bent to the ground, took handfuls of dirt, and smeared himself with them. He tied a ragged piece of cloth over one eye. Rubbing more dirt into his hair and face, he then leaned forward and twisted himself into a bent and ugly form. He boarded the *Pelican* and began the long siege of waiting.

He sat in a dark-shadowed corner of the ship and watched Jeffrey and Leslie board and go below to their cabin. He was still seated there when the soft sound of bells across the water told him it was midnight.

He watched a buggy come to a stop in front of the gangplank, saw Kristen step down and look up at the ship. From the pale glow of the ship's lights he could see the

535

fear and revulsion on her face; yet she walked slowly and deliberately up the gangplank. He knew she was making this sacrifice for him and he wanted to hold her more desperately than he ever had from the moment he had met her.

He made his way to her with a stumbling and awkward gait. If she was in the least frightened of him she gave no sign.

"Please," she said softly, "will you tell Mr. MacIntire I am here?"

"Yes, mum," he mumbled and moved away carrying the sweet scent of her perfume with him.

He went to Jeffrey's cabin and, in delivering the message, fooled Jeffrey as well. He then went back and ushered Kristen to Jeffrey's cabin. He hated to leave them alone too long, but he had one other thing to do first. With a broad smile on his face he made his way to Leslie's cabin. Leslie was startled when the door to her cabin opened and closed. She spun about to look at the man who leaned casually against it. At first she was angry; then recognition began to fill her eyes.

"Morgan!" she gasped.

"At your service, my dear Leslie," he said.

"You . . . you're . . ."

"Dead? Hardly. I never felt more alive than I do at this moment. Oh, I'll admit I don't look very well, but I'll mend that . . . as soon as I've taken care of you, my evil little witch."

She knew what he intended and she opened her mouth to scream only to find herself gripped by a strong arm, a heavy hand over her mouth. Within minutes, he had her bound and gagged and placed on the bunk.

Her wide frightened eyes watched him as he washed away the dirt and stood looking down at her. She could tell there was no pity in the deep blue gaze that looked mockingly at her. Then he turned, and as silently as he had come, he was gone.

Several of Jeremy's men had been placed among Jeffrey's crew. They would make sure he and Jeffrey were not interrupted.

He stopped just outside Jeffrey's cabin door and Kristen's voice came to him.

"What good would it do you to keep me, Jeffrey? I loathe you, and I will die before I let you touch me."

"Oh, my dear, I've heard those brave words from women before, but with the proper ah . . . treatment and incentives, they have always changed their minds," Jeffrey's cool arrogant voice replied.

"You pitiful man," Kristen said softly. "Is that the only way you can get a woman's love, by force, or by money? I feel sorry for you."

A sharp slap was heard through the door and a liquid flame shot through Morgan.

"Little bitch, I shall teach you to talk to me like that. In a week, I shall have you crawling at my feet."

Morgan swung the door quietly open. Jeffrey was standing with his back to it and Kristen was facing it. At the movement she looked at the door and her eyes widened, first in shock, then recognition, then brilliant glowing joy.

"Morgan!" she cried.

Jeffrey spun about, his eyes darkened with surprise and a curse on his lips.

"You! How did you get here?"

"Did you think I was dead?" Morgan said, deep amusement in his voice. "I'm very much alive. I'm here for two things. To take back what is mine . . . and to kill you."

"You fool, you are surrounded by my men."

"Do you think so? Call for help and see who comes."

Jeffrey could read clearly the truth in Morgan's eyes.

"The *Falcon* is off your port bow with guns aimed at you. Your reign of terror is over, Jeffrey. You have lost."

"Bastard!" Jeffrey shouted. In one quick move he whipped a wicked-looking knife from his waist and grabbed Kristen as she tried to run past. He held her about the waist and the knife touched the skin of her throat.

"Don't be a fool, Jeffrey," Morgan said, but his worried gaze held Kristen's eyes, sending her a message of love and courage.

"You will have your men lay down their arms. You will signal the *Falcon* away . . . or I will kill her."

"If," Morgan said coldly, "you harm her in any way, I will take a long time killing you. That I swear."

"Move out of my way, Morgan. We're going on deck where you will do what I have told you."

He took a step toward Morgan, pushing Kristen in front of him. His eyes on Morgan, he did not give Kristen enough consideration. Suddenly she dropped heavily. Unprepared for the shift of weight, Jeffrey's attention shifted to her, trying to grasp her again in his arms. At that moment, with the swift movement of a cat, Morgan leaped. As the two men's bodies clashed in combat, Kristen darted aside. She stood and watched spellbound as they battled. Jeffrey showed the first dawning of real fear, and Morgan, a white-hot rage that knew nothing now but the primitive urge to kill.

They battled ferociously . . . each searching for a vulnerable place to end his enemy's life. Finally, Morgan's hands gripped Jeffrey's throat. Jeffrey slid to his knees as his eyes began to bulge and his vision darkened. Morgan did not see or hear anything but the gurgling sounds of the man he intended to kill.

"Morgan, stop!" Kristen shouted. She tried to draw him away, but her slim form was no match for his.

Desperately, she came beside them and forced her body slightly between them. She reached up and took Morgan's rage-filled face between her hands.

"Morgan, my love, my very dear," she said in a tear-filled voice. "Do not kill, Morgan, I beg you. Let justice take care of him. Please Morgan, look at me. I love you, Morgan, I love you."

Vaguely, her words seemed to reach him. He blinked as he looked at her, aware for the first time of what she was saying. Slowly his hands loosened their hold and Jeffrey lay on the floor gasping for breath.

"Kristen," Morgan said softly in an anguished voice. Then he gave a half-laugh, half-sob and reached for her. His arms crushed her to him and his hungry mouth found hers in a deep fulfilling kiss.

"It's over, Morgan, it's over."

"Yes, love, it's over. We will take these two back to let them face the justice they deserve. For us, I know an island. . . ."

"Oh, yes, Morgan, let's go there. Let's start over as if they had never entered our lives."

"Captain Black will sail away on the *Falcon*. Lord Morgan Grayfield will go home with you. We'll marry and all the past will be buried."

"I love you, Morgan," she whispered softly as his lips touched hers again in a sweet and gentle kiss that spoke only of the future and their love together.

The *Falcon* did disappear, carrying with it the notorious Captain Black who was never heard of again.

Jeffrey and Leslie paid with their lives for the crimes of murder they had committed.

Owen and Jane sailed for Scotland with Ian and Douglas after promising to return soon for a visit.

The wedding of Lord Morgan Grayfield and Kristen Seaford had been celebrated widely. Everyone commented on the beauty of the bride and the obvious happiness of the handsome young groom. No one seemed to know where they disappeared for their honeymoon, but everyone wished them happiness including the little boy they had immediately adopted and who, with Morgan's parents, waited patiently for their return.

# Epilogue

The island was small, lush, and green. It rang with the laughter of the two who walked its beaches, played in the surf, and loved the moonlit nights away.

The cabin was small, but it was all the young couple wanted. Despite their wealth, this place was where they found happiness.

They lay together now, talking in whispered tones as lovers do, as if they were afraid someone would intrude on their happiness.

"All you have told me of your escape, Morgan, is hard to believe. My prayers must have found you. I prayed so hard."

"It's amusing, the reactions of Ian and Douglas, not to mention Owen's when I refused to tell them how I got free." He laughed.

"I thought Owen was going to do you bodily harm." She giggled.

"That," he replied, "was the only reason I finally told him. I do believe he meant to carry out his threats."

"Oh, Morgan," she whispered. "How close we came to losing each other!"

"I know, love, it is a thing that still frightens me. I have to hold you close just to keep proving to myself we are here and you are mine."

SYLVIE F. SOMMERFIELD

Their lips blended in a gentle giving kiss. Strong arms held her close as their kiss grew more deep and passionate, promising her that they would forget yesterday, but that there would be a tomorrow . . . and all the tomorrows of a future filled with love and the joy of having each other forever.

## MORE ENTRANCING ROMANCES
### by Sylvie F. Sommerfield

**DEANNA'S DESIRE**           (906, $3.50)
Amidst the storm of the American Revolution, Matt and Deanna meet—and fall in love. And bound by passion, they risk everything to keep that love alive!

**ERIN'S ECSTASY**           (861, $2.50)
Englishman Gregg Cannon rescues Erin—and realizes he must protect this beautiful child-woman. But when a dangerous voyage calls Gregg away, their love must be put to the test. . . .

**TAZIA'S TORMENT**           (882, $2.95)
When tempestuous Fantasia de Montega danced, men were hypnotized. And this was part of her secret revenge—until cruel fate tricked her into loving the man she'd vowed to kill!

**RAPTURE'S ANGEL**           (750, $2.75)
When Angelique boarded the *Wayfarer*, she felt like a frightened child. Then Devon—with his captivating touch—reminded her that she was a woman, with a heart that longed to be won!

*Available wherever paperbacks are sold, or order direct from the Publisher. Send cover price plus 50¢ per copy for mailing and handling to Zebra Books, 475 Park Avenue South, New York, N.Y. 10016. DO NOT SEND CASH.*

# BESTSELLING ROMANCES BY JANELLE TAYLOR

**SAVAGE ECSTASY** (824, $3.50)

It was like lightning striking, the first time the Indian brave Gray Eagle looked into the eyes of the beautiful young settler Alisha. And from the moment he saw her, he knew that he must possess her—and make her his slave!

**DEFIANT ECSTASY** (931, $3.50)

When Gray Eagle returned to Fort Pierre's gates with his hundred warriors behind him, Alisha's heart skipped a beat; would Gray Eagle destroy her—or make his destiny her own?

**FORBIDDEN ECSTASY** (1014, $3.50)

Gray Eagle had promised Alisha his heart forever—nothing could keep him from her. But when Alisha woke to find her red-skinned lover gone, she felt abandoned and alone. Lost between two worlds, desperate and fearful of betrayal, Alisha hungered for the return of her FORBIDDEN ECSTASY.

**BRAZEN ECSTASY** (1133, $3.50)

When Alisha is swept down a raging river and out of her savage brave's life, Gray Eagle must rescue his love again. But Alisha has no memory of him at all. And as she fights to recall a past love, another white slave woman in their camp is fighting for Gray Eagle!

*Available wherever paperbacks are sold, or order direct from the Publisher. Send cover price plus 50¢ per copy for mailing and handling to Zebra Books, 475 Park Avenue South, New York, N.Y. 10016. DO NOT SEND CASH.*